ONLY A GLOW

the white warrior series: book one

Nichelle Rae

Cover art by Pro Book Covers
Edited by Tanya Egan Gibson

The White Warrior Series

Book I: Only a Glow
Book II: The Blaze Ignites
Book III: Steady Burn
Book IV: Doused
Book V: Embers Under the Ash (Coming Soon)
Book VI: Fire of the World (Coming Soon)

Other Books by Nichelle Rae

Frost Burn
Lights Fall

PROLOGUE

The Shadow was nearly upon him, and he felt utterly frozen. Why? It couldn't be fear. Could it? He'd never felt fear before. But his legs were shaking, and his chest was constricted to the point that he could hardly breathe. It *had* to be fear.

Nearly panicked, he desperately searched inside himself for some strength, a shred of courage, but found nothing. The Light Gods had abandoned him! A void occupied the place where They had been. He was barren inside. Why leave him today of all days?

The Shadow rose a hundred feet into the sky like a black tidal wave. As he stared into the pit of darkness and evil, only one rational thought passed through his mind: he had to protect the Sword. Bowing his head when the Shadow began to crash down toward him, he closed his eyes and vanished from the battlefield.

He opened his eyes to find himself alone next to a burned-out husk of a birch tree on a tiny island of land surrounded by stagnant gray water. He dropped to his knees, sending ash and dust floating up around him. Guilt and shame devoured him. He had abandoned his army. Men, women, Salynns—millions of souls who had put their faith in him, had followed him, had died for him—he'd just left to The Shadow.

He clenched his fists so hard that his arms shook as he brought them up to his face. But he'd done what he'd *had* to do. He had to protect the Sword! It was the only link the Light Gods had to this Shadow-stricken world. It was the only thing that mattered.

He sighed, lowered his hands, and shook his head. It was upsetting that fear had defeated him, but it was alarming that the Light Gods had left him vulnerable to such fear. Why *today?*

Suddenly, a bright white light appeared behind him. He spun to face it and quickly covered his eyes. It was absolutely blinding.

"You have dishonored us!" a female voice cried.

The Light Gods! As he forced himself to squint against the brightness, he realized with horror that indeed, after seven thousand years, They had abandoned him.

"No," he replied in a stunned whisper. "My only intention

was—"

"SILENCE, COWARD!" the voice screamed. "As punishment, you will be a mere human from this day forward, but you will not age or die until after you have a child—one who will finish what you failed to."

The thought of his child facing the great Shadow frightened him more than he could express in any language he knew—and he knew them all.

"No!" He threw himself on the ground before the Light. "Please don't doom my kin to such an end!"

"It is decided," the voice replied. "You have forsaken your crown and thus have lost it!"

The white light stretched down toward him like a massive hand reaching from the clouds. The light brightened as it lifted him off the ground, and he felt his power draining away. Sickness and weakness overcame him, as if the very blood in his veins was being pulled from every inch of his body. When it was over, the hand dropped him on the ground, making ash rise around him, and the light vanished as quickly as it had appeared.

He crawled to the stream and stared down at his new reflection in disbelief. The Light had taken everything from him—his power, his color, and his crown.

Something heavy banged against his leg. He looked down to see the Sword still hanging at his belt in its scabbard, unchanged. Realizing that it was meant to be passed to his future child, he wept until he could hardly breathe.

For seven thousand years he had fought and clawed to restore the influence of Goodness and Light in the world. The number of cracks and crevasses he had searched in that time was unimaginable, even to him. But it was why he'd been created.

His child, however, would be mortal, and he or she wouldn't have the luxury of seven millennia of experience to try to accomplish what he could not. Most frighteningly, he wasn't sure the Light Gods would even back up his offspring in the battle when it occurred. The Nameless One was backed by the Shadow Gods. What chance did a mere mortal—his child—have without the help of the Light Gods?

Anger and bitterness consumed him, drying his tears and drowning his grief, and with each minute that passed he became more determined to never have a child. He would not doom his kin to such an end.

ONE

———◦⟨∞⟩◦———

I knew every sound our woods made. I even knew about sounds that my father didn't notice. So any sound out of place was like a clap of thunder to my ears. When I heard the thunder this morning, I knew the threat was there. But I wasn't prepared to find myself in the toughest fight of my life.

I couldn't understand it! I had at least five inches on this creature, and there was no way he had as much training as I did. My whole life was training! So why was I having to fight so hard? I was panting with exhaustion from the effort. I didn't pant!

Clink! Clank! Swish! Clank! Clink!

I couldn't even get a good look at him because he moved so quickly. I only knew that he was a small human boy. His footing was so precise and perfect that I was almost daunted—and that made me angry.

My father had taught me that rage and emotion took a warrior's mind out of a fight, causing mistakes. But not mine. When my father and I dueled, the angrier I became, the more precise my attacks were. My mind also became clearer, not foggier. This shocked my father—which said something, because nothing shocked my father.

All right. Playtime was over. This boy had no idea who he was dealing with. Among the thousand things my father had taught me in my short thirteen years, one was how to maneuver my body with kicks, punches, blocks, turns, twists and organized combinations of all of these to avoid an attack. This empty-handed fighting style was my father's and mine alone. It was his greatest advantage over his enemies. It gave me the advantage here, too.

When the boy swung his sword in a downward arc again, my left leg shot up, connecting with his wrists and stopping the swing. I instantly jumped and spun, swinging my opposite leg around so my heel smashed square into his cheek. He went flying to the ground. Before he could recover, my sword was barreling down toward his chest. He would have been dead, had something not grabbed my wrist and jerked my arm backward. I gasped in surprise and looked up to see my father gazing down at me.

"Well done, Azrel."

I knew how to read his eyes exceptionally well—it was like seeing written words on a piece of parchment—so when I met his gaze, I realized he had *planned* this attack on me. I looked down at my defeated foe and was horrified to realize that the boy couldn't have been more than ten years old. He had shiny straight black hair that fell to his cheekbones in the front, and was slightly longer in the back. His eyes were an unreal periwinkle color, a strange delicate blend of purple, gray, and blue. I'd never seen such eyes. Then again, my father's gray eyes—and my own blue ones, reflected in the looking glass on our wall and in still water when I bathed—were the only other ones I'd ever seen.

I snatched my wrist from my father's grip and stood, straightening to my full height, a pitiful five foot five compared to my father's six and a half feet.

"What's going on?" I demanded, placing my hands firmly on my hips and glaring up at him. Why had he suddenly decided to have this child fight me? It insulted my abilities and, well…I'd almost lost!

"You fight well, Ortheldo," my father said to the boy, ignoring me. My jaw would have dropped, had not my teeth already been clenched so tight.

Ortheldo picked himself up off the ground. "Thank you, sir."

All I had to do was glare at my father—and oh, what a glare it was—for him to again meet my eyes. "We'll talk at home," he said, and then invited Ortheldo to come along.

I curled my lip as the boy accepted my father's invitation with a beaming smile. They started for home, and I fell behind them, brooding silently. How had this ignorant boy almost beaten me?

"Why are you so upset?" my father asked over his shoulder. "You fought well."

"Yes, you did," Ortheldo piped in.

I clenched my teeth so hard I was surprised they didn't break. My father had been my only companion my whole life, so my social skills were obviously less than perfect. Besides, I was hardly feeling gracious toward this child who had nearly beaten me in a duel.

My glare shifted to the boy. "Nobody asked you what you

think! In fact, I don't think my father was talking to you at all. So, mind your own business."

Okay, maybe he was just being nice, but who was he, this strange little child, to say anything about *my* fighting abilities?

I expected him to break down into tears, but he just looked back at me with calm detachment, and I noticed for the first time that there was sharpness in his eyes—a maturity and wisdom, even severe pain there. He had to have been through a lot for his young eyes to possess such clarity. I had an urge to apologize for my harsh words, but my pride was still bruised.

On the way to the cave, my anger gave way to a strange sense of insecurity. I'd never encountered another being, human or otherwise, in my entire life. Why was this boy here now? How did he get here? How long was he going to stay? Where was he from? I clenched my teeth and crossed my arms tightly across my chest, not liking this sudden and, so far, unpleasant change in my life.

It had always been just my father and me. My entire world up until now had consisted of my father teaching me about war—fighting techniques, swords, bows and arrows, and everything else he knew about violence and gore. Then there were my regular lessons, like learning all the languages of Casdanarus as well as how to use different plants, even seemingly useless weeds, to heal the sick or wounded and make low-level potions. Sword dueling was what I loved, though. It had been my whole existence since I was born.

I knew the unique calling of my life, so it frightened me that this boy could be younger than me and still be as well trained as I was. He didn't have the same calling I did. There was only one White Warrior. I shook my head, frustrated with myself for allowing my insecure thoughts to drift to this stupid boy again.

When we finally arrived home, the three of us had a very long talk. My father started off by telling Ortheldo a lot of his own history, all the stuff I already knew about, like The Nameless One: the great Shadow that had ended my father's glory days. Ortheldo listened and seemed to understand much of what my father said, though I was very uncomfortable about him sharing such sensitive information. I soon found out, however, why Ortheldo understood so well.

Ortheldo was a runaway. That much I had guessed. But I

learned that day that he'd run away from Dwellingpath, the most powerful human city in Casdanarus. Recently, it had fallen into disarray and darkness. I also learned that Ortheldo was not merely a citizen, but the heir to the throne. At hearing this, I suppressed a flinch.

A member of the ancient royal family of Dwellingpath had defeated The Nameless One 3,000 years ago, after my father had left the battle. That meant Ortheldo's very own ancestor was responsible for saving the world. To this day, though, it remained a mystery how a mere human, with no magical power, had done so.

Curious about why this young prince had left his home, I questioned Ortheldo quite a bit that day. I could see it hurt him to speak of such things, but he was cooperative and answered my questions anyway. I learned a lot about him, maybe more than I wanted to. I started to pity him, but at the same time, I respected him for what he had lived through. Yes, he was only three years my junior, but he was probably just as mature as I was, maybe even more so because of it. His actual age didn't reflect in his eyes. Thinking about that made me feel a little better about his having almost won our duel that morning.

His difficult story began with the decay of Dwellingpath. His mother had fallen ill and died, and Ortheldo's father had become so grief stricken that he'd willed himself to die, too. His death had left Ortheldo's much older brother, Socrat, to rule. Under Socrat's greedy rule, the kingdom began to fall apart, and he treated Ortheldo with incredible cruelty, beating him without reason, starving him for days, and even torturing him. When the boy refused to go into detail about that, I didn't press him.

Those years of abuse drove Ortheldo to meet secretly with an old sword master. "After two years," he explained, "I felt confident enough to face my brother." Ortheldo sighed and scratched the back of his neck in clear sign of discomfort. "Socrat was about to hang me by my wrists again, when I drew the blade I'd hidden under my cloak. I dared him to try to touch me, threatening that I'd kill him if he came close enough. Socrat just laughed and drew his sword."

"Weren't you afraid?" I asked. "I mean, being so young and facing such horrible person? A person of such power?"

"No," he said simply, shaking his head as he stared at the floor. "His killing me would have been better than what I was living through."

I told myself that the pang of pain I felt for him was just my imagination. "Go on. I'm sorry I interrupted."

He gave me a fleeting smile before he continued. "'When this is over, you'll get the beating of your life and you won't eat for a month,' Socrat said to me. So, we started to duel." Ortheldo closed his eyes hard. "Socrat was winning. But when I was almost done for, he got cocky. He drew his leg back and prepared to whale a kick to my ribs." The boy shook his head, opened his eyes, and stared at the floor again, lost in the memory. "So, I raised my blade—and he shoved his foot right into the tip of it."

I grimaced at the thought of a sword being shoved up my foot, but I also felt a sense of satisfaction for Ortheldo's sake—a sensation I again tried to convince myself wasn't really there.

"He screamed in agony and fell to the floor as I staggered to my feet." Ortheldo bowed his head and closed his eyes. "He was quickly silenced when I cut off his head."

My eyes bulged. For a moment I thought I'd hallucinated those last words. This young child, practically a baby by human standards, decapitated a man?

"My satisfaction quickly turned into terror, though," he went on, looking at me with wide eyes, as if the body of his beheaded brother were lying at his feet. "I had just killed the King. It didn't matter that he was a horrible, cruel older brother; the King had been murdered." He shook his head, keeping his frightened eyes on me. "I thought I'd be hung for sure. Or worse, tortured again and forced to live as if I'd never killed my brother." His gaze finally shifted to the floor in what looked like shame. "So, I fled." After a brief moment, he looked up at my dad. "Your father found me in the western border of your woods."

I stared at him with newfound admiration that I desperately tried to hide. This boy, at ten years old, had traveled from Dwellingpath, to my woods, alone. Dwellingpath was thousands of miles to the west of here.

I cleared my throat, trying to cover up how impressed I was by this feat. "Why would you leave though? If the King was dead, wouldn't that make you King?"

"But I'm the one that killed him."

I shrugged. "Maybe the kingdom would have been glad to have Socrat dead."

"I wasn't about to stick around and find out whether they'd hang me, or torture me, or welcome me with open arms!" he cried defensively, a small tremble in his voice.

I was close to arguing with him, but decided not to press the issue. Listening to him, though, I realized that we were quite alike. We'd both grown up at a young age. Both of us had been forced into the wild, but for different reasons. Also, though I'd be the last one to admit it, we both needed a friend.

"Azrel," my father said, "Ortheldo will be staying with us for quite some time. He wishes to be trained with a sword as well as you have been. Obviously, he will not be returning to Dwellingpath." He nodded at Ortheldo. "He will be your dueling partner from now on. I will train you both to be great warriors"— he sighed—"as I once was."

My eyes went wide. Why had he said that?

Ortheldo smiled at me. "Yes, I know who your father was." My eyes got bigger. "He told me when I first revealed my own identity."

I scowled at my father. How annoying. Why did he have to reveal such a personal and private thing to this boy? Though the question burned on my tongue, I wanted to go to sleep sometime today, so I let it go.

I wondered all that night why my father would take in a child like Ortheldo and share his deepest secrets, which he'd only ever shared with me. Maybe my father did it because he knew what it felt like to live in fear, exiled and shamed by his peers, regardless of what his side of the story was. My father knew all too well what it was like to have to run and hide because others didn't understand his motives.

I suppose my father's heart reached out to Ortheldo, and in a strange way, mine did too. Soft emotions weren't things I often felt, so I didn't know how to define what I was feeling. Nor did I try to. I just had to accept the fact that I now had a new dueling partner. Whether that was a good thing or a bad one, I wasn't yet sure.

TWO

I laughed. "Come on, Ortheldo," I taunted playfully as I took a swipe at his head. He parried it, but then missed my cross-counter, under which he had to duck. "It's like you're not even trying."

After another brief parry, he left himself wide open for my foot to connect with his chest, of which I took full advantage, kicking him gently into the large oak tree behind him. There he conceded the bout and stuck the tip of his sword into the ground.

I held my arms out to my sides and smiled. "What's the matter with you?"

He sighed heavily and leaned against the tree, staring at the ground. I realized then that he was really disturbed. Seven years had passed since he'd entered my life. He was eighteen now and I was twenty, and we were close enough to know when the other was unfocused and off his or her game. We could usually help each other out of it, but something felt downright wrong today. Ortheldo seemed…sad.

My father called us into the cave. Ortheldo glanced at me as he pushed himself away from the tree, and I saw in his eyes that he knew something I didn't—something grave.

I stepped in front of him before he passed me. "What is it?"

"What?"

I gave him a flat look. "Don't play dumb with me. What's wrong?"

He gave me a sad smile. "Curse you and your ability to read eyes so well." I studied his eyes, looking for an answer, but he took hold of my shoulders, turned me around, and guided me firmly in front of him so I couldn't see his face as we headed to the cave. "You'll find out," he said sadly, making my heart race in an unpleasant way.

When we entered, my father was sitting on his bed with a miserable expression. I stopped in my tracks, staring at him in horror as Ortheldo passed me. Something was wrong. The air felt somehow thick and heavy with…I didn't have a good word for it, except perhaps dread. Across his lap was something long and thin and wrapped in white material.

My father looked up at me slowly, as if he didn't have the strength to raise his head. "Sit in front of me, Azrel."

Confused, I slowly took a seat on the cave floor at his feet.

"This is the moment I've dreaded your entire life," he said somberly. "It's my fault that you must bear this burden, and I'm so very sorry."

He unwrapped the white material and revealed a mighty double-edged sword resting on his knees. My eyes widened. The fine silver blade bore engravings of a flame traveling up the sword with an eye on each side. The hilt was something I never could have imagined—a solid diamond. It wasn't simply a hilt with diamonds *in* it—it was a diamond hilt! Because diamonds were smooth, the hilt looked like it would be hard to hold onto in battle once your palms got sweaty, but yet I somehow knew it wouldn't be. There was something special about this weapon. I could tell.

I reached for it in awe, but my father quickly pulled it away. I looked up at his face, only to see two tears fall from his eyes. My eyes bulged. Never in my life had I seen my father cry! The sight of it made my heart clench with a new emotion I could only identify as fear, something I had *never* experienced in my life, though I felt this fear more for him than I did myself.

He looked past me at Ortheldo. "Ortheldo, please sit next to Azrel." He obeyed. "Azrel. Ortheldo. I have taught you much over the years. All I ask is that you remember my teachings and use them wisely. Can you do that?"

"Yes," Ortheldo and I both answered softly.

My father nodded. "Azrel, after I hand you this sword, you will gain what you need." I opened my mouth to ask him what he meant, but he held up his hand, silencing me. "You will find out when I hand it to you." I closed my mouth and nodded. "After I hand it to you, you must leave this place immediately and never return."

I started to shake. "What?" I asked, as an unfamiliar burning sensation started to form behind my eyes. "Why do I have to leave?"

"You must travel to The Pitt and seek out your mother, Priweth."

My mother? What did she have to do with anything?

So many strange emotions were running through me. My world had turned upside down in a matter of minutes. I didn't even want to touch that sword if it meant having to leave everything I'd ever known! I didn't want to live among strangers in an unfamiliar land! I wasn't about to voice that to my father, however. I wouldn't dare.

"Ortheldo," my father continued softly, "will you travel with Azrel to The Pitt? See that she arrives safely?"

"Of course, I will," he responded in a rough voice.

"Thank you." My father's eyes turned to me once again. "Azrel, you still have much to learn, but you will not learn all of it alone. You will be guided along your path until you know your place. You will find out more of this when you leave here." He paused and stared at me intently. "Azrel, I need you to make me a promise before you take this sword." I nodded reluctantly. "Promise me that you will never, ever, give anyone a reason to call you a coward." He shook his head slowly. "Don't ever let yourself make the mistake I did by allowing myself to be labeled one. Be brave. Promise me this before I hand you this weapon."

I nodded and swallowed heavily, trying to force a large burning lump down my throat. "I promise, Father."

What was about to happen to our lives?

My father nodded and finally offered the weapon to me. His hands and lips quivered when I hesitated to take it. I studied his face and his eyes and saw that he was reluctantly handing me this sword. He didn't want me to take it. Before I could read his eyes well enough to find out why, he closed them tightly and tightened his jaw as if bracing himself for a hard hit.

I swallowed again and then slowly stood, wondering what awaited me. I tentatively reached my hand out and rested it on the diamond hilt. It was smooth and cool and sparkled magnificently in the little bit of sun that seeped in through the front entrance of the cave. I wrapped my fingers around it and picked it up. The sword was lighter than I would have guessed it to be, and it balanced beautifully in my grasp. I held up the blade and stared at it in wonder.

Suddenly, the metal exploded into a white fire! My first inclination was to drop it, but my fingers held fast! I couldn't let it go! The white fire expanded in every direction, crawling across the floor and up the walls until I was completely surrounded by it!

Immense fear gripped me unlike anything I'd ever felt. I was going to be burned up! I tried to back away, but I backed right up into a wall. Before I could scream, I realized that the fire wasn't burning me. It didn't do anything at all but fill the cave, until white light was all I could see around me.

Two separate streams of white fire came from the sword, like hands reaching to touch my face, and I felt a strange rush of power enter my veins. I gasped from the intensity of it. My head rolled back and my eyes closed as I absorbed whatever was being done to me, or given to me. The power spread from the heels of my feet to the tips of my hair. I felt an amazing rush of knowledge surge through me, too, and suddenly I knew what this sword was. I knew what I was becoming! It was the sword my father had mentioned— the sword that he himself had wielded 3,000 years ago. The power now inside of me was the same magic that had been sucked away from him.

I was becoming the White Warrior!

I knew that my father had taken me into seclusion to keep my existence a secret from the greatest Evil that he'd ever faced and so he could train me in preparation to fulfill my calling to destroy that Evil. But I didn't know I would have the help of magic when that day came! The gift of the White Fire had been passed to me. The earthly incarnation of the Light Gods.

Wait. Gift? Often my father referred to it as a burden, a curse from which he'd had no escape. Now it was mine.

As the power oozed into my skin, coursed through my veins, and penetrated my soul, a voice spoke to me from inside the light.

"Azrel, you have been given the gift of the White Warrior. All Light and Goodness shall be bound to your soul from this day forth. Use this gift wisely, for your father foolishly dishonored his crown—the crown that you must earn back. You have great powers bestowed in you, yet because of your father's cowardice, your magic has been limited. You shall not receive your crown, nor have the privilege of all your magic, until you have proven yourself worthy. You are powerful but not yet invincible. Death can still come to you through human means. Only when you have earned your crown will you become fully immortal. Let no evil corrupt your soul or touch this Sword, for doom will befall all should you weaken. Fare well with this gift, Azrel, for it is unique, and it is yours alone."

I heard all the words, but the only ones that mattered to me were the ones used regarding my father and his actions: "foolishly," "cowardice," "dishonored." I didn't like those words, and it burned my blood to hear them associated with my father, a great man.

I glared into the light, unable to see anything, yet making sure my defiance was clear. "Don't ever talk about my father that way again."

The light disappeared slowly, and the cave came back into focus. Out of the corner of my eye I saw a strange white figure standing beside me. Reflexively, I spun around and thrashed my sword at it, only to have the white figure shatter at my feet. It was just our looking glass! With wide eyes, I stared into what was left of it on the wall.

The white figure was me!

My heart raced as I gazed at what I'd become. It looked like my reflection, but at the same time, it wasn't. My long brown hair was now a pure shining white that softly glowed. In fact, a delicate white halo of light seemed to shine around my entire being. My skin even looked whiter. My eyes weren't blue anymore. They didn't have any color, not even a small black pupil. They were just two pure white lights that glowed brighter than the rest of me. I brought my hand up to tenderly touch my face, just to be sure that what I was seeing was real. I felt my hand on my cheek, but I still could not connect my own touch to what I was seeing in the shards of the mirror.

I looked down to inspect my new white clothing. It was silky and soft, but ridiculously tight. I thought it might be hard to move in, but as I wiggled around and stretched, I found it incredibly easy. The material was as flexible as I was. I felt straight and aligned, very in control of what my body was doing, almost as if I had no clothes on at all. The top looked like a shiny white corset, beautifully decorated with glittering white intricate designs across my chest. A thick, white cloak lay on my shoulders, falling gracefully to the back of my ankles. On my feet were the most dazzling boots of white leather, with a layer of white sparkles glittering just beneath the surface. A master leather worker could not have crafted them. On my hands were the most intriguing devices I'd ever seen: fingerless white gloves. The thick cloth extended up past my wrists, and on each hand three white metal pieces jutted out from my knuckles into claw-like knives about six inches long.

Looking in the mirror again, I saw a small diamond brooch in the shape of fire fastened to my top. I touched it lightly with my fingertip and wondered why it was there. Maybe a mark of distinction? Though it would be hard to mistake the White Warrior for someone else.

When I finished my examination, I thrust the sword into the white, diamond-studded scabbard attached to my white leather belt, and turned to my father. The sight before me nearly sent me to the floor.

He lay on his bed with Ortheldo leaning over him, grasping his shoulders. The look of utter loss on Ortheldo's face made my limbs go numb.

I could barely think. What was wrong?

I rushed to Ortheldo's side and gazed down at my father. He was whiter than the white of my garments, and his breathing was labored.

"Please forgive me, Azrel," he said in a choking whisper, "for dooming you with this curse." I wanted to silence him, but didn't dare. "Keep this shameful secret. Tell no one about it until you know more of it. You will know when to use it. Be brave, and know this, if you know nothing else: you have allowed me to be alive with your presence. Since you were born, I've felt that life could not have been more fulfilling, more glorious, more worthwhile, or more generous. I could not have been more blessed than to have met your mother and spent these last years with you. I love you very much, my beautiful daughter. My warrior."

An invisible fist was closing around my throat. I couldn't even let out the burning sob that wanted to explode out of me.

Before I could say a word, his eyes closed, and his breathing stopped.

My eyes went wide, and my breath started coming in rigid pants. I cupped his face in my hands, staring at him in disbelief and horror. This...this wasn't happening. It wasn't! How could this be? How could he be...dead? He couldn't! The man had lived for thousands of years! He couldn't be gone! Not so suddenly! I needed him now more than ever!

This wasn't real! My father…my daddy…was…

As my jaw clenched so hard that my face trembled, a thought suddenly occurred to me: the sword had taken him from me. My father had passed me the White Warrior magic, and it had killed him. My father, my guardian, my teacher, my best friend…was gone. I'd never hear his voice again, never see his handsome smile, never feel his strong hand pat my shoulder when I'd done something well. All because of this blasted sword!

Shaking with grief, I clutched my father's shirt in my trembling fists and threw my head back and screamed at the top of my lungs. There was nothing else I could do. My father was gone. One of the only two people I'd ever known in my life was gone.

I cursed that sword! I cursed this power! It had taken everything from my father once, and now it had taken everything from me!

I would have gone mad and destroyed the entire cave, and probably myself, had Ortheldo not yanked me into his arms right then and held me. Both of us knelt on the floor, shaking in each other's arms, and I started to cry for the first time in my life. Ortheldo didn't, though. Perhaps he was too numb, or maybe he felt like he needed to be strong for me. Ortheldo had lost a father, too, after all. I squeezed him tighter, a gesture he returned.

My father, my daddy…he would never be coming back to us.

———

We buried him that morning at the entrance of the cave so that his spirit might ward off any intruders. The deed would have been simple had I used my new power, but Ortheldo and I decided against it. My father hated the white fire, and to use it to bury him seemed disrespectful. I transformed back into the brown-haired, blue-eyed Azrel I'd been before the sword had been handed to me, and we buried him with our bare hands. We dedicated the rest of the day to carving my father a proper headstone. Then, remembering his words about leaving, Ortheldo and I gathered all our weapons and whatever else we might need for a long journey and left the cave as the sun was setting.

We both took a long last look at our home, our refuge, and I recalled the memories, lessons, and twenty years I'd spent growing up here. It sank in that my world was coming to an end, and once again, I cursed that sword and magic. I decided right then and there that I would never use them. They needed to be kept secret, and by the Light and the Shadow Gods, I didn't want to use them any more than my father had wanted to give them to me. I would remain the same Azrel I'd always been—only fatherless.

I eventually bowed my head and turned away, continuing to walk with Ortheldo. We were going to endure a lot of travel time on our feet, but I wasn't concerned about that. Instead, I was becoming frightened about going off into the unfamiliar.

Fear was not a feeling I liked very much, and my father had told me to be brave, so I drove down the fear inside me, forcing it back into the chasm from whence it had emerged. Come hell or high water, I was not going to be afraid!

Little did I know that high water would be something that I would fear greatly.

THREE

Ortheldo and I had been traveling on foot for over a month. Unfortunately, our journey was taking place during the worst winter Casdanarus had seen in many years. We estimated that by foot it would take us at least six months, maybe more, to reach the general vicinity of The Pitt. We had no choice but to press through.

A horrible blizzard swirled around us one day as we came to the bank of a river. We thought it might be the Ambuel River, but we weren't completely sure since we couldn't see two feet in front of us. The section in front of us wasn't very wide, as the branches of the trees on either side of the bank nearly touched. The Ambuel River was known to be deep, though, and famous for its rapids and currents.

With our cloaks wrapped tightly around us, we warily approached the bank. The river was frozen enough to hold a little snow on top of it, so we thought we could cross there.

Ortheldo walked ahead of me to test its thickness and came back in moments. "It's good! We can cross!" he yelled over the howling wind. Slowly and carefully, he and I tiptoed onto the slippery surface, the biting chill icing my bones as solidly as it iced the river.

I started to relax a bit when the opposite shore came into view, but then something suddenly felt wrong.

A sudden shadow of dread grew in my mind. It almost felt like physical pressure, like a hot wind passing through my brain. A sick feeling of darkness consumed my thoughts, and I knew something wasn't right.

Before I could get the words out to Ortheldo that we should turn back, a large branch, one almost as large as a tree itself, lost its battle with the weight of snow, ice, and wind.

Our heads snapped up as the branch careened toward us, and we jumped out of the way right before it crashed into the ice, breaking it apart.

I fell onto the ice, the cold of it penetrating my clothes, making me shiver. My hands burned with cuts from having broken my fall.

After gathering my senses, I unsteadily found my footing and made my way to Ortheldo, who was picking himself up off the ice.

"Are you okay?" I yelled.

He nodded a reply. "Are you?"

I nodded.

Before either of us could say anything else, a sudden gust of wind came up. Ortheldo was tall and thickly built, so he kept his footing. My body, while still muscular, was thinner, and absolutely no match for this wind. It blew me off balance, and with the slippery ice under my feet, I went flying backward into the broken ice and splashed into the water.

Submerged, my body screamed in pain from the cold.

I clawed for the surface, and when I popped back up through the hole again, I screamed aloud. With my hair in my eyes and my arms flailing about, I reached for something, *anything* to hold onto and pull myself out! In my panic, I just barely felt Ortheldo's hand trying to grasp mine. Before he could take hold of me, though, something gripped my ankle and dragged me under the water and ice again. Suddenly the thing clamped down hard, and I felt teeth in my flesh!

I screamed in pain, releasing what little air was in my lungs. Some filthy river creature had me! I kicked at it with my free foot and felt a slick, scaly surface under my boot. Opening my eyes, I saw the long tail end of a Vec Fish—a giant half-snake, half-fish fresh water carnivore.

Looking up, I saw the water above me moving and realized I wasn't under the ice anymore. I reached behind me and pulled a dagger from the top pocket of my pack. With my lungs burning for air, I thrust it up into the underbelly of the beast. It jerked once and then released me before swimming off, leaving a fading trail of blood behind.

I scratched for the surface and exploded out of the water, gasping in a breath of freezing air. I wasn't trapped under the ice, but I was in the rapids! I desperately tried to cling to a passing rock, but the current took me under again in a mind-boggling rush. I held what little breath I had, and there was nothing for me to do except endure the freezing, merciless pain of the river, and my throbbing ankle. The feeling in my fingers and toes vanished. I surfaced periodically, and each time I did, I could only take in what air I was granted before going under again.

I tried to look for Ortheldo as the river swept me farther away, but my view didn't last long as the current took me under again and again, barely giving me enough time to draw air.

I struggled for what seemed like years to get to the shore. My traveling pack weighed me down, and I'd never really learned to swim, so my movements were more flails than strokes. My eyes started to roll into the back of my head, and the pain just made me want to give up. But no! I had to hold on! I had to endure this! I had to get to the bank!

I must have been carried at least two miles downriver before I finally collapsed on land. I was beyond any measure of cold, lying face down and soaking wet on the snowy riverbank. Wind and snow still swirled around me, and I was in agony. My pack, seeming to have tripled in weight, was crushing my already laboring lungs and I was forcefully, painfully drawing in breaths. I began to feel ice form all over my body, as if I were growing another hard, cold, thin layer of skin. I didn't even attempt to move my fingers or hands. For all I knew, they had been cut off.

I started to believe that this was it. I was going to die here.

One rational thought was left to me. I slowly slid my hand down to my hip and took hold of the hilt of the sword my father had given me. "Evil will never get it. It's safe. I won't fail you, Father," I whispered as I shivered on that bank. I whispered it repeatedly, as the white snow around me faded into darkness.

———

"So here at last is where I find you," a soft voice said.

I came to consciousness and immediately wished I hadn't. I was in so much pain! I heard footsteps but could not open my eyes.

Strangers! I thought weakly. *The sword!*

The hilt felt warm, and I was still holding onto it.

Good. They'll never get it if I hold on.

Unable to open my eyes, I used my other senses—or what was left of them. My body was frozen solid, and I had no feeling in my legs. I could still hear the river rushing behind me. That meant I was still lying on the riverbank. The blizzard had stopped, but a pile of snow had accumulated on top of me. I wondered how long had I been out here. I wondered how I was even still alive.

I focused on the sound of the stranger's boots crushing the

snow as he neared me. "Stay away," I said. "You'll never get it. I won't let you have it. Stay away." I spoke in such a soft, weak voice that I doubted I could be heard. My lips cracked and bled when I moved them, and I winced in pain.

My pack was lifted off my back—somehow, without my arms moving—and I was tenderly rolled onto my back. My clothes and skin cracked and crunched from the layer of ice that had formed all over me. It was painful to be moved. Only the Light Gods knew how long I'd been frozen in that same position. A hand slid under my legs and another behind my back, and someone picked me up. My head hung heavy, feeling ten times its weight due to the snow and ice frozen in my hair.

I ignored the pain and bent my thoughts to the sword. "Stay away. You'll never get it," I said again softly, as I was held tenderly in a pair of arms.

"Show me your eyes, young one," a kind male voice said.

I felt a hand rest on my forehead. Beyond any will of my own, my eyelids lifted, and my blurry vision was filled with a pair of soft blue eyes. My vision came into focus a little more, and I saw that it was an elderly man with a kind smile hidden by a long white beard. How he had picked me up and was holding me with one arm, I couldn't guess.

Despite his kind appearance I held fast to the sword. "You'll never get it. I will fight you if I must," I said, barely above a whisper.

I didn't convince myself any more than I did him. My words only made the man's smile widen.

"You are in no shape to be making threats, young Azrel," he said. "But lucky for you, I mean you no harm. I'm here to help you."

"You know who I am?" I asked in soft surprise. I'd lived such a sheltered life. How did this stranger know me? Then Ortheldo came to my mind. He must have found help! "Ortheldo!" I gasped, meekly struggling to free myself from the man's arms and run to him, wherever he might be. "Where is he? Is he okay? I must see…"

"Shh, shh," the man said gently. "You are weak and delirious. Hush now. I'm going to make you well."

Before I could give him a piece of my mind for calling me

delirious, darkness claimed me again.

FOUR

I awoke again to the sweet sound of music and soft singing. It was such a lovely thing to hear, but it quickly became the last thing on my mind when I realized the sword wasn't in my hand!

I sat straight up in the massive bed in which I was lying and searched for it. I didn't have to look far, thankfully. It was right at my side on the bed, with a shear white material wrapped around the hilt. I impatiently ripped the material off, dropped it onto the floor, and breathed a sigh of relief when the diamond hilt was in my hand.

I looked around at where I was. The bed could fit four people across it with room to spare. It was covered in a lovely gold silk cloth with deep green woven throughout it. Matching gold woven pillows were behind me. It was quite luxurious compared to what I was used to—a cave. Looking down at myself, I found that I had on a beautiful cream-colored nightgown with lace trim and floral embroidery. Though it was lovely, I felt like a fool wearing it. I was used to sleeping in pants and a long-sleeved top. This was so…feminine.

Looking around, I had no clue where I was or how I'd gotten in this room—if it could even be called a room. There wasn't any glass in the windows, no doors, and no roof. Streaks of yellow sunlight shone down through a thick, full canopy of golden leaves above me that grew from rich, brown tree branches.

Leaves? I thought. *But it's winter.*

I was basically sitting outdoors, but there was no snow. The temperature was rather warm actually.

Three tree trunks bunched tightly together protruded through the floor of my "room" and bore beautiful carvings, long scarred over, of various leaves, fruits, flowers, and vines. The walls looked like any normal wooden ones in any ordinary house—except that they stood only four feet tall. Empty archways rose from the top of the short walls like glassless windows. Since it was easy to see over the walls, the empty archways only served to add architectural splendor to the place. Empty archways also rose from the floors to serve as doorways leading from one "room" to another and out onto a small balcony.

Warm, sweet-smelling air blew softly around me, and I felt as if I could breathe more easily than ever just by being here—wherever "here" was.

Gazing over the balcony, I could make out a partial view of the land surrounding me. It consisted of a large, still body of water below, high rugged golden cliffs above in every direction, and waterfalls. In my immediate line of sight, there were at least three rushing down the rock walls. I appeared to be up in some trees that sat on the edge of an island in the middle of a wide lake.

I couldn't see much more from my bed, but I tried to imagine what I couldn't see. The land looked as if nothing, not even time, could touch it. It seemed young and new and yet somehow ancient at the same time. I was enthralled.

"Hello, Azrel."

I spun my head in the direction of the voice and held up my sword to ward off an attack—one that didn't come. What I saw nearly made my jaw drop to the floor. I clenched my teeth against doing so. A woman stood beside my bed, but she couldn't be a human. Her face was so beautiful, so flawless, that it was like nothing I could have ever imagined. Her hair looked like spun gold, falling in graceful spiral curls to below her waist. Her dress of deep golden-tan floated gracefully about her ankles, and the white lace trim complemented her pale face and rosy cheeks.

She smiled kindly at me. "My name is Isadith. I have been taking care of you."

"Where am I?" I asked, not lowering my sword or my suspicion, despite her kind blue eyes.

"You are in my homeland of Galad Kas. Please be assured that you are safe here, as is your sword."

I knew of Galad Kas. It was a Salynn city. I was in a Salynn city? Isadith was a Salynn? I stared at her and all her loveliness and finally took notice of the white Sallybreath flowers in her golden hair.

Sallybreath flowers were a magical kind of flower that grew from the hair of every Salynn. The color of the Sallybreath flowers depended on which realm the Salynn belonged to; Galad Kas' flowers were white. It was the easiest way to tell apart a Salynn and a human, other than the fact that Salynns were far fairer than humans. There were a few more subtle qualities that differentiated them, too, like stealth, speed, and strength that exceeded any human's capability.

Looking at Isadith, I realized my father hadn't been kidding when he'd said that Salynns were, by far, the fairest of all beings. Seeing them in the flesh was much more enchanting than beholding pictures of them in books.

Wait—had she mentioned my sword being safe? How did she know that it was precious to me? Though I hated it with every fiber of my being, I knew how important it was.

As I narrowed my eyes at her, another figure walked into the room. "So, she has finally awoken, has she?" His voice was slightly familiar.

Despite the warm sun, the man wore a heavy, velvet deep-green hooded robe tied closed at the waist with a shining golden belt. His long, white beard and hair rested upon his robe like fresh snow on a grassy field. Examining him a moment, I suddenly remembered the soft blue eyes I had seen on the riverbank.

He smiled. "And she is already on the defense, I see."

At first I wondered what he meant. Then I realized I was still holding up my sword. Having no idea what was going on or what these beings had in mind to do with me, I was still positioned for attack. I wouldn't let myself become a victim.

"Who are you? Why am I here? Where's Ortheldo?" I asked.

"Will you withdraw your sword first so that I may give you your elixir?" Isadith asked, producing a vial of dark brown liquid.

I curled my lip at the foul-looking substance and at her having told me to lower my defense. "No! I won't withdraw my sword, and I sure as bloody hell won't be drinking that!" I threw off the blankets and advanced toward them with my sword raised. Though they outnumbered me, they backed away. "I have things to do, places to go, and people to find," I told them. "So, if one of you will be kind enough to give me my traveling clothes, I'll be gone."

"Please calm yourself. No one means you any harm here, White Warrior," the old man said.

I took in a sharp breath. White Warrior? What the...? How could he possibly know? It was supposed to be a secret. Only Ortheldo, my father, and I knew of the white curse.

"If you will rest and drink your elixir, I will explain everything to you," the old man said, as though he could read my thoughts.

Too curious to argue, I lowered my sword and sat back down on the bed. Isadith handed me the vial and I choked down the liquid as quickly as possible. With a kind smile, Isadith left the room. Her moves were so graceful that I couldn't help but to watch her walk away.

The old man pulled up a chair to my bed. "First of all, my name is Beldorn, and it is a pleasure to meet you," he said with a wide grin.

I could almost hear him add, "Even though you just threatened my life," and I cracked half a smile.

"I'm sure many questions linger in your mind, doubtless the first being how I know you are the White Warrior. Well, there is a simple answer to that: I was friends with your father." My eyes widened. "You may recall him saying that you would not learn your place all on your own?" I nodded. "Well, he was speaking of me. He asked me to guide you on your path since he would not be able to. He wanted me to teach you more of what you need to know about the world you have never seen and about this powerful gift that has been given to you."

I mentally scoffed at the word "gift."

"Despite how your father may have felt about it or what he said to you about it, it *is* a gift," Beldorn said, seeming to read my thoughts again. "You will realize this someday."

Sure I will, Beldorn, I thought, wondering if he could thought-read sarcasm.

"Upon our first meeting, just after you were born," he continued, "he told me everything about himself and you. We had regular meetings over the past twenty years, during which he updated me on your progress and we finalized plans.

"I was supposed to meet you soon after you left the cave, but the endless snowstorms hindered me. When I finally was able to set out, you were long gone, and I went searching for you. That's when I discovered you on the riverbank. Finding you in such peril, I guessed that if you had any magic at all, it would be the only thing keeping you alive. So I aided you in opening your eyes to see what color they were, since white eyes occur when the White Warrior's powers are in use. Your eyes were white, confirming who you were."

I looked at him, replaying his finding me on the bank and recalled his lifting my pack off me without moving my arms and picking me up and holding me up with one arm. That was only possible with magic. Then it dawned on me that Beldorn was a Wizard—another race my father had taught me about. They were the most powerful of the magical races. My father didn't teach me very much about them, though, because according to him Wizards were complex beings and each one was as different as the next.

Beldorn sat in silence for a few minutes, deep in thought, before he spoke again. "Your father asked me to teach you, though I'm not sure *what* he expected me to teach you. You already know everything you need about your gift. You know it must be kept a secret, you know—"

"Yes!" I interrupted heatedly. "And it's such a well-kept secret, isn't it? For instance, you, Ortheldo, and Isadith know about it. Who else will find out? Why not tell everyone in Casdanarus?"

"Palponer, Isadith, Ortheldo, and myself are the only beings who know. Your secret will not be exposed by the Salynns or me. It's too important that it be kept a secret."

"Palponer?" I cried. "Who is he, and why does he know? And why do any of you care if it's kept secret? Its secrecy is important to my father and me, for our own reasons. What difference does it make to you?"

He stared blankly at the opposite wall as if he wasn't listening to me, and I started to grind my teeth. My father and I had our reasons, all right. We didn't want anyone to know because the White Warrior was the most hated being in the world. No one would want it revealed that she had the "gift" that once belonged to "the greatest coward in the history of Casdanarus," as was written in some of those history books. The "gift" was shamed and spat upon by all. I didn't want to be shamed and spat upon just because, beyond my control, it had been passed to me. Why my father and I had to bear this burden, I'd never know.

"Palponer is the Lord of Galad Kas," Beldorn finally answered, ignoring my other questions.

I was so frustrated. My father had said to keep it secret, and now Beldorn was saying to keep it secret. If its secrecy was so important to everyone, why did everyone know about it?

I looked away, dreading to ask the next question, "What's become of Ortheldo?"

There was a quiet pause before Beldorn replied, "We don't know. We've found no trace of him."

I squeezed my eyes shut, and that strange burning feeling returned to them, indicating that I was about to cry. I had lost all that was familiar in my world. Ortheldo was the only thing left I could call home, and now he was gone.

I suddenly felt very cold and alone. I drew my knees up and wrapped my arms around them, curling into a tight ball to keep out the bitter cold of emptiness. I hoped beyond hope that he was okay. My Ortheldo, whom I had thought of as only a dueling partner, had truly been my best friend, my only friend. I'd never gotten the chance to tell him how important he was to me, how much he had meant to me. He and my father had been my whole world. I missed him and wanted him here. I needed his comfort and his handsome face. I needed to hear his voice tell me everything would be okay.

As a droplet of water slid down my cheek, I heard a thoughtful hum come from the Wizard. I snapped my eyes open and scowled at him. "What?" I barked.

"How often do you cry?"

I narrowed my eyes. "Why?"

"Because the White Warrior cries white tears."

Confused, I touched the teardrop on my face and looked at it. It was indeed white water. Perhaps it should have shocked me, but it didn't. If white fire existed, why not white water as well?

"I would counsel you to avoid crying at all costs. But if you find yourself in a situation where you must cry, hide your face well. You can't give away your secret."

I wanted to cry a river of tears for Ortheldo but decided I'd better get into the habit of never crying for any reason.

"Well, Azrel, you need your rest," Beldorn said, rising from his chair. "We will stay in Galad Kas for a few months, allowing you to mend and the winter outside of this place to end. Then I will take you traveling for a while and teach you what I can." He started to make his way out of my room. "After that I will take you to The Pitt, where you will live with your stepfather, mother, and brother."

My heart stopped. "Brother?" I asked, looking at him quickly.

What was he talking about?

Beldorn stopped at the archway and turned back to look at me. "Yes. You have a younger brother. Your mother's second child."

"What?" I whispered.

Beldorn saw the look on my face and chuckled. "I see you are intrigued."

"I have a brother? I've never had a brother before," I said, sounding ridiculous.

Beldorn laughed. "Yes, I know. Rabryn is his name, and he's anxious to meet you."

My eyes went wide and butterflies seemed to erupt in my stomach. "He knows I exist?" I said. "He knows I'm coming?"

Beldorn nodded. "As does your mother." My eyes went wide. "You've been out cold for two weeks. In that time, I traveled to The Pitt and told them of your coming. Rabryn was just as surprised as you are, and very excited." A thoughtful look came over his face. "That's the impression I got anyway, when he started jumping around the house singing your name."

I laughed loudly. I'd never laughed so hard in my life, but the image of a small boy I'd never met before jumping around and singing my name made me laugh so hard that my sides ached. I felt so strange. Why was this brother, my brother, such an exciting thing to me?

I had a brother. I was a sister!

Beldorn smiled at my outburst. "Would you like me to tell you about him, or do you wish to be surprised?"

I composed myself enough to speak. "I would love to hear more about him. Would you mind?"

"Not at all," he said, coming back into my room and sitting down in the chair again. "I will also tell you more about your mother and their way of life. It's very different from what you're used to."

I grinned and listened to all that Beldorn had to say about The Pitt, my mother, and my brother…Rabryn.

———

After two months, spring started to bloom outside of Galas Kas, and Beldorn decided it was time for us to leave. I almost didn't want to. It was so lovely and peaceful here. Because I was so used to solitude, it felt strange being around so many beings at once, and I often avoided the Salynns that called this place home and went off by myself. Isadith was the only Salynn I grew relatively close to. We spent the most amount of time together.

At her request, I even taught her some swordplay, showing her some techniques that my father had taught me. She seemed to genuinely enjoy my teachings, which I thought odd for a graceful, female Salynn. Yet I felt a sense of pride being able to teach Isadith, who was thousands of years old, something she didn't know.

When we simulated duels, I thought of Ortheldo.

It burned my heart that I didn't know what had happened to him. It burned even more that I might never find out. I missed him. I missed his pretty eyes and his bright, warm, handsome smile. I missed his voice telling me what a great warrior I would be and, when things got tough, how much faith he had in me.

I spent a good amount of time with Beldorn, too. I learned to respect him and even befriended him. But I couldn't bear to lose another person close to me, so I kept a good distance between us. I think he sensed this and left me alone quite a bit.

As I packed my weapons and belongings for travel, Isadith came to my "section," as I'd fondly come to call the rooms in the trees.

"Hello, Azrel," she said kindly.

"Hello," I replied and returned her smile, though I'm sure it was as transparent as the glassless archways around the room.

"I wanted to see you before you left. I have a gift for you."

"A gift?" Confused, I turned toward her. "Why?"

She came toward me holding a deep-red Salynn cloth across her palms. "It isn't much, but I thought you could use it."

I took the gift from her long, slender hands and opened it. In the cloth lay a beautiful Salynn knife with a small strap and hilt. My eyes went wide at the sight of the gorgeous, perfectly shaped blade. But the short white strap was too small to pass as a belt. I was a bit confused about what to do with it.

Isadith took the small strap into her hands and crouched down in front of me. "I had it made for you." She wrapped the strong leather Salynn strap around my left thigh and fastened it, positioning the hilt on the outside of my leg. "You attach it to the top part of your leg, where you can have discreet access to it." She straightened and smiled at me while I examined the blade in my hands.

I'd learned from my father that Salynn goods were very powerful and masterfully crafted, so this blade would most certainly come in handy. I studied the metal and noticed that the slightly curved foot-long silver blade bore lovely engravings of words in the Salynn script.

"A star shall shine on the hour of victory for the mighty warrior," I read aloud in the common tongue and then smiled at her. "Thank you, Isadith."

She smiled back. "I won't hinder you any longer. Beldorn is waiting."

With that, she left my section. I slipped the beautiful blade into the hilt attached to my thigh and finished packing with a heavy heart.

A great gathering of Salynns saw Beldorn and me off. They all wished us well as we packed our supplies on Beldorn's horse, Lómarandil. She was a beautiful stallion who had a silver coat and a light gray mane. Before coming here, I'd never seen a horse in the flesh, and I now thought no creature could ever be as beautiful and powerful as a horse was.

When we finished loading our traveling gear, Beldorn mounted. I hesitated, gazing at the ground, trying to push away the fear of going into the unknown again.

From behind, a pair of hands rested on my shoulders. I looked back to see Lord Palponer smiling down at me. I'd only met him a few times during my stay, but they were always lengthy and pleasant meetings. His face was slender and youthful, and his white Sallybreath Flowers were almost invisible against his straight white hair that cascaded past his shoulders, accenting the golden crown he wore on his brow. His eyes were a lovely pale gray color, and were kind, making me feel safe and comfortable. His white robes swished around his feet with each graceful move, and the string of pearls he wore around his waist dangled down the front of his robes, truly giving him a lordly air.

"Farewell, Azrel," he said softly, placing a hand on the top of my head in a gesture of blessing. "May your paths be green and the breeze blow at your back."

I put my hand upon my chest and bowed low at the waist to

him, swallowing my pride to show respect to the one who had given me a place to mend. Though he had been present at the battle when my father fled, he didn't scorn me or treat me badly for being what I was.

"Thank you for everything, my Lord," I said.

I mounted in front of Beldorn, and we said farewell. The Wizard squeezed his legs against Lómarandil, and she leaped forward into a soft gallop straight toward the water's edge. My stomach knotted, and I wondered if Beldorn planned to make her swim to the shore. We hit the edge of the water and started galloping *over* it.

Eyes wide, I looked down as we rode over the surface on an invisible bridge. The calm water under Lómarandil sparkled and rippled in the sun, but her hooves clopped loudly as if she were riding over a solid surface. I was impressed. Salynn magic was no doubt very powerful and wonderful if this was possible. What a great protective measure for Galad Kas—an invisible bridge!

"The bridge moves as well," Beldorn informed me, reading my thoughts again. "It is constantly circling the island so enemies can never guess where it might be."

I nodded, though I barely heard him. I was glad Lómarandil was under me and Beldorn's arm was around my stomach, or I might not have been able to cross due to my new, deeply rooted fear of water. I could never, ever cross this bridge on foot. Not when the only thing I could see under me was the water itself.

I looked over my shoulder for a last glance at Galad Kas and saw Isadith standing high upon a branch at the edge of the island. She raised her hand to me in our final farewell, to which I waved back. Then, with a longing and heavy heart, I faced forward again and rode into the unknown.

FIVE

Beldorn and I traveled together for over a year to many places that I'd only seen and read about in books during my studies. We didn't see everything, of course—that would have taken years. But every place I did see was magnificent. We came across realms and towns, from the simple to the exquisite, and all were different and special in their own way. I saw races and species that I'd only ever read about. There were creatures in some places that I hadn't believed existed until I saw them with my own eyes.

Due to my lack of social graces and my not being used to being around large numbers of people, which still made me nervous, I didn't interact much with others, but I did explore the lands.

Queen Sauryavia of Fayithjen Forrest, a land that lay just outside the border of Miick, wouldn't tolerate my preference for solitude, though, and insisted I spend as much time with her as I could. This made me really uncomfortable. Despite having my guard up, I became relatively close to her.

It wasn't heartbreaking to leave, but going off into the unknown was always hard for me. Maybe it always would be.

One random day during our travels, a large party of mounted figures was riding toward us on the other side of a clearing we were crossing. I narrowed my eyes against the bright sun—or perhaps at the brightness of their armor. It had to be the armor because the metal they wore shined brightly in a rainbow of movement. The array of colors was breathtaking! No two colors were the same in the large fleet, which I found very interesting. I didn't know so many colors existed. I didn't know metal could be dyed either. It had to be magical.

"Beldorn, who are they?"

He looked out across the plain. "Ah, those my dear, are the Gleo`gwyns."

"Gleo`gwyns?" I thought about that for a moment. "That's Salynnian for 'Metallic Riders,' isn't it?"

"Indeed."

I nodded. It seemed fitting. I vaguely recalled my father

mentioning them.

"They are a mix of races that do nothing but ride the lands and help travelers in need. They know much about woodlands, plants, and beasts—even more then you might, Azrel."

"Travelers in need?"

"They can bring food if travelers are hungry, water if they are thirsty, aid if they are injured, or protection if they are attacked. They often tend to village emergencies, such as a fire or famine, if a village has a dry season. In ancient days, they were mainly used for carrying messages for soldiers of Light because they, and their horses, have unnatural abilities to endure long, hard rides with almost zero rest. They can make extremely speedy retrievals and returns."

"Protection? They don't seem like they could be violent, even to protect someone."

"They are generally peaceful people, but if the need occurs, they will fight and kill to protect an innocent traveler or merchant. When they win a battle, they burn the bodies of slain enemies. It's how they remind foes of their battle prowess, which is formidable, despite how peaceable they seem."

As the Gleo`gwyns passed us across the distance, the one I assumed to be their leader, who wore shiny, deep-red armor and a crown of what looked like leaves and berries, gave Beldorn a little nod in greeting. Beldorn waved in reply.

We came to a Salynn realm called White Veilvin. The entire land seemed to have a gentle white glow about it, as if the souls of every living thing were reaching out to embrace the day. The grass there was a periwinkle color, which sadly reminded me of Ortheldo's eyes. Small gold flowers sprung up across the grass like scattered confetti, and the leaves atop the mammoth trees, which looked like distant relatives of birch trees, were light pink.

The Sallybreath flowers that grew from the hair of these Salynns were gold, which meant they were the most powerful of all the Salynns. I became disenchanted quickly, though, when I found out what these particular Salynns there were like. Yes, they were very powerful, far more than those in Galad Kas, but they were also serious, cold, boring, and downright rude. They never sang, or danced, or told stories like the Salynns of Galad Kas. They thought they knew everything, and believed their decisions were always right.

My personality clashed hard with theirs, and things became interesting during our visit. I decided to stir up their quiet lives a bit and made a spectacle of myself. I started arguments, complained about the food, and dueled with any Salynn who wanted to challenge me, usually hurting them before winning the bout. I poked fun of their clothes, the way they walked, and their grim expressions. I absolutely hated it there.

One Salynn who really annoyed me, was Masinyel, the leader of White Veilvin. The King had disappeared fifteen years ago, but fifteen years meant nothing in the lifespan of a Salynn. He might as well have disappeared yesterday. In the King's absence, Masinyel was the one everyone answered to. She knew about my magic, which alone would have annoyed me, but everything about her bothered me. She was a very unsettling individual. It didn't help that her main—and pretty much *only*—interest in me involved trying to convince me to change permanently into my White Warrior form, which I adamantly and loudly refused.

Beldorn lightly scolded me as we rode away, saying that it would probably take three new generations of Salynns to forget about my visit. I took it as a compliment.

We stopped hither and yonder on our trek back west, even passing Galad Kas again, until we reached Rocksheloc Mountain, the largest mountain in Casdanarus. It stood proud and alone on the eastern edge of the Mongerst Mountain range. Calling this mountain "massive" would be an understatement. Rocksheloc was a Humount realm, and because of my affinity for mountains, I desperately wanted to stop there. Alas, Beldorn said we didn't have time.

We passed through Narcatertus, the largest human village in Casdanarus, soon after. I hated the place the second I laid eyes on it, even from a distance. It was a cesspool of humanity. The number of people alone was suffocating. Luckily, we didn't stay overnight at some fleabag inn there. Instead, Beldorn and I camped at the mouth of Crox Pass, just inside the Mongerst Mountains.

That night, Beldorn said he was taking me home.

Home. That word didn't seem quite right to describe The Pitt. What was a home? A place to live? A place where you were surrounded by loved ones? I began to wonder about how the people at "home" were going to take to me. Would they accept me? How were these simple but, so I was told, kind people going to react to someone so different from them? How was I going to react to people so different from me? I lost a lot of sleep while we traveled through Crox Path. There was no way to answer my questions yet, so I just decided that I would adjust to whatever treatment I got from them, positive or negative. I had to.

Beldorn and I eventually came to the woodland that surrounded The Pitt and rested for the night near a small stream. Dusk was falling as I gazed into the forest that would take me to my mother. It was a road I felt reluctant to take, probably because I was only used to two ways of living: solitude and travel. Staying in one place for a long length of time with crowds of beings constantly around frightened me. I wasn't going to admit I felt fear, though. My father had told me to be brave, and I would do my best.

The thought of my father still made me sad, but looking at the road that would take me to my mother, I couldn't deny a small stir of joy at recalling how he'd looked when he'd first told me about her.

After he had fled that fateful battle, he'd traveled Casdanarus for a long time, avoiding every man, Salynn, and being in between, for fear of being recognized. The hatred and resentment toward him was widespread and strong, even after 3,000 years. His chosen isolation over such a vast length of time, however, started to make him go mad. It got to the point where he thought about slitting his wrists to end his misery. At the same time, however, he realized then that he had to somehow rejoin society.

Reason told him that if he did this, he would need to live in a very small and secluded place, which brought him into the woods. After hundreds of searches and many empty woodlands across Casdanarus, he decided that slitting his wrists might indeed be an option.

While in the woodland that I sat in now, he trudged on for endless days and miles, trying to park up the courage to actually do it. Finally, weak, tired, and maddened, he dropped to his knees and took out the sword, resting the edge of the blade against his skin. As he put pressure on the blade, anticipating the peace and oblivion of death, he suddenly noticed an opening in the trees ahead of him.

Stunned, he stared for a long time into the opening fifteen feet in front of him. It hadn't been there a minute ago. He removed the blade from his wrist and hastily stumbled toward it. He emerged into a land that he'd never seen before. The man had seen every blade of grass in Casdanarus three times over in 3,000 years of travel, and yet he'd never seen this land.

He marched down the grassy cliffs and quickly encountered the inhabitants, who seemed only slightly surprised by his arrival. Everyone received him well, considering he was a complete stranger.

The land he had found was called The Pitt. It was small and secluded and perfect for him. The name fit the location because the village rested at the bottom of a lush green bowl of land, but my father said it seemed a harsh name for somewhere so lovely. He learned quickly that the people liked it that way. Evil rumors about a place called The Pitt kept others away from it, and they enjoyed their solitude.

He named himself Gworrent, and on the day he arrived, the people gave him a house whose previous owner had recently passed. He felt strangely safe among these people. They didn't know who he was or, more importantly, who he had been. That alone made the decision to stay easy.

A celebration was in order after he'd been living there for a few days, a party they held every year to celebrate the coming of the spring season. That night he met my mother, Priweth.

"One look into her piercing blue eyes and suddenly I could not have enough of her. It was something I'd never felt before," my father told me.

They started spending a lot of time together, and unfortunately, he had to lie about his past so he wouldn't reveal his former identity. He feared he would lose her if she knew about his reputation and the scorn that people felt for him. As time wore on, though, his past became a distant memory. All he cared about was his future with my mother.

One night, my mother called to him and told him some news— news that should have been joyful, but chilled him to the bone. "We're going to have a child," she said.

My father told me he cried when he heard the news, though at the time I could not imagine him doing so. I never saw him cry until the day he died. Now I could see it so clearly.

My mother had tenderly wiped away his tears and asked what was wrong. My father took her hands in his, looked her in the eyes, and said in a choking sob, "Priweth, I've lied to you."

That night he revealed everything to her. He told her who he really was, what had happened to him, and what the female voice from the light had told him about him having a child to finish what he should have.

"Priweth," he said, "I have to take our baby far away as soon as he is born. Evil will be hunting him, and I need to train him properly so he might be able to face it."

My mother broke down into tears at the thought of losing me and her beloved in one foul blow. Seeing her cry as deeply as she did made him wish he had slit his wrists in the forest—something that made me want to slap my father when he told me. My mother, however, was gracious and understanding and knew it was for the best. The simple secluded life of The Pitt would not prepare a warrior to face the Evil that she now knew awaited her child.

"So be it," she sobbed.

They held each other close that night, making plans. They decided that on the day I was born my father would take me away in the middle of the night. In the morning, my mother would claim that they had gotten into an argument and he'd stolen me while she'd slept to make her regret defying him. They both cried at this plan because it meant that my father would never again be welcome in The Pitt.

As painful as it was, this was their decision. It was the only way to get me out of there without divulging that my father was taking me into the woods to train me to face the greatest Evil the world had ever seen.

At last, during a cold sunrise in December, I was born. My mother named me Azrel, which meant "victory" in the ancient Salynn language. My father fell face down on the floor and cried until he couldn't breathe because I was a girl, and his daughter would have to take up the sword and face the Evil he could not. He regretted every decision he'd ever made in his life—all of which seemed to have brought his daughter to this horrible fate. Women of this world were not warriors. He knew, though, that if he didn't at least try to prepare me for my path, I would be doomed to meet my end before long.

Late that night he prepared a horse with all the supplies he and my mother had purchased for my care. My father came back to the house and found my mother holding me for the first and the last time. She was sobbing heavily.

"Why can't I go with you?" she begged as tears flowed down her cheeks.

My father kneeled before her and petted her hair. "Priweth, I don't want to expose you to this Evil," he said. "It burns my heart that my daughter has to face this, all on account of my failure." He shook his head. "I don't want anything to happen to you, or Azrel, but at least *you* can be safe here."

My mother nodded and painfully handed me to my father. He took me into his arms and then gazed at her. "In an instant," he told me years later, "I memorized every curve and every freckle of her face. Then I said the most painful words in my 10,000-year existence: 'Goodbye, my beloved Priweth.'"

She rested her hand on his cheek and said, "My heart will never belong to another." Then she looked down at me, kissed me, and whispered softly, "Goodbye, Azrel, my beautiful baby. I love you more than you know."

My father got up and silently left the house with me. My mother watched from the doorway as he mounted his horse and sped off into the night with a heavy heart and a maddening longing to stay.

My mother sounded like a sweet lady, but she was still a stranger to me, and I was still a stranger to her. By this time tomorrow night, though, I would have met both her and my brother.

My brother. I smiled again at the image of a young boy dancing around, singing my name. But my smile vanished when I thought about the possibility that he might not like me once we met. What if my mother didn't like me? What if I only caused her pain because I reminded her of my father?

The "what if" questions kept me awake all night. As the sun slowly lit up the forest, I wondered what awaited me in the land I was about to enter: acceptance or rejection? Oddly enough, my biggest concern was not rejection from my mother, but from my little brother.

When the sun traveled to the eight o'clock hour, Beldorn finally awoke. He took one look at me and said, "Something troubles you."

I didn't take my eyes from the woods as I nodded.

"I know what it is, I think," he said, getting to his feet. "We can talk about it when we get going, if you wish. Right now, we're going to have to reevaluate how you look."

Confused, I looked up at him, and then down at myself. I *was* rather grubby. The toils of travel showed up very clearly in my appearance.

"I'll bathe in the stream," I said and stood.

Beldorn stopped me and presented three small vials of odd-looking liquid. "From Isadith," he said. "This one"—he held up the vial of purple liquid—"you put in your hair first." He held up the dark pink liquid next. "This one you put in your hair second." Finally, he held up one that was pale orange. "This one, you wash your skin with." He handed them to me along with a soft, lavender-colored Salynn cloth and a new set of clothes I hadn't seen before. "She wanted you to look your best when you met your family."

I shook my head, stunned, then smiled up at Beldorn. "Thank you."

He patted my shoulder and I headed down to the stream to find a still and shallow place to bathe. I found one only a half a mile downstream, and after soaking in the water, I popped the cork of the first vial. The smell invaded my senses. It was lovelier than anything I'd ever smelled before, and I felt a rush of exhilaration that warmed my heart and soul. Oh, I wanted to stay in that stream and smell those liquids until the sun went down.

After drying off, I was happy to discover that the smells didn't fade. I also noticed that my skin and hair had never before felt so soft and so clean. I felt renewed, strong, and almost beautiful. Even the outfit Isadith had sent with Beldorn made me feel lovely. It consisted of a dark blue satiny tunic with gorgeous, delicate vine embroideries along every hem, dark gray leggings, a matching gray belt, and new black boots.

I was so beyond grateful to her for these gifts. Maybe if my appearance wasn't upsetting, I would be accepted more easily.

When I returned to camp, I found Beldorn packing up Lómarandil. He stopped suddenly when he spotted me, and he smiled brightly. "Well! Don't you look radiant, Azrel."

"Thank you," I replied instead of rolling my eyes at the compliment like I usually did.

But I *felt* radiant! I hoped this feeling would never go away.

SIX

I felt sick. Night had long fallen as we came to the edge of lush high cliffs that towered over The Pitt. My stomach churned as Beldorn eased Lómarandil down the steep, grassy cliff side to the village below.

The cliffs formed a perfect oval around the small land populated by perhaps three hundred people. A waterfall to the right cascaded down the only rocky cliff side, joining with a stream below that bisected the land into two parts before emptying out through a short cave to the left. Six wooden bridges spanned the length of the stream. No roads were visible, just well-traveled paths worn away by wagon wheels. Some were more worn then others, especially where the bridges met the land on each shore.

All the houses dotting the land looked very similar. None were either exceptionally big or small—just comfortable, simple, one- or two-story houses, varying only in shape. Almost all of them had a flower garden somewhere on the property. Short, gnarled, odd-looking trees I'd never seen before dotted the land. Some bore fruits, others flowers, adding to the natural beauty of the place.

We reached the bottom of the bowl and started making our way through the village, passing the two largest buildings, each of which had a big plot of land. One clearly was used for farming, and the other to raise pigs, goats, and sheep. We also passed a small blacksmithing building, a linen shop, a leather shop, and a butcher's shop. The place was completely self-sustainable, with no need for trade beyond the cliffs.

My heart was pounding in my head as we rode through the village. We crossed one of the bridges and traveled one of the well-worn trails until Beldorn stopped in front of a house that sat within a ten minute walk of the waterfall. I turned my gaze to the house—the one I would call home for the Light Gods only knew how long.

It was built on top of a small, raised parcel of land. A short flight of eight cobblestone stairs led to the front door. We walked up them now. I felt dizzy the entire way.

Standing at the front door, I saw that all the lights in the house were off. "Well, I guess they aren't home," I said, trying to get out of this any way possible, though I knew I sounded ridiculous. "We should come back tomorrow. Or maybe next week. Just to be sure they're here."

Beldorn gave me a stern glance over his shoulder and knocked on the door with his staff. My heart seemed to skip a beat with every knock. A light came on inside almost immediately, and footsteps could be heard coming toward the door. My face grew hot with nervous tension and I felt like I was going to be sick. On impulse, I stepped behind Beldorn. I knew I wouldn't be able to hide for long. If nothing else, my pounding heart would give me away.

I felt like such a child, so vulnerable to whatever was about to happen. And, okay—I finally admitted it—I was scared. I really didn't like fear. Worse, I didn't like not being in control or the feeling of helplessness. What had happened in the river was a perfect example—thrashing around in rushing water while being swept away against my will. It was the worst feeling a human being could experience. Having my father die, losing my best friend, and being taken to live in an unknown land with a mother I'd never met— all of that was a lot like being in that river, and I hated it.

The doorknob rattled, and I heard the door creak open. A soft female voice came from within. "Beldorn! How lovely to see you again."

Beldorn bowed slightly, almost revealing me. "Hello, Priweth."

As they exchanged greetings, my mind kept screaming, *Run! Run away! Get away while you can! You don't have to face rejection! Leave! Just jump on Lómarandil and ride like the wind. Go! Go!*

"Azrel." Beldorn's soft voice brought me out of my terrified thoughts of escape. I looked up to see him gazing at me over his shoulder. "Your mother wants to meet you."

I swallowed hard and dropped my chin to my chest. Taking a deep breath, I gathered all the courage I had left in me and stepped out from behind the Wizard. Slowly, I raised my head to look at my mother.

She was absolutely stunning! No wonder my father had loved her so much. It had been twenty-five years since he'd first met her, and she was still radiant. Her thick brown hair was tied up in a knot with loose strands caressing the sides of her face and neck. Her white chemise outlined her perfect figure and danced around her bare feet. I had her blue eyes. In fact, I looked a lot like her, but my figure wasn't as elegant. I was more muscular than she was, and taller.

As soon as she looked at me, her legs buckled and she fell to her knees in the doorway. Tears filled her eyes, and her chin quivered as she gazed up at me. I resisted the urge to shift uncomfortably at her reaction.

"Azrel," she whispered. Her throat bobbed in a hard swallow. "I'm so happy to see you."

After a little nudge from Beldorn's staff, I took a step toward her. "Hello...Mother," I said hesitantly. The word "mother" tumbled out of my mouth awkwardly. I'd never said it to anyone before.

Holding back hysterical sobs, she slowly reached out to take hold of my hand. Gazing down at it, she tenderly caressed the back of it, as if making sure I was real and solid to her fingers. She looked up at me again and, using the doorframe for support, pushed herself to her feet. She stared at my face for another moment and then, with a cry, threw her arms around me and sobbed into my shoulder.

I stood frozen and confused as she trembled against me. At last I lightly placed my hands on her back, feeling odd at having a stranger hold onto me as if her life depended on it.

Sensing my apprehension, she pulled away and wiped tears with one hand, keeping the other on my shoulder. "I'm sorry, I'm sorry. I don't mean to rush anything. I wanted you to get used to this change first, but"—she looked at my face and placed her elegant hand on my cheek—"I'm so happy to see you. Oh, I've thought about you every single day since"—she tripped on her words—"well, since you left."

I could tell she didn't want to say "since you were taken away."

Smiling gently, she caressed my cheek and the side of my hair. "Oh, my daughter." She gazed at me a little longer before looking up at Beldorn, prompting me to face him as well. "Thank you so much for bringing her here safely. Do you have time for a cup of tea?"

Beldorn smiled. "No, thank you, Priweth. I have a long road ahead of me and must be off."

"Oh, all right. Thank you, Beldorn," she said as she placed her arm gently around my shoulders.

Beldorn bowed slightly again. "Goodbye, Azrel. Until our next meeting."

"Goodbye, my friend," I said, swallowing back tears. "Thank you for all that you've done for me." He smiled before he turned and walked back down the cobblestone steps. I watched him mount Lómarandil and ride out of sight.

I picked up the pack holding all my belongings and faced my mother, feeling empty and alone at having my friend, my partner for the past fourteen months, just ride away as if we'd meant nothing to each other. Once again, the rug of familiarity had been pulled out from under my feet, and I hated it.

My mother smiled at me and stepped inside the house. "Come in, please."

I walked through the doorway. It wasn't very bright. A single oil lamp above the doorway glowed softly, and I could make out the general set-up of the simple house.

Right in front of me was a staircase to the second floor. The hall at the top turned to the right out of sight behind a wall. A cozy living room was just to the right of the staircase. I took a step toward it and gazed around. An unlit fireplace took up the middle of the back wall, with a comfortable looking couch to the left of it. In front of the couch was a short table that stood on a lovely woven throw rug. Another chair, hidden in shadows, faced the table as well. To the left of the stairs was a room that I guessed was a kitchen, though it was dark. From the light provided, I could make out a dining table surrounded by high-back wooden chairs, and saw the edge of a wash basin on the right wall.

"Are you hungry or thirsty?" my mother asked, looking rather nervous.

I shook my head and continued gazing around, taking a few steps into the living room. My eyes fell again to the chair, and I noticed a small figure curled up in a blanket with its back to me.

Excitement boiled up in my chest as I took my pack off my shoulder and set it on the floor. "Is that...?" I asked, not taking my eyes off the little sleeping figure.

I felt my mother's tension ease a bit. "Yes, that's Rabryn," she said softly and walked past me to the chair. My heart skipped a beat at the mention of my brother's name. "He wanted to wait up for you," she said, going to stand behind it, "but the poor thing was exhausted." She smiled, and then bent over the back, and gently shook his shoulder. "Rabryn. Rabryn, darling."

The shadow stirred a bit and a soft voice asked, "Is she here yet?"

I couldn't believe those were the very first words he had to say! A warmth toward him grew inside me unlike anything I'd ever felt before. He really wanted to see me.

My mother brushed her hand over his forehead. "Yes, she is."

Rabryn sat up, suddenly wide awake. "Where? Where is she?"

"Right behind you," my mother replied.

Rabryn's head spun around. My breath caught in my throat, and I nearly collapsed at the sight of his face. He was the most beautiful thing I'd ever seen. He had the biggest, brightest pair of blue eyes. His face, in general, was just indescribable—perfectly proportioned, with a shape that gave him an otherworldly look, and light skin that looked like liquid peach marble. His short brown hair was a mess, giving him an innocent look that matched the innocence his eyes. He was so beautiful.

I would have run up and hugged him, but he was at me first.

"Azrel!" he cried and ran up to me.

I laughed and crouched down with my arms out, and he jumped into them at full speed, almost knocking me over. I wrapped my arms tightly around him and stood, holding him against me in an airborne hug before crouching down again and placing him back on his feet. I stayed low to keep him at eye level and smiled. "Well, it's nice to meet you, too, Rabryn."

He beamed and then petted my hair and my cheek. "You're so pretty!" He inhaled deeply through his nose. "You smell good, too!"

I laughed. "Why, thank you."

He placed his hands on his hips and looked at me questioningly. "So, you're my big sister, huh?"

My heart leapt at being called a big sister. "Yes, I am," I said, squishing his nose with my finger.

He giggled and brought his hands up to his nose. His eyes then dropped down to the sword at my belt and Isadith's gift attached to my leg. His eyes went a little wide. "What are those for?"

I had to forgive him. He and his people led simple lives. Swords and battle knives were of no use to them, so seeing one of each attached to a woman's body like she was about to charge the frontline probably looked strange.

"Those are for me," I replied. "I use them to protect myself."

"Protect yourself from what?"

He seemed genuinely interested, which I found odd. He didn't need to know about the evils of the world though, so with a smirk on my lips, I stood and drew out my sword. "From little brothers who attack big sisters with hugs!"

He let out a rather girlish scream and ran off. I laughed and chased him to the far wall, where he suddenly bent down in front of a pile of neatly stacked firewood and picked something up. I laughed out loud when I realized it was a hand-crafted wooden sword. He faced me in a battle stance—a pretty good one for a child who had never seen a sword fight.

My mother laughed behind us. "Sword fighting is Rabryn's favorite game."

A challenging smirk spread across my brother's face. "It sure is."

I raised an eyebrow. "Oh, really?" I took a battle stance of my own. "Well, have at it, little brother. If I break your sword, I'll make you a new, improved one," I said with a wink.

With that, Rabryn swung his sword at me. He fought as any child amateur would of course, but I let him play it off for a few minutes to release some of his energy. After a bit of fun, I hewed the tip of his sword off and knocked it out of his hand in the same move.

He looked at me, shock filling his piercing blue eyes. "You really know how to sword fight?"

I smiled proudly and sheathed my sword. "Yes, I do. My father taught me."

"Wow!" He ran to our mother and pulled on the front of her nightgown excitedly. "Mama, mama! Can I go outside and play sword fight with Azrel? Please? I'm not tired!"

My mother giggled and then cupped Rabryn's face in her

hands and kissed his forehead. "You may not be tired, my darling, but I'm sure Azrel is. She's had a long journey and needs to rest. You can play with her tomorrow."

Rabryn turned to me. "You've traveled very far? How long have you traveled? Will you tell me about it? I've never left home, but I'm going to be an explorer someday!"

I laughed. "I've traveled quite a bit, and it will take more than a day to tell you all the places I've been to."

"Wow!" Rabryn exclaimed again and looked up at our mother. "Can Azrel sleep in my bed tonight, Mama?"

She kissed his forehead again. "Of course, dear." She turned him toward the staircase and gave his bottom a little swat. "Now go to bed."

He raced past me and up the stairs, his bright eyes on me the whole time. "Don't be too long. You need your rest."

I laughed and shooed him up the stairs. My mother smiled softly as he disappeared.

"I'll bet my last coin that he keeps you up all night talking."

I returned her smile. I glanced down, not really wanting to bring up the next subject but knowing I needed to. "Is my stepfather here?"

Her eyes became sad, and she glanced away. "Yes. He's upstairs sleeping." She looked back at me and forced a smile. "He wanted to be awake when you arrived but...well, he's a hard worker, you see, and he—"

"He doesn't want me here because I'm a reminder of your first love, Gworrent." I interrupted, reading the truth in her eyes. She looked at me apologetically and pressed her lips together, to which I smiled. "Mother, if we are going to have a relationship at all, we can't start out by lying to one another."

She chuckled in relief. "Okay," she nodded. "You're right. I'm sorry." She walked toward me and took my hands into hers. "I just didn't want you to feel you weren't welcome here." She rested a hand on my cheek. "You are welcome, my dear, more than you know. Derweldo"—she shrugged—"he just needs to adjust. I chose not to wake him because I wanted you to feel somewhat comfortable coming into this home."

I nodded. "Thank you, but I don't want you to think you have to protect me. I was taught to protect myself very well. If Derweldo won't accept me, that's up to him."

"He will accept you. He'll learn to love you, just as I do." She paused and pulled me into a hug. "Oh, my daughter. I can't tell you how happy I am that you're here with me." She held me a moment and then pulled back. "It's been over twenty years, and you've grown up so beautifully. Gworrent did a marvelous job. Not that I would expect anything less from him." She smiled. "I'd really love to talk to you about, well, about your father, and your upbringing. Your life, basically." She chuckled. "How is your father?"

I looked down and swallowed past the lump in my throat. Why hadn't Beldorn told her? "He died," I said heavily.

"Oh, dear Gods," she squeaked, bringing her hands to her mouth. "I'm so sorry, darling," she said, placing her hands on my shoulders. "I can't imagine how you feel, having spent your whole life with him. Goodness knows I wanted to die when he left The Pitt, and I'd only known him for five years."

I nodded. "He was a wonderful man, teacher and father."

"I wish things hadn't turned out the way they did. I loved your father very much."

I nodded. "He loved you, too."

She smiled and looked at the floor, and I could practically see the memories of her time with him passing through her eyes.

After a moment, she finally looked at me with a sad smile. "I know I can't replace the twenty years you had with your father, but I'm hoping you can learn to love me just as much." Her eyes glazed over. "I love you, Azrel. I do. I never stopped. You are my baby girl." Two tears fell down her cheeks, and she shook her head as she caressed the sides of my hair. "I wish I could have seen you growing up. Will you give me that chance, Azrel, my daughter? A chance to be your mother? Allow me do what I can to make up the long years I've missed with you? Years I will regret for the rest of my days."

My heart was overflowing with emotions I could hardly sort, but tenderness toward this woman, my mother, seemed to dominate them all. I nodded. "I will."

She pulled me into another embrace. "Thank you. I hope I can make you happy here. I will do my very best."

I smiled and hugged her back. What a good feeling it was, holding my mother. My mother. I had a mother, and for the first time I actually realized that fact. I already loved her. She was my flesh and blood, the woman who had borne me and then had had me ripped away from her. But I had her back now. We had each other.

She pulled away and gave me a playful smile. "You'd better get upstairs before Rabryn has a fit." We both chuckled.

"I won't fit, Mama," a small voice said. We both turned to see Rabryn sitting on the stairs, looking at us from between the banister bars. "I like watching you happy."

My mother tried to suppress a smile and placed her hands on her hips. "I thought I told you to go to bed."

"I did go, but Azrel was taking so long, I came to see what was keeping her. Then I heard you talking all nice and crying happy tears and hugging, I just sat and watched. I like it when you're happy."

My mother sighed and smiled fully. "Oh, my darling boy. You make it impossible to stay angry with you."

"Of course I do," he said with a wide, toothy grin. "That's how I stay outta trouble."

My mother and I laughed hysterically together. I caught the small jerk of her head, and we both ran after the little rascal, making Rabryn scream and run up the stairs. We were close on his heels, until he went into the first door on the left and shut it. My mother and I were left clutching our stomachs in the hallway.

Just then, another door opened to the left and I felt eyes on me. I looked to see my stepfather standing in the doorway at the end of the hall. I wanted to gasp at the sight of him. He wore only a pair of sleep bottoms, so I could see that he was very attractively built. It wasn't a bulky, muscular build, but a lithe, trim one. His dark blonde hair was disheveled, falling to graze the sides of his neck. He was beautiful. I could see where my brother got his handsome looks. Rabryn, however, didn't have his father's brown eyes. He had my and my mother's blue ones.

Derweldo smiled, though it was clearly forced. "Well, well! What do we have here?"

Rabryn peeked out of the door. "Daddy!" he cried and ran to his father.

Derweldo smiled genuinely as he picked up Rabryn with a playful growl and tossed the small boy over his head and across his shoulders, so that Rabryn's stomach was against the back of his neck. "Hey, buddy. Why aren't you in bed?"

"Beldorn brought Azrel! See?" Rabryn replied, pointing at me.

Derweldo looked at me and smiled tightly again. "I do see."

"I'm sorry we woke you up," I told him.

"Not at all. I wanted to be woken up to greet you." He looked at my mother. "Why didn't you wake me?"

"Dear, I know you worked a lot this week, and tonight was the only night you'd get to sleep a decent number of hours."

He set Rabryn down on his feet and then took my hands into his and leaned in to kiss my cheek. "Welcome."

"Thank you."

Derweldo suddenly caught sight of the sword and knife at my hip and thigh, and his smile vanished.

"Azrel knows how to sword fight, Dad! You shoulda seen her downstairs! She's going to teach me how to be a real sword fighter!"

"Is she now?" Derweldo shamelessly gave me a fake smile, not bothering to hide his distaste for me anymore. "Well, I'm glad you managed to arrive safely. I look forward to getting to know you and seeing my wife reunited with her long-lost daughter. I know it makes her very happy."

I nodded stiffly. "Thank you for allowing me to stay in your home," I said as genuinely as I could, but the look in his eyes told me he understood my hidden message—the message that said, "I know this is your home, and I know you don't want me here, but too bad."

He forced another smile and nodded once. "Of course." He looked down at Rabryn and ruffled his hair. "You get to bed, okay?" Derweldo looked at my mother. "Don't be too long." My mother nodded, and he looked at me again. "Sleep well."

"You, too," I replied, keeping my gaze even. He nodded again and turned back into the bedroom, shutting the door behind him.

My mother led me into the room Rabryn had entered, and I got ready for bed. I had expected her to give me a nightgown, in which I would have felt very uncomfortable, but she gave me pants and a top. I smiled as I put them on.

Looking down at my discarded clothing, I eyed the sword my

father had given me and suddenly remembered the powers that I harbored. Being here had almost made me forget about them. I ran my fingertips lightly along the smooth diamond hilt and decided in that moment that I would forever wear it at my side. Though The Pitt seemed safe enough, and I would look strange with it, I couldn't let my guard down, ever. I knew what Evil waited for me. I'd put my other weapons away, certainly, and the magic that went along with my sword—forever, if possible—but the sword itself would go wherever I went. It was too important to be hidden away and forgotten about. Besides, I had a feeling I was going to be idle here in The Pitt for a while, and I needed to keep up my knowledge of how to handle it.

Rabryn and I crawled into his rather large bed, and he immediately cuddled up in my arms. My mother "tucked us in"— that's what Rabryn called it—and then kissed us both on the head. I'd never been fawned over before, and it felt strange. But I figured I'd better get used to strange things here. I was in a whole new world now.

"Sleep well, my dears," she said as she left the room.

No sooner had the door shut than Rabryn spoke. "Will you tell me about your travels now? I'm not sleepy, and I'd like to know where you've been."

I giggled. "Very well, little brother." I drew him close to me and began my tale. As I spoke, he took a strand of my long hair and twirled it around his little fingers.

That night, and in the following days, I told him everything about all the different places I'd been and people I'd seen with Beldorn. I told him all about my past, my father, Ortheldo, and Isadith, everything except The White Warrior part.

In all our long years together, and through all our long talks, no matter how close we got, I never breathed a word to him about it. It was the only secret I ever kept from him, and I had a bad feeling it was going to turn around and bite me in the rear end one day. It pained me to keep secrets from my brother, but I had no choice.

If Rabryn found out about it, I was sure he'd be in danger somehow. That alone made me bite my tongue whenever I was tempted to tell him anything about it. I would not allow any harm to come to him, ever. Not mental, physical, or anything in between.

He was too special to me, and I loved him too much.

SEVEN

Eight Years Later in The Pitt.

"He's here, Azrel!" Rabryn called from somewhere in the forest.

Finally! I thought, and quickly made my way through the trees toward the sound of Rabryn's voice. I emerged to see him standing with a familiar green-robed figure on horseback.

"Looks like I've come just in time," Beldorn said as he dismounted, clutching his usual white staff in his hand. "The celebration is tonight, isn't it?"

"It is," my brother replied happily.

Rabryn stood nose to nose with the Wizard now. He was so tall and handsome at seventeen years old, though his bright blue eyes still held much of the gentle innocence from his childhood, which made me happy. That some of it had been lost, though, was my fault. But I didn't want to think about that today. It was supposed to be a happy day.

Rabryn looked over at me, and Beldorn followed his gaze. Rabryn had just enough time to smile at me before I bolted full speed toward the Wizard. "Beldorn!"

I was so happy to see his unchanged face. Both of them laughed as my brother jumped out of my path before I could trample him. I threw my arms around the Wizard's neck and held him tightly. He laughed and returned my embrace.

"You should try harder to knock me over next time, Azrel," Rabryn teased, "or I might think you were losing your aggressive touch."

I grinned. "Silence, boy. Can't you see I'm reuniting with a dear friend?"

Rabryn chuckled.

Beldorn gave me a squeeze and then gently pulled away. "Azrel, you are stunning! You look more and more like your father every day."

He meant it as a compliment, but it wasn't. Not here.

My smile melted, and I looked at Rabryn, whose sad gaze met mine. "Yes," I said softly, "so I'm told." I bowed my head while

58

my brother came up beside me and put a comforting arm around my shoulders.

Beldorn's eyes shifted from me to Rabryn and then back to me. "Are you still being ridiculed because of your father?"

Beldorn didn't mean being ridiculed about being the White Warrior. No one, not even Rabryn, knew about that. He meant the general treatment I got here because of my father.

Due to the story that my mother was forced to make up about my father kidnapping me, they believed that I had inherited an evil disposition from him, and that frightened them…immensely.

I had a few strikes against me that validated their fears and made things worse for me. For one, it was well known—though I didn't know how—that my father was a sword master and that he had taught me some serious swordplay. People in The Pitt didn't like warfare or weapons, and they sneered at me for always carrying a sword at my belt. To them, weapons only brought trouble, which meant *I* brought trouble.

It didn't help matters that I'd also passed my fighting knowledge on to Rabryn in "secrecy." We hadn't, in fact, tried to keep it secret; the community had just decided to imply it to put more emphasis on my "deviant nature." The truth was that I really liked teaching my brother how to use protective tools. He favored the bow more than the blade, though, and he handled it like a master already. When the Evil hunting me decided to rear its ugly head, it gave me piece of mind to know that my brother would be able to defend himself.

The biggest strike against me was that I didn't age. I had arrived here at barely twenty-one years old, and though I was now twenty-nine, I still possessed the young, vibrant face of a twenty-year-old. Some thought it was evil sorcery I'd picked up from my father, which was actually almost true. I'd retained the youth I'd had when my father had handed me the sword and power of the White Warrior.

Though I wouldn't admit it, I'd feared that this extreme rejection of me would eventually include my mother and Rabryn. It never did, though. In fact, they'd both gone to great lengths to defend me. The abuse toward me was the reason for the lost innocence in my brother's eyes. After my mother and Derweldo had died of illness, only he had remained to defend me, which had taken a toll on him. He'd suffered a lot in his attempts to defend and protect me, and though most of his attempts had been in vain, he'd never stopped trying.

The hatred for me evolved and deepened, and the rumors about me became downright absurd. Things started flying around about how I was "forcing" Rabryn to learn to fight, that I "cast a spell on him" to make him protect me as fiercely as he did, and that I had turned him into my own personal "slave."

When the abuse reached a tipping point, I'd finally made a desperate attempt to get some peace by establishing myself as someone to be feared. It had been my only recourse. I'd brought my sword to a local girl's neck, threatening her and anyone else that even looked at me crossly, reasoning that no one would approach someone they feared and call her a "miserable waste of halfway-good flesh" or harm her. It had paid off.

As I'd established myself as someone to keep far away from, the insults and abuse eventually stopped. There were still some gutsy enough to say something now and again, but I could deal with that. I'd decided before arriving there that I would adjust to whatever treatment I got, positive or negative, and that's just what I did.

I completely blamed that cursed sword for all of this! I could swear its only reason for existing was to ruin the lives of those who possessed it. It had ruined my father's life when he ran from battle to protect it. Now it was ruining mine by causing the people of The Pitt to hate me in a way that I didn't think possible. All to protect the blasted thing!

I sighed as I looked at my brother. Today I didn't want Rabryn to be unhappy on my account. Tonight was The Pitt's annual celebration of the first day of spring. Celebrations were always when my brother was happiest, so I was going to do my best to keep him happy. He couldn't be happy if he knew I was upset.

So, when Beldorn asked if I was still being ridiculed, I smiled and jumped into his arms again. "It doesn't matter. You're here." I hugged my brother. "Rabryn is here, and everything is wonderful."

That worked. Rabryn and Beldorn laughed.

We spoke merrily as we headed down the grassy cliffs toward the land below, mostly discussing Beldorn's travels. Being so adventurous when he was younger and having a big sister who'd had adventures in her life had helped shape Rabryn's eager and curious appetite today.

Much of the time my brother and I had spent together was devoted to little adventures we had in the woods above the cliffs, where no one of The Pitt ever ventured. We'd often gotten into light trouble with our mother for running off. Though I'd been certainly old enough and skilled enough to take care of him, I suppose deep down she just hadn't wanted to give the townspeople something else to sneer at me about.

"I'm happy to report," Beldorn said to my brother, "that The Pitt's existence still remains an evil rumor or unknown at all."

"Oh, blast!" I cried. I threw my arms up into the air and slapped my thighs. "And after all the trouble we've gone to, to make our existence known throughout Casdanarus."

That sent Beldorn and Rabryn into hysterics.

We passed people busily preparing the town center for the party, and I was glad most were too preoccupied to notice me. But then I saw two women, Clyryan and Seana, off to the side of the trail pointing and laughing at me. I was vaguely aware that Rabryn and Beldorn's conversation had stopped. The girls began to mock me by using their broomsticks to start a fake and cruelly exaggerated sword fight.

I took a breath and sighed. "This is where I leave you two." Rabryn glared at the girls as I hugged Beldorn. "I'm glad you're here, my friend." I took Rabryn's hands in mine and forced a smile, pretending it didn't bother me. In a way, it really didn't. "I'll see you later," I said and kissed his cheek.

I turned off the main trail back toward the cliffs that served as the natural walls of the land, but served as a cage for me since I was stuck here for the time being. The woods above them where I found some solitude and freedom.

____

Night fell, and the party was in full swing. The music was loud, filling the entire bowl, and everyone was drinking, dancing, and having a grand old time.

I sat a good distance away under an arthol tree, the short, gnarled species of the land. I knew I wasn't welcome there. Still, I smiled, watching Rabryn and Beldorn at the party. Rabryn was chatting up with the few friends he did have left, despite who his sister was, and Beldorn was happily telling stories to the children.

Beldorn was an outsider like me, but he was welcome here because he was well known. He was also a mere passerby rather than a citizen. Plus, he didn't have the association with my father, or his reputation, that I did.

I watched the party for a bit, but eventually I turned my eyes up the cliffs toward the woods. Leaning comfortably against the tree, I sighed and picked a long blade of grass to chew on. I daydreamed about the lovely lands I'd seen years ago, lands I longed to see again, people I longed to see again. It was something I caught myself doing more and more frequently lately.

I eventually heard footsteps coming toward me, and I felt friendly, loving eyes on me. I knew it was Rabryn. Without looking at him, I smiled.

"If you've come to try and persuade me to go down to the party, you've wasted your time." I turned to look at him. "You were never good at persuasion, little brother."

He gave me a playful look of offense, like my suggestion was completely absurd. "I haven't come to persuade you to do anything."

My grin widened. "You were never good at lying to me, either."

He smiled. He was dressed in his "party clothes," as he called them, though they weren't much different from his regular attire. They consisted of a dark-blue tunic with a gold lace sash tied loosely about his waist, the knot hanging gracefully to the side, dark maroon leggings, and black boots. His brown hair framed his face, the front ends just reaching his cheekbones and the back worn longer to the nape of his neck.

I studied his lovely bright blue eyes and didn't like what I saw in them. "What's wrong, Rabryn?" I asked, my eyebrows dropping in concern. I knew when something bothered my brother. I barely even had to read his eyes to tell.

His smiled faded, indicating that I was right, and he eased himself to the ground next to me. He stared down at his lap, and I could tell he was struggling to get the words out.

"What is it?" I asked.

"Well," he sighed and looked up at me, "to be honest, it's

you."

"Me?" I scoffed and looked away with a smile. "And I thought it was something important," I said trying to lighten the mood.

"It *is* important!" he shouted. I looked back at him in surprise. He never spoke to me like that. Seeing the expression of shock on my face, he softened his tone. "It's important to me."

Clearly this was not some run-of-the-mill distress he was feeling. I got on my knees, fully facing him, and gave him my full attention. "I'm so sorry, Rabryn. I didn't mean to upset you. What's wrong?"

He sighed. "It's just"—he struggled to find the words—"I know well enough that you are very hated here." He sighed again. "You used to come to *me* when you were upset or hurting, but now you just go into the woods. Like today," he said quickly, as if fearing I'd interrupt him before he could get it all out, "when Clyryan and Seana were mocking you, you didn't talk to me. You seek more solitude in the woods than you ever have, and I'm worried that…that…" His eyes filled with emotion. "I'm worried that I'm losing you in some way. I'm worried that someday you're going to go into those woods and never come back."

I couldn't believe he was saying that to me. I smiled and pulled him into my arms. He hugged me close. "Rabryn," I said gently, "you're not losing me. And you, of all people, should know that I wouldn't go *anywhere* without you." We both chuckled and pulled out of our embrace.

A flicker of sadness rippled through me, and I sighed, sitting back on my heels while I tried to think of a way to explain this to him. "When I go into the woods, it's not only because I want to get away from the hatred people have for me here. It's more than that."

My voice trailed off as I wondered how I could explain this to him without telling him about who, or what, I was. As I chewed my bottom lip, an idea formed.

I drew out the sword and gazed at it across my hands. "I have a great gift, Rabryn," I said softly. "I know so many wonderful things that other people don't know about because of the time I spent with my father." I sighed. "But the knowledge I possess is of no use here, so I go into the woods to try to make myself useful. I need to feel like…like I have a purpose besides a dart board of hate." A smile formed on my face. "I feel that kind of worth when

I go into the woods. Even just by doing a simple deed such as"—I shrugged and tried to think of an example—"I don't know, mending a bird's broken wing, or something." My smile widened. "I can do that. I have that skill."

I paused and gazed down at my sword, then laughed softly. This was stupid. Rabryn was generally accepted here. He was one of them, born and raised. He didn't know what I was talking about, and I was never good at explaining what my emotions were anyway. It was even harder while trying to hide something—like the fact that I felt like I could be more useful if I killed the Evil hunting me and hopefully bring honor back to my father's name.

"I'm sorry," I said. "I'm probably making no sense to you at all."

There was a brief pause before Rabryn spoke. "Azrel, look at me." I looked up and saw him smiling. "Who am I?"

"What?" I asked, confused.

"Who am I?" he asked again.

I began to question his mental health. "You're Rabryn, right?" I asked with an awkward smile, wondering if that was the answer he wanted.

He chuckled. "That's my name. But who *am* I?"

I shifted my gaze from side to side to see if there was anyone around that could save me from this nut. "You're my brother?" I asked warily.

Rabryn smiled. "That's right, I'm your brother. Give me a little credit." He crossed his arms and smirked. "I understand you just as well as you understand me. This isn't a one-way sibling-ship, you know."

I chuckled. "I know that." I sighed and pulled him into an embrace, thinking that he couldn't possibly understand me because he didn't know me as thoroughly as I knew him. I had one big secret, and the day it surfaced was a day to dread.

"I'm glad I decided to talk to you about this," he said and pulled away. "I was getting worried."

"Thank you for caring about me so much, Rabryn."

"Always." He smiled playfully. "So will you come to the party now?"

We both laughed because we both knew that was a dumb question. Of course I wouldn't.

"Absolutely…" His eyes widened in disbelief that I might say yes. "Not!" I added. We laughed again. "You should know better than that," I teased, peering at him with one eye.

"I do know better," he said with a smile. "I just thought I'd try."

"I won't go to the party, but will you do me a favor?"

"Anything."

"Stop worrying about me!" I cried and gently shoved his shoulders. We both laughed again.

"Now it's my turn to say, 'You should know better than that,'" he said with a smile.

I returned the smile. I did know better—I knew he'd worry about me no matter what I told him to do.

I ruffled his soft brown hair. "Well, go have fun at least."

He kissed my forehead and stood. "As you wish, your majesty," he said in a noble tone, bowing deeply at the waist and making an exaggerated sweeping motion with his arm. I chuckled and watched him walk back to the party.

As I looked out at the village center and saw all the happy, smiling faces, an overwhelming desire to be there came over me. There was so much warmth and joy just a short distance away, and I wanted to be among it with my brother. Suddenly, I didn't care if they wanted me there or not.

"Rabryn!" I hollered and got to my feet. He turned around. "Wait up," I called out and jogged toward him.

His smile was filled with pleasant disbelief as I approached. He offered me his arm. "Shall we?"

I laced my arm through his and smiled. "We shall."

EIGHT

⊶⟨∞⟩⊷

AZREL

I was pretty thrilled as we headed down to the party, but as soon as we entered the ring of firelight, the joyful feeling seeped away. Nasty and fearful looks, and some curious ones, were shot in my direction. Everyone near me moved away as I approached, like I had some deadly disease they could catch by being within ten feet of me.

What had I been thinking?

I sighed and let go of Rabryn's arm, forcing myself to smile at him. "Go on. I'll be fine here."

He glared at the men and women standing nearby and then sighed as he looked back at me. "Are you sure? I'll be more than happy to stay with you if you want."

I tried to laugh, but it was hollow. "That's the last thing I want. I see you enough. I don't need you dangling at my side here." I tried to hide the quiver in my voice, though I felt hateful eyes burning into me.

Rabryn sighed. "If you need me, I'll be over with Beldorn." I nodded, and he kissed my cheek and walked away.

I sat on top of the nearest picnic table, resting my feet on the seat and my elbows on my knees as I gazed around. Anyone whose face my eyes scanned turned away. Some people sneered before going about their business. Some whispered, some pointed, but none approached.

Rabryn took a seat with Beldorn and the children, who surrounded a fire listening to stories. Rabryn whispered to the Wizard and pointed in my direction, no doubt telling him that I was here. Beldorn looked at me, surprised, and waved. I waved back and returned to surveying the crowd.

After a few unsettling minutes, I was about to go back to my arthol tree when an explosion came from the campfire where Beldorn and my brother sat with the kids. I watched, horrified, as a yellow and orange transparent figure appeared in the fire. The thing stood eight feet tall, with claws on its hands and toes that were nearly two feet long, and nails like knives. Its face resembled

66

that of a bat with bites taken out of parts of its squished-in face. Thin, needle-like teeth protruded from the top and bottom of its mouth, nearly cutting open its own nose and chin.

Looking on with wide eyes, I searched my memory and realized I was seeing a Gorkor! Or, it looked like one, anyway. But Gorkors were solid creatures. This thing looked like an orange ghost of one.

The beast let out a ferocious roar that echoed into the night, and terrified people began running in every direction, tripping over each other, and things, in a mad dash for safety.

My breath caught in my throat when the creature stepped out of the fire and started walking right toward Rabryn! My brother slowly began backing away from it, his eyes wide, too dumbfounded to move quickly. He was weaponless! He always left his bow and arrows in the woods where we practiced.

Without another thought, I sprang from my seat and ran toward the creature, violently knocking aside anyone in my way. Drawing my sword, I leapt on top of another picnic table in one bound, putting the Gorkor's thin waist within my reach. I spun my body around with full force and sliced through its belly.

My sword hit nothing! It was as if I had cut air!

With my body spinning and no solid surface to slow my momentum, I nearly fell flat onto the grass, but I regained my footing just in time. I looked back at the monster and saw Rabryn fall to the ground. The thing was right on top of him.

"NO!" I screamed.

Suddenly the creature vanished and Rabryn stood up from the ground, looking wide-eyed in my direction. "What? What's wrong? What is it?"

I flinched at his bewildered expression. He was acting as if nothing had happened! My eyebrows knitted together as my heart started pounding.

"What do you mean, what's wrong?" I shouted.

Rabryn's face drained completely of color when he saw me standing on the table, my sword in my grip. His eyes were huge, and his fist was over his mouth like he was about to throw up.

"Azrel," he began softly, placing his palm gently on top of my boot. "I was just reenacting a story Beldorn was telling to the children." My eyes went wide. "That monster was just Beldorn's magic. Not real."

My heart stopped, and heat invaded my cheeks so quickly that I felt faint. My sword suddenly felt too heavy to hold up, and the point sank down, resting on top of the table, with me barely holding the hilt.

Wonderful.

Suddenly laughter burst out all around me. I gazed around helplessly at the hysterical crowd. I actually felt more confused than embarrassed. Weren't these the people who had just *run* from the same pretend creature? They had thought it was real just as much as I had, yet *they* were laughing at *me?* Running from a fake creature seemed more of a reason to laugh than trying to kill one, especially when it was going after a loved one.

I looked at Rabryn again, who looked up at me helplessly. "I'm so sorry," he said in a whisper. "I didn't..."

I cut him off by sheathing my sword and jumping off the table, roughly shouldering through the hysterical crowd, not caring if I knocked people to the ground.

"Azrel! Wait, please!" Rabryn called.

He was quickly in front of me, studying my face. I felt defeated more than humiliated but tried not to let it show in my expression. Having no words to comfort me, Rabryn pulled me into his arms and held me. I hugged him back in a halfhearted embrace. The laughter rang out all around me, prodding me toward tears that I refused to allow to spill. I held them back. I had to.

"I'm so sorry," Rabryn whispered.

Something in his voice provoked me to pull away and look at him. He was in tears.

"I didn't know that you..." he began in a soft voice, but faltered and bowed his head, shaking it weakly.

Rabryn seemed more stung by their laughter than I was. Pain inflicted on my brother would not be tolerated. Not by me.

My defeat quickly turned to anger, and I picked out the nearest voice, which was behind me to the right. "Poor Azrel didn't get to use her cute little sword to save the world from a pretend creature!" Clyryan laughed with Seana. "How ever will she sleep tonight?"

I slowly turned toward Clyryan. All at once, the crowd went silent and watched me with fear growing in their eyes. I ignored it as I slowly approached Clyryan with a smile.

"Dear Clyryan," I said in a saccharine tone, "saving the world wasn't my intention at all." I tilted my head in the direction from which the monster had faded. "I just thought that hideous creature looked an awful lot like you, and I was going to put it out of its misery."

Clyryan's cheeks flushed crimson, and hatred filled her eyes. I could have stopped there, but hearing Rabryn snicker behind me encouraged me.

I sighed and assumed an expression of mock sympathy "But alas, it seems the poor creature realized its peril and put itself out of its misery." My brows went up. "Maybe you should follow its example."

Rabryn burst into laughter. I smirked triumphantly at the silly girl and turned back toward him. Ah yes, I could ward off a verbal attack with the best of them.

Clyryan, determined to have the last word, yelled after me, "You miserable, worthless waste of halfway-good flesh!"

I froze in my tracks. That was it. The gloves were off. She obviously needed a reminder that you didn't insult someone who can take your life in the blink of an eye. They all did.

She and Seana were laughing hysterically behind me. Out of the corner of my eye I saw that I was standing next to the silverware table. Piles of forks and spoons and...*knives* were within my reach. I discreetly reached out with my right hand, keeping it hidden behind my cloak, and took hold of two knives. After positioning them correctly in my hand, I spun and hurled them at her with all my strength.

The crowd screamed in horror, but Clyryan didn't have time to scream before the knives were buried in the wooden pole behind her, a centimeter away from each side of her head. She was frozen in shock.

I drew out my sword and walked up to her, relishing the fear in her eyes as I lightly ran the tip of my blade up her torso and neck, placing it under her chin so firmly that she was forced to raise her head to avoid getting stabbed. She strained her wide eyes downward to see me as I brought my nose within inches of hers.

"The next time you cross me," I hissed, "I won't miss."

I backed away a few feet and then spun around while sheathing my sword. I quickly made my way as far from the party as I could manage, with Rabryn right at my side.

———

We sat silently in the dark woods above The Pitt, Rabryn's hand clasping mine. I gazed into the deep shadows of the forest, lost in my own thoughts: thoughts of escape, thoughts of my father, my travels, even my mother.

At long last, Rabryn spoke. "It's my fault," he said softly. "I shouldn't have..."

I squeezed his hand to silence him. "No one is to blame for that."

He was silent another moment. "Thank you," he said then.

I looked at him, confused. "For what?"

"Protecting me the way you did."

I laughed without mirth. "Oh yes! You were in *so* much danger."

"You didn't know that I wasn't in real danger," he countered softly, "yet you still stepped in to fight for my life."

I smiled at him and looked out into the woods again. "I will always fight for your life."

We sat together quietly until the silence was broken by footsteps. My entire body tensed up at the unexpected sound. No one ever came up here. I felt Rabryn go rigid as well.

I strained to listen and realized that the sound wasn't coming from the direction of The Pitt; it was coming toward us from outside it! A ripple of shock went through me and I shuddered from an icy chill.

"Rabryn," I said so softly that I wondered if he heard me at all, "don't make any sudden moves, but stand up slowly." He nodded his understanding, and we stood up, not daring to crinkle a single leaf as we did.

I stared hard into the blackness of the forest for a moment, unable to see anything. Who or what could possibly be coming at us from the *outside*? It wasn't every day, or even every few years, that guests came to The Pitt from beyond the woods.

"What is it?" Rabryn whispered to me.

I responded by bringing my finger to my lips, and I continued to search the darkness. Moments passed, and ever so slowly the sound drew nearer, snapping sticks and crunching leaves with every heavy step. Whatever it was, it wasn't making any real effort to remain silent.

I rested my hand on the hilt of my sword, tensing my body and my senses to full awareness, getting battle ready. My eyes strained into the blackness to see something, anything.

Finally, I detected a shadow not too far ahead staggering forward in the moonlight. The shadow was hunched over and seemed to be breathing heavily in a struggle to stay alive. The body teetered for a moment, and then a shoulder rested hard against a tree trunk. It held itself there for a moment as Rabryn and I watched, unsure of what to do. The head then tilted up, and the figure stared at us for a long moment. Suddenly, the entire shadow fell forward to the ground with a dull thud.

Rabryn and I looked at each other, then rushed over to the fallen figure. Rabryn was the first on his knees at the stranger's side. He was face down on the ground, and by the moonlight that the canopy allowed, I could see that his tunic and leggings were torn to shreds and that he had long stripes of blood covering his back and continuing all the way down to his calves. They were very clearly lashes from a whip. Fresh ones, too, not even a day old.

I glanced around the woods. What thing could be so violent as to cause this type of massive damage and be this close to The Pitt? We were more than a week away from any civilization! Why and how were these wounds fresh?

"Roll him over," I instructed, feeling an uncanny worry for this person.

Rabryn pushed and I pulled, rolling the stranger onto his injured back. His breathing was shallow and heavily labored, revealing that he was at least alive. The slivers of pale moonlight that managed to penetrate the dense treetops didn't give us much to work with, but as I ran my hands up and down his body feeling for weapons and broken bones, I kept finding more cuts.

"We can't help him here," Rabryn said. "We have to get him back to the house." He paused and kept a steady gaze on me. "How do we do that?" His cluelessness was endearing.

I looked back at him. "I guess we have no choice but to carry him."

"That's great, for the person who doesn't carry him," Rabryn said dryly.

I flashed a smile despite the situation, and at that moment I felt the gentle touch of fingertips on my cheek. I jumped and looked down at the stranger.

A thin ray of moonlight lay across his eyes, which he'd managed to barely open into slits. The look in them was so strange. Before I could read them, they closed abruptly, and his hand fell limply to the ground. Rabryn and I would have thought him dead, but the sound of his breathing relieved us of that concern.

"Let's both lift him. Together we can carry him," I said, still feeling the tingle of the fingertips on my cheek.

Rabryn nodded and slipped both of his arms under the stranger's. I picked up his legs, and we began our journey to the house. We carefully carried the unconscious man down the steep grasses to the plane, keeping ourselves hidden in the shadows to avoid attention. The man grew increasingly heavier as we walked, which was expected. Sweat was trickling down our brows and backs by the time we entered the front door.

"Couch!" I barked, very ready to put him down.

"You don't have to tell me twice," Rabryn said with a grunt.

Had my face not been so strained from the effort of carrying the man, I would have smiled. We laid him on the large couch.

"Basin of water and a cloth," I ordered as I took my cloak off and covered the man. Without question, Rabryn went to the kitchen. "No lights!" I called after him.

I wanted to keep all the main lights off so that no one would think we were doing anything evil or strange. We would have been asleep by now had we not stumbled upon the man.

I kneeled on the floor in front of him and thought about all the wounds on his body. Unfortunately, I knew I'd need at least a little light to mend them all, so I went to the mantle above the fireplace. We kept nothing up there except some paintings and an oil lamp.

I was groping for the lamp when I heard a strange noise behind me. I paused in my search to listen, but all I heard was the sounds of Rabryn getting water. I went on searching for the lamp. When I took hold of it, the sound came again. It sounded like a strained, whispering voice coming from the stranger. I grabbed hold of the lamp and turned around to look at the man on my couch.

"Azrel," it came again.

I almost dropped the oil lamp. Had he said my name, or were

my ears deceiving me?

"Azrel," it came more clearly.

My eyes went wide, and I started shaking. He had indeed said my name! How did this person know my name?

I slowly walked over and gingerly lowered myself to sit atop the short table in front of the couch.

"Do I...know you?" I asked.

The shadow of his head bobbed up and down in a slow nod.

My heart was pounding. How? How could this outsider know me?

I pulled the lamp onto my lap and frantically lit it. Pale orange light reached into the dark shadows of the night. As the light brightened, it seemed to illuminate the very shadows of my past. My hand came up to my mouth as I looked at his face.

Was this really happening? Was I really seeing this?

His face was pale and bloodstained, and some parts were swollen, but it was unmistakable. His well-defined cheekbones, his square jaw, and the unreal periwinkle eyes that were like a window to his soul were all framed by raven black hair.

"Ortheldo?" I whispered in disbelief.

His lips curved up into a weak smile. "Hi, Azrel."

He was alive! Barely, but he hadn't perished that snowy day on the river. He was actually here with me. I practically threw the lamp aside and fell onto my knees in front of the couch, cupping his face in my hands. My eyes washed up and down his beautiful face, unable to believe that I was actually seeing him again. My partner. My dear friend.

My friend! I had a friend in this hateful world! I had someone that I'd grown up with, someone for whom I cared greatly and who cared about me. Someone who took me away from the recent nine years and brought me back to the good times when my father was alive.

I caressed his cheeks with my thumbs and just stared at him. I didn't know what to say. What could I say? I was so overwhelmed with joy to see him that I couldn't speak. My friend, my only partner as a girl, was here with me again.

Rabryn broke the silence when he cleared his throat. I hadn't noticed him come in. He had a sheepish grin on his face. "I take it you know him?"

I laughed and quickly wiped my eyes to get rid of the tears that had formed. "Yes, I do! Rabryn, this is my friend Ortheldo." Rabryn's eyes went wide as he looked down at him. "Ortheldo, this is my brother, Rabryn."

Ortheldo nodded weakly in greeting.

I suddenly felt wet, gooey warmth under my hand that rested on his chest. I picked it up to see blood staining my fingers, and my eyes went wide.

"Oh, Gods!" I exclaimed. I'd been so caught up in seeing him again that I'd forgotten he was badly hurt. I quickly jumped into action, pulling my sleeves up and tying my hair back into a messy knot to keep it out of my way while I worked. I brought the short table closer to the couch so I could easily tend to him. "Just lay still, Ortheldo," I said softly. "I'll take care of you."

It took more than two hours to dress the small cuts all over his body. When I finished, I wanted to ask him the hundreds of burning questions I had, but the sound of his steady breathing stopped me. I stared at him as the lamp cast a soft glow over his sleeping face, giving him such a youthful glow. He was twenty-six now. After that day on the river, I'd had so many questions about what could have happened to him, and I'd often wondered if I could ever find him if I tried. All those questions could be put to rest now. I ran my fingers through his hair and smiled down at him.

After a moment, I stood and reached for the blanket draped over the back of the couch and covered him. I sighed fondly. I couldn't wait until I'd be able to speak with him.

I felt a comforting arm encircle my shoulders, and Rabryn rested his head against mine. "Come on, you need to rest. He'll sleep through tonight and probably all through tomorrow, too." We both chuckled. "It's time for us to sleep. It's been an exhausting day."

The memory of everyone laughing at me returned, but it didn't hurt nearly as much as it had earlier. While Rabryn guided me up the stairs, I cast a gaze over the railing down at Ortheldo below and smiled.

NINE

I woke up to the most beautiful morning I'd seen since arriving in The Pitt. The sun was warm and bright, and a soft, warm breeze blew in through my window, caressing my face and swirling small strands of my hair up into a merry dance. I sighed in contentment and then finally threw my blanket off me and went toward the bathing room down the hall. I lit the fire under the tub to start heating it and went to the hand pump to fill it. It took forever, but eventually it was full. After testing the water and deciding it needed a little longer to heat to my liking, I returned to my room to pick out my clothes.

I chose a satin outfit that was much fancier than what I'd usually wear, but this wasn't a usual day. It consisted of silky white leggings, a sky-blue tunic, and a white lace sash that my mother had given me. I grabbed my sword, its white belt and diamond studded sheath, and the nicest pair of black boots I owned, then went into the bathing room again. After making sure the water was hot enough, I extinguished the fire, stripped off my nightclothes, and slowly lowered myself into the soothing water.

I was enjoying my bath immensely when a knock came on the door. I sighed. "Yes?"

"Beldorn is downstairs," Rabryn said through the door. "He needs to speak with you immediately about last night and our visitor."

I let out an exasperated sigh and rested my head on the edge of the tub again. So much for enjoying my bath. I loved the old man, but he had horrible timing.

"All right," I said, clearly annoyed. "I'll be down shortly."

Last night. The memory of everyone in The Pitt pointing and laughing at me should have upset me, but it didn't. I was too overjoyed about the arrival of our "visitor" to care.

I quickly washed my hair and skin with the vials Isadith had given me so long ago. Though I emptied them every time I bathed, I always came back to find them full again. They smelled as sweet as ever and always refreshed me, making me feel ready for anything. I hummed a merry tune as I dried myself off, quickly dressed, and made my way downstairs.

I gazed over the railing at Ortheldo. He was still asleep. If it were possible, he seemed even more handsome in the light of the day, despite the visible cuts and bruises. Beldorn was sitting in the chair across from the short table, opposite where Ortheldo slept, and Rabryn sat on the short table facing the Wizard.

"Good morning," I said cheerfully as I bounced off the bottom step and went to the couch.

I barely heard their responses as I gazed down at Ortheldo's face. Bending over, I smiled and ran my fingers through his dirty black hair and caressed his cheek. I wished he'd open his gorgeous periwinkle eyes, just so I could see them.

Beldorn cleared his throat to get my attention. I turned back to him and flushed crimson when I saw them both watching me. "Sorry," I muttered, pulling Ortheldo's blanket up to his chin and taking a seat next to Rabryn on the short table. "Now, what is so important, Old Man, that you had to interrupt my bath?" I teased.

"You are in good spirits despite last night's events," Beldorn said.

I smiled and shrugged. "There was more to last night than being humiliated." I gestured behind me. "Look at who's sleeping on my couch."

"I can see," he replied with a smile. "That is actually one of the two things I wanted to speak to you about. But first I wished to apologize for making the image of a Gorkor appear to attack your brother."

"There's no need, Beldorn. Everything turned out wonderful. What do you need to tell me about Ortheldo?"

"What you want to know about Ortheldo would be best told by him when he wakes. What I need to speak with you about is what Ortheldo was bearing."

Tension suddenly hung in the air like an invisible fog. I didn't like Beldorn's foreboding tone. Dread and confusion slithered through my soul like a snake, and my stomach sank at the thought that this perfect day was about to be ruined.

"Okay," I said, my eyebrows drawing together. "What was Ortheldo bearing?"

Without a word, Rabryn reached into the pocket of his gray

leggings and pulled out what seemed to be a necklace. It was a simple chain of white metal, but my attention was diverted to the single gem dangling from it. It was a white jewel that resembled the white diamonds on the hilt of my sword but wasn't quite the same. This jewel was perfectly round and a little larger than a small marble. But the most distinct oddity was the soft orange glow emitting from deep inside it. Rabryn held it out to me, and I gently took it from him.

"What in Casdanarus is this?" I asked.

"I plucked it out of the stream near where we found Ortheldo," Rabryn said. "The orange glow made it rather noticeable."

"How long have you been awake?" I asked, aiming for a teasing tone and trying to salvage what could still turn out to be a good day.

He smiled in reply. "A little while."

"It was good fortune that Rabryn found it," Beldorn went on. "My guess is that whatever evil did this damage to Ortheldo, did so because he had this necklace, and they wanted it."

"How do you know Ortheldo had it?" I asked.

"I don't. These are just guesses."

I lightly clasped the gem. To my surprise, it seemed to pulsate with warmth, as if life was churning inside of it. "Wow," I managed after finding my voice. "Why was it in the stream, though?"

"Beldorn and I guess Ortheldo chucked it in the river to hide it," Rabryn said, "in case whatever was pursuing him managed to kill him."

My heart twisted. "So, someone wanted this necklace enough to kill for it?"

Beldorn looked at me, his blue eyes intense. "Someone or some*thing*," he said, the edge of his voice sharp enough to cut steel.

I narrowed my eyes on the jewel and pondered what kind of evil was lurking around here. It had to be someone, or some*thing*, that was really bored because nothing dark and dangerous ever came this far west.

"These are only guesses, Azrel," Rabryn said gently. "We won't know anything for sure until Ortheldo wakes up and tells us what happened."

I looked over my shoulder at Ortheldo, wondering what in the world had he been up to since we parted. And why had he been bringing this weird necklace here?

"I came by this morning to see if you were all right after last night," Beldorn said. "When I saw a strange, severely injured man sleeping on your couch, naturally I went upstairs and woke your brother to have him explain. He told me what happened and took me to the place where you found Ortheldo. I went to the edge of the woods to try to discern what might have happened. Rabryn decided to investigate as well and found the necklace in the stream. Together Rabryn and I have discussed what may have taken place."

Rabryn picked up the story. "We guess he threw the necklace into the stream just as he entered our woods, which is when he was attacked. Then the stream carried the necklace down to where I found it." Rabryn shrugged. "We didn't find much evidence of his pursuers besides hoof prints in the mud on the outskirts of the woods. The forest must have been too much for the attacker's horse, which is probably why Ortheldo escaped."

I closed my eyes and held my hand up in surrender, the amount of negative information coming at me overwhelming. It took me a second to digest it all. "Okay, but why *here?*" I asked, jabbing a finger to the floor. "Why was Ortheldo coming *here?*"

The tension seemed to thicken. Beldorn held his narrowed gaze on my face while speaking in a meaningful tone. "The Pitt is the best place to keep things hidden," he said. "Secrets, perhaps?" His eyes narrowed more. "Isn't it, Azrel?"

My eyes went wide. What was he doing? I looked at my brother and saw his face flooding with confusion. I didn't want him to know. He'd be devastated! He'd hate me!

I looked back at Beldorn and scoffed as if he'd said something absurd. "If you say so, Beldorn." I got up from the short table and turned to check on Ortheldo, putting my back to him and hoping that would silence him.

"You know exactly what I'm talking about, Azrel," he said sternly.

You'd think a Wizard would get a clue!

I spun around and watched him stand up from the chair. He suddenly seemed much bigger for some reason, as if his presence filled every corner of the room. The air around me felt heavy and thick and ominous.

Rabryn stood as well. "What does he mean, Azrel?" His sad tone was more heartbreaking than his pained expression.

My mouth moved up and down awkwardly as my eyes shifted all over the room, anywhere but his face. He had trusted me for years! Now he suspected I kept things from him. Eight years of love and trust would go out the window if I told him, and any respect he had for me would disappear once he knew what I was. I couldn't lose Rabryn that way! He was everything to me: my brother, my friend, my confidant. I couldn't lose what we had, and by The Gods I was going to hold onto it for dear life!

"I have no idea, Rabryn," I said, giving the Wizard a wide-eyed dangerous look.

"Azrel!" Beldorn yelled, making me jump. I stared at him in disbelief. Had he seriously just yelled at me like that? "I told you there would come a time when you would know when to reveal yourself and to whom!"

My breath quickened, not so much from fear of Beldorn, but from fear of losing my brother's love. Rabryn's eyebrows were drawn together, his eyes confused and hurt. I didn't want to hurt him, but now I had no choice. I'd never been so enraged in my life. Feeling blinded by it, I lost all sense of time and reason. The only one left who'd given me a chance here, the only person left who loved me, was about to be betrayed by me. I clenched my teeth and fists, glared at Beldorn, and let loose my rage.

"That's right!" I screamed, throwing my fist in his direction. "You *did* tell me I would know when to reveal myself, and now is not the time!" I pointed an accusing finger at him. "You said that I would know when to reveal *my*self, not that *you* would do so!"

Beldorn's stern expression faded, but his steady gaze held mine, which only enraged me more. *He* wasn't just about to lose everything, *I was*! I started trembling violently and lost all control of my words. My head was reeling with words to scream at him, to scream at everybody!

"How could you possibly know what it was like to keep this horrible secret from the one person I could trust and who trusted me? Who loved me! You don't know how it feels being hated by every person you live with except one! I wanted to tell him *my* way, not yours! I wanted to tell him when *I* was ready, not when you decided I should be!"

My screaming went up an octave to the point that my voice broke. The screaming wasn't enough! I felt ready to burst with agony and rage. I felt tears forming behind my eyes and desperately tried to hold them back, but my world was coming to an end. I was going to lose Rabryn!

"How could you make me do this to him?" I screamed at the Wizard. "Now I'm going to lose the one person in my life who matters! The one person who loves me! He'll hate me now, thanks to you! I'll have no one!"

That last high-pitched scream sapped all my energy. My knees buckled and I hit the floor hard, my body collapsing over of my legs. Drained and weak, I rested my forehead on the floor. When my tears—my white tears—spilled over, my hands immediately went up to cover my face. I hadn't cried in nine years, not since Beldorn had told me not to in Galad Kas because the color of my tears would give away who I was. My entire body shook violently from the heaving sobs, sobs that left me almost unable to breathe. I thought I was going to go mad, or throw up from the sudden loneliness and defeat I felt.

I was suddenly pushed upward by my shoulders and then crushed against a chest. I clutched at the back of his shirt, desperately needing something to hold onto as my sobs came out in agonizing yells. My frustrations, built up over the years since my father died, all spilled out in this moment. The loss of Ortheldo, the loss of my mother, the very life I lived here. Every single tear that I had wanted to cry over the past eight years in The Pitt all came out at once. Tears poured forth from all the insults, from all the hateful abuse, from all the loneliness—and now from the loss of Rabryn.

My entire life was like a nightmare that wouldn't end. Today had started out so beautiful. Couldn't I have enjoyed this day, this *one* day, without something rotten happening in my world?

A hand rested on the back of my head. "Azrel," Rabryn said close to my ear. I was surprised to realize it was Rabryn who was holding me. "You will never lose me. I swear to you. I could never, ever hate you. Do you understand me?"

He sounded sincere, and I'm sure he was. That allowed me to gain a bit of control over myself. But the nagging thought that he didn't know what I was yet made that splinter of hope crumble. Everyone hated the White Warrior.

I felt a third hand gently rest on my back. Thinking it was Beldorn, and knowing I owed him an apology, I slowly pulled away from Rabryn. Keeping my head down so my tears stayed hidden, I leaned to the side where I was gently being guided. I expected to feel Beldorn's soft velvet robe, but my cheek rested against a bare chest.

I jerked away and saw Ortheldo kneeling on the floor next to me. He looked down at me, those periwinkle eyes obliterating every barrier in my soul. My eyes went wide as I looked up at his face. Unable to stand being parted, I slowly leaned in and rested my cheek on his chest and let him hold me. It had been so long since I felt his arms around me.

When I had calmed down enough to breathe normally, I gazed up into his face again. He was ashen and groggy, and his facial injuries consisted of a badly swollen black eye, a jagged cut from his eyebrow up into his hairline, two long splits in his lip, and a long abrasion under his chin and jaw. He smiled despite his injuries. I rested my hands on his cheeks, scanning his face as if my eyes were still trying to believe what they were seeing.

There were so many things I wanted to say to him, but I was completely lost for words and only managed a brilliant, "You're awake."

His smile widened, and his thumb gently wiped a white tear from my cheek. "I've missed you so much," he softly.

The feelings that came along with seeing him now were not the same feelings I'd had when we left our cave nine years ago. They were stronger now, and something I'd never felt before. Being able to see him and touch him once again stirred up more feelings than I knew how to sort.

I smiled and threw my arms around him. "I have missed you more than you could possibly know," I choked out, trying to contain my joy. I rested my hand on the back of his head, only to feel a bump the size of a fist and some welts of dried blood.

I opened my eyes and pulled away from him. "What in the world happened to you? Where have you been? Do you feel okay?"

He chuckled and ran the back of his finger down my cheek. "I feel better thanks to you and your brother." He looked past me, giving Rabryn a warm smile. I could feel my brother's eyes on me as he waited for what I had to tell him. I tried to muster the strength to turn and face him.

To buy some time and emotionally prepare myself for what I had to do, I kept my eyes on Ortheldo. "Come on. You need to lie down and rest."

Ortheldo nodded, and I started to help him to his feet. Without a word, Rabryn positioned himself on the other side of him, and we both helped him back onto the couch.

Once Ortheldo had been covered up again and was resting comfortably, I finally faced my brother. He was staring at me with anticipation. I looked down. I didn't know if I could do this. I didn't want Rabryn to know the horrible thing I was. It was bad enough that I had kept something from him for years, but admitting the truth would be worse.

For a few moments, I tried to decide how to tell him, but my mouth suddenly felt dry. "Rabryn," I began with great effort. "I'm not everything I seem."

He looked at me, confused, but so far there wasn't any scorn or anger in his expression, just curiosity.

I swallowed hard, trying to moisten my throat and feeling so small and insignificant. Once again, matters had gone beyond my control, and I hated this feeling of helplessness more than ever.

I wasn't going to be able to speak the words. So, with a sigh, I figured it would be best to just show him. I walked around the living room and closed all the drapes and shades. As the room darkened, so did my mood. I rested my forehead against the last window, closed my eyes, and took in a deep breath, trying to prepare myself for what I was about to do. I dreaded using my magic again. Nine years. It had been nine years since I'd touched it.

I finally turned around to face the three of them. After taking in a deep breath, I drew my sword. Bringing it up over my left shoulder, I released my magic, and the blade exploded into white flames, making Rabryn jump. I arced the sword down and across me, slicing the air in front of my torso. The air split open, and white fire poured out like water gushing from a broken dam. As the flames spilled silently to the floor, a breeze from nowhere started to swirl the fire around my feet and then up around my body. The unnatural element cocooned me, and I felt myself changing and transforming, revealing to everyone in the room the horrid curse that my father had passed on to me.

Finally, the white flames extinguished, and I let out a slow breath and bowed my head in shame. I didn't look at any of their faces, especially not Rabryn's. "This is my secret," I said solemnly.

It was silent for a moment. Then Rabryn spoke. "That's no reason to hate you," he said, as if it was absurd that I would even consider it. My eyes snapped up to meet his. He was sincere, but his eyes were also wide, as if he was struggling to believe what he'd just seen. "So, you have magic powers. I'd keep that a secret, too, if Beldorn advised it."

Rabryn didn't hate me after all! I had kept a secret from him, but he didn't seem angry about it. Suddenly the realization hit me that Rabryn had never heard of the White Warrior.

The Pitt was an incredibly sheltered place, so the war against The Nameless One had probably only been a whisper to them when it happened. 3,000 years had passed since then, and the whisper was long forgotten. None of these people, certainly not my brother, knew that the White Warrior was the most hated being in the entire world.

Rabryn suddenly threw his head back and laughed. "Well, Sis, show me what you can do!"

He still loved me! I could have cried from relief! My world hadn't come to an end!

I smiled sheepishly at his unexpected request. "I would, but I don't even know what I can do."

"You don't know how to use your magic?"

"I know how to use it. I just don't know what it's capable of."

Beldorn smiled, looking like his gentle, kind, benevolent self again. "Look around, Azrel. I'm sure you'll be able to find something to demonstrate to him."

My eyes shifted around the room and rested on Ortheldo. He was pale, wounded, and weak, but he gazed at me with a smile. Wondering if I could heal his injuries, I grinned.

I started making my way over to him to try, but Rabryn gently took my upper arm, stopping me. His eyes scanned my face as he cautiously reached up to stroke strands of my white hair and touch my white, glowing face. He looked at me as if to make sure his eyes weren't playing tricks on him. Then, releasing me, he began laughing. My smiled widened at his lovely reaction.

Still smiling, I sat down on the edge of the couch next to Ortheldo. "You have a lot of explaining to do, my friend." He nodded. "So, let's make you well and get started, shall we?"

I gently placed the broad edge of my still-flaming sword against Ortheldo's forehead, and he drew in a sharp breath. Thinking I was hurting him, I almost pulled my sword away, but then he relaxed and smiled as he started to glow with soft white light. I watched the swelling and discoloration around his eye and jaw fade away and the cuts disappear. I felt the wounds close on his back, arms, and legs, completely healing him.

I assessed Ortheldo's appearance, thinking he really needed to wash when this was done, when suddenly, without my command, the white light grew brighter. When it finally died down, his wavy black hair was clean and shiny, as was his skin. He even smelled good, like he had just bathed.

His eyes were so bright and clear and alert when he opened them that my heart stopped. The pain and fatigue had vanished from them, making them even more unbelievable than I had remembered.

He sat up and gazed down at himself. He spread his hands on his bare chest and then patted his skin and head in various places, feeling for the bumps and cuts and bruises that were no longer there.

"I don't feel anything," he exclaimed. "No pain, nothing." His brows suddenly dropped. "Well, that's not entirely true. I do feel hungry." We all laughed. He smiled at me with such warmth that my insides turned to liquid. "Thank you."

My heart skipped a beat at the sound of the soft, genuine gratitude in his voice and the intense way he looked into my eyes.

"That was incredible, Azrel!" Rabryn exclaimed behind me. "Do you think you could make breakfast appear on the table, too?" We all laughed again.

"I could try."

"Actually," Beldorn interrupted, "I think it best to turn back into your regular form now, Azrel. You should not use this gift frivolously. Remember, it still must be kept secret."

He seemed a bit worried. Though something deep inside me told me to listen, I really wasn't in the mood. "Just a moment," I said with a mischievous smile.

I took my sword in my hand and pointed it in the direction of the kitchen. A flash of white light filled the kitchen, and a hardy breakfast appeared on the table—ham, eggs, potatoes, hot cakes, and apple juice.

I gave Beldorn a sly grin. "You don't really think I'd cook breakfast the hard way, do you?"

Beldorn lips tightened, and a stern expression came over his face. I ignored it. It served him right for yelling at me and forcing me to reveal my secret to Rabryn.

I changed back into my normal form, sheathed my sword, and grinned at them all. "Let's eat!" I said cheerfully.

Maybe my powers weren't so bad.

Wait. What was I thinking?

Reality iced through me, and my mood became grim as I vividly remembered what my magic had put my father through. Nothing good came from this power. Sure, I could heal, but I didn't like the idea of using my magic even for *that* purpose. What had I been thinking, putting breakfast on the table? I scowled down at the weapon at my hip, wondering what horrible thing would come of my mistake. For all I knew the food was poisonous. I scolded myself for using my magic so carelessly. That shouldn't have happened. It would *not* happen again.

TEN

Rabryn went upstairs and grabbed a set of his clothes for Ortheldo to wear. They were way too small, as Rabryn was lithe and lean and about four inches shorter than Ortheldo, who was muscular and bulky. Beldorn fixed that, though, with a quick spell. Ortheldo then pocketed the mysterious necklace, and we went into the kitchen to eat.

Ortheldo sucked down his breakfast faster than any man I'd ever seen. I wondered how long he'd gone without food before we'd found him. He was in good spirits, though, despite what he'd been through.

Beldorn didn't eat. He stayed quiet and broody as he gazed out the window. The windows in the kitchen, to my dismay, had been open when I'd made breakfast appear, but I didn't think too much of it. I was still too busy kicking myself for using my magic at all.

When Ortheldo had eaten his fill, he sat back in his chair and sighed. "Thank you, Azrel. That was wonderful."

I stood and took his plate. "You're welcome."

As I took Rabryn's plate, that strange, good feeling at seeing my friend alive and here with me bubbled up again. It had been nine years since I'd last seen him, but it felt like no time had passed at all. His eyes were still the same; his smile, everything, was still the same.

Realizing I was staring at him, I practically jumped out of my skin to quickly look away. As I passed him on my way to the washbasin, though, he gently took hold of my elbow, stopping me. I turned to look down at him. He squeezed my arm reassuringly and smiled. I managed to smile in return, letting something warm and wild and very new stir in my chest a little when I looked at him. He let me go, and I moved to the washbasin. I put the dirty dishes in it and gripped its edge to try to compose myself and force down the emotions that flooded through me at the sight, smell, and touch of him.

Finally, I turned back, attempting to keep my expression and voice neutral, and pulled up a chair next to him. I couldn't contain my curiosity any longer. "All right, now tell me everything that has happened to you since we unintentionally parted on Ambuel."

I hoped his tales would be positive, but his face clouded over. Memories of hard times skimmed across his eyes, and my smile faded. He'd been through so much already, dating from way back to when he was a kid. I hated to think that he'd been through more hardship.

Rabryn saw the change of our moods and leaned in closer to listen to what Ortheldo had to say. Beldorn stood and went to the window, still gazing out expectantly, though I knew his ears would be turned in our direction.

Ortheldo sighed and then looked down and took both of my hands into his. "I searched for you for a long time after you fell. I went up and down the Ambuel, finding no sign, no hope that you were even alive. But I knew you had to be, or else we were all in big trouble. A world without the White Warrior would be a dead world."

I shot a glance at my brother to see if his expression changed at the mention of the White Warrior, but there was no change.

"I had already gone without supplies or food for days, but I was going to find you no matter what it took. I had to. I kept searching until my legs couldn't hold me up anymore. When I finally collapsed on the bank, the Gleo`gwyns found me."

I didn't know what to do with myself. How could I react to that? Emotions gathered and formed a lump in my throat. He'd searched for me until he was near death? Guilt rippled through me as I wondered why he would do such a thing. Something else rang in my memory, too—the Gleo`gwyns. Those were the rainbow-clad riders that Beldorn and I had passed during our travels.

"They saved my life," Ortheldo continued. "When I was well and knew more about them, about how they traveled the lands constantly, I asked if they'd seen any sign of you. They had nothing solid to tell me, but they mentioned rumors they'd heard about 'a lady from nowhere,' and other things of the sort. I had a feeling the rumors were about you and followed them until they brought me to Galad Kas, but you'd left there months earlier. They said you were on your way home with the Wizard Beldorn, but of course, I didn't know where your home was because the maps your father drew had been with you when you fell into the river." He sighed. "I should have been content knowing you were in the good hands of a Wizard but"—he looked down at my hands holding his and caressed the backs of them with his thumbs—"I still missed you and feared for your safety every day. I promised myself I wouldn't stop searching until I found you." He looked up at me again and smiled. "It took me nine years, but I finally have— completely by accident, of course," he said with a small chuckle.

I couldn't laugh with him, though. I felt overwhelmed and dizzy. He'd searched for me nonstop for nine years of his life? It sent my mind reeling! Why? How could he have been so bent on finding me? Driven to do so not for months, but for years!

Rabryn's voice broke the silence. "Ortheldo, how did you come about the necklace and our woods?"

Ortheldo exhaled heavily and leaned back in his chair, rubbing his face with the hand not holding mine. "How I came across The Pitt is a bizarre story." He looked at me. "I remembered your father saying that The Pitt was significantly hidden in woodlands. I'd already been down this way and had searched every forest that I came across, including this one, and I hadn't found anything. I swear that some magic protects The Pitt. Otherwise I should have run right into it years ago."

Magic around The Pitt? "My father said the same thing." I didn't realize I'd said it aloud until both Rabryn and Ortheldo looked at me.

"What did he tell you?" Ortheldo asked.

I shrugged. "Just that he was desperate to find some secluded race to live with peacefully. He said that if he hadn't found The Pitt he probably would have died of madness or killed himself because he couldn't be alone anymore." I hoped I'd chosen my words carefully. I didn't want to hint to Rabryn that my father had been temporarily immortal and had lived for thousands of years.

Ortheldo nodded. "You saw my injuries. I was nearly dead as well." A thoughtful look crossed his face. "Maybe the magic only allows beings in life-threatening situations to see it or enter it."

My eyebrow cocked up thoughtfully as well. "Maybe."

"Because soon after I entered the trees, my attackers stopped and searched as if they'd lost sight of me. But I could see them as plainly as they *should* have been able to see me."

Now that the possibility presented itself, it seemed ridiculous to think that there *wasn't* a magic barrier around The Pitt. How else would these people have lived so long in perfect solitude? Then again, Beldorn came and went as he pleased. Perhaps because he was a magic user, he could cross the magic barrier without life-threatening circumstances.

How odd that I'd lived here for eight years and had never known that magic surrounded the borders. Rabryn had lived here all his life, so he had to be more shocked than I was...or was he? Gazing at my brother, I saw his expression was unchanged. He didn't seem at all impressed that magic of some sort seemed to protect the lands of The Pitt. Had he already known, or did he just not care?

"How did you come across that necklace?" I asked.

"That's even more bizarre," Ortheldo said, shaking his head. "It was a couple months ago. I had fallen asleep. Nothing seemed out of the ordinary, except that it was the deepest *and* the most restless sleep of my life. I can't explain it, but it was as if I were split into two people, with one of me asleep in one world while a second me was wide awake and walking around in another. It was no dream, that's for sure." He paused as his eyes took on a faraway look. "The me that was awake was standing in a place of green light." Ortheldo narrowed his eyes and shook his head slightly. "There was nothing else, just wall-to-wall green light. In the distance, though, something started coming toward me. 'Take it,' a voice said. As the shape drew closer, it took the form of that necklace. 'Take it,' the voice said again. Suddenly I realized it was your voice."

I flinched. "Me? I never left here."

Beldorn interjected without turning away from the window. "You might not have physically left, but your subconscious can leave you when you sleep."

I smirked at his back. "Have you gone batty, Old Man?" I waited for a response but got none. He didn't even move. He just stood there, silent as stone, watching and waiting.

I looked back at Ortheldo and saw that distant look in his eyes again. "I grabbed the necklace and looked around for you, but no one was there. Then I heard the echo of your voice once more." His eyebrows dropped in disturbed confusion. "You said, 'This has been lost, and I entrust it to you. Find me. You must find me or we all die. Head west and I will meet you there.'" He shook his head. "When I awoke, I thought it had all been a very realistic dream, but then I found the necklace in my hand." He paused a moment and shrugged almost casually. "Of course, after that I headed west, but I wasn't alone anymore. Something was pursuing me now. I could feel it in my bones, its presence growing stronger the farther west I went." He sighed and ran his fingers through his hair. "As soon as I set sight on your woods, I was attacked by two Legan'dirs."

I sucked in a breath and my eyes got so wide I was surprised they didn't roll right out of my head. Beldorn even turned around at the mention of Legan'dirs. They were the foul souls of evil things, more ancient than time—the very first creations of the Shadow Gods. The name Legan'dirs was the Salynn word for "Phantom Riders." They were spirits that knew no boundaries, no limits. They could pass through solid objects with no effort, yet they wielded solid weapons that could harm flesh. What they did was solely for their own benefit. They didn't even serve the Shadow Gods any longer.

"How did you survive?" I whispered in shock. My disbelief wouldn't let me speak any louder.

Ortheldo nodded. "That's why I strongly believe some active and intelligent magic surrounds The Pitt."

There was no doubt about that now. Ortheldo otherwise would be dead. Why *wasn't* he dead? The Legan'dirs should have killed him.

"I ran as fast as I could toward the woods, hoping to hide somewhere in the trees. Legan'dirs are fast beasts, though, so they caught up to me quickly. They brought out whips and clubs from inside themselves and put them to use. I fell to the ground, but I knew I had to reach the woods in order to have any chance of survival. I got up and was knocked down repeatedly until I was so weary and in so much pain that I didn't think I'd be able to get up again. That's when, for the second time, the Gleo'gwyns were there to aid me."

Thank the Sky Sanctuary for the Gleo'gwyns! I made a mental note that if I ever met them I would thank them immensely for all that they'd done. Ortheldo should not have survived this encounter.

"The Gleo`gwyns surrounded the Legan'dirs, allowing me enough time to run to the woods and escape. I think some of them may have died while helping me," Ortheldo said sadly. I wanted to comfort him, but he quickly continued. "I was only a few yards from the opening of your woods when I heard your voice call out to me."

My eyebrows dropped again. Why was he hearing me all over the place?

"'Throw it in the stream,' you were telling me. Your voice was so quiet and distant that it was as if it was being carried by the wind alone. It wasn't sharp and clear like when you'd given me the necklace. Anyway, I looked to my right and out of nowhere, a stream was flowing where there had been land before, so I chucked it in."

"That's Blind Creek," Rabryn said.

Ortheldo nodded at him. "Very fitting. Your people named it well." His eyebrows dropped in curiosity. "Is the stream also hidden by the strange magic that protects The Pitt?"

Rabryn nodded. "The magic *is* intelligent, as you guessed. It hides our land at will, expanding and moving. It reveals The Pitt to people in dire need wherever they might be in the woods."

My eyes grew wide. He knew! Rabryn had always known that a magic barrier protected The Pitt, but he'd never told me!

"I think it's time you told Azrel *your* secret, Rabryn," Beldorn said without looking our way.

I snapped my eyes to my brother again. What?

Rabryn looked from the Wizard back to me with...was that a smile on his face?

My jaw nearly dropped. He had kept a secret from me? We had lived together for eight years! I'd watched the boy grow up! What secret could he have *possibly* kept from me?

Ortheldo glanced from me to Rabryn, wondering what was going on.

Rabryn shifted his sly gaze from me to Ortheldo. "What happened after you chucked the necklace into the stream?"

He was keeping me in the dark! I was going to murder him! I could only take one thing at a time, though, so when Ortheldo glanced at me as if wondering whether he should go on, I tore my eyes away from my brother and nodded at him.

"Well, I entered the trees and the Gleo`gwyns retreated, with good reason. The Legan'dirs pursued me but then stopped almost immediately, like they had lost sight of me. So I just started walking. By the end of the day I was exhausted, and in a lot of pain until"—he smiled at me—"until you finally met me as you promised you would."

That was so strange. I'd never said I would meet him anywhere. Nevertheless, I smiled. "I'm glad you're safe now."

Then we both looked at Rabryn.

His turn.

He knew what I wanted, so I just sat silently, waiting. He kept a sheepish grin on his face, and his eyes told me I was going to find his secret funny, in a twisted sort of way. He was enjoying this. That was for sure.

I couldn't take it. "Well, speak, little brother!" I cried. "Or are you trying to drive me mad?"

He chuckled and shot a glance at Beldorn before looking back at me. "Well, big sister, it seems we've both got some skill at keeping secrets."

I smiled despite the slight sting of those words. "Apparently so."

He sighed heavily and slapped his hands down onto his thighs before he stood. "Well, as it was best for you to show me your secret, it's also best that I show you mine."

He closed his eyes, and a sparkling gold light started to form around him. My eyes went wide! He had magic! My brother had magic!

I watched in astonishment as the gold light deepened, then almost solidified, until a wall of shimmering gold light hid him from view. After a moment, the gold wall dripped down to the floor, melting away as if water had been poured on top of it, leaving Rabryn standing there...only in very different form.

I jumped up from my chair so quickly that I knocked the thing to the floor. Then I nearly tripped over it as I backed away, staring at him with my mouth about as wide as it could be. I couldn't think! I couldn't find my voice for what seemed like forever.

Finally, I managed aloud, "You have to be *kidding* me!"

My brother threw his head back and laughed. No wonder he

was grinning! Rabryn's brown hair now fell pin-straight all the way to the middle of his back, with the top half pulled back into a long braid. Two other braids were at each temple, tucked nicely behind his ears, and *gold* Sallybreath Flowers dotted his hair!

My brother was a Salynn. *A Salynn!*

He now wore a beautiful cream-colored silk tunic, a heavy cream-colored cloak, and silver silk leggings that were tucked into very familiar, yet odd looking, shoes on his feet. They were of a loose brown material that extended up to the middle of his shins, fastened by silver leather thongs crisscrossing all the way up to secure them. A silver leather belt was cinched at his waist, and a silver leather quiver was strapped to his back with a belt that came across his chest. The quiver was full of at least two dozen masterfully crafted white wooden arrows. The matching white bow beside them was perfectly formed and adorned with delicate and bold filigree carvings.

"Surprise," he said with a soft smile.

I couldn't move. I couldn't think. My brother wasn't just any Salynn; he was a Salynn from *White Veilvin!* Given the stories I'd told him, he *knew* that I didn't care for the Salynns there. That was why he had smiled before changing. My brother, the closest person to my heart, was kin to the people I couldn't stand!

I drew my sword and pointed it at him, trying desperately to keep from laughing as I pretended to be angry with him. I wanted to explode with laughter from the irony. "Explain yourself, you rotten Salynn!"

He laughed loudly again. Unable to stand it a moment longer, I burst into laughter with him. We were in tears of hysteria, and it took us a while to compose ourselves. I couldn't believe he was a Salynn!

Once we calmed down, I stared at him, still in disbelief. My gaze washed over him again. "How is this possible?" I suddenly became worried. "Wait. Are you still even my brother?"

"Unfortunately for you, I *am* still your brother." We giggled, and I thanked the Light Gods that we were still related. "The explanation is easy: my father was a Salynn from White Veilvin."

"Oh," I said in understanding. "Well, yes, I suppose he would have to be. But, I mean, how old are you?" I asked. After all, Salynns lived thousands of years. I could only manage little questions at the moment. I was too stunned to think of anything better to say.

"I'm still only seventeen years old. I'm half human, and I picked up a human lifespan from mom." He wrinkled his nose. "Which stinks."

"Why?" I chuckled.

"Well," he shrugged. "Wisdom and power comes with age and experience. I'm young, and I'll die young, which won't give me much time to become wise or powerful or allow me to experience things like regular members of my kin can." He paused and stared at my face, which I was sure betrayed my feelings of helplessness. "I'm everything you've known me to be, Azrel, except my race. I was born and raised here. I have lived here my whole life. I've never gone anywhere outside of this place. I barely know how to use my magic. I just happen to be a Salynn living in The Pitt."

"So, you've never seen White Veilvin, your homeland?" That sentence sounded so strange that I could barely get it out. This was my brother. He'd lived here his whole life. He didn't seem to belong anywhere else. He shook his head in reply. "So, you're a seventeen-year-old Salynn who knows nothing of your kin, nothing of how to use magic, nothing of how to survive as others of your race do? You're completely useless outside of The Pitt, and you don't know how to use a weapon besides what I have taught you? Is that right?"

He grinned. "That's about right."

"Wow," I said in disbelief. I'd thought all Salynns were the same, especially the ones in White Veilvin. "What made your father come here?"

Rabryn shrugged and sat on the edge of the table with his arms crossed. "He never talked about that. All he said was that he disguised himself as a human and came to live here because he was needed. He met mom, married her, and had me." He shrugged to drive home the point that the explanation was simple. "He turned me into a human as soon as I was born because he didn't want the people here to know what we were, for obvious reasons. My father knew about your 'kidnapping,'" he said, making air quotes with his fingers, "and he didn't want to see mom lose another child. So, he used his powers to hide my race until I was old enough to do it myself."

"But how did your father die then?" I asked. "Salynns can only die if killed by another or if they will themselves to die. Derweldo and mom fell ill."

Rabryn sighed and glanced down at the floor before looking back up at me. "I honestly don't know. My only guess is that because he'd been in human form for so long, he became mortal."

What a day! First Ortheldo came back into my life after nine years, then I used my powers for the first time in that long, and then I learned that my brother and stepfather were truly Salynns.

A thought suddenly came to me. "You said you don't know how to use your magic, but you used it to hide your race."

He grinned wolfishly. "I've actually used it twice."

I was confused for a second, and then it dawned on me. "You put the magic barrier up around The Pitt, didn't you?"

Rabryn's grin widened. "The first barrier, when The Pitt came into existence, was some Ancient Wizard's doing that allowed magical beings to find it at will. After you arrived, though, Beldorn decided that the barrier should be made stronger. Magical beings shouldn't be able to find it. Beldorn couldn't construct a barrier that strong alone. I couldn't strengthen it alone either, because I was so young and because my father hadn't taught me anything about using my magic besides transforming. So Beldorn and I did it together."

I was flabbergasted. I barely made myself speak the next words. "Why did the barrier have to be stronger only after I arrived?"

As Rabryn was about to answer me, that dark shadow formed in my mind, like a hot wind passing through my brain. I hadn't felt it in years—not since establishing myself in The Pitt as someone to be feared and not tormented. The shadow seemed to pass over my brother's face in the same instant. We both snapped our heads to the window where Beldorn stood. Something was very wrong! We could both feel it.

Beldorn faced us, his eyes just as wide. "Time to go," he said and rushed out of the kitchen toward the living room.

"What's wrong?" I asked as he feverishly gestured for us to follow him. Rabryn and Ortheldo didn't hesitate. I went to the window instead.

"Azrel! Get away from there!" Beldorn hollered.

I pushed aside the curtain and saw with horror an angry mob gathered outside my house. Every person in The Pitt must have been out there. They were holding torches, pitchforks, axes—anything they could muster up as a weapon. And these people didn't like weapons.

"Gods," I whispered.

Suddenly a rock came flying through the window and hit me squarely in the cheek. Pain exploded in my face, and my neck muscles jerked unnaturally fast as I fell backward onto the floor from the blow. Little slivers of glass ripped my cheek open into small jagged cuts that burned like fire. The next moment insane banging started to fill my ears. I painfully craned my neck toward the front door in time to see the tips of axes come through it. They were trying to get in!

The sound of breaking glass exploded in every direction as more rocks and burning torches were thrown in through the windows. Was this a nightmare? Had I not woken up this morning?

Suddenly Ortheldo and Rabryn were both at my side, frantically pulling me to my feet and hurrying me into the living room to the back of the house where Beldorn was. We all huddled against the wall between the fireplace and the staircase, waiting for them to break down my front door.

This was madness! Fires from the torches were now burning in various areas, and my entire house was a racket of noise. Why was this happening? Had they seen Rabryn transform? No, they wouldn't have had enough time to gather the entire population in three minutes.

Realization washed over me in a cold sweep from head to toe. Someone must have seen the flash of white light through the kitchen windows when I'd made breakfast appear.

I clenched my teeth and cursed myself for being so stupid, then cursed that stupid sword for existing! Once again I was in pain, hurt, because of this sword. No, this was beyond hurt. Now I was going to *die* because of this sword. No, even more so, my friends were going to die because of it. This was my fault. I had just killed my only two close friends and the last of my family.

Suddenly I was falling backward as if I had been leaning against a door that just became unstuck. I hit the ground, and when I opened my eyes, we were all outside. I scrambled to my feet and gazed at the gaping hole in the back of my house. Before I could look too long, the people finally broke down the front door and were streaming in. Others who had seen us fall through the hole were coming around the sides of the house. For a moment, I was paralyzed in shock. They were determined to kill me! The look in their eyes made me believe that I had no chance of surviving.

Finally, I began to run.

The mob was heavy on our heels. This was ridiculous! We couldn't outrun them. Plus, where were we going?

I screamed this question to Beldorn, to which he said, "To the stables!"

"Stables?" I cried, ignoring the flaming pain in my face. "We don't have horses here!"

"I took the liberty," he replied.

I looked over my shoulder just in time to see a man lunge and take hold of one of my sleeves. It was Bloters, The Pitt's butcher. My body jerked, doubled over, and halted as all his body weight hit the grass. I desperately tried to jerk my arm free. I clawed his hand and pulled as hard as I could but to no avail. I couldn't breathe! The mob was drawing closer. They'd have me on the ground in a second.

"Time's up, witch," Bloters growled, and I screamed in terror.

Suddenly, Ortheldo appeared by my side. With all his strength and brawny body weight behind his left arm, he threw such a hard punch into Bloters' jaw that I heard the butcher's facial bones break. Bloters went face down into the grass, hard, with blood exploding from his mouth. Ortheldo grabbed my arm and pulled me along beside him. My lungs felt like they were going to explode from fear and the strain of running for my life. A sharp pain formed in my right side, cutting my air intake to a minimum.

When we reached the bottom of the eastern cliffs, I was astonished to see a stable with four horses inside it.

"Azrel, Forfirith is yours. Ortheldo, Urylia. And Rabryn, you have Eleclya."

Sure! That would be easy! We would have no problem picking out which horse that we'd never seen before was ours.

When we ran into the stables, though, we found that three of the horses had nametags hanging from their necks. I would have laughed, had the absence of air in my lungs allowed it. I should have known better than to underestimate Beldorn. Forfirith was a tan stallion with a black mane and a small white diamond in the middle of his forehead. Eleclya was the white and dark gray spotted stallion with a silver mane. Urylia was a dark brown and white stallion with a white mane. Beldorn's horse was the same one he'd always ridden, Lómarandil. All the horses were stocked to the brim with traveling supplies and weapons.

We mounted our assigned horses, and Beldorn turned to us. "Hold on tightly now."

Not daring to disobey him, Ortheldo, Rabryn, and I gripped the reins hard. In a flash, all four horses bolted from the stable, heading straight for the mob, as there was absolutely no way around it. I was bracing myself to run a few people over when suddenly they all seemed to stop, and we blew past them at an unnatural speed. Beldorn had to have cast a time spell. When I looked over my shoulder, my suspicion was confirmed. The people all turned their heads more slowly than they should have, and their feet hovered in the air for a few seconds before touching the ground again.

We were safe, but guilt and helplessness rippled through me when I caught sight of my mother's house in flames, burning to the ground behind me. I wanted to scream in agony for her, for my brother, but numbness set in, denying me the chance.

Faster than the wind could blow we were up the western cliffs and waiting at the edge of the woods. The world slowly became clearer as time caught up to us.

"That was amazing!" Rabryn hollered.

I sat in silence. My face still burned and throbbed, and I could feel little drops of blood snaking their way down my jaw and neck. My mind was blank except for the image of fire consuming the place that had been home to Rabryn and me—the only place I had been able to call home since leaving the cave.

"Beldorn, Azrel's bleeding," Ortheldo said.

"I'm fine." My voice surprised me by coming out in a low, raspy whisper. I wasn't fine, but the pain I felt wasn't anything I didn't deserve.

"Come here," Beldorn said.

Without any direction from me, Forfirith walked to him. I didn't care. I felt so lost and empty that I couldn't care. What was going to happen now? What was I supposed to do? Why did everyone I love have to suffer because of me and this stupid sword?

I barely felt Beldorn's velvet hands cup my face. Slowly, the burning pain in my cheek and neck faded, the jagged cuts closed, and the sticky blood disappeared. He removed his hands, and only the tingling sensation of his magic lingered on the surface of my skin. I didn't deserve to be healed, but I thanked him anyway.

"Come, we haven't much time. I must get Azrel away from here. Her welcome has, unfortunately, worn out." Beldorn's expression was sympathetic. "Azrel, you may never be able to return here, as they might kill you. You could destroy them all if you wished, but I don't believe you are that kind of person."

I didn't want to agree with him, but he was right. Besides, I'd vowed never to use my powers again.

"They believe I'm an evil sorceress," I said, forcing myself to speak and explain myself to Ortheldo. My throat felt so dry and thick that it took effort to talk.

Beldorn nodded. "They have good reason to believe so."

"Gods of Light!" Rabryn cried in disgust. "They have no proof! They've *never* had proof!" He looked at me intently. "You're not evil!"

Poor Rabryn. He still didn't know what I was. I was evil. Not intentionally, but the "gift" was evil, and the "gift" belonged to me. Did he not see what I'd just done? Our mother's house—*his* house—had been destroyed because of me.

Beldorn gazed steadily at Rabryn. "A passerby saw the flash of white light through the kitchen windows after Azrel made breakfast appear and alerted the entire land. They have reason to believe she is a sorceress of some sort."

"Still," Rabryn countered, "if they'd only allowed Azrel to show them that she isn't evil! They couldn't even manage that?"

No. But I couldn't blame them. I probably wouldn't have given me a chance to explain anything if I were them.

"It doesn't matter, my dear boy," Beldorn said gently. "You know they have thought Azrel evil since the day she arrived." Rabryn glanced away, knowing it was true. "This was a good enough excuse to get her out of their land. You and I and Ortheldo see it as a horrible act, but you must understand that they believe what they were doing was right. They believe Azrel to be evil, and destroying evil things is the right thing to do. They saw the white flash—"

"And they came after me." I cut him off in a low voice, not wanting to hear any more about how unwanted and evil I was. I knew it all well enough.

Beldorn caught my gaze and nodded. "And they came after you," he conceded, catching my hint for once.

I glanced away. "I'm sorry I didn't change back into my regular form when you told me to. I now realize my mistake."

"As is the case with all mistakes," he said gently, "you have to make one to realize you have made it." I nodded in agreement, though I didn't feel comforted. "Come now. We must go."

We dug our heels into our horses' sides and entered the woods at a full gallop. I'd never felt so pained about leaving somewhere in my life. I'd been upset about leaving the cave, but at least it hadn't been burning down as I'd walked away. The only home Rabryn had ever known was gone, and it was my fault.

"Where are we going?" Rabryn asked.

"To the edge of the woods where we can make plans," Beldorn replied.

The edge of the woods was an entire day's ride. Oh, well. I was too numb to argue. I felt so small and defeated. The smell of smoke lingered in my nose, and I silently begged my mother to forgive her daughter for the horrible thing she was—the thing that had caused this unforgivable mess.

ELEVEN

We rode the rest of the day and a little way into the night before resting a few miles inside the forest border. I stayed away from everyone that night. I couldn't even look my little brother in the face. The three of them stayed away from me as well. I could feel their pitying glances, but I couldn't meet their eyes.

In the morning we rode for a few hours until the opening of the forest presented itself. Beldorn stopped and dismounted. I waited a moment, staring toward the opening that led to the outside world. A world I hadn't seen in eight years. A world my brother had *never* seen.

I allowed myself a shred of joy at seeing it, the wide open plain, the sunlight streaming down, warming the yellowish grass that was just starting to come back to life for the spring. Looking out, it fully dawned on me that I was out of my cage. The Pitt was a full day's ride behind me. I was free!

Accompanying that joy, though, came the fear of venturing into the unknown again. I really hated fear. It only made a bad situation worse and sucked the joy out of something that was actually really wonderful. So, I stopped my fear dead in its tracks. I shoved it deep down inside of me and locked it away. I couldn't afford to be afraid, especially when the lives of those close to me were involved. Once we left the secluded safety of this place, things could get very dangerous for Rabryn. He was completely unprepared for what awaited him out there. I couldn't be afraid. Not now. Not when my brother's life was on the line.

A strange sensation rose up inside of me. It was like a light suddenly shone on my soul, or out of it, filling me up as I stared defiantly toward the opening of trees. A strange sense of self came with it, too, and an image of the White Warrior popped into my head.

No! I shoved that thought away along with the fear. I hated that sword! I hated my magic! As I pushed the image away, the light filling me up drained away, too. I didn't care. I'd rather feel empty than feel this curse.

As I dismounted, my eyes immediately went to my brother. He was still in his Salynn form, gazing out at the opening with big, frightened eyes. A heavy sense of responsibility weighted my shoulders. The only life he'd ever lived, the only world he'd ever known, was a day behind him, and the largest part of it had been burnt to the ground. I hated bringing this on my brother. He didn't deserve it.

I walked over and nudged him with my shoulder. "It's not as bad as it looks," I said, trying to cheer him up.

He looked at me with a forced smile and nodded before he put his arm around me and guided me off to the left, where Beldorn and Ortheldo had gone.

We made our way through the ferns and bushes and other various plant life of the forest. My boots crunched loudly on the dead leaves and sticks, but Rabryn didn't make a sound when his Salynn shoes stepped on the ground. He may not have been raised a Salynn, but he already had the traits of his kin. All Salynns were very light on their feet. It was one of their many subtle trademarks, along with their sharp senses and amazing fighting abilities.

We walked a short distance until the trees ended abruptly, revealing a short but steep hill, with Blind Creek flowing below. The stream was about sixteen feet wide and no more than two feet deep. It wasn't very impressive, but it was nice looking. Rocks of all shapes and sizes jutted out from the surface, causing the water to make a soft gurgling sound that calmed me. I drew in a deep breath through my nose, smelling the cool, fresh morning air, and sighed.

At the bottom of the hill, we let the horses drink. Then all of us gathered on a large flat rock, half of which was on land, with the other part of it gradually sloping down into the water.

"All right, Beldorn," Rabryn said after he had taken a seat. "What do we do now?"

"Ortheldo, do you have the necklace?" Beldorn asked, getting right down to business.

I glanced over my shoulder as Ortheldo pulled it out of his pocket and handed it to the Wizard, who tenderly took it from him. When I turned to admire the stream again, Beldorn sighed. "This is how you bring honor to you father's name, Azrel."

I snapped my head around so fast it was a marvel that my neck didn't break. What had he just said to me? Had I heard him correctly?

"What are you talking about?" I asked with wide eyes.

After all the years I'd spent idle, sitting around doing nothing, I was suddenly being offered the opportunity to do what I was born to do—bring honor to my father? Had the time come? Finally?

The old man regarded me with somber blue eyes. "Honor your father by returning this necklace to its owner."

My eyes narrowed suspiciously. It sounded too easy. "How?"

Beldorn held up the gem in his fingers. "This jewel is very old. It's even more ancient than history can recognize."

Great. I just wanted him to tell me what I needed to do so I could get on with it. Hopefully this would be a short history lesson.

"In the beginning of Salynns' time"—oh, definitely not short—"when the first Salynns walked Casdanarus, they explored mountains. One mountain they mined, long since pummeled flat by time, harbored endless numbers of these jewels. When they stumbled upon these treasures, the Salynns had no idea of their value. Further exploration of the caverns revealed various healing aids. Healing plants grew right from the jewels; healing spells and recipes for healing elixirs were carved right into the mountain walls. The healing aids were everywhere."

I slowly sat myself down on the rock. "So, the necklace has healing powers."

"Yes and no," Beldorn replied bobbing his head side to side. "It does not only harbor healing powers; it *is* the power of healing." I blinked, wondering if he meant what I thought he meant. "Everything that has the power to heal is bound to this jewel, for everything that can heal was born from it."

My eyes went wide as I looked at the tiny gem with newfound astonishment. This thing was the power of healing? That sounded insane!

"In early times, the jewels' magic was used for the purpose for which they were created, to heal the wounded and ill. But when the Salynns of old realized the jewels' immeasurable value, they became greedy. They stole them from the walls of the mountains, hoarding them and hiding them for their own purposes and selling them for countless amounts of gold to helpless ailing families. Slowly, though, the Salynns began to realize that if the jewels were not put to healing use for an extended period of time, they would lose their orange glow and die. Once a jewel dies, it cannot be brought back to life. The glow is the jewel's soul." Beldorn's eyes were steady as he spoke in a low, meaningful tone. "If all the jewels die, then the ability to heal dies with them."

"Okay," I said carefully, not fully sure I understood where he was going with this. "Then we'd better get to finding the rest of these gems and start putting them to use, don't you think?"

Beldorn pressed his lips together and sighed softly. "This jewel is the last of its kind."

"What?" I barked.

"Greed and time have killed all the rest. However, this one jewel holds the souls of every other jewel that existed before it, giving it the power of the hundreds of thousands of others that once lived." His voice dropped low. "Which makes it hundreds of thousands of times more powerful, hundreds of thousands of times more valuable, and hundreds of thousands of times more desirable."

I swiped my hand across my mouth, pinching my lips together briefly as I tried to grasp the gravity of what he was saying. "So, basically, if this gem dies, we lose the ability to heal. Is that what you're telling me?"

His grim, eerie tone of finality sent shivers down my spine. "Because this jewel is the last of its kind, those who fall ill or are wounded after its death will not heal." My eyes went wide, and he sighed. "For everything that has the power to heal is bound to this gem."

A terrible silence fell upon our little group. Then my brother spoke hesitantly. "But…people can heal. The body has the power to heal itself without spells or plants, doesn't it?"

Beldorn nodded. "It does. But I'm concerned about the fatal injuries and illnesses that call for the need of magical healing." He sighed. "And with the evil times that are on the brink, these magical aids are desperately going to be needed."

Another silence fell, but Ortheldo broke it. "You said Azrel can return the necklace to the owner. What did you mean?"

"The owner of the jewel is the only one who knows how to activate its power, can preserve its life, and protect it."

I small bit of relief dripped through me. "Okay, great. Who's the owner?"

Beldorn shook his head. "I don't know."

I stared at him a moment, then threw my arms out to my sides and climbed to my feet. "Well, that's just great! So what are we supposed to do? Search Casdanarus on a wild boar chase and hope that the gem doesn't die before we find a person that we don't know we're looking for?"

"You will find this person. I have faith that you will."

I laughed without mirth and vigorously rubbed my forehead with the heels of my hands. He was putting the fate of Casdanarus in the frail hands of hope and faith. Had he lost his mind?

"What was the point of this idiot necklace owner if she could lose something so crucial to the fate of the world?" I asked.

Beldorn's eyes narrowed almost suspiciously. "What made you say 'she'?"

"What?" I flinched. "I don't know. It doesn't seem likely that a man would oversee a piece of jewelry, and Ortheldo said he heard a female voice when it was given to him."

"I said I heard *your* voice," Ortheldo argued.

I rolled my eyes. "Well, it wasn't *my* voice. It was a female voice."

"Very well," Beldorn said. "You are at least looking for a woman who is the keeper of the necklace. That narrows your search considerably."

I looked at him stunned. "Beldorn! Don't trust a conclusion based on my off-handed comment."

"Your first instinct was to say it was a woman. First instincts rarely lead you astray."

I sighed in frustration. Instinct had nothing to do with it, but I didn't bother arguing with him. "Okay. Fine. Let's go find the owner," I said with a helpless shrug.

"You should be aware that news of the necklace has already reached evil ears; hence, the Legan'dirs' presence this far west." His face scrunched as if he'd bitten into a lemon. "You can imagine what Shadow creatures would do if they had the power of all healing in the palms of their hands."

"But you just said only the gem's owner can activate the gem's power," I said.

Beldorn shrugged. "For all we know, they could have the

jewel's owner in their custody already. Or, if they took hold of it, they could just let the gem die."

I shook my head in frustration, crossed my arms, and turned to look out over the water. What a situation. Either let some evil thing get hold of this necklace and everyone dies, or I don't get the necklace to its owner in time and everyone dies with the gem anyway.

"How did the Legan`dirs know I had the necklace, though?" Ortheldo asked.

"Beings of pure Shadow can feel the presence of an equally pure source of Light—like the healing jewel. The opposite is also true—a being of pure enough Light can feel something of pure enough Shadow. The two extremes are constantly at odds. Each is like a force of invisible pressure on the other. The pressure increases as the two pure forces get closer together. Unfortunately, this ancient natural law makes the jewel easy for Shadow beings to find."

"Great," I said bitterly, facing them. "So, let me see if I have this straight. I have to try to find a person I've never met or seen before, though I have no idea who the person is or where to go. All the while, every evil creature in existence is on the hunt for this necklace, which, by the way, is easy for them to find. Plus, this necklace is dying, and we have no idea how long it's going to live. Is that about right?"

Beldorn nodded. I let out a hollow laugh. Well, if I was going to die, I might as well die trying to restore honor to my father's name. "Okay," I said with finality, "any *hint* of where I can start?"

"First," Beldorn said, standing, "you must get some updated maps of Casdanarus. Head to Rocksheloc Mountain. I will go ahead of you to get the Humounts started on drawing some new maps. You should be there in two weeks and five days. After that, you may want to make your way to Triple Peaks. Candletars may be able to point you in the right direction."

"Fine." I held my hand out to Beldorn, who handed me the necklace. "I'm gone," I said, pocketing it. I passed all of them as I headed back to the bank toward my horse. I figured I might as well get on with my death; that was all that seemed to be waiting for me on this ridiculous venture.

"You'll need help!" Rabryn cried, jumping to his feet.

I smirked at him over my shoulder. "No, I won't."

I gathered up my horse's reins and turned him toward the hill, but Ortheldo stood in my path, his arms crossed stubbornly. My brother appeared beside him, his body language the same.

"I have not searched for you for nine years only to see you for two days and have you head off on your own," Ortheldo said firmly.

I narrowed my eyes. "This is *my* responsibility. Not yours. The last thing I need is a death or two on my conscience. Least of all the deaths of my best friend and my brother."

I felt bad about what I was saying, because he *had* searched for me for nine years and I didn't want to leave him anymore than he wanted me to leave, but I couldn't let him put himself in danger.

Ortheldo clenched his teeth, closed his eyes, and took in a deep breath through his nose. I'd seen him do that a million times. It was how he kept his patience in check. My father would often be teaching him something new, and if he couldn't get it right, he would do that...and then try again.

When he opened his eyes, he looked at me with a steady gaze. "I'm going with you, Azrel, whether you like it or not. If I die, at least I won't die alone." He narrowed his eyes, daring me to argue with him.

I sighed heavily and looked at Rabryn.

He shrugged. "You're stuck with me, too, Sis."

His body language and tone let me know that while I could argue all I wanted, it wouldn't do me any good. I'd seen him like this before—stubborn.

I looked away from them, annoyed. Why did they want to come? Now I was going to be worried sick for the both of them the entire time. But I could tell they weren't going to pay attention to anything I had to say in protest. I knew them both too well to take that look in their eyes lightly. I supposed the company would be nice, too. Besides, neither of them really had anywhere else to go.

I looked back at them and shrugged a shoulder. "Fine. Let's go." I started leading Forfirith past them up the hill.

I caught Ortheldo grinning and nudging my smiling brother with his elbow. Both of them were rather proud of themselves for having won me over so easily. They really hadn't won anything, though. I was just too tired to have a long, drawn-out argument.

Beldorn was the last one up the hill with Lómarandil. When he arrived, we all mounted our horses. Beldorn and Ortheldo kicked them into a full gallop and headed toward the opening in the trees. Rabryn and I lagged behind, gazing after them. Those two were used to the world outside of The Pitt, so there was no hesitation on their part. For my brother and me, though, it was a little harder.

"Are you okay?" I asked Rabryn. He had never been this far from home.

He licked his lips and nodded before smiling at me. "Let's go."

We tapped our heels into our horses' sides, and they bolted toward the opening at a full gallop. My heart was thundering against my chest as I watched the end of the trees approach.

Finally, sunlight exploded on my face, and the free breeze of the open plain whipped my hair to one side. I was free! Free from judgment, free from hatred, free from the people of The Pitt.

The sensation was so overwhelming I thought I might burst. Instead, I let out a loud scream of exhilaration! Standing up in my stirrups, and bending over Forfirith's neck, I speed him up. With a toss of his mane, and a powerful neigh, Forfirith ran.

"That a boy! Ya!" I hollered. I laughed as we blew flat past Beldorn and Ortheldo, who also laughed.

It felt so good! I was finally free!

TWELVE

As much as I wanted her to, as much as I tried to make it so, Azrel never belonged in The Pitt. Her dynamic upbringing had sparked a fiery nature that was too wild for The Pitt. The simplicity, the ideals, and the rigidness of the people and the place just hacked away at her spirit, piece by agonizing piece. I did my best to avoid thinking about the things she'd been through, but it was always there in the back of my mind.

Though her spirit may have wilted during her time there, it was far from dead. We were only a day away from the woodland border and it was already getting stronger with every mile she put between herself and that land. As she stood in the distance with Forfirith, the moonlight lent her a fair silver tint, and my keen eyesight allowed me to see that she was smiling...and *talking* to her horse.

Yes, my sister was *talking* to her horse.

I made a mental note to ask her what she was saying to him, and of course make fun of her for it. But I smiled more at the fact that she seemed at peace, and content. No one deserved peace more than Azrel.

I, however, was far from at peace. I was terrified. Beldorn had left us all before nightfall, which seemed to increase my anxiety. We were on our own now.

I couldn't stop my heart from pounding and my legs from shaking. The thought of having nowhere to go, nowhere to turn, no place to call home, wasn't anything I'd faced before. The mob at The Pitt had seen me as a Salynn. My heart sank, knowing that the people who I had grown up with, people I had known my whole life, hated me now. I shuddered, recalling their faces in that mob, twisted with such hatred and murderous rage toward my sister. I'd become a stranger to them in that moment, and they to me.

I knew Azrel blamed herself for everything that had happened, but no one was at fault. It had been just an ugly turn of chance, and there was nothing to do about it except deal with it.

That was one thing Azrel had taught me at a very young age.

"Chance is what makes life hard, but there's nothing you can do except deal with what it gives you." It's how she explained how she'd dealt with her torture in The Pitt—and it *was* torture, though we didn't talk about it much these days.

I was trying to deal with this turn of chance, but I was failing miserably. The very air that blew around me felt alien. Even the ground I sat on felt unfamiliar. I didn't belong here. My home was hundreds of miles away. Everything I'd ever known was hundreds of miles away.

"You're quiet."

Ortheldo's voice made me jump and spin. I hadn't realized he'd sat down next to me. I turned my eyes back to Azrel in the distance. "Just thinking," I replied, not wanting to let on that I was afraid.

"Scared?" he asked.

Apparently, I didn't have to let anything on. I smiled a little. "Terrified."

He surprised me by nodding. "Me too."

I looked at him, relieved that I wasn't the only one. But what did *he* have to fear? He'd been in this world before. "What are *you* afraid of?"

Ortheldo shrugged casually as he gazed out toward Azrel. "A few things. Failure mostly. What about you?"

I drew my knees up and wrapped my arms around them, taking one of my hands into the other. "Not too much...just everything."

He surprised me again by chuckling, which made me chuckle and put me more at ease with this stranger.

Before I realized it, I spoke again. "When I was a kid I wanted to be an explorer, but," a wave of sadness came over me as I gazed toward my sister, recalling all the times I'd been denied a childhood because of what I had to watch her go through. "Then I grew up." I pressed my lips together and sighed. "I've never left home before and, truth be told, I'm scared to be out here."

Ortheldo nodded. "It's a scary place out here."

I scoffed lightly, but smiled at him, too, finding his candor oddly comforting. "Thanks a lot."

He smiled at me in return. "Sorry, but to say anything else would be a lie." He shrugged and looked out toward Azrel again. "It's not all bad out here, though. You can take comfort in that."

I nodded. "Thanks. I will."

There was a silent pause between us. Then, "Is she *talking* to that horse?" he asked.

I laughed. "Yes. Yes she is."

Ortheldo smiled and looked at me. "I wonder if she expects an answer." We both laughed.

"Children," Azrel's called out across the distance, "you can stop talking about me now." Ortheldo and I stopped laughing and looked toward her with wide eyes. How could she have possibly heard? She was too far away!

"We weren't!" I called out to her.

"Don't try to lie to me, little brother," she replied. "You never could manage it. Besides, I can hear you as plainly as if you were standing right next to me. And no, Ortheldo, I don't expect the horse to answer me."

Ortheldo gazed at her with a wrinkled forehead. "Light Gods, that sword must have heightened her senses beyond your level."

His words gave me an opening to ask the question that had been burning in me since Azrel had turned into that white figure at the house. "What is she, Ortheldo?" I asked, lowering my voice to a level I hoped Azrel couldn't hear. He didn't answer right away, and I turned to find him looking a bit perplexed. "That white person she turned into. What is she?"

He gave me a small sad smile. "I don't think I'm the one you should be asking."

I nodded and looked back at Azrel. I hadn't expected Ortheldo to tell me, but there was no harm in asking.

Azrel and her horse started back toward us from the creek. I wondered if she would tell me if I asked. I didn't think so. She didn't seem to like the magic she possessed. In fact, she seemed to hate it with every fiber of her existence. Yet, she always carried that sword at her belt. In the eight years I'd known her, not a single day had gone by that she was without it. But if she hated it so much, and it had brought on the scorn of The Pitt, why had she bothered?

Something irked me about it. I knew only that her father had given her the sword just moments before he died and that it obviously possessed some white, fiery magic.

Not for the first time, I sighed in frustration at how little I knew. I'd missed so much growing up in The Pitt. Something told me I *should* know what that sword was—and who my sister was—but I didn't. I hadn't even been told why the magic barrier around The Pitt had needed to be strengthened after Azrel had arrived. "You'll find out someday, my dear boy," Beldorn had said, "just not today." I'd been only nine years old at the time, but I wished I knew now. If she was in danger, I wanted to know about it.

Azrel put Forfirith with the other two horses and then plopped down on the grass in front of us. She gazed up at the night sky with a soft smile on her lips.

It had been a long time since I'd seen her without the pinched, hard lines of stress and loneliness on her face. My sister was an incredibly beautiful woman, but she didn't know that, or she didn't care. In a way, I wished she did, just so I could tell her how jealous the women in The Pitt were of her.

"You know," Azrel said, "I can't remember the last time I admired the stars."

I turned my eyes upward. I couldn't remember if I had ever admired the stars. They were too easy to take for granted. Catching a glimpse of Ortheldo out of the corner of my eye, I noticed he wasn't looking at the stars at all. He was looking at my sister. He gazed at her like she was the only thing in the world he could see, or even desired to see. It made me smile.

Ortheldo was a strange character, and I was really looking forward to unraveling the mysteries and secrets around him in time. I respected him greatly already, and I'd only known him for two days. The fact that he'd searched for Azrel for nine years made me like him even more. He cared for her a great deal, and that was important to me. Not many people cared for my sister.

Azrel let out a heavy sigh and looked at us. "Okay, Ortheldo, you're going to have to boost my memory of travel and direction." Ortheldo smiled broadly. "How do we get to Rocksheloc?"

"Crox Path," he said without a thought.

"Okay. Yeah, I remember Crox Path," Azrel said. "And that would be..." Her voice drifted as she sat in thought. "I want to say northeast of here."

Ortheldo beamed proudly. "You would be correct."

Azrel gave a jerky nod. "Very good." She froze suddenly. "Wait." She looked at Ortheldo skeptically. "Crox ends at Narcatertus, right?"

"It does."

Azrel curled her lip in dismay and a bit of disgust. "If we keep northward of Crox, we can avoid it, right?" Ortheldo nodded. "Okay. Good. We'll do that then."

"What's wrong with Narcatertus?" I found myself asking before I could help it. I felt so foolish, and the last thing I wanted to do was draw attention to my ignorance.

"Oh, it's nothing really evil," Azrel began. She paused abruptly when she caught my eyes. She studied them for a moment and smiled. "Don't feel foolish for asking questions, Rabryn."

She could always see what I was thinking when she looked into my eyes. She'd done it since forever, so it didn't shock me anymore. It actually made me feel good that she knew me that well. She could answer my questions or make me feel better without my saying or doing a thing.

"Narcatertus is a human town," Azrel said, "full of very dirty, rough, and rude people. There are a lot of disruptions and crime, but nothing truly evil."

Ortheldo took a deep breath and stood. "All right, you two get some sleep. I've got first watch."

I nodded. "I'll take the last."

Tension filled the air, and I looked up to see Ortheldo and Azrel exchange an odd look. Azrel looked at me and shook her head. "You don't have to take a watch, Rabryn."

My eyebrows dropped. "Why not?"

"Ortheldo and I can manage."

What was she saying? I already felt like useless baggage these two had to carry around. The least I could do was take a watch.

"And I can't?" I asked, making it clear that I was insulted.

"It's not that, Rabryn," Ortheldo said, squatting beside me. "We're just worried about you."

"Well, don't be!" I said more harshly than I intended.

"Rabryn," Azrel said gently, "we know you've never left home before. We don't expect you to take a watch." She smiled. "You said yourself that you're useless outside of The Pitt." My heart started to sink. "What if you come across something that you can't handle?"

I couldn't deny the sting that came with the thought that my sister didn't feel she could trust me with her life. Was I that useless? Was I that undependable?

Seeing the hurt in my eyes, Azrel's smile wilted and she clutched my arm. "Oh, Gods! I'm so sorry, Rabryn. I didn't mean to upset you."

"Then let me take the last watch, and I'll forgive you."

She swallowed hard and looked up at Ortheldo, wanting his input. Ortheldo tilted his head to the side and opened his palms, allowing her to make the decision. She looked back at me, and I made a point to put the hardest, most determined look I could manage into my eyes. I wanted her to feel sure and safe that I wouldn't fail her.

A nervous smile slowly spread on her face. "Okay. I'll wake you after my watch."

I smiled at her. "Thank you."

Azrel nodded and went to lie down. Ortheldo tapped my shoulder. "Don't forget what I told you about it being a scary world out here." His tone was soft, but his eyes were hard and intense. "I admire your courage for offering to take a watch, being so new to the outside world and all." He shook his head slowly, his eyes intently holding mine. "But courage is useless unless you can summon it when you face real danger. You have to be able to think and make split-second decisions that determine life or death." He held up a finger to me. "Remember, every Shadow creature in the world can feel the presence of that necklace." His voice grew low and serious as he pointed to Azrel. "And that necklace is in Azrel's pocket."

I swallowed heavily and suddenly wasn't so eager to take a watch.

"There are many dangers out here that you don't know about," Ortheldo went on. "You have to be prepared to face them. Don't let your guard down for *a second!* Always expect that something is coming, and know that you should be ready for it. Do you understand?"

I nodded. "I understand," I said in a choked whisper.

Ortheldo smiled. "Like I said, I admire your courage. Just stay armed, prepared, and alert, and everything will be fine."

I nodded again and watched him walk off into the darkness toward the small patch of cluttered trees just beyond our grassy clearing. In a soft whoosh, I let out the breath that I didn't realize

I'd been holding. Watching him walk away, I felt a sense of pride ripple through me. A man like that trusted *me* to stand guard. Every step he took was filled with purpose and pride. I bet he never let his guard down, not even in his sleep. A small part of me hoped I could be like him someday, so self-assured and worldly. It was a shame the people of Dwellingpath didn't have him as a leader. They didn't know what they were missing.

I went to my sleeping mat beside Azrel's and lay down, gazing up at the sky. Ortheldo's words echoed in my head: Stay prepared, armed, and alert. Always expect something is coming. Life or death decisions in a split second. The necklace is in Azrel's pocket.

"I won't wake you if you've changed your mind," Azrel suddenly said. I looked over at her. She was on her side facing me, her head resting in the crook of her arm. "It's okay if you have. You've never been in a situation like this before. I'll understand."

I grinned. "I'll be fine. I was taught to wield a bow by the best."

She smiled at that.

I looked at the sky again and lay in thought for a moment. "Azrel," I said, "what was that white figure you turned into?"

She was quiet, so I looked over at her. Even in the gray moonlight I could see her face was drained of color. At that point I didn't expect her to answer, but I wanted her to know it was on my mind.

She swallowed hard before saying, "I don't know, Rabryn."

My brows dropped. Okay, I wasn't expecting her to answer me, but I certainly wasn't expecting her to *lie* to me. Anger heated my cheeks and my teeth clenched. She knew very well the answer!

"What do you mean, you don't know?" I fired, propping myself up on my elbows. "You don't know what you are? You don't know where it came from? Getting a power like that at some point in your life would have been hard to miss!"

"Rabryn, please," she squeaked, her eyes squeezing shut.

I turned to my side and glowered at her mercilessly. "Please what?"

She rolled over onto her opposite side, putting her back to me. "Please just go to sleep."

Now I *had* to know what it was! The truth deeply troubled her, and that scared me out of my mind.

"No! I want to know what you are! I want to know why you hate your gift so much. I want—"

"Gift!" she screamed and spun on me. Her expression was like none I'd ever seen on my sister's face before. She looked more animal than human. I could almost see my death in her eyes. "How would you know if it's a gift? You don't know anything about it! How dare you call it a gift!"

I was stunned. Her breath was heavy, her eyes were bulging, and her arms trembled with the will to not lash out at me. That brief second was enough to make me forever fear being on the wrong end of my sister's anger. I pitied anyone and everyone that ever angered her enough to earn a taste of her blade.

I swallowed and withdrew into myself from fear. "All magic is a gift, Azrel," I managed meekly.

Apparently that was the wrong thing to say.

"No!" She jumped to her knees, looking like a wild cat about to pounce. Her fingernails even dug into the grass. "Some magic is a curse!"

I hadn't known my question would upset her so much. Behind the rage, I saw the pain that I had inflicted, and I desperately wanted to take it back—if not for her sake, then for the sake of keeping my own skin intact. I couldn't think of anything to say. She had never spoken to me like this before, let alone yelled!

"I'm sorry, Azrel," I said, my voice trembling. "I didn't mean to upset you like this. It's just...I just don't appreciate my sister, my best friend, lying to my face."

Her eyelids fluttered and then her eyes went wide with what appeared to be alarm. She looked around her like she'd forgotten where she was, and then she looked down at her hands. After pulling her fingers from the dirt, she gazed at them like they had betrayed her somehow.

I swallowed heavily. "You don't have to tell me, Azrel. Just please don't lie to me about it. I pried because I didn't understand why you did so."

I really hadn't meant to upset her like this. Clearly the anger and hatred she had for her magic went deeper than I'd thought. Based on her reaction, it was probably too deep for me to even comprehend.

She brought a hand to her mouth and pressed it firmly into her face like she was about to throw up. "I'm sorry, Rabryn," she whispered, her voice muffled by her hand. "I shouldn't have yelled at you like that. I didn't mean to frighten you. I'm so sorry." After a moment, she lowered her hand and nodded. "I do know what my magic is." Her eyes squeezed shut. "It's...*I'm* called the White Warrior." She opened her eyes and shook her head. "But please don't ask me anymore right now. I'll tell you when I'm ready. I'm sorry I lied to you. I swear it won't happen again."

I gave her a small smile and peered at her with one eye. "Be sure that it doesn't."

She smiled, though the lingering terror in her eyes made it looked forced. She nodded. "Get some sleep. It's a long, lonely time doing a watch. You'll need your rest."

I nodded. "Goodnight, Azrel."

She lay down. "See you in a few hours."

I nodded again and lay down with my back to her, thinking about her extreme reaction to my question. Whatever her magic was, it was a problem for my sister on levels I didn't even understand.

And that made it a problem for me.

THIRTEEN

―――――(∞)―――――

RABRYN

It felt like I'd only been asleep for twenty minutes when a hand gently shook my shoulder. I opened my eyes and found myself gazing up at Azrel.

"Your turn."

I closed my eyes again and tried to comprehend how much sleep I'd actually gotten. It wasn't much. I sighed and groggily sat up, stretching my arms high above my head and arching my back. I let out a big yawn and tried to rub the blur of exhaustion from my eyes.

"Are you sure you want to take a watch? I'll do it for you," Azrel offered, gazing at me in deep concern.

I smirked, still rubbing one eye. "I just might take you up on that." Without a word, she stood and started off into the darkness again. "Whoa, whoa!" I quickly got to my feet and took her arm, stopping her. "I was only joking."

She seemed disappointed. "Oh." Then she gazed at me with concern again. "Are you sure you're up for this?"

I stretched my arms over my shoulders one by one as far as they could go to get myself fully awake and alert. "Azrel, I'm not letting you stay up for two-thirds of the night. You're going back to sleep." I took her hand and guided her back to her bed. "Besides, I won't be able to sleep now anyway."

She lay down on her mat as I crouched to get my cloak, bow, and arrows. I felt her eyes on me as I did. Standing, I drew an arrow out and notched it into my bow, showing her that I was prepared. "Everything will be fine, Sis."

"Please be careful," she begged. "If you sense anything that doesn't feel right, and I mean anything, wake me up. I won't be angry if it turns out to be nothing, okay?"

My smile widened, and I bowed deeply to her, making an exaggerated sweeping motion with my arm before placing that hand on my chest. "Yes, your majesty." I always did that when she gave me orders. She smiled and seemed to relax a little as I walked off into the night.

As our little camp shrank behind me, I began to wonder if I *was* up for doing a watch. I entered the small patch of trees I'd seen Ortheldo go into earlier that night, and glanced around nervously, checking everything from treetop to root tip.

"Well, this was a really good idea." I said softly, needing the comfort of a human sound.

I found a low rock that allowed me to keep an eye on the camp in the clearing, yet stay hidden, and sat on it. I wondered if that was what I was supposed to do.

Stay alert and armed. Always expect that something is coming and be ready for it. Never let your guard down. Life or death decisions in a split second. Ortheldo's words haunted me as I sat alone in the dark. I supposed that had been Ortheldo's goal—to keep me on edge. It was working.

But then time slowly dragged into eternity. We were only about thirty miles from the frontier of woods surrounding The Pitt — the safest, quietest, most boring place in all of Casdanarus. What could really happen here?

Moments after I wondered that, I heard footsteps. I froze. The footsteps were followed by a strange airy sound I couldn't place.

A wave of nervous heat went through me from head to toe, and I slowly stood. I didn't dare make any sudden moves. My eyes darted left and right in time with my racing heart.

More footsteps. Then that airy sound came again, and I realized it was laughter, like children giggling in the distance. It was so soft, as if the sound were carried by the wind alone.

Suddenly quick footsteps raced behind me. I spun around trying and catch a glimpse of the being, but it moved too fast. I saw nothing.

I desperately attempted to keep my breathing under control, trying to listen while my eyes darted around in the darkness. Every inch of my skin seemed to tingle with fright. I strained my eyes but saw nothing. The longer I stood there unable to see what was near me, the more the fear took over. It began to throb in my head and ears like a steady, banging drum. It was almost painful.

Again, footsteps shot around me from left to right, and again I spun around. Nothing. Then the airy giggle returned, sounding like something from a nightmare.

My pride was smashed to dust. I needed help. I tried to call out but only managed to make odd guttural noises deep in my throat. I couldn't call to Azrel for help!

Footsteps darted behind me again, closer! They were so close this time that the wind from the speed of the being moved my cloak.

Then, from the corner of my eye, I saw a shadow leaning against a tree. I spun quickly to face it. It was a black, dense shadow, the size of a small child, but I couldn't see details of a face. I heard more airy giggles, but my eyes didn't leave the silhouette.

"Rabryn," a terrifying raspy whisper said, filling my ears.

My heart stopped. It sounded like a child, but the voice was not human. It echoed eerily in my head and made me feel like I needed to wake up from a terrible dream. The voice seemed to fill my entire skull, making my reason hazy and leaving me distraught. I couldn't think. I knew nothing but fear in this moment. So much terror! I had no memory. I didn't know who I was or what I was doing. I only knew that I was scared. I felt like I was about to go mad. The fear was consuming me, eating away at me painfully!

Suddenly, from one last rational part of my sanity, Ortheldo's words exploded like lightning through my mind. "Stay alert. Be ready for anything. Be prepared and everything will be fine."

I suddenly remembered that I had a weapon in my hand. I yanked an arrow from my quiver, fit it to the string, and pulled it taut.

The airy voices and laughter stopped immediately.

I gathered all the courage I had left, though it wasn't much, and put it into my voice. "Speak, little one!" I managed harshly.

I tightened my jaw and tried to harden my eyes, but no doubt my fear betrayed me. My lips felt dry, my tongue thick. I heard the creek nearby and suddenly longed for a drink of water.

The small figure didn't move, didn't speak, and didn't giggle. Then three more shadows appeared among the trees, all of them looking like silhouettes of young children.

I tasted the sweat forming on my upper lip, and more dripped down my face. The immeasurable terror consumed me again. My breathing was rapid and shallow, and I thought if I didn't die of fear, I would suffocate. I couldn't take a deep enough breath, though I tried. My lungs burned for the air they weren't getting.

Pain pulsated in my head, and my body trembled violently.

I felt a hand close around my throat—but nothing was touching me! Slowly I felt the pressure of small fingers pushing into my skin. My arms were locked in firing position, but I couldn't fire! My joints were locked!

"Rabryn," came a steady voice, "back away."

It was a familiar voice, a real voice. The sound of something real washed relief through me. It didn't fully erase the terror I felt, but suddenly the hand disappeared from around my throat. I could breathe again.

The four shadows suddenly threw their arms up in the air and their heads back, and they let rip screams of agony that I could feel in my bones. The terror of the sound made me freeze again. I winced as pain exploded in my mind. My temples pounded uncontrollably. The screams seemed to reflect the pain I felt in every inch of my body.

Somehow, I had enough reason to know that I needed to take a step back. I tried, but my legs didn't move. Nothing moved! I was paralyzed!

A new panic boiled up inside me. I couldn't escape these things even if I tried! I was trying, and I wasn't moving!

"Rabryn," a second voice said calmly, but sternly. "You *have* to back away. You have to *make* yourself move."

The calm tone of the voice managed to calm me a bit, and suddenly my leg snapped up from the ground as if it had become unstuck, and I took a step backward. I still couldn't look away from the shadows, and my arms were still locked in firing position, but I didn't care! My leg had moved!

Suddenly the little shadows all clutched their heads and doubled over as if they were in great pain, and they screamed even louder. The sight alone was terrifying, even without their eerie shrieks!

The fear returned, and as it did, my legs stiffened again and the panic of not being able to escape returned. I could only stare at the shadows in horror.

"Do you remember," the first voice said, "when Mother took us to the waterfall for picnics?"

I didn't know how she could think of that right now, or be so calm in the presence of these things, but the memory did come. I could see the waterfall cascading down the brown cliffs in epic majesty while we ate peaches and Mother's special cucumber sandwiches.

As the memory flashed in my mind, my leg jerked up from the ground again, and I was able to take a step back.

The creatures screamed again and began bouncing up and down at the waist abnormally fast. Spikes of terror impaled my soul again, and my legs froze.

"Just keep thinking about those picnics," Azrel said smoothly and calmly. "The waterfall. The sweet peaches. Mom's smile and her laugh."

Her voice and the memory sent another wave of calm through me. But rather than using my freedom to take another step, I used it to look to the ground. Taking my eyes off those things alone relieved me, and my legs started moving more easily as I backed away.

Finally, I found myself standing between Ortheldo and Azrel. Both had their swords in their hands as they looked toward the shadows. Without a glance or a word, they took hold of my upper arms with their free hands. The solid feel of their touch sent overwhelming relief through me, washing away the unbelievable terror I felt. I let out a long, heavy breath as my entire body unlocked, relaxing almost to the point of liquefying. I was surprised my knees didn't collapse under me. My arms hung limply at my sides, and I dropped my bow and arrow to the ground, my fingers having become too limp to grip them.

I closed my eyes in relief, and when I opened them again, the shadows were gone! Gone! Just like that! As if they'd never been there.

As I stared in disbelief, Azrel spun to face me and firmly grasped my other arm. "Are you okay? Did they hurt you?" she asked, resting her hands on my cheeks.

I felt my face flush with hot embarrassment and shame as Ortheldo picked up my bow and stepped up beside her. I couldn't even look at him. After griping and arguing with them about taking a watch, I'd failed. I was so angry with myself for being so bloody useless.

"I'm fine," I managed in a frustrated growl.

I braced myself for them to start in with some variation of "We warned you." And why not? I deserved it.

Instead, Ortheldo clapped me on the shoulder. "Well done," he said, beaming proudly. My sister looked just as proud and happy.

I was beyond confused. "What?"

"Few in the entire world can draw a weapon after a Feariter has targeted them," he explained.

I was flabbergasted. He was praising me? I could have gotten us all killed by those things, and the two of them had to rescue my pathetic hide!

"They had no way of harming Ortheldo or me, so you can put that concern out of your mind," Azrel said, reading my eyes. "And us helping you is nothing to be ashamed of. You did well."

I couldn't decide if she was being serious or just trying to make me feel better.

"Why could they only harm me and not you?" I asked.

Azrel laced her arm through mine, and we began walking back to camp. "Had I known those things were this far west, I would have warned you." She glanced up at Ortheldo. "It seems our situation is worse than Beldorn knew." Ortheldo's lips were pressed together in a thin grim line as he nodded. That wasn't comforting to hear, but I kept my mouth shut. "Feariters come from the Black Mountain way in the east. They're pretty harmless if you know about them."

Harmless? I wanted to laugh out loud.

"They basically feel a nearby presence of fear, no matter how small, and seek it out," Azrel went on. "When they find it, they frighten you even more, building up your fear until there is enough of it for them to control, which gives them control over you. They can paralyze you, make you go mad, or do anything they want until they kill and eat you."

"What?" I cried, my heart jumping into my throat. "I was almost *eaten* by those things?"

Azrel nodded. "That's why Ortheldo and I spoke to you in the calm, steady way we did, hoping it would calm you down enough so you could break free from their control."

"They use fear to control their prey," Ortheldo piped in. "If there is no fear, or not enough, they have little or no control. Azrel and I know how to stay calm the moment we hear those things giggling at us."

I couldn't believe this. They were talking about those things so casually. I felt a pang of anger and jealously that I hadn't known any of this. I wanted to be able to know what was what without batting a lash. I wanted to be able to defend myself against these evil things roaming about.

Ortheldo winked at Azrel. "Nice touch, planting a calming memory in his head."

Azrel flashed him a smile and looked back at me. "I'm sorry I didn't tell you about Feariters. I had no idea they were around here. If I had, I wouldn't have put you on a watch. This is my fault."

"I'm still impressed you managed to draw your weapon," Ortheldo said before I could offer a word of comfort to my sister. "When a Feariter has control of someone, the victim very seldom manages to do anything, let alone draw a weapon. The Feariters usually have complete control within seconds and obviously wouldn't allow you to do anything that could cause them harm, like drawing a bow."

"Why didn't you just slice them up instead of talking me down?" I asked.

Ortheldo shook his head. "You were too deep in their control. If we attacked, they would have had you attack us."

"And even if we had somehow managed to spare you and kill them, you would have just died with them because they had such a firm hold on you," Azrel said softly.

I pressed both of my fists to my forehead, trying to control my patience with myself. Was I going to die because some evil thing attacked me and I didn't know what to do? I wanted to know everything there was to know about creatures like the Feariters, but suddenly I was tired. The terror of dealing with those things had wiped me out. I looked up at the night sky, and my heart sank when I realized I still had to finish my watch.

I stopped abruptly and turned around to head back into the trees, but Ortheldo and Azrel were both quickly in front of me.

"What are you doing?" Azrel asked.

"It's still dark. I have to finish my watch."

"Oh, no you don't!" Ortheldo said, turning me around back toward the camp and guiding me forward by my shoulders. "You just mind wrestled with Feariters. It's harmful for you to stay awake right now. Besides, you'll just pass out anyway and be useless as a guard."

Though I wanted to argue, I didn't. I let them lead me back to camp, vaguely aware that they were taking my quiver off my back and making me comfortable. My vision was blurry as Azrel brought my blanket to my chin and kissed my cheek.

"I'll take the rest of the watch," Ortheldo said, sounding miles away. He crouched down beside me and rested his hand on my shoulder. "You are too brave for your own good, my friend. Too brave."

It was the last thing I heard before I fell into blissful sleep.

FOURTEEN

I tilted my face up into the waterfall, letting it wash away my anxiety over almost having lost Rabryn to the Feariters last night, and the exhaustion of having argued with Ortheldo over who would finish Rabryn's watch. I'd managed to convince him that I hadn't been tired. It was the truth. I'd been too shaken to sleep. I was paying for it today, though. I'd been in an utter daze of exhaustion as I'd walked upstream to find a place to bathe and had found these cliffs with a waterfall.

I stood on the surface of a huge rock that jutted out from the main land, the main waterfall to my left, while I cleaned myself under a smaller, gentler branch of it. Behind me was a forty-foot drop to the stream below.

The cold water was waking me up. I sighed and leaned forward, crossing my arms against the cliff in front of me and resting my forehead against them. I'd almost lost my little brother last night. It had taken all my strength to stay calm after having seen my little brother so helpless. Rabryn was okay, though. That was all that mattered.

I jumped when fingertips grazed my shoulder. In a blink, I grabbed my sword that I'd stuck point-down into the moss and spun.

"Hey! Whoa! It's me," Ortheldo cried, jumping back with his hands up.

I let out a breath, closed my eyes, and stuck the point of my sword back into the moss. He should have known better than to sneak up on me.

"You never cease to amaze me," he said with a small smirk.

I looked at him with my brows drawn in confusion. "What?"

"How can you be even *more* beautiful without clothes on?"

I rolled my eyes and shook my head. "Shut up."

Had it been any other handsome man standing next to me while I was naked, I would have been embarrassed. Growing up, though, my father had set daily schedules for us. While some activities and lessons shifted daily, one thing had always remained the same: bathe in Gegnar Stream at sunrise. Ortheldo and I had seen each other naked every day for seven years. Oddly enough, there had never been anything sexual about it. Our training had been so intense, and we had both always been so focused on it, that those kinds of things just never developed, or mattered. Which was why I didn't understand why he was looking at me the way he was right now. Something new was in his eyes, something I couldn't place, and that made me cringe a little.

"What are you doing here? Where's Rabryn?"

"Back at camp."

My eyes bulged. "You left him alone? What's the matter with you?"

"Relax, Azrel. He's fine. He's a young man. You can't babysit him."

I pointed a finger at him. "Don't tell me how I should treat my brother."

Ortheldo's gaze became sympathetic. "He needs to learn how to take care of himself, especially on *this* journey."

"Take care of himself?" I said flatly, placing my hands on my hips and fully facing him. "You're telling me this after what happened last night? Ortheldo"—I held out an open palm in the direction of camp—"he couldn't even withstand what most people consider harmless creatures. How well do you think he'll do when we get down to business with the *real* Shadow creatures in Casdanarus? There are far more deadly things out here than Feariters, and you know it."

"Rabryn didn't know about the Feariters. I think if—"

"You're right," I interrupted. "He didn't. That makes him unable to take care of himself out here. Had we not been there, he'd be dead. He's from The Pitt, Ortheldo. 'Dangerous' doesn't exist in their vocabulary. He can't survive out here alone."

"He needs to learn," he said gently.

"Not on his own," I barked.

Ortheldo sighed and gave me a small smile. "You'd think I'd know better than to argue with you." I glared at him. "Please, just trust me," he insisted. "Your brother is fine. You know Feariters only hunt at night."

I shook my head, annoyed. "Fine. I'll finish my bath and head back myself."

"Here. You might need these," he said.

I looked back at him as he bent over a pile of linens on the ground beside him. He picked up a large blue cloth, a small lavender cloth, and three small, familiar vials of liquid and handed them to me.

"Thank you," I said, reaching for them and placing them on the ground next to my sword, out of reach of the waterfall.

When I looked back at him, he began stripping off his own clothes. Unexpectedly, my heart started to race as I watched him gently toss them to the ground, piece by piece, next to a deep red cloth still folded on the ground. I couldn't stop my eyes as they moved slowly up and down his body as he dropped his pants. He was so handsome, with broad shoulders that went down into a V-shaped torso, rippling with muscles all the way to his waist. His hips were small, and his buttocks was firm and tight. Below that were thick, muscular thighs that led down to strong, shapely calves.

When I raised my eyes back up to his face, he was grinning. "Looks like I'm not the only one pleasantly surprised after all these years."

It escaped—a girly, stupid-sounding giggle. I quickly cleared my throat, forcing my stupid smile away, and peered at him skeptically. "You're not joining me to bathe. I was here first."

His brows furrowed, the smile still on his face. "Bathe? I came here for a swim." He approached me, coming so close that our noses nearly touched and he had to look down at my face. My heartbeat quickened to a pace I didn't think was possible to experience and still live. "Care to join me?" he asked in a weirdly sultry voice with a playful smile on his lips.

At those words, I shrank back into myself and turned away from him, facing the cliff wall in front of me. "You know I can't swim." Small prickles of panic ran up and down my arms and legs at the memory of being swept away by the Ambuel.

"I'll teach you," he said gently.

I shook my head, avoiding his eyes, and pretended to be more interested in finishing my bath. The last thing I wanted to do was flop around in water like an idiot while he tried to teach me to swim.

Splash! I spun around at the distant sound and saw Ortheldo

was gone. *He didn't!* I thought. I got on my hands and knees and crawled to the edge of the rock, looking down the forty-foot cliffs to the stream below as Ortheldo's head surfaced. He'd jumped!

"Wooo!" he shouted as he flipped his hair out of his eyes.

"Are you crazy?" I screamed at him.

He laughed, the gentle sound echoing off the cliffs in the gorge. "It feels great! Jump for it, Azrel! I'll catch you!"

"You're mad!" I yelled in disgust, though I was smiling.

He laughed again, and I watched him swim to the shore. He pulled himself out of the water at the mouth of the steep, winding path that led back up the cliffs, and cupped his hands around his mouth. "Would you mind throwing my cloth down?"

I grinned and shook my head in disbelief as I turned around to retrieve it. When I did, I saw the black hem of a robe right in front of my nose.

I screamed and jerked backward. I wasn't scared. I wasn't! I just needed to think. Was I under attack? Where was my sword? I crawled backward to allow myself some time and room to think.

Another longer scream escaped when I ran out of ground and I fell onto my back, almost plunging over the edge of the rock and down with the main waterfall. I was trapped!

I was contemplating a jump to save my life when I saw a black robed figure down on one knee with a bowed head. "Forgive me, Missstress. I didn't mean to ssscare you." The airy hiss of the voice made me imagine what a snake would sound like if one could talk.

Seeing the figure in a submissive position calmed me a little, and I found my voice. "Why…why are you kneeling?"

Then the head lifted.

In the effort to hold back another scream, I squeaked, and my eyes nearly popped out of my sockets. Not from fear, but from disbelief.

It was not a human face that looked up at me. The skull was of human size, and the skin was a peachy human color, but it wasn't skin that covered the creature. It was scales. Scales covered the long mouth, too, and the abnormally long neck. Yellow eyes bulged from under hairless brows, eyes with vertical diamond-shaped pupils. A forked tongue hissed out of the mouth when it spoke.

It was a snake's head! It was a snake looking up at me with a two-foot-long flexible neck!

"Are you not the one who hasss the necklace?"

"I…I have it, yes, but it doesn't belong to me. My friends"— my throat seemed to close on me, and I tried to swallow past the lump—"and I are on a journey to find the owner and return it."

"I am here to help you, Misssstress."

The creature rose to its human feet and walked toward me. I felt helpless, paralyzed, as it reached into the fold of its black robe with its human hands. I closed my eyes, waiting for pain and death. Instead, a soft, satiny material draped around my shoulders.

I sucked in air and opened my eyes. The huge snake face was directly in front of mine, making me jerk back. When I looked down to see what was on me, I saw a beautiful white satin robe draped around my shoulders. I looked back into the snake's eyes. Unable to stand that for long, I gazed at the creature's chest and quickly slipped my arms into the robe, clutching it closed with my fists to hide my nakedness.

"Thank you," I managed breathlessly, attempting to look at the face again.

"I am Norka, Misssstress. You have nothing to fear from me."

"Why are you calling me Mistress and kneeling before me? That isn't necessary, Norka." I was stunned at how my voice sounded, so proper and confident. I hadn't even thought about those words before I'd spoken them.

"My Missstresss, the Blue Dragon Laroevith ssaid I must kneel in your wake and addresss you properly." The long split of the mouth seemed to curve up in a smile. "I decided to do as sshe wanted ssso I wouldn't lose my head." The creature leaned forward and seemed to peer at me meaningfully. "My neck isss too easy a target," it whispered almost playfully.

I laughed at the truth of that.

Over the roar of the waterfall, I heard distant commotion—the sound of two pairs of feet running madly toward me. "Ortheldo and Rabryn," I whispered, looking over Norka's shoulder toward the trees on the mainland.

"What did you sssay, Misssstress?"

I stood and tied the robe closed. "Please, no more of this Mistress nonsense. My name is Azrel."

Norka didn't move. "A pleasure, Azrel."

"Oh, don't say that yet," I said. I bent and took Norka's hands into mine. They seemed to me masculine, and I decided in that instant that he must be male.

I straightened and guided him to his feet just as Ortheldo and Rabryn burst through the trees. Both of them were breathless and armed with bows. When they saw Norka, they faltered, staring in horror and amazement. Ortheldo's clothes were haphazardly thrown on, and he was still barefoot and soaked in sweat. He must have run the entire length of the path up the cliffs to the camp to get clothes, Rabryn, and his bow, and then run straight here.

"Azrel," Ortheldo said in a rough whisper, still panting. "Get away from it." Rabryn looked too stunned to blink, never mind fire his arrow.

"Lower your weapons," I said. "This is Norka, and he's only here to help. This is my brother, Rabryn, and my friend, Ortheldo."

"Did he hurt you?" Rabryn asked, finally finding his voice.

I smiled playfully and planted my hands on my hips. "Do you think he'd still be alive if he had? He only surprised me. That's why I screamed."

Rabryn's expression softened a bit, but he didn't lower his weapon. Ortheldo held Norka with a hard glare, not softening a bit.

"What do you want?" he asked.

"I only wisssh to help the Missstress."

"Why do you want to help?"

I saw a fire in Norka's yellow eyes that outmatched Ortheldo's. It didn't appear to be directed toward Ortheldo, instead seemed to be aimed inward, toward himself. Regardless, it was clear that Norka didn't like the question and wasn't going to answer.

"Ortheldo, Rabryn, please go on back to camp and start packing up the horses."

"Already done," Rabryn said, still staring at Norka.

"Well, go anyway. I need to finish my bath."

"I will *not* leave you alone," Ortheldo said firmly.

"No need to worry, sssir Ortheldo. I'll be with her," Norka offered gently.

Ortheldo's eyes narrowed. "That's what I'm afraid of."

"Ortheldo," I said and approached him, "go back to camp. I'll be fine." I gave him a playful smug smirk. "I'm a grown woman.

You can't babysit me."

Ortheldo tensed up in annoyance. "This is different!"

"How so?" I prodded.

Big mistake.

"Because it is!" he screamed at me. "Why do you have to be so damn headstrong? Why can't you once, *just once*, accept the protection offered to you?"

I stared at him, stunned. Where was this coming from? "Because I don't need it," I replied, a bit perplexed.

He clenched his teeth and looked at me with wide eyes full of rage and a bit of fear. "Fine." He looked behind me and pointed at Norka. "But know this, snake. If you harm her in *any* way, you will be *begging* me to kill you before I'm done with you." He spun around and headed back through the trees toward camp.

Rabryn watched him go and then looked back at me. "What was *that* about?"

I shook my head, still stunned. "I have no idea." After a moment, I jutted my chin toward the direction of camp. "Go with him, Rabryn. I'll be fine."

He gave a little nod, and with a last glance at Norka, he headed into the trees.

I shook my head, not sure whether to be furious with Ortheldo for such a reaction, or touched. I turned to face Norka and saw him sitting with his back to me on the far edge of the rock with his legs dangling over the side. His long flexible neck allowed him to crane his head back to look at me. "I'll keep my back turned while you bathe, Missstress."

I forced a smile. "I told you, there is no need to call me Mistress. Azrel is fine."

He simply nodded and turned away, but not before I caught a flash of deep sadness in his yellow eyes. I dropped the white robe onto the ground and got under the waterfall.

"So where are you from, Norka?" I asked, reaching for the first vial of Isadith's liquids.

Norka's head seemed to sink in a shameful way. "I am from Fayithjen Forresssst," he replied quietly.

Relief instantly flooded through me. Of course he was! How could I have forgotten? All Fayithjens were half human, half creature. More importantly, they were harmless.

"Ah, Fayithjen," I said, recovering from my stupidity, "that's a lovely land."

Norka turned his head slightly toward me, his eyes averted. "You've ssseen it?"

I nodded as I rubbed the first liquid into my hair. "I visited there once, a long time ago. Maybe you remember having two visitors about eight years ago? Me and a Wizard?" Norka's head dropped even lower. "Fayithjen is so far east, though. What are you doing here? How did you even find us?"

Norka was silent for a long time. After a while, I decided he wasn't going to answer and glanced at my sword to make sure it was easily accessible. I rinsed out the purple liquid, picked up the vial of dark pink liquid, and rubbed it into my hair. Leaving it in, I took the last vial of orange liquid and poured it into the lavender cloth to begin washing my skin.

"Those liquids sssmell lovely, Azrel," Norka said as I rinsed myself off.

I smiled. "A Salynn from Galad Kas gave them to me."

Norka nodded. "Sssalynn gifts are usually very sssspecial."

His voice was sad and distant. Something seemed to deeply trouble him. I had a lot of questions, but I figured I'd better bide my time. No need to spook the poor creature.

I stepped out of the waterfall and wrapped the large light blue cloth Ortheldo had brought me around myself. "Especially when one offers the gift of friendship."

Norka slightly turned his head toward me again. I went to him and squatted beside him. His eyes widened when I gently placed my hand on top of his.

"Friendship is a gift I would like to offer you, too, if you let me," I said. He looked down at my hand as if to make sure I was really touching him in such a gentle way and raised his head again slowly, looking into my eyes. "But I can't befriend someone I don't know. Or worse, one who won't *let* me get to know him."

He swallowed heavily. "But I hardly know you, and I ssstill wish to befriend you."

I smiled sympathetically. "Unfortunately, your eagerness to befriend me, especially when I bear something of great value, makes me suspicious of you."

I started to place my other hand on his shoulder, but before I even touched him, he flinched and cowered back as if I were going to strike him. My heart bled for him. I wondered what had happened to him to make him so sad and frightened. I slowly lowered my hand onto his shoulder, and he opened his eyes when he realized I wasn't going to hurt him.

"If you open up to me and tell me about yourself, I won't find it so difficult to befriend you." I looked into his eyes. "Will you tell me about yourself at all?"

He seemed to smile. "We should get on the road first."

I smiled in return and nodded. "Fair enough. It's a long road, and we'll have plenty of time to talk."

Norka nodded, and we both stood. For the first time, I realized I came to just below his shoulders. Deciding not to let that intimidate me, I started getting dressed and gathering my things. I paused and stared down at the deep red cloth that Ortheldo had brought with him for himself. I sighed and picked it up, wondering if he was truly angry with me. I'd have to talk to him. Then, with Norka in tow, I set out through the trees toward camp.

The boys were fidgeting with their horses when I returned. I packed away my cloths and vials on Forfirith and then went to Ortheldo. He refused to look at me, pretending to focus on adjusting his saddle. I held out the deep red cloth, pressing it firmly into his chest and waiting for an explanation to his outburst.

His face softened as he took it. "I'm sorry," he said, draping the cloth over the saddle. He crossed his arms on top of it. "Azrel, I didn't mean to yell like that. It's just"—he finally looked at me—"when I heard you scream, it felt like my heart had been ripped out of my chest." He looked at me intensely and shook his head. "I can't lose you again. I can't." He sighed. "I felt so helpless standing at the bottom of the gorge, unable to get to you." He sighed. "I didn't mean to take anything out on you. Can you forgive me?"

I smiled. "Of course," I said and embraced him. He sighed heavily and embraced me back.

I never wanted to let him go.

The sudden realization that I never wanted him to leave my arms caught me off guard. But my body relaxed against him in a way it had never really done before, like if I turned into liquid Ortheldo would still catch me. It was such a…safe feeling.

Safe. That was something I wasn't used to.

But I liked it. A lot.

I snapped to my senses. What was I doing? I pulled away quickly and backed away from him a little. That had been an embarrassing show of affection. But I found that I had to stare at his chest to quell the urge to touch him again and melt into him.

"I'm sorry," I said, without meeting his eyes.

"For what?" he asked, making me look up at him. "I've never enjoyed a single moment in my life more than that."

I didn't know what to say. I didn't want to call him a liar, though I believed he was one. Nothing good came from being around me. He knew that better than anyone.

"You smell amazing!" he said, changing the subject. "What is that?"

I chuckled, grateful to him for defusing the awkwardness. "The vials you brought me were a gift from a Salynn friend of mine."

"I'll have to remember to thank her for such gifts."

I laughed. "Let's go."

As I passed my brother on my way to my horse, I caught a glimpse of impish amusement in his eyes.

I rolled my eyes and gave his shoulder a small shove. "Shut up," I said, and he laughed.

Forfirith nudged me with his nose when I stood in front of him. I smiled and petted his cheek. "Hey, boy, I need to ask you a favor. We have someone new traveling with us. Would you mind letting him ride on you?"

"There isss no need, Azrel," Norka said. I turned and saw him mounted on his own steed of a beautiful red color with a red mane to match. "Thisss is Red Wing."

My eyes went wide as I looked at the stunning animal. "Wow! She is beautiful."

Norka smiled a little proudly. "I will ride behind to keep an eye out."

My brows dropped. "I thought we were going to chat on the road?"

"The road isss long. We'll have plenty of time."

My eyes narrowed. "Okay."

I didn't like the idea of having my back to him, but maybe he needed me to show some trust first. It was a risk, but one I was willing to take for now. The boys and I mounted our horses and began a light canter across the clearing, Ortheldo on my right and Rabryn on my left. I glanced back at Norka, who rode a few paces behind us, and then faced forward again.

"I don't trust him," Ortheldo said.

"I'm beginning to question my trust as well."

"What is he?" Rabryn asked.

"He's a Fayithjen." I replied, keeping my eyes in front of me.

"A Fayithjen," Ortheldo muttered and shook his head. "What's he doing so far west? How did he even find us?"

I reached into my pocket to be sure the necklace was there, then shook my head. "I don't know. My best guess is that he felt the presence of the necklace and followed it here."

Ortheldo looked at me quickly, seeming a little surprised. "Well, I'm glad to see you're not letting his kind manner blind you to that possibility."

I smiled. "I wasn't born yesterday, Ortheldo."

He returned my smile. "No, you weren't."

It was quiet a moment before Rabryn asked, "What's a Fayithjen?"

I could tell by the look on his face that he felt stupid for having to ask questions. I smiled at him encouragingly. I wanted him to ask questions. The more he knew, the more prepared he would be out here.

"Fayithjens are half-human, half-animal creatures. They live in Fayithjen Forest far to the east. They are generally peaceful people. They can appear as full humans or, like Norka does, in their half-creature form. They all have the qualities of their animal counterpart. For instance, their ruler, Queen Sauryavia, is half owl. That makes her wise and noble; thus, she possesses great qualities for a leader."

Rabryn looked at me with wide eyes. "I didn't know there were such creatures!"

Ortheldo and I laughed, making Rabryn redden. "No, no," I said quickly. "We're not laughing at you. You need to ask questions. There are just so many creatures in the world, many stranger than Fayithjens, and your reaction to them should be enjoyable."

"As I told you last night," Ortheldo said, "it's not all bad out here."

Just most of it, I wanted to say, but I held my tongue.

"All right, master travel guide," I said to Ortheldo, "how far is it to the mouth of Crox Path?"

"Five days."

I gave a jerky nod. "Okay. Let's get going."

We sped up our horses to a soft gallop. I hoped Norka would eventually decide to ride up with us. He and I had a lot to talk about.

FIFTEEN

I tightened the messy knot my hair was in and tucked the loose strands behind my ears before returning to sharpening my sword. Sitting on a log just inside the ring of firelight, I tried to keep myself from glancing up at Norka. It was our second night on the road, and we hadn't shared a word since he'd joined our journey. It was making us all a little edgy, and we kept our weapons ready. During the day Norka always rode far behind us. At night, he sat a good distance away, always out of the firelight, keeping himself firmly tucked in the shadows. I don't think he slept, and he didn't eat.

I glanced up from my work to gaze at his silhouette twenty feet away, where he sat against a tree in the darkness. Why would he say he wanted to talk and then not come near us?

As I sat in thought, Ortheldo came over and offered me a plate of hot food. I smiled graciously at him and took it. He sat himself on the log next to me, and we ate a couple of bites. The only sounds in the forest were bugs and birds chattering. Shafts of pale moonlight shone down through newly budding leaves, illuminating spots of the forest floor where rocks and logs were partially hidden by dead brown leaves and low scattered plant life. It was a dense woodland, but it wasn't stuffy and tight. Air flowed easily through the trees when the breeze blew.

This place reminded me a lot of the woods of The Pitt. I thought about those peaceful moments up in those woods where I wasn't scorned or hated. No eyes could glare at me in those woods, and I actually had a few friends. No human friends of course, but friends nonetheless. Birds, deer, and even a few squirrels would come to visit me.

Ortheldo's voice roused me from my thoughts. "Your buddy over there is going to starve to death if you don't feed him."

I swallowed a bite of food. "If you're so worried about it, go offer him something to eat."

Ortheldo shrugged. "I'm not worried, but I know you are." He took a bite. "Besides, I already tried to offer him food." He looked at me and smiled. "But he sssaid he doessn't eat that ssstuff."

His mocking of Norka's voice was dead on! I bit my lip to keep from laughing while I backhanded his shoulder. "Jerk," I muttered.

He smiled as he chewed, then looked at Norka again. "Go find out what his problem is. I'd rather not learn the hard way what he *does* eat."

I wasn't sure I wanted to find out either.

After a few more bites, I placed my plate on the ground and stood, then sheathed my sword before heading toward Norka. I squatted down to bring myself to his eye level. "Are you hungry? We have more than enough food to share."

"Thank you, Azrel, but I don't eat that ssstuff." I smiled to myself at the resemblance to Ortheldo's imitation.

"Well, I can make you something else if you'd like. What do you eat?"

"Flesssh," he hissed.

My smiled melted, and I had to force my voice to stay neutral. "What kind of flesh?"

"Raw."

My hand instinctively went to the hilt of my sword, and my entire body tensed up on alert.

Norka seemed to smirk. "Don't worry, I don't like human flessh. It's too tough."

I wanted to laugh but didn't know if I should. He didn't like human flesh, yet he must have eaten some to know he didn't like it.

"Oh. Well, that's good." I regained my composure slightly, clearing my throat nervously. "Why don't you go hunting?"

Norka seemed to deflate a little. "I don't know how."

"You don't?" I shook my head in confusion. "Then how are you alive?"

He sighed. "I wasss born into a wealthy family. I never had to hunt for food because ssomeone alwaysss did it for me. I never had a reassson to learn." He bowed his head. "I never thought I'd be on my own."

I was tempted to prod him for more information, but I left it at that. It must have taken a lot for him to tell me that little bit. I'd take the answers as I got them, as he felt comfortable giving them.

Slowly I'd peel away the layers surrounding this unhappy creature. "I can teach you to hunt."

His snake eyes snapped to meet mine. "No!"

I jumped at his voice. When he realized he'd practically yelled at me, he softened his tone. "I mean, uh, no, thank you, Azrel."

I was a bit shaken and confused by his reaction but kept it to myself. "Why not?"

His eyes went to the ground as if the answer would be at his feet. "Well, uh, sss, I don't know. I mean, I can't hunt."

My brows dropped again. "I just said I would teach you."

He looked up at me in pure panic. "I can't! I mean, you sssee"—his eyes darted around until finally resting on my sword— "I don't have a ssword."

I smiled trying to comfort him. "You don't use a sword to hunt. You use a bow. I can teach you how to use that."

Norka began wringing his hands together. "I don't have a bow!" he said, his eyes brightening at having come up with another excuse. "Ssso there! You ssee? I can't!"

"We have three. Rabryn or Ortheldo will let you use one."

His eyes went wide and darted around, clearly searching for another excuse.

I knew he was hiding something, and I wanted to see him run out of excuses. Was he really that desperate to get out of feeding himself? Apparently so, and I wanted to know why. I'd have to choose my words carefully, or he wouldn't tell me.

"Norka, are you not hungry?"

He smacked his lips together as if he'd just tasted something bitter. "No, I am hungry. Its jusst..." His voice trailed off. I tried to get a lock on his eyes to see what he was trying to tell me, but he closed them in defeat. "My Missstress forbade me to eat while I was with you."

"What?"

He looked at me intently. "She ssaid that she would be very angry if I ate."

I tilted my head, peering at him intensely. "Oh, you must be joking," I said in a throaty voice of utter disbelief.

What kind of Mistress forbade her subject to eat while on a mission to help another? Did this Mistress think Norka would be taking food out of our mouths?

I stood up. "Let's go," I said firmly, indicating the forest with my thumb. "We're finding you some food."

"But my Missstress—"

"Your Mistress isn't here. I was the last person you called Mistress; therefore, I make your decisions now. I've decided we're taking you to find some food. Now let's go."

I started back toward camp to get one of the boys' bows. I was completely enraged with this Mistress Laroevith! Dragon? Baa! I'd slice her in half if I got the chance. No wonder Norka was so distant and terrified. He'd probably been abused and starved by this Dragon. Why would this beast send Norka on a mission to help us, only to put him in his grave by denying him food? I wondered if he had gone without food all the way here. No, this Mistress said he couldn't have food while he was with us. He didn't hunt, so he must have been given enough food to last until he reached us. My heart wrenched for the poor creature.

When I reached the fire, I crouched down to gather my bow and arrows and strapped them on my back. Ortheldo and Rabryn were sitting on a log finishing their supper.

"How is your Fayithjen friend?" Rabryn asked before taking another bite.

"Fine. But you're not going to believe this. His Mistress—"

I stopped. Something wasn't right. Norka was a Fayithjen. Fayithjens didn't have any Mistresses besides the queen, and I knew the queen. Sauryavia wouldn't do this to him.

Wait. What had he said his Mistress' name was?

Laroevith. A...

I froze. Memories of some of my teachings hit me like a rock to the head. Cold realization wrapped around my throat, ready to strangle me—which would be a merciful fate compared to what could actually happen. My eyes widened, and I breathed quickly as nervous heat filled me. Sweat formed on my upper lip, and the door to my fear cracked open.

"What's wrong?"

"What about his Mistress?"

I barely heard them speaking as I slowly turned my wide, fearful gaze behind me to Norka's nearing shadow. His eyes flashed dangerously yellow as he passed under a beam of moonlight.

His Mistress.

"Ortheldo," I said and began to tremble with uncontrolled terror. "What do you remember about Blue Dragons?"

I wondered if his memory would match mine.

It did.

The metallic ring of his sword being drawn snapped me to my senses. The numbing silence of the night was broken, and my fearful trance along with it. The sound of our movements seemed to fill the entire forest.

Sword or bow? Sword or bow? The choice flew through my brain. I went with the bow since it was already in my hand. As I notched an arrow and spun around to face Norka, I caught a glimpse of Ortheldo at my side. His eyes were wide and his sword was in front of him, though we both knew drawing weapons against Norka would be useless. Rabryn jumped to his feet and fit an arrow in his bow, understanding nothing except that we were very frightened.

Norka's shadow stopped abruptly when he saw all of us on our feet. He stood in silence, watching us. Somehow the silence was even more frightening than an actual attack would have been.

"Ssso, Azrel," Norka said. "You've figured it out at last."

The door to my fear cracked open further. My legs started to tremble, and drops of sweat snaked down the back of my neck. I felt my heartbeat in my head, and my cheeks and jaw burned from my fiercely clenching my teeth to keep from screaming.

What was he going to do to us?

Norka advanced a few steps, and the three of us stepped back the same distance. The shuffling of our frightened feet filled the forest, which seemed to have suddenly gone otherwise silent. Where were the birds and bugs that had chattered so merrily before?

Norka stepped over a log we'd placed next to the fire and sat down. His elbows rested on his knees, and his hands dangled limply between his legs. He stared into the firelight for a moment and then looked up at us. "When I firssst told you the Blue Dragon wass my Misssteress, I'd hoped you would figure it out."

I didn't even have to look at Ortheldo to know his rage spiked at that revelation. I also knew that if we somehow lived through this, I was going to get a sounding out from him to last me the rest of my life. I would deserve it, too. Had I mentioned the Blue Dragon before, Ortheldo would have understood the danger and spared us this. How could I have been so stupid?

"At firssst I thought you'd just never heard of the Blue Dragon. But now I sssee that you just have no memory."

He was mocking me! I gritted my teeth, slammed the door on my fear, and took a daring step toward him. If I was going to die tonight, it was going to be with honor.

"Why would you *want* me to find out that you're a criminal?"

He gazed back into the fire, holding his hands over the flames to warm them. "Tell me, Azrel, what made you remember tonight who the Blue Dragon was?"

"I realized you shouldn't have a Mistress in Fayithjen besides the queen. That led me to think of who you said your Mistress was. Laroevith, the only Blue Dragon in existence, and the mistress and warden of Tribletwel"—I clenched my teeth—"Casdanarus' prison for dangerous beings who have committed offences of magic."

He nodded. "Better late than never, I sssuppose."

"Now tell me why you'd *hoped* I would find that out."

Norka looked up at me from under his scaly brows, and the depth of the sadness in them made me almost gasp. It was an empty, hopeless kind of sadness that seemed infinite. "Because I'm innocccent."

I sneered. "Of course, you are. They're all innocent in Tribletwel. Tell me, Sorcerer, how an 'innocent' being such as yourself got stuck in a nasty place like Tribletwel." My voice dropped menacingly, and I pulled my bowstring back farther. "And you can also explain what you're doing here. Since you're so 'innocent,' you certainly haven't come for the necklace."

Or my sword, I wanted to add, but didn't. It was best not to put any ideas in his head. He might not know of it.

Norka gave me a steady gaze. "Do you think weaponsss can harm me?"

I felt my insides shrink. Of course, they couldn't, but I held my ground. "If you don't answer my questions, we're going to find out."

"If I wanted to kill you, don't you think I would have done ssso by now?"

"Who knows what tricks you animals have up your sleeves?"

I expected him to strike me dead right then, but he only sighed, sounding exhausted. "Will you not lower your weaponsss?"

"No," I growled at him. As useless as this weapon was against a magic user, I still felt safe holding it.

Norka sighed again. "Very well. If it makesss you feel better, you may keep them."

That sentence burned my blood. I hated that it was true, that he was letting us, *allowing* us, to keep our weapons.

"I will answwer your first quessstion," Norka said. "I hoped you would realize what I was when I told you the Blue Dragon was my Mistresss, in hopess that you would kill me." He took in a deep breath and closed his eyes. "Can you even fathom the thought of an innocccent being dealing with living in a place like Tribletwel?"

"Innocent?" I shrieked. "How can you—"

The second his yellow eyes opened and rested on me, I felt a ball of air form in my open mouth, filling it like a gag to keep me silent. There was no air was in my lungs! I dropped my bow and fell to my knees, clutching my throat. He was choking me!

Ortheldo suddenly came into view as he ran toward the snake with his sword ready for a strike. I wanted to scream at him to stop, but I couldn't make a sound. No sooner had he entered my view than he was thrown from it by another force of Norka's magic.

I couldn't breathe! I was dying! No air! Burning pain! I desperately clawed at the inside of my mouth and throat to try to make some kind of hole, some portal for air. I needed it! I lost all sense of reason and time. I was going to die, all because I was too stupid to have put two and two together. Everything was going quiet, and the edges of my vision turned black.

Suddenly the gag was gone. My upper body collapsed over my knees and I sucked in loud gulps of air, smothering the burning pain, then coughed it out. I was barely able to hold myself up on my elbows. *Just wait*, I told myself. *The burning will subside. The death will subside.* I couldn't believe I was alive.

As my senses returned, I heard howls of pain. My heart stopped, and my eyes shot up to survey the woods. Please don't be Rabryn or Ortheldo! Please! It was Norka. He was on his knees, hunched over in terrible pain, and clutching his head. His howls made my insides twist with agony.

What had happened?

Ortheldo, lying on his back to my right, was just coming to. Black charred arrows littered the ground in front of me. I followed them with my eyes until I saw Rabryn on the other side of Ortheldo. He was on his knees staring at Norka in wide-eyed terror. I crawled to him as fast as I could, unable to trust my legs yet.

I cupped his face gently in my hands and turned his eyes away from the snake to me. "Rabryn, are you hurt?"

His mouth moved up and down awkwardly for a moment before he spoke. "He burnt them," he replied. "Every single one I shot. They didn't get near him."

"It's okay," I said, pulling him into an embrace.

"You curssssed bratsss!" Norka yelled.

I looked over and saw Ortheldo standing behind Norka, pinning his arms to his sides with those powerful thighs. One hand lifted the creature's chin, while the other held a sword to his long neck.

"I didn't want to hurt you!" he wailed. "I jussst wanted you to lissten to me!"

I stood and helped Rabryn to his feet, and we walked over. Norka's eyes landed on me, silently pleading with me to believe him.

"Should I make it quick and slit his throat? Or go for his belly so we can watch him bleed to death?" Ortheldo asked.

"Why were you screaming like that?" I asked Norka, ignoring Ortheldo.

Norka's eyes closed. "Becaussse the Missstress has a leassh on me. If I usse my magic, she ssenses it through the leash and ssends me pain as punisssshment." He opened his eyes and looked up at me. "I didn't want to do what I did. I just wanted to sssilence you for a moment. But then thessse two attacked me and had to defend myself. Magic iss all I can do." A single tear zigzagged down his scaly face.

I couldn't deny the sympathy I felt for him. "I almost died with your gag in my throat. Were you trying to kill me?"

He dropped his eyes closed again and shook his head with the little freedom Ortheldo's hold allowed. "No," he whispered. "I wass dissstracted by thessse two and accidentally left my magic in too long."

Ortheldo leaned over Norka to stare down at his face. "We don't believe you." He added pressure to the edge of the blade, and a drop of blood trickled down the snake's long neck.

The bottom part of Norka's mouth began to quiver, and another tear fell down his cheek. I wanted to cry for him. Maybe he was telling the truth.

"Let him go, Ortheldo," I said softly.

His head snapped up to me, and he stared at me for a moment. "What? But —"

"I said let him go!"

Norka's eyes opened, and he looked from me to Ortheldo, wondering if he was about to live or die. Ortheldo glared at me for a moment. Finally, with a growl of frustration, he removed his sword from Norka's neck and stormed off into the woods.

Norka bowed his head as another tear dripped down his long nose. "Do you think I'm out here becaussse I'm free?" he asked and looked up at me. "I'm not. I'm sstill a prisoner. The leassh on me hass no limitsss." His sniffed and squeezed his eyes closed. "I didn't want to hurt any of you. Leassst of all you. You have been ssso kind to me."

I did the last thing in the world even I expected I would do. I dropped to my knees and hugged him. He quickly and eagerly accepted my embrace, and his sobs broke free at last. He seemed to be crying out years of built-up emotion—pain, loneliness, fear, and maybe even betrayal. Perhaps he really was innocent of his charges. All of it came out at once. I knew how that felt. After years and years of trying to be strong, suddenly out of nowhere you collapse. All strength disappears at that point, as if it had never been there to begin with.

I wanted to cry for him, but I still didn't trust him. He could not be allowed to see my white tears. He would know what I was, and that could be very dangerous for the world.

A soft, airy giggle in the distance perked my ears to their keenest. I wondered if anyone else heard it. It came again as a shadow flashed in my view from behind Norka. My eyes went wide as I felt the lingering fear that had exploded in me when I'd realized Norka's identity.

Feariters.

"Don't move," I whispered, trying desperately to stay calm.

"I hear them, too," Norka whispered back.

Rabryn!

I slowly pulled away from Norka and looked back at him. He glanced around with big eyes. I took a deep breath and tried to control my voice. "Rabryn. Stay calm." He looked at me, his eyes still big. "Just think about our picnic, and you'll be safe." He nodded, took a deep breath, and closed his eyes.

I couldn't help my own fear. I knew about Feariters, and I knew to stay calm in their presence, but it was so much easier when you had never heard their eerie, nightmarish giggles—because you only heard those if you were a target. I closed my eyes and forced my breathing to steady. I couldn't become a victim to these creatures.

The giggles faded, but they were soon replaced with screams of agony far more terrifying.

Terror shot through me and I became paralyzed. They had me! No! I could not die like this! I had to think of something.

Ortheldo.

I smiled inside at the thought of him. He was angry with me right now, but I didn't care. I let my mind drift to that safe, intimate moment when he'd held me in his arms. The safety I'd felt in that moment swept through my heart and soul like a cleansing breeze that obliterated the Feariters' hold on me.

The next thing I knew, a hand was on my shoulder. I snapped to awareness to see Rabryn crouching beside me. "They're gone."

I looked around. There were no shadows, and the screams had stopped. I looked up at him with a playful smirk. "I'm glad you didn't get yourself eaten."

He smiled. "I'm glad you told me to think of our picnic."

I turned my attention to Norka. "Are you okay?"

He nodded and sniffed, then wiped his cheeks with the sleeve of his robe.

"Okay. I'm ready to listen to you now, and you'd better spill your guts before Ortheldo comes back and spills them for you."

He let out a small laugh. "What do you wisssh to know?"

"Why are you here?"

"I was sent by my Missssstress to help you."

"Why?"

"Becaussse I volunteered to go."

That wasn't what I meant, but it was interesting. "Why?"

Norka sniffed and sat himself comfortably on the ground, crossing his legs. Rabryn sat across from him and I sat beside Rabryn. "As I told you, I am innocent of my chargesss. I would have gone on a mission to help Hathum himself if it meant I could escape Tribletwel."

My heart clenched and my eyes went wide. That was the wrong thing to say, at the wrong time, to the *wrong* person!

Seeming to realize how inappropriate that statement was, he nervously began wringing his hands. "I'm sssorry. I ssshouldn't have said that."

"Go on," I said carefully.

"Rumorss of the necklace's lossss are everywhere. Evil iss already on the hunt for it. My Mistresss had a vision that you were going to need help. Well, I'm happy to ssay that ssshe favored me among all the prisssoners. I have been her personal asssistant for decades, doing odd chores for her, like cleaning and some eassy errands. I think she may have ssomehow known that I didn't belong there." He paused. "She first wanted me to go into the wild landss and fetch someone sstronger than me for this misssion, but I volunteered myssself, and she agreed. She supplied me and told me where I would find you...and ssshe told me of my death."

"What do you mean, she told you of your death?" I asked.

"It meansss I'm sssomehow going to die in this effort to help you."

"You're what?"

"I'm going to die sssomehow on this trip. I will never again return to Tribletwel, which is the bessst news I'd heard in yearsss, and the main reason why I volunteered to go."

I wanted to change the subject and quickly. I didn't want to hear about someone being happy about dying. "Why the leash? And why won't she let you eat?"

He glanced at the ground. "I'm still a prisoner. She still hasss a responsibility to keep me under control, so she put the leash on. And I'm ssstill obligated to sssuffer for the crimess I was convicted for, so ssshe wanted me to starve. She gave me only enough food to last the time it took getting to you. After it ran out, I wasn't allowed to eat. That way I wouldn't return to Tribletwel at all. Either I'd die of ssstarvation or die helping you. Either was fine with me."

Now I asked the question to which I wasn't sure I wanted the answer. "What were you convicted of?"

He sighed softly. "Murder and treassson."

I swallowed past the lump in my throat as Rabryn tensed up. "Who were you convicted of murdering?"

He squeezed his eyes closed, and his shoulders sank. "My wife." I smothered a gasp, and Rabryn took a firm hold of my hand. "She was Queen Sauryavia's chief advisor, Hethana. She was murdered, and I wass framed for it."

"How? How were you framed?" I managed to whisper.

He cleared his throat and regained a bit of his composure. "In our bedroom—where ssshe was found dead—were papersss, the handwriting forged to look like mine. They ssspoke of plots and deviousss plans to use my magic to overthrow the Queen and her council, making me ruler of Fayithjen. A diary, also forged, ssspoke of Hethana finding out about my plotsss and threatening to tell the Queen. According to the diary, I had to kill her." He looked up at me, his yellow eyes large, and his voice dropped to a whisper of pain. "I would never have harmed her. I loved her, and Ceco."

I was overwhelmed and very afraid to ask my next question. "Ceco?"

He drew up his knees, circling them with his arms, and rested his chin on top of them. "My daughter."

I realized I was gripping the hilt of my sword hard, and my other hand was squeezing Rabryn's fingers almost hard enough to break them. I wanted to kill something, anything! I wanted the real murderer to pay! As I thought about declaring war against Fayithjen, that familiar light loomed up from wherever it hid and shone through my soul, reminding me of the White Warrior's existence. I pushed the thought away.

"Was Ceco"—I struggled with the words—"was she..." I couldn't bring myself to say "murdered."

Norka shook his head. "I don't know. After my wife was found, I never sssaw my daughter again. I was thrown in the dungeonsss to await my trial. I have reassson to believe that she essscaped her mother's killer though." He slipped a finger in the top of his black robes. "Cccceco inherited the curse of magic from me. When I awoke one night in the dungeons, I found thisss around my neck."

He pulled out a necklace from his robes. It wasn't made of a precious jewel, but it was no doubt priceless. It was a child's craft of beads woven through a leather thong to make a red heart. I wanted to scream in agony for this poor being. His baby girl must have made it for him!

"She gave thisss to me two weeksss before her mother was killed." He smiled wistfully in remembrance. "It took her a month to make. She tried sssso hard to keep it ssssecret, but I caught a glance of her working on it from time to time. She concentrated ssso hard and had to redo it many times until she believed it wasss perfect. I never took it off once she'd surprised me with it." His smiled faded as he tucked the necklace away. "When the guardsss came to take me in, they stripped me of everything—my jewelsss, my clothesss, and my Cccceco's gift. I guess sssomehow she used the curssse of magic to return to me the most precious thing I had left in the world, though I wasss behind barss, and heavily guarded." He shook his head. "I never taught her how to use the magic ssshe had. Ssshe was too young. But somehow ssshe figured out how to do this."

I closed my eyes, not wanting to know the answer to my next question either. "How old was Ceco?"

His yellow eyes glanced up at me. "Three."

I brought my fist to my mouth and squeezed my eyes shut as I fought against the bile that rose in my throat. This creature had lost everything. His entire world was gone. No wonder he had that bottomless pit of sadness in his eyes. All he wanted to do was die. Who could blame him?

"Norka, I am so sorry," I whispered, my emotions choking me from speaking any louder.

When I opened my eyes, he was gazing down at my hand resting on top of his. I hadn't even realized I'd put it there. He gently took my hand and caressed it as if savoring the feel of me for the last time.

"Thank you," he said. "Thank you for lissstening to me. You may kill me now."

Both Rabryn and I snapped to attention. "What?" we cried in unison.

"You may kill me now," he repeated in a low voice.

I stared at him. "I'm not going to kill you!"

His wide eyes snapped up to meet mine. "What? Why not?" The words sounded more like a plea for me to reconsider than an actual question.

Because you don't deserve it! Because you've suffered enough! Because you deserve a chance at happiness like everyone else! Because I couldn't kill you even if I wanted to now! I wanted to scream all of these at him but didn't. Death was what he wanted. Making excuses for him to live and encouraging him to live would only provoke an argument. It might even depress him more, if that were possible. I had to approach this differently.

I stood, firmly placed my hands on my hips, and looked down at him. "Because you have yet to make yourself useful to me. Laroevith sent you to help me, so help me you shall. You will not see the end of my blade, or the end of your life and misery, until you earn it from me. Or until it's granted to you on your quest as your Mistress predicted. Do you have a problem with that?"

Norka looked down pitifully and shook his head.

My heart sank, but I held my ground. "Rabryn." He looked up at me from the ground. "I want you to take Norka into the woods and teach him to use a bow as I've taught you. Kill him some food so he can live long enough to make himself useful to me."

Rabryn's eyes flicked nervously to Norka before he nodded.

I pulled my quiver and bow off my back and gave them to Norka. "You can use mine."

He hesitated before gingerly accepting them. He was awkward and careful with the weapon, as if he feared he might break it—or more so, that it might suddenly come to life and break *him*.

I faced Rabryn as he got to his feet and took his chin firmly in my grasp. "Don't you dare go far into these woods," I warned. "I had better be able to *smell* you nearby. Do you understand?"

An odd expression passed over his face, and for an instant, he looked like he was going to argue with me. But the expression vanished as quickly as it had appeared, and he only nodded.

I watched them both disappear into the dark woods, hoping my brother would be okay and still wrestling with whether it was wrong to trust Norka. Maybe his story was all a lie.

No. I was good at reading eyes, and he was being truthful.

I gazed into blackness of the woods and sighed, dreading what I was about to face. I crossed my arms over my chest, grimacing at the thought of trying to explain myself to Ortheldo. I suddenly wished I'd kept my bow.

SIXTEEN

ORTHELDO

She was coming. I could feel her presence even before I heard her footsteps crunching dead leaves and snapping sticks. She paused behind me, no doubt assessing what kind of mood I was in.

I kept my gaze on the bubbling water in front of me, refusing to look at her. I had simmered down a bit, but I was still torn between strangling her for not telling me that the Blue Dragon was Norka's Mistress and grabbing her face and kissing her because she was safe.

Without a word of greeting, she stepped over the rock I was sitting on and sat down beside me. "It's nice here," she said. "I'm glad you went to the water. That always cools your moods."

I shook my head in disbelief and smiled. She still knew me so well after all these years. Water usually calmed my temper. It was a characteristic dating back to when I was growing up with Azrel. Our cave had been near water, so whenever training got rough, I'd go for a walk down to the stream or Azrel's father would *send* me for a walk to cool off.

I wrestled with the fact that I wasn't sure I knew *her* so well anymore. Having gotten to know her again over the past few days, I realized that though she was still the same in many ways, she was fundamentally different in others.

The Azrel I knew was strong, vibrant, controlled, careful, and fearless. She loved life and had a fight in her that no one could match. This other Azrel, this "new" Azrel, was temperamental, fearful, careless, and had little control over her emotions. Blowing up at both Beldorn and Rabryn the way she had was evidence of that.

I tried to think of explanations and reasons for this new Azrel, but came up with nothing. From talking to her brother, I'd learned that she'd been relentlessly hated, feared, and shunned by the people of The Pitt. Perhaps this new Azrel was a result of that.

There was definitely something going on—something deep that I didn't understand yet. I wished I could know what it was so I could help her. I had to find out how this new Azrel had come to be.

"The Feariters were here," she said.

I nodded. "I heard them." I kept it to myself that it was the thought of her that had saved me.

"They must have sensed our fear when we realized what Norka was."

I nodded in agreement. There were so many things I wanted to say to her, but I decided to start with the most obvious. "Why didn't you tell me the Blue Dragon was Norka's Mistress?"

There was a pause as she picked some grass from the ground and fiddled with it in her fingers. "I forgot."

"How could you forget something like that? I'm surprised you don't remember the exact date, day, and time your father taught us about Tribletwel."

She sighed. "I don't know."

I studied her profile in the moonlight, drinking in her beauty. A Salynn's fairness couldn't hold a candle to Azrel. I considered her eyes, which appeared dreamlike, even in profile. That incredible shade of blue became even more striking in the silver light. I had to remind myself to breathe.

She finally looked at me, and we stared at each other for a long time. My feelings for her billowed on the edge of explosion as I took in every curve of her face. *See it*, I silently begged her as my eyes trailed down to her gorgeous lips. *See it. Please see it.* I adored the way her strong, elegant cheeks curved down onto her jaw. *Do you see it?* I wanted to hold her hands forever. *I love you. Please see it.* I wanted her body next to me for the rest of my life. *Read my eyes.* I wanted to inhale her skin far more than air. *I love you, Azrel.* I wanted to run my fingers through her long hair until I couldn't move anymore.

It didn't take long for her to turn bright red and look away from me, like she had the other times I'd put what I felt for her in my eyes. I worried that if I didn't say it aloud soon, I might never get the chance. But now didn't feel like the right time.

I sighed softly and looked over the water. Then she rested her head on my shoulder. "Are you okay?"

I was surprised and confused at the same time. "What do you mean?"

"I saw Norka throw you."

"Oh," I said in a half laugh and then kissed the top of her head. "Please. I've suffered worse knocks than a shove from a harmless Wizard."

She lifted her head and looked up at me with her eyes shining bright and a soft smile. "Harmless? You heard his story?"

I nodded. "I stayed close in case you needed me, so I managed to overhear everything. I believe him." I pressed my lips together and sighed. "I'm glad you stopped me from killing him this time, but if he hurts you again, even *you* won't be able to talk me out of spilling his guts. Do we understand each other?"

She gave me a gentle smile and nodded.

I nodded, too. "Good."

The snap of a bowstring, and a cry of death from a nearby animal, broke the silence of the night. Both Azrel and I turned in the direction of the sound.

"What was that?" I asked.

"Rabryn took Norka hunting for food."

My brows went up. "You actually let him go alone?" I was thrilled that she was taking my advice and not babysitting him. The fact that she'd let him go alone in the woods with Norka was a big step.

With a smile of satisfaction, she looked at me again. "I threatened Rabryn's life if he went beyond my smelling distance."

My shoulders sagged. She hadn't *quite* taken my advice.

Rabryn neither needed to be protected nor wanted to be. I could tell every time Azrel attempted to do so. True, he was too brave for his own good. He insisted on taking a watch every night, even though he was unfamiliar with the dangers out here. For Light's sake, he'd even managed to draw a weapon after Feariters had targeted him! That alone spoke volumes about his potential and his courage. And he was a Salynn on top of that. He needed to get a good feel for his surroundings and his own instincts. He needed to learn to trust himself to make decisions, the right decisions, in the world. Azrel was stalling his development by being overprotective and not allowing him to take the risks he needed to take to harden his disposition.

I didn't want to provoke another argument about this with her, though, so I changed the subject to something else that would get my head bitten off. "Why don't you tell your brother what the

White Warrior is?"

The sudden tension in the air almost took my breath away. Though she hadn't even moved, it felt suddenly as if she were ready to pounce on me any second.

She didn't look away from the water. "Because he doesn't need to know," she said tensely.

It was clear she wanted me to drop the topic, but, like her, I had a stubborn streak. "Oh, really? Pray tell, why is that?"

She spun on me. "He just doesn't need to know!" she screamed.

Ladies of The Light, I hadn't expected that! I jumped at her reaction, the feral look on her face making me want to swallow my tongue for speaking. But determination to get to the bottom of this overrode my fear.

I slowly shook my head, looking at her with my eyes wide. "Don't you ever yell at me like that again," I said in a slow, low voice. "I asked you a question, and I want an answer."

She seemed to shrink back under my challenge, but only for an instant. Then her eyes narrowed and she slowly stood up and looked down at me with her hands balled into tight fists at her sides. "Don't you dare presume to think you can give me orders," she said in a throaty voice.

The Gods knew Azrel and I had had our share of heated arguments growing up, but this was nothing like those. This was the new Azrel I was dealing with. I didn't know how to handle this one, except to hold my ground.

Refusing to look like a scolded puppy, I slowly stood. Our six-inch difference in stature allowed me to look down at her. I refused to let this new Azrel intimidate me into submission and compliance. She should know me better than that.

"Azrel, if you don't tell him, I will."

Her moves were like lightning. Screaming wildly, she grabbed the front of my shirt in her fists. With impossible strength, she picked me up off my feet and slammed me hard into the tree trunk behind me. Pain exploded in the back of my head, and my vision flashed black for an instant.

"If you ever threaten me again, I'll make you rue the day you were born," she said in a low growl.

I couldn't even focus on my surroundings. My vision faded in and out. It was like she was killing me by sheer force of her will.

Suddenly she let go, and I helplessly crumbled to the ground like a puppet with cut strings. Blood dripped down the back of my neck, soaking into my shirt. Only when I found myself gasping for air did I realize she'd somehow cut off my breathing, too.

Dizzy and in pain, I wearily looked up at her. Her eyes were wide and she pressed her hands against her mouth as she looked down at me, seeming to just realize what she'd done. She spun around, ran to the stream, and threw up. I staggered to my feet and bent over her, holding back her hair as the contents of her stomach emptied into the rushing water.

This new Azrel was terrifying. It didn't seem right to fear the woman that I'd grown up with—the woman I loved. No. The Azrel who'd just attacked me wasn't the Azrel I knew. That Azrel was unpredictable and clearly dangerous. I had to find out what was happening. Something was gravely wrong.

As I listened to the water moving and Azrel heaving, a thought occurred to me out of nowhere: Did she hate her own magic? My entire head was throbbing, but I tried to think through the haze. Azrel only lost her temper when asked about the White Warrior, which had to do with her magic. Could she hate it so much that she would deny it as a part of herself, burying it inside so she didn't have to acknowledge it?

I sighed, wondering if that theory was even plausible. But nothing else made sense. The blow to my head might have cracked something loose. It hurt enough to be true. Whatever was wrong, I had to find a way to help her.

"I will tell you how you can help."

My heart jumped into my throat at the unexpected sound. A voice that was not really like a voice had spoken. I glanced around the woods. First to my left—nothing. Then to my right, where a white shapeless form materialized beside me. It was barely there, much thinner than fog. It was like a glowing wisp of mist, or steam from a boiling pot, only quite still.

"If she does not accept her gift, and who she is, the world will perish into the depths of darkness."

What...who are you? I wanted to ask, but my disorientation didn't let the words pass my lips.

"That's not important now," the voice said, apparently

reading my thoughts. *"What is important is that Evil is about and in search of the healing gem. Gibirs and Gorkors have been unleashed, and you have already encountered Legan'dirs. These creatures have been seen across Casdanarus, and peaceful lands are beginning to whisper of war and a Second Shadow."*

My teeth clenched. There would *not* be a Second Shadow! Not as long the White Warrior lived—and she was right in front of me.

"Look at her," the voice said gently, almost sadly. I gazed down at Azrel. She was doubled over the stream with her hands crossed tightly over her stomach. *"She is a pitiful shadow of what she should be, and you know it."*

The pain in my head intensified. It felt like someone was pounding a burning wooden stake into the back of my skull with a mallet.

"A Second Shadow will occur if Azrel fails." I looked back at the mist. *"You must remind Azrel who she is. She has a job to do but has forgotten much of what her father taught her—the Blue Dragon, for instance. If she is not reminded, even in the smallest ways, everything will end. You must remind her how to be the person her father trained her to be. If not yet the White Warrior, then a warrior at the very least. She will walk her own path eventually, but you must begin by showing it to her."*

How? I asked. I couldn't believe I was having a mental conversation with a patch of glowing white mist.

"Use the evil that is lurking about. Remind her of what she is. She has forgotten." With that, the mist disappeared.

I stared in disbelief at where it had been and tried to decide whether I had hallucinated it.

The sound of Azrel's sobs brought my attention back to her. She had sunk to her knees, still clutching her stomach. I got on my knees beside her, glad to have the weight off my feet, and tried to gather her in my arms.

She weakly resisted my embrace. "Don't touch me," she sobbed pathetically. "I don't deserve to be comforted by you."

"Why?" I asked softly. "Why do you think that?" I desperately wanted to hold her, to ease her pain, to find out what was wrong.

"Because I'm evil!" she wailed, throwing her head back in grief, and numbly pushed me away.

Her words penetrated my soul, and I stared at her, stunned.

Her? Evil? I gently shook my head. I'd never seen her like this, so helpless, and desperately upset. It terrified me that someone as strong as Azrel could become so horribly vulnerable. I knew the warrior she was born to be, the warrior she was trained to be, and the warrior she had been before we'd lost each other. I needed that warrior to come back. *The world* needed that warrior to come back if whispers of a Second Shadow were stirring.

I crushed her to my chest. "You listen to me, Azrel. You are not evil. Do you hear me? You're not!" I tried to sound convincing, but the tremble in my voice at witnessing her distress betrayed me. "Is that why you won't accept who you are or tell Rabryn about it? Because you think you're evil?"

"I almost killed you!" she cried, still trying to resist my embrace. "I *am* evil!"

My heart stopped. I was right! She hated her magic. She believed her power to be evil! But how? How could she think that the very essence of the Light Gods, her white fire, was evil? Black fire was the evil power of the Shadow Gods. She knew that!

When the realization dawned on me, I squeezed my eyes closed and held her tighter. It was because her father had died as soon as she'd received the gift of her white fire. Everything good in her life had ended the moment she'd received that sword. Things seemed to have just gotten worse since then, though I doubted I had the full picture of what she'd been through in The Pitt.

I suddenly realized the importance of what the mist had said to me. Azrel needed her white fire magic, but she could barely stand to mention it, let alone use it well enough to defeat any Shadow creatures or beings. I needed to remind her who she really was.

Suddenly, I heard Norka and Rabryn coming through the woods toward us. Azrel yanked herself away from me and leaned over the stream to splash some water on her face, removing any evidence of her tears. She got to her feet and turned to face them as they came through the trees behind us. Glancing over my shoulder, I saw Norka with a bloody sack over his shoulder, probably his dinner, while Rabryn looked on in concern.

"Hey," Azrel said brightly, "how did your hunting lesson go?"

"Great," Rabryn replied half-heartedly, looking guilty, as if he knew he'd interrupted something. "Norka needs more lessons, but he's not a bad shot."

"Did you kill your supper yourself?" Azrel asked.

"No," Norka replied, staring at me. "Massster Rabryn is a good ssshot though. I will learn quickly."

I tried to stand, but the pain in my head was too much.

"Shit!" Rabryn suddenly cried. "Ortheldo, you're bleeding!"

I knew. I could feel it soaking into the back of my shirt.

"Watch your mouth," Azrel said as she appeared by my side with her eyes wide. "Sit down. I'll get some plants to help you."

With her help, I got off my knees and plopped my rear end down on the ground as the world became a pool of black that came and went. An apology was in order, though, and I forced myself to focus on Norka as he came to stand beside me.

"I'm sorry you've had to endure so much suffering, so much loss. I hope you can forgive me for judging you too quickly and harshly."

He nodded somberly. "I forgive you." He looked at Azrel. "Excussse me, Azrel. I will heal him."

I wanted to look up at him again, but now I was feeling nauseated as the fading world started to spin.

"But your Mistress will send you pain," Azrel said, her voice filled with concern.

I barely heard her as I began to give into the peaceful, painless black that wanted to take me.

"His injury was my doing. It's only right that I undo it," Norka said.

It wasn't his doing, it was Azrel's. I wanted to tell him so, but even if my voice had worked, I would have felt like I was betraying Azrel somehow.

"It's not your fault, Norka. It's—" Before Azrel could say "mine," Norka cut her off.

"There is no exsssscuse for what I did. He hasss shown me kindnesss, so I will do the ssame for him. The pain doesn't lasst long, and he might die before you can gather and prepare your plantsss."

My vision flushed with black. Whatever conversation was going on, I wasn't a part of it. I fell backward. I felt the vibration of sound. Someone was yelling, but I heard nothing.

Suddenly a hot stinging sensation filled my skull as a hand

took hold of the back of my head. I winced but then quickly relaxed as healing magic flowed through me. Slowly I came out of the darkness, and then the pain was gone.

I sat up, fully alert, to Norka's screams of pain. I cringed when my gaze found him kneeling on the ground, clutching his head in his hands as if he were willing it not to explode. He was enduring this for me. After what I'd done to him, he'd healed me. I wished his pain would end quickly.

Azrel flashed into my view and gathered the trembling snake in her arms, whispering soft words of comfort. "It's okay. It will pass. Thank you, Norka. Thank you. You'll be okay."

His screams quickly ceased and he looked around, surprised. "It'sss… It's gone!" he said in disbelief. He sat back from Azrel and stared at her with big eyes. "The pain should last longer than that, but as ssssoon as you touched me, it went away. How did you do that?"

"I—I have no idea," Azrel stammered.

It was quiet for a minute, since no one knew how to explain that, so I took the opportunity to get on my knees in front of Norka and rested my hand on his shoulder. "Thank you, my friend."

He smiled at me and placed his hand over mine. "You're welcome, friend."

Rabryn sighed heavily. "All right, it's late. Time to go to sleep. I'll take first watch."

We all got to our feet and made our way back to camp. Azrel and I fell behind Norka and Rabryn. "I have no right to ask for your forgiveness," she said, crossing her arms across her chest and staring shamefully at the ground. "I just get you back, and then almost lose you again to my own hand, of all things." She looked up at me. "I'm so sorry," she whispered. "I can't think of any words to tell you how sorry I am. I didn't mean for that to happen. I tried to stop it."

I stopped walking and stared at her in astonishment. Tried to stop it? What did she mean by that? She stopped walking as well and looked up at me in a way that made me forget my own name.

"If you can't forgive me, I don't blame you."

I had to swallow before speaking. "Tell me what made you do that. Then I'll decide whether I can forgive you."

She nodded. "That's fair." She shrugged. "But I don't have an answer for you. When you were questioning me, I felt..." She paused and shook her head. "It's hard to explain, but I felt myself shrink inside, like I was depleting somehow. And then"—she continued shaking her head like she couldn't find the words—"I lost control. A part of me was screaming to let you go, to not hurt you, and...I don't know, it felt like something else was controlling my actions, my words, like I was a bystander in my own body." She crossed her arms tightly over her chest, "It was weird."

So here was a new mystery to solve.

"What made you stop when you did?" I asked.

She shook her head again. "I don't know. I'm so sorry, Ortheldo."

I nodded and put my arm around her shoulders as we started toward camp again. "It's okay. I forgive you. You were clearly not yourself and didn't know what you were doing. I know you wouldn't do that to me on purpose."

Then how did you do it? I wondered silently.

"Thank you, my friend," she said and rested her head on my shoulder again as we continued through the trees.

SEVENTEEN

AZREL

The sun was out this morning, but it wasn't very warm. All of us wore our cloaks except Norka, who always wore only his plain black robes. I gazed at Ortheldo riding ahead of me, looking dashing in a dark blue tunic, black leggings, and black cloak. Had it not been for Norka, Ortheldo might not have seen this day.

I couldn't take my mind off what had happened last night. How could I have done that to him? I'd almost killed him! *Killed him!* I couldn't even *conceive* of it! Yet it had almost happened. The very thought provoked tears.

Something was terribly wrong with me. I'd always known that. Now I had the proof. Last night, somehow, I had cut off his breathing just after slamming him against the tree and cracking his skull open. I had felt myself thinking to cut off his air, but it wasn't my thought. It had seemed to come from somewhere else, and somehow I had acted upon it. How could I have even *thought* of something like that in the first place?

I shook my head and tried to think about something more pleasant. My gaze turned to my brother. Norka rode beside Rabryn for a nice change, rather than trailing behind us in the rear. Right now, they were laughing and talking together about going hunting again for lunch. They had already gone out together this morning to catch Norka's breakfast. It was nice to see Norka acclimating and my brother making a new friend.

My thoughts turned dark again when I looked at Ortheldo riding in front of me. He had forgiven me for last night, but I worried that a part of him was still angry with me. I couldn't blame him, though. I was angry at myself.

Suddenly that shadow of dread grew in my mind—that sort of weird pressure in my brain that told me danger was near or something was about to go terribly wrong.

"Norka!" Rabryn cried out.

I spun around to look behind me. Rabryn was alone, and Norka was tearing up dust as he rode away in the direction from which we'd come. I hated this shadow but was also grateful for it, as it served as an advance warning system that allowed me to prepare for something awful.

"What happened?" I barked, my guard going up.

Rabryn shook his head. "I don't know. We were having a fine conversation when he suddenly looked out ahead of him, stared for a moment, and said he had to go. Then he just…" Rabryn's eyes grew wide, seeming to feel the shadow, as I had, now that he didn't have the distraction of Norka's conversation. "What's wrong?"

I searched the clearing through which we were riding, but there was nothing for miles around us except the edge of a small thicket of woods to our right. If anything was coming at us, it would be from that direction. I moved Forfirith around Ortheldo, who had stopped riding, and Rabryn pulled Eleclya up next to me. We both looked over at Ortheldo, who was sitting stone still, staring out ahead of him like he was seeing something both dreadful and amazing.

"What is it?" I asked.

Ortheldo finally looked at me. "We need to turn south here. Come on!" He checked Urylia to the right and sped off toward the small woods. Rabryn and I exchanged glances, knowing that was probably the best area to *avoid*, before riding after him.

"I have a bad feeling about this!" Rabryn shouted for us both, dodging tree branches as we entered the woods.

"So do I!" Ortheldo called back. "That's why I felt we should turn south."

"Of course. What was I thinking?" Rabryn muttered. "A foreboding feeling comes from some direction, so the best thing to do is turn toward it. How foolish of me."

I grinned at him. He was so bloody cute sometimes. He could easily be considered a man at seventeen years old, but he was still my goofy, wisecracking baby brother.

Ortheldo came to a stop. He looked around the woods for a moment, standing in his stirrups as he gazed around like he was expecting someone to approach. He sat again and beckoned us to dismount quietly. We obeyed, crouching down on the ground beside the horses. Ortheldo crept spider-like to a group of bushes near the edge of the trees that looked out over the south side of the clearing we'd just left. After exchanging another look, Rabryn and I followed and cautiously peered over the top of the bushes.

I flinched when I saw a large band of Gibirs walking carelessly over the plains. "What the hell?" I whispered.

I couldn't believe it! What were Gibirs doing *here* in the west? As soon as the question went through my mind, I felt stupid. I knew exactly what had brought them out here—the necklace. But that didn't make seeing them any easier. Western Casdanarus was the cleanest, most pure side of the land, utterly free from Shadow's influence. Seeing these Shadow creatures walking in open air, *here*, made my stomach flip over.

Gibirs were about as tall as an average man and had considerable bulk. They bore revolting black boils and blemishes all over their sickly dark green skin. The sight could make one vomit. They had black bellies, black spikes jutted out from their hunched spines, and their arms hung low in gorilla fashion. Unlike Gorkors, Gibirs could speak, but they were not very intelligent creatures.

"What are we doing here?" I whispered to Ortheldo. "They aren't in our path, so we can avoid them easily."

"Prepare for battle," he said without looking away from the pack on the plains.

"What? Why?" Ortheldo looked over at me with a cool gaze of playfulness and annoyance. I curled my lip. "Don't look at me like that." He didn't stop. "What?" I whispered. "Can't you see that we are largely outnumbered?"

"I can see that you've lost your nerve, Azrel."

"Excuse me," I said, feeling as if I'd been slapped in the face. I didn't want to admit it, but he was right. I didn't know about him, but I'd never been in a battle like the one he was suggesting.

"You know that we're skilled enough to take these Gibirs. You're just afraid."

My eyes narrowed. He knew I hated the word "coward," so he was careful not to use it. But implying it was almost as bad. I would always remember my father's last few words: "Don't ever give anyone a reason to call you a coward."

I sighed through my nose and glared harder at him. "Strap on your weapons then." Ortheldo beamed a smile and walked to Urylia to prepare.

My glare followed him, but from the corner of my eye I saw Rabryn hold a finger up to object. When I stood and walked away, he dropped his arm dumbly to the ground. "And we're starting this unnecessary battle because *why?*" he asked.

I looked down at him as I approached Forfirith. "You stay here. I don't want you in this."

Rabryn nodded. "Sounds good to me. Just be careful."

Ortheldo smirked at me as we both shed our cloaks and draped them over our saddles and started unpacking our weapons. He wasn't entirely serious about implying I was afraid. He just knew that saying so would make me have to prove him wrong. I really didn't know if I was up for this, though. I couldn't keep my knees from shaking. Was I really about to do this? My first real battle.

Ortheldo hummed happily, showing not an iota of doubt or worry. It was irritating how much he was enjoying this. I clenched my teeth and wondered why he felt the need to start a battle with the Gibirs anyway. I guessed that perhaps he wanted to see what remained of my fighting abilities. I didn't expect very much from myself, and hoped he didn't either.

With my quiver strapped to my back, my bow in hand, my Salynn blade at my thigh, and my sword at my belt, I walked through the trees along the edge of the clearing without glancing at Ortheldo. After passing a few trees that didn't fit my needs, I stopped under one that was perfect. I pulled my hair up into a messy knot and then leapt up and grabbed a low branch. Pulling myself up, I scaled the tree until I found a place that gave me a good view of my targets, kept me well hidden, and gave me some strategic flexibility.

I looked back down to where I'd left the boys, and I saw Ortheldo searching the treetops for me. He wouldn't be able to see me, though. I'd made sure of it. He nodded, his expression now impressed, and stepped out of the woods toward the Gibirs.

They drew their weapons immediately, but Ortheldo remained unaffected. He stood right in their path and crossed his arms. "Shouldn't you all be cowering in caves? Your small, scattered bands are no longer threatening."

"Kill the Human! Slice him! Stab him! Death to the Man!" the Gibirs yelled.

My muscles tensed, and I loaded two arrows in my bow. My brain was a whirlwind of emotions as I drew the string to my cheek. I had never been in a battle with anything like Gibirs.

Be brave.

My father's words echoed in my ears, and I let my nerves settle. I had to be brave. They were only Gibirs. Unfortunately, the shadow in my mind kept me from being completely calm. Something bad was going to happen, but there was no turning back now.

"Actually," Ortheldo said, "we'll save you the trouble of finding shelter and just kill you all."

Thwip! I released the two arrows and watched them fly down through the trees and hit the two Gibirs I was aiming for. I couldn't believe it! I could still hit an intended target, even from this distance.

The Gibirs' attention quickly turned from Ortheldo to the woods. They wasted many of their precious arrows shooting blindly at the trees trying to kill me, but I was already on a lower branch of a neighboring tree.

Thwip! Two more arrows plunged into two Gibirs' throats.

I began to feel comfortable with my bow and even smiled a little, happy to know I hadn't lost all my skill after all.

Again, the monsters shot blindly at tree branches, but I had already jumped to the ground.

Thwip! Two more Gibirs dead.

This feeling was incredible! The thrill of battle had never flowed through my veins before, and feeling it now was intoxicating, especially being as highly trained as I was. I loaded two more arrows and launched them with the expertise my mind and body now remembered I had. I fit two more arrows onto the string and drew it back as I walked out onto the field to join Ortheldo.

As I walked, the bow seemed to mold in my hand, and it felt unimaginably comfortable in my grasp. I was in total control. I had the power here. I wasn't helpless like I felt in the rest of my life.

"Ah." Ortheldo sighed, rubbing his palms together briskly as I approached. "This should make things a bit more fun, don't you think?"

"Oh, I plan on enjoying myself thoroughly," I replied, not shifting my eyes from the Gibirs.

And I would, too. Too long had I been a victim of circumstances out of my control. Too long had I felt hopeless and low. Not here. This was my territory. I didn't just mean the battlefield either. I meant western Casdanarus. These foul things did not belong in a place so lovely, peaceful, and pure.

"So will I," Ortheldo said.

A moment later he drew two blades from his back with a flourish and tore through the nearest Gibirs with his skilled hands. I released my two arrows, killing two more, then dropped my bow and pummeled into the battle bare-handed.

Something took over then. Something else. Something strong and fearless. I caught a glimpse of what I used to be and what I was meant to be. Each close call I managed to ward off with my unique empty-handed fighting style brought forth vivid and lovely memories of my father teaching me to do such things. I couldn't believe I still remembered the techniques!

After I'd killed a dozen or so, though, my muscles started aching. I hadn't used them in such a way for a long time. Instead of recoiling from the burn, though, I welcomed it. It felt so good to use my muscles like this again.

When the next Gibir approached, I spun around, bringing my leg up and smashing the heel of my boot into its soft temple. He fell dead. Spinning again, I brought my elbow back and smashed in the sharp front teeth of another. After that, my right arm swept up under its chin, curling around its neck. I pulled it back, snapping the bone in half. I did the same with four other Gibirs that dared come close enough. Spin, punch, block, kick, snap. The Gibirs had no chance. None!

My muscles relentlessly screamed in agony until I couldn't ignore it any longer. I'd been idle too long. I had to rebuild the strength I once had.

I pulled out my Salynn blade and began hacking through the Gibirs with it. The lovely metal of my knife was soon spoiled with black blood. Nonetheless, the number of living Gibirs diminished.

Suddenly I was attacked from behind. Before realizing it, I was down on all fours with the weight of a body on my back. I tried to reach for my sword, but one punch to the side of my face made the world an explosion of colors. Two more hits to my rib cage knocked the air from my lungs. The hits came harder as I tried to gather my senses.

With a quick thought, I pushed all of my weight up onto my

palms and toes and spun around, landing hard on my back with the Gibir underneath me. It remained undaunted and slammed its fist into the side of my face again. I slammed my elbow back into its face, loosening its grip on me, and then did a backward somersault so I could look down at its face. I planted a hard left hook into its slimy jaw, but then a jab square up into my mouth sent me flying onto my back in the grass. The Gibir was instantly on top of me with a blade drawn and aimed at my throat.

Oh man! I was way rustier than I'd thought. My muscles screamed in pain. Slowly, though my arms trembled with the effort to stop it, the knife inched toward my neck.

Suddenly an arrow exploded from the Gibir's chest, splashing my forehead with its blood. It fell to the side, and I sat up quickly, expecting to see Ortheldo with a bow aimed in my direction. But it was *Rabryn!*

I sucked in a deep breath. What was he doing? I wanted to scream at him for being so stupid!

I realized then that there were still four Gibirs not being managed. Before I could gather my wits and get into the battle again, a creature beyond my reach loaded its bow and aimed directly at my brother.

Scrambling to my feet, I ran toward Rabryn as fast as I could move. I just had to pull him down! I just had to get him on the ground and he'd be safe! My mind was racing, but time seemed to stop altogether.

I couldn't move fast enough!

My brother might die!

No! He couldn't!

I just had to reach him!

Run, you fool! Run faster!

I heard the twang of the bowstring and then the sickening *thunk* sound of the arrow going deep into Rabryn's left side. He screamed in agony, and his body went flying backward to the ground.

Grief, as fast as lightning, raced through my mind. I let it go with a scream that thundered through the clearing and echoed off the mountains that were still a two-day ride away.

The image of my little brother being impaled went through my mind over and over again, torturing me until I fell to my knees by his side. Panic surged through me, numbing me from any reasoning. I couldn't breathe. I couldn't think. My vision blackened with the horrid reality that my brother could be dead. Dead!

"Never...been...shot before."

I sucked in air as my world came back to me. It was bright and colorful, and Rabryn was alive! His face was twisted in anguish, his hand resting around the arrow wound, but he hadn't been killed on impact. He was still with me. I could save him!

As my mind started to work again, I knew Ortheldo was trying to manage the remaining Gibirs and needed me.

I leaned over my brother and firmly cupped his face in my hands. "Don't you dare go anywhere, even into death without me."

Suddenly his eyes shifted passed me and went wide. "Behind you!"

I turned just in time to see the glare of a blade swinging for my neck. My powerful reflexes allowed me to duck quickly enough to avoid it. My instincts kicked in, and I did a backward somersault to avoid a downward blow from a second Gibir. By the time I was on my feet, Ortheldo was dragging one of them away.

I looked over at my brother. Seeing him on the ground, bleeding, filled me with utter rage. I felt it boil into every pore, corrupting every inch of my body and soul. Every fiber that made me a living, breathing human being was heated with the sensation. Slowly I looked back at the Gibir. It seemed daunted by whatever it was seeing in my eyes.

War was my territory. Battle was my playground. And by the Gods of Light, this Gibir would not see the blue sky of another day.

I clenched my teeth, baring them like a wolf, and pulled my sword free. The creature blocked my initial blow, but my Salynn blade came down so fast that I barely saw my own arm move as I sliced through its forearm, cutting off half the limb. Black blood sprayed my clothes and my face, and the Gibir screamed in anguish before dropping to its knees. I glared down at it and crossed my sword and Salynn blade at its neck. With a scream, I pulled them apart, popping off the Gibir's head like a dandelion blossom.

I quickly scanned the field to make sure nothing was moving and then hurried to my brother's side again. He looked bad. He'd already gone pale and was struggling to breathe.

"Hold on, baby. Hold on."

Ortheldo kneeled across from me on Rabryn's other side, and I lost it. I slammed my fist so hard into Ortheldo's jaw that blood splashed onto the grass.

"This is your fault!" I screamed at him. "You had to fight the Gibirs, didn't you? You couldn't just walk away, could you? Damn you!" I shook with the effort of screaming the last two words.

I couldn't help realizing that this was the second time in two days I'd hurt Ortheldo badly. But no! This was different. Last night was my fault. This was his!

"Azrel...Azrel," my brother wheezed from the ground. "Please don't...be angry with him. I joined the fight on my own. It's... my fault."

I was shaking with rage and fear. That was so like him, taking the responsibility for his own actions.

I glared at Ortheldo as he slowly and shamefully dragged his thumb across the split I'd just put in his lip. "Help me save my brother's life and I'll find it easier to forgive you." He looked up at me. "Water."

He nodded and hurried toward the trees where we'd left the horses. He'd know where to find some.

I looked down at my brother again. "I have to go find a plant that will help you." His brows dropped in what seemed like confusion. I took off my cloak, covered him, and put my Salynn blade in his hand. "I'll be right back. I'm just going over to the trees." I kissed his forehead before running toward the small woods. My heart was racing. Every moment meant my brother's life.

As soon as I entered the trees, I started searching for some Roogle Root. It wasn't easy to see, especially with my eyes filling with tears. Knowing that crying would only make my search more difficult, I forced them back. I spotted a mixed patch of plants and got onto my knees to sift through them. I thought I'd found the right leaves for a moment, but when I uprooted the plant, a sour, dead smell filled my nose.

"Oh, for Heaven's sake!" I cried and threw the bundle against a rock. It was Roogle's twin, Rouge Root.

The Rouge plant gave off a very unpleasant smell when uprooted. Roogle, however, gave off a soothing, sweet smell. It was the best way to tell the difference between the two when searching in low light. The other difference was that Roogle had dark blue veins running through the leaves, while Rouge's veins were black.

A few agonizing moments later, I found more mixed leaves, and at last I pulled up some Roogle Root. I ran back into the clearing toward my brother. Ortheldo was already there, kneeling by Rabryn's side. My brother's eyes were closed.

No! No! He couldn't be dead! "Rabryn! Rabryn!" I screamed and ran even faster.

"He's okay. He's okay, Azrel." Ortheldo assured me as I fell to my knees at his side. "He's just weak."

Rabryn opened his eyes into slits and looked up at me. "Azrel."

I smiled briefly and then set right to work ripping the leaves off the Roogle Root. I glanced at the small cloth and three bowls on the ground that Ortheldo had already pulled from our packs, and started filling one bowl with the leaves.

"Where's the water?" I asked, not taking my eyes off my work.

"Right here," he said and set a glass jar down next to my knees. I nodded and continued tearing the leaves off the stem.

When I finished plucking the Roogle leaves, I noticed Ortheldo squirming a little uncomfortably on the other side of Rabryn. He clearly wanted to say something but was afraid of provoking my anger again.

Finally, he spoke. "Azrel, in order for the Roogle Root to work, the water has to be warm. Forgive me, but he might not make it through the time it takes to build a fire and heat the water."

I ignored him as I poured an even amount of water into each remaining bowl. What did he take me for? We both had learned about healing plants from the same man.

I picked up one of the bowls, and began to whisper a spell I'd learned a long time ago from Beldorn. Fire ignited in my palms, and steam instantly rose from the water. Ortheldo looked at me, surprised for a moment, and then cleared his throat and pretended not to be impressed.

I put the Roogle leaves into the bowl of warm water and began mixing it with a blunt rock. Soon I had a bowl full of hot dark green paste.

I set it down, leaned over my brother, and caressed his clammy cheek, knowing that what I had to do next was going to cause him excruciating pain. "Rabryn," I squeaked. His half-closed eyes shifted up at me. "Rabryn, I have to…" I sniffed and cleared my throat. "I'm going to heal you, but I have to…" I squeezed my eyes shut and then looked at him again. "I have to pull the arrow out."

He looked anxious for a moment before squeezing his eyes shut tightly. "Just do it quickly," he whispered hoarsely.

I swallowed back my tears and took hold of the arrow's shaft. Suddenly, Ortheldo's hand was on top of mine and we looked into each other's eyes. "*We* have to pull out the arrow."

I swallowed heavily again and nodded. "One…two…three!"

We both began to pull. Rabryn's jaw dropped in a silent scream as the arrow started to come out painfully slow. It was barbed! They'd shot my brother with barbed arrows! Tears leaked from Rabryn's eyes and I could see him mouthing, "Stop. Stop. Stop!" though his voice wouldn't work. I had to get this arrow out now! I pulled harder, ripping pieces of my brother's innards out with the barbed tip.

When it finally dislodged, Rabryn's scream ripped through the sky and tore my soul to shreds. "It's okay, baby. It's okay! I know. I know," I squeaked. "The arrow is out. You're going to be fine."

I immediately began to clean the wound that was now gushing blood. Before he could bleed to death, I scooped out a heaping handful of the Roogle Root paste and put it over the hole. The blood flow stopped immediately. I spread the paste around his skin to protect it, using every bit until I was scraping it out of the bottom of the bowl.

Rabryn fell asleep almost instantly. A side effect of Roogle Root. I crawled over to where he lay his head, lifted it slightly, and rested it on my knees. Then I soaked the small cloth in the bowl of cold water and placed it on his forehead to reduce the temporary fever he would endure as another side effect of Roogle.

An awkward silence fell, and I looked at Ortheldo. He was on one knee, looking down shamefully and completely unable to meet my eyes. With a sigh, I reached for the bowl of paste and scraped out what I could. "Come here."

He looked up at me and, without question, leaned forward. I

put the tiny bit of Roogle Root that I could get out of the bowl onto the cut in his lip that I'd caused. I sighed. "I'm sorry I hit you. It wasn't your fault. He joined in on his own."

"Thank you," he said softly.

"But why couldn't you just go around them?" I half asked, half whined. "Why did you have to stop and fight?"

He searched for an answer a moment and finally said, "I don't know. I thought it would be fun."

I shook my head. "I've never been in a battle like that before. I didn't even know what I was doing."

He smiled. "Well, you were superb for your first time out."

I smiled a little at him. He stared at me, seeming to search my face for something, but before I could say anything, he started walking the battlefield, pulling arrows out of the bodies. I gently rested my brother's head on the ground and began to help.

It didn't take long to realize how stiff my muscles were. Even just bending down slightly to grasp an arrow and pull it out sent fiery hot pain through my back, neck, shoulders, and butt. I rolled my shoulders and did my best to subtly stretch them out, but it didn't help much. I would feel this battle in my bones for the next month.

The silence between Ortheldo and me was smothering. Perhaps he was still angry with me about last night. I cleared my throat to speak. "Where do you think Norka went so suddenly?" Ortheldo just shrugged in response. A tightness of guilt filled my chest. He *was* still angry with me about last night. I tried to harden myself against his resentment, but I knew I deserved it.

It was early afternoon once all the arrows had been collected. "We should go," I said, dropping the ones I had into my quiver.

"What?" Ortheldo asked, appalled. "Rabryn is in no shape to travel."

Figured. When he finally did decide to speak to me, it was to argue.

I looked at him, annoyed. "I'm sure Rabryn would want us to keep moving. Unless you think he'd rather lie here among these corpses while they start to rot in the afternoon sun. I bet they'll smell lovely by lunch time."

"He's going to be asleep all day," Ortheldo said, ignoring my sarcasm.

I faced him with my hands on my hips. "What makes you think I don't know that? We were taught everything we know by the same man, weren't we?"

He shrugged and looked down to pluck another arrow out of a Gibir. "It's been a long time."

He didn't have to say what he really meant. It was written all over his face: You forgot all about the lesson with the Blue Dragon, and look what happened with that.

I shook my head and went toward my brother. "Just put Rabryn on Forfirith with me, and you take Eleclya. Think you can handle that?" I asked over my shoulder.

I thought I saw him smile broadly as he plucked the last arrow out of a Gibir. I ignored him and went to my horse to start packing things.

When I was done, Ortheldo picked my brother up off the ground as easily as if he were lifting an infant and brought him over to me. I struggled a bit at getting my brother's limp body up onto my horse's back in front of me, and once we were both mounted I had a hard time trying to keep him balanced against me.

Ortheldo noticed. "You're sure you want to travel with him like this?"

With the back of Rabryn's head resting on my shoulder, I took up my horse's reins and glared down at Ortheldo. "Let's go."

With a smile and a shake of his head, he mounted his horse and collected Eleclya's reins. We were off again, and Norka was still nowhere to be seen.

EIGHTEEN

Three hours before sunset we rode alongside a small, gentle creek that turned with the dirt path we'd found and followed—the first sign of civilization in four days. Against the horizon, only a day's ride away, were the jagged mountain peaks of the Mongerst Mountains.

Oh, they were beautiful. I hadn't seen a mountain in eight years. Now, there was an entire range of them before my eyes. I couldn't wait to reach them.

As I absorbed the sight of the mountains, my brother lifted his head from my shoulder and gasped softly. I immediately stopped Forfirith and looked at him. He was finally awake.

"They're beautiful," he said softly.

I smiled, realizing he'd never seen a mountain before.

Ortheldo pulled up beside me. "What's wrong?"

"Rabryn's awake. Help me get him down."

Ortheldo dismounted and came to Forfirith's side. He put his hands under my brother's arms and slowly pulled him out of the saddle. Rabryn looked like a toddler being pulled off a pony ride.

I dismounted quickly and helped him. "How do you feel?"

Rabryn grinned at me. "I'll probably be better once I've eaten something."

Ortheldo and I chuckled.

"Sit him down by the creek. I'll get us something to eat," I told Ortheldo.

As Ortheldo helped my brother, I led all three horses to the water to drink and then gathered up a little snack from our packs, some fruit, dried meat, and nuts. I went back to the boys, and we all sat next to the water and ate.

I expected my brother to remain weak and pale until we got him more advanced medicine, but he appeared to be gaining strength and color with every passing moment. I was grateful but confused. With as much damage as that arrow had done, with as much blood as my brother had lost, he shouldn't be doing so well so quickly. Soon, though, he was sitting up by himself and laughing with Ortheldo about the battle. I suppose they sensed my growing concern, as both of them eventually looked at me.

"What is it, Azrel?" Rabryn asked.

I looked up from the torn, blood stained section of his shirt and into his bright blue eyes. He shook his head, silently asking me what was wrong. I looked at Ortheldo, who also shook his head.

I pressed my lips together. "Lie back and lift up your tunic, Rabryn."

Confused, he complied with my request. I crawled over to inspect the wound, and my eyes got wide. "Dear Gods," I whispered.

"What is it?" both asked, Ortheldo sounding curious, while Rabryn sounded concerned.

I looked at Ortheldo. "Come look at this."

"What?" Rabryn insisted.

Ortheldo crawled over, and his brows went up with interest. "Wow."

"What?" Rabryn asked more urgently.

"Your wound," was all I could say.

Rabryn sat up and looked at his stomach. "Yeah. It looks great."

Great? It looked phenomenal! There was nothing left of it but a large bruise! Granted, it was an exceptionally large bruise, spreading from his stomach all the way around to his back like a giant black and purple ink stain, but his skin had closed. Roogle never closed a wound so fast! Especially a wound that was nearly fatal. There wasn't even a scab left—just smooth, black and purple skin.

"What did you do? Did you use some of that mysterious white magic you showed me at home?" he asked a little mischievously.

"What? Oh. No," I replied, still distracted by the healed state of his injury. "I just put some Roogle Root on you."

"What?" Rabryn asked, dismayed. "A plant?" His tone made me look up at him. He was angry. "You used a plant instead of your magic?"

I had no idea why he was angry about that, but I didn't want to talk to him about my magic, so I got to my feet and started toward the horses.

"Gods, Azrel," he said after me. "Did you *want* me to die or something?"

I froze for a moment. Without thinking, I spun around and slapped him hard across the face. "Don't you *ever* accuse me of wishing you dead! Ever!"

Stunned, I could only stare helplessly at Rabryn as he slowly looked up at me, hurt, and surprised. I'd never struck my brother before. I couldn't even look at Ortheldo.

Just walk away, I had to tell myself.

I headed toward Forfirith again, shaking. What was wrong with me? I had nearly killed Ortheldo last night, and then I'd struck them both in the face in the same day. Why was this violent side of me suddenly rearing its ugly head? I hated it!

I rested my forehead against Forfirith's face. "He just doesn't know what I am. If he did, he'd understand why I hate my magic so much."

Forfirith made a whining noise and jerked his nose in Rabryn and Ortheldo's direction a few times.

"What?"

He did it again.

I looked at them as they slowly packed up. "You think I should tell my brother what I am?"

Forfirith made a gentle almost purring sound and rested his nose against my chest, as if trying to comfort me.

"But what if he hates me?"

Forfirith blew out a forceful breath, stomped his foot, and pushed my shoulder forcefully with his nose, as if daring me to believe that could be possible.

Well, why not tell Rabryn? I pressed my lips together thoughtfully and petted my horse's nose. So many "what ifs" were up in the air, and I didn't want them to come crashing down on my head. I couldn't deny that I had to tell him sooner or later. Why not sooner, before he found out from someone else and didn't understand?

I sighed and caressed Forfirith's cheek. "Okay, boy. Okay. I'll tell him."

Rabryn and Ortheldo were walking toward me to pack up their horses. Rabryn looked down when he tried to step around me, but I placed my hand on his chest, stopping him. "I'm sorry I slapped you."

He looked at me for a moment and then nodded. As I stared into his handsome blue eyes, I suddenly wasn't so sure about telling him. I chewed my bottom lip nervously as I ran the "what ifs" through my head again. He was watching me and could likely tell I had something on my mind that I wanted to say. He probably knew what it was, too, and that I was hesitating to do so.

His eyes suddenly softened as he related a message to me through them. *Trust me*, it said.

I sighed heavily, and I wearily dropped my head between my shoulders. Here went nothing—or maybe everything. I looked back up at him. "Rabryn, please sit down."

He eagerly sat himself on the ground. Ortheldo sat right next to him. I would have laughed if I weren't so nervous.

I sat across from them and drew up my knees, wrapping my arms around them. "Rabryn, I didn't use my magic to heal you because I hate my magic." I paused and waited for a reaction but saw none. "My father went through a lot to protect it, and it betrayed him. After that"—I swallowed heavily—"it killed him."

Sympathy washed over his face, and I blew out a breath to try to compose myself. It had been a very long time since I'd talked about my father.

"The White Warrior you saw at home? It isn't just a form I take when I use my magic. It's who I am." My nerves were threatening to choke off every word I had to say, and I swallowed them down with force. "It's who my father was."

The question came into his eyes: *Who is the White Warrior?*

"The White Warrior is an incredibly rare and powerful being. In fact, there have only been two in the history of mankind. My father…and me."

Rabryn's brows shot up with interest.

"When my father was created —"

"Created?" he interrupted.

I sighed and shook my head. "I'm sorry. There's so much to tell that I don't even know where to begin."

"That's okay. But what do you mean when you say your father was *created*?"

"My father was never born. He was created by the Light Gods." Rabryn's eyes widened. "I'm talking handcrafted by Them. He described waking up among the Light Gods as like being in a cloud and on the sun at the same time."

"Wait. Were you…created?" Rabryn asked hesitantly.

I shook my head. "No. I was born."

He appeared to relax a little at that.

"My father was created during a time of incredible darkness, when an intelligent force of destructive Shadow called The Nameless One obliterated everything in its path and the Shadow Gods ruled the world."

Rabryn's eyes narrowed. "What?"

"This was eons ago," I said, waving my hand dismissively so that he wouldn't panic too much about what I was saying. "During that time, there was nearly nothing left of Goodness and Light in the world, or in anyone, which made it difficult for the Light Gods to intervene. Without enough Goodness to wield, the Light Gods couldn't move to help. Any beings of Light in the world were either too afraid to act or were imprisoned or enslaved by Shadow forces and *couldn't* act." I sighed heavily. "The people of Light had to be released before the Light Gods could rise against the Shadow Gods." I shrugged helplessly. "That's what my father was created for."

"To take on the *Shadow Gods?*" Rabryn asked.

"Not right away. He had to set the people of Light free first, so the influence of the Light Gods could be restored and They could help him in the battle against the Shadow Gods."

"Your father dealt directly with the Gods?"

I shrugged a little nervously. "Not only that, but my father was armed with the power of the Light Gods."

"What?" he asked in a sharp whisper. I could tell he was having a hard time wrapping his mind around this.

"That white fire magic you saw?" He nodded. "That's the earthly incarnation of the power of the Light Gods." His eyes went wide. "The very power of Light and Goodness itself."

He stared at me for a long time before he drew up his knees, rested his elbow on top of one, and cupped his cheek in his hand. He looked over at Ortheldo like he was searching for confirmation. Ortheldo closed his eyes and nodded.

Rabryn looked back at me. "And *you* have this power now?" I nodded. "Holy Gods of Heaven." After another long moment of staring at me, Rabryn crossed his legs on the ground again. "So,

I'm assuming your father won the battle since"—he gestured around—"obviously the Shadow Gods don't rule the world." I scratched my temple with a fingertip and felt my face scrunch up. "Or not," he said picking up on my discomfort.

I closed my eyes and sighed softly. Almost there. I was getting closer to the really difficult things I had to tell him. I wasn't ready for this.

"The first thing you have to understand is that the Light Gods took a huge risk in creating my father. During this time of incredible darkness, They actually removed all Goodness and Light from the world, all of it, including from the hearts of Their people, and put every shred into creating him."

Rabryn grimaced a little. "Wait. While the Shadow Gods ruled?" I nodded. "Then how was your father able to restore any Light to the world?"

"Hope," I said plainly.

"Hope?" he asked with a faint trace of disgust. "How did that work?"

I almost smiled. I was just as disgusted with the notion as he was. First of all, hope, especially back then, was rare and flimsy. Second, hope wasn't exclusive to Light beings. I'm sure the Shadow Gods *hoped* they would enslave the world forever. Hope was a fragile silly thing, but that it was all that my father had to work with to restore Goodness to the world spoke volumes about what he'd accomplished. He had restored the balance by himself and raised an army of hundreds of millions for the Light Gods.

"Anyone with hope left in his or her heart he found, he helped, he cared for, and he fought for, which strengthened that hope until it became Goodness and Light, which the Light Gods could then use to influence the world—or more notably, the hearts of other people. Slowly but surely, over thousands of years, my father's Light expanded into an army of hundreds of millions."

"I'm guessing the more influential Light became, the weaker The Nameless One got."

I nodded. "Until a balance was struck. Then it was time for my father to face The Nameless One himself."

Rabryn peered at me with a narrowed gaze of curiosity and concern. "I have a feeling that didn't go very well."

I stared at him. I wasn't going to be able to continue. I couldn't do it. My heart was pounding too loudly, and I started breathing heavily. I didn't want him to know! I didn't!

"Azrel," Ortheldo said gently, drawing my attention. "Keep going."

I swallowed heavily and quickly looked back at my brother. "You *have* to understand how important my father's existence was! How important the safety of his sword was!" I said with a clear tone of desperation. "All Light, all Goodness, was bound to him and his sword. All of it. Goodness and Light only existed at all because *he* did, because *his sword* did. If The Nameless One had killed him and gotten a hold of his sword, all Goodness and Light would have ceased to exist. The Light Gods would have ceased to exist. A Shadow being, of any kind, cannot *touch* the sword of all Goodness." I swallowed heavily and drew out the blade from my belt. "This sword."

Rabryn's eyes went wide as he looked down at it, then back up at me, and then down again.

"This sword is the only reason Goodness and Light exist, even now. That's why I always carried it with me, despite how I was treated for it." I sighed and replaced the sword in my scabbard, trying to prepare myself for the next words.

"The Nameless One was very powerful. And the day they faced off"—I shut my eyes—"my father left."

"He left?"

"Yes, left!" I screamed. "Ran off! Disappeared! The final, and most important battle of his existence, and he ran away!"

Here it was. The moment of truth. Was my brother going to hate me like the rest of the world hated my father? Even after he'd singlehandedly pulled it out of the most relentless, darkest Shadow reign in history?

"Your father was the bravest man alive," Rabryn said.

I sucked in air through my clenched teeth and my eyes went wide. "What did you say?"

"You heard me," he said firmly.

"You...you don't think him the biggest coward in history? A traitor deserving 1,000 years of torture for his treachery?"

"No," he said in disgust. "Who would think that?"

I scoffed. "Gee, I don't know, Rabryn. Maybe the hundreds of millions of beings on the battlefield that watched him vanish.

Maybe every single generation of every single race since then who reads, or someday *will* read, all the nasty things people have written about my father in history books. You tell me."

His face softened with understanding. "And you're the White Warrior now."

I looked away, unable to manage a reply, not even a nod of my head. I felt empty and stiff. I hated telling him this. I hated what I had. I hated that stupid sword.

"Azrel," my brother said softly, drawing my attention. "I understand why you didn't want to tell me, but I want you to know that I don't think your father was a coward."

My eyes filled with tears at his sweet, genuine tone.

"It took a lot of courage to do what he did, to leave and let others think what they would, no matter how horrid. He did what he was created to do, and that was to protect the sword, to protect all of Goodness. He fulfilled his duty." Rabryn sighed. "He also passed the sword on to a worthy successor."

My throat closed and, though I tried to stop them, my tears finally spilled down my cheeks. He didn't hate me. He didn't believe of my father what the rest of the world did.

Rabryn shifted to his knees and rested his hand on my cheek, wiping my tears with his thumb. He stared firmly and unashamedly into my eyes. "There is no other person in the world more worthy to protect all of Goodness and Light than you. You've already sacrificed a lot for this sword. You and your father both. You both risked scorn and hatred and abuse in order to protect it."

I started to tremble.

"From where I sit, both of you are more than worthy to bear the title of the White Warrior."

I sniffed, and he leaned forward to kiss my forehead as more tears dripped down my cheeks.

"Thank you, Rabryn," I said, my voice shaking. He pulled away and smiled at me. He knew now. My brother knew, and he still loved me.

"Question, though," he said and sat back down across from me. "How was The Nameless One defeated if your father didn't kill it? I would think something that powerful could only be killed by something equally as powerful."

I wiped my face free of tears. "Owasyn, the king of

Dwellingpath, killed it."

"A human?"

I nodded. "Ortheldo's ancestor."

Rabryn looked at Ortheldo. "Your ancestor defeated The Nameless One?"

Ortheldo shook his head. "I have nothing to do with that life, that land, or that history." There was an edge to his tone, so Rabryn wisely turned back to me.

"How? If your father couldn't kill it, how could a human?"

I shook my head. "To this day no one knows."

He looked confused and curious, shaking his head a little as if he wanted to pursue an answer but didn't know where to start. "Okay. So, The Nameless One was defeated, apparently a long time ago. So that leaves you to do what?"

"The Nameless One was destroyed, but not its creator."

"Creator?"

A shiver ran down my spine. "A very powerful Shadow Wizard named Hathum."

It had been a long time since I'd spent any time brooding over that name. Hathum was the evil that waited for me somewhere out here. Hathum was the evil I was born to destroy.

Rabryn looked at me like he almost didn't believe me. "So you, my sister, are supposed to destroy the creator of the most destructive Shadow force in all of history and time?"

"Oh, it gets better than that," I said with false brightness. His eyes narrowed. "Because my father failed in killing The Nameless One and left the battle, the Light Gods took away his magic, forcing him to live as an immortal human being until he had a child who would finish what he should have. That child is me, a mortal."

"You're *mortal?*" he asked, appalled. I nodded. "But you don't age."

"I can still die."

"The Light Gods kept you *mortal?*"

I nodded again. "And they also limited my magic."

"What?"

I nodded again. "My father, when he was created, wore a stunning diamond crown. Not a crown with diamonds in it, but a crown created from a solid diamond. When he handed me the sword, the Light Gods told me that They were limiting my magic and that I would remain mortal until I earned that crown back."

"How are you supposed to do that?"

I shook my head. "I wish I knew."

"Oh, you've got to be kidding me," Rabryn said and looked away, shaking his head, barely keeping his rage and fear for me in check. I could see his mind spinning with the facts of what I was dealing with. A mortal with limited magic was expected to kill the most powerful immortal Shadow Wizard in the history of the entire world. Another reason to hate my magic—as if I needed another one.

It stayed quiet for a long time until Ortheldo spoke. "Azrel," he said in a shaky voice.

Both of them looked up past me with wide eyes. I was about to turn around when an unmistakable shadow appeared over me, and my eyes went wide, too.

"Norka," I said.

"He just materialized out of nowhere!" Rabryn cried, standing up quickly. Ortheldo did, too.

I slowly looked over my shoulder to see him standing over me with a smirk on his snake face. We stared at each other for what seemed like eternity, my heart pounding so loudly that I was sure Norka could hear it. I was not ready to face Hathum. Not like this. Not as a mortal with limited magic. But now Norka had the power to expose me. If Hathum found out I was alive, or even existed, I was done for. The Light Gods, Goodness and Light, and the world as I knew it were all done for.

Finally, he spoke. "I knew there had to be a reason why I was sssupposed to addresss you as Missssrtress." He got down on one knee and bowed low, stunning me stupid. "The White Warrior has been returned to usss. The Light Gods be praisssed!"

I slowly got to my feet and faced him. "Were—were you behind me the entire time?"

He looked up. "I wasss."

"How?"

He stood and pulled the hood of his black robe over his head, and I watched him fade from sight. I jumped back and drew out my sword, searching for a shadow, a ripple in the air, anything! I didn't know what he was up to.

"I'm not going to hurt you."

All of us jumped and spun around as the sound of his voice suddenly came from behind us. He appeared once again, drawing back his hood.

"These are magic robes. I can turn invisssible without using my own magic and reccceiving the pain Missstress Laroevith sends me. Ssshe gave it to me before I left. I knew it would come in handy."

"Why did you ride off before the battle with the Gibirs?" Rabryn asked angrily before I got the chance to ask my question.

"A voice told me to ride away. Ssshe said, 'Don't let the creatures sssee you or you will be recognized and feared, and what needs to be accomplished won't be.' I haven't the ssslightest idea what she meant, but sssomething inside my heart told me to obey. I'm sssorry if I angered you, Masssster Rabryn."

"You didn't anger me. I was worried."

Norka seemed completely taken off guard by that, blinking dumbly a few times before replying, "I apologize."

"Why were you eavesdropping?" Ortheldo hollered before I could speak. He looked ready to tear Norka's throat out with his teeth.

"Would you have told me this sssecret otherwise?"

"Did you think that maybe there was a good reason we didn't want anyone to know?" Ortheldo responded with a glare.

I stepped in front of Norka. "Norka. I need to know if you will keep my identity a secret."

His scaly brows dropped. "Why must it be kept sssecret? The world needsss to know you've returned to us. Rumorsss of a Sssecond Shadow are circulating, and creatures of the Shadow Gods are being ssseen cross the land."

"Please, Norka." I closed my eyes, trying to rein in my patience and also prepare myself to slit his throat if he didn't do as I asked. "For the sake of Goodness, you can't tell anyone who I am. No one can know yet. It was my father's dying request. The Wizard Beldorn also wished it. Please, will you keep this a secret?"

His features softened, and he took up a bundle of his robes, held it up to his chest, and bowed deeply at the waist. "I will keep your ssssecret, White Warrior. I give you my word."

I sighed in relief. "Thank you, my friend."

Ortheldo and Rabryn relaxed as well.

Norka grinned as he straightened himself up, and his mood became brighter than I'd ever seen it. I considered his eyes, and for the first time I saw a sliver of hope in them. "I'm glad you're back, White Warrior."

I smiled uncomfortably.

"Well!" Norka said brightly. "Are there any warriors among usss who are hungry?"

"Well, we just had supper," I began. "But if —"

"Supper?" Ortheldo interrupted a little playfully. "You call dried meat, fruit, and nuts a supper? Come on," he said, clapping Norka on the shoulder. "Let's go hunting for some real meat."

I smiled as the three of them started gathering hunting supplies from the horses.

"Coming, Azrel?" Ortheldo asked.

I shook my head and rolled my shoulders back. "No, thanks. Norka can use my bow. I think I'm going to stay here and work my aching muscles. I'll have a fire ready when you get back."

As the boys headed for the trees, Norka stepped up in front of me. "I am honored to be using your bow."

I smiled and tried not to look as uncomfortable as I felt. "Kill something big with it."

"I will try."

He followed the other two across the road, and I went to Forfirith. I pulled out a pair of light leather gloves and took out my Salynn blade. I cut the fingers off the gloves, then cut off ends of my pants to free my legs, and finally cut the sleeves off my tunic and tossed them aside. As I was putting my hair up in a knot, I heard a whistle. I spun around just in time to see Norka lower his fingers from his mouth. Rabryn and Ortheldo started laughing.

I rolled my eyes and looked at my horse. "Jerks," I muttered. He made a noise like a soft chuckle.

"Hey Azrel!" Ortheldo called. I turned to face them with my hands on my hips. "Have I told you lately what an amazing pair of legs you have?"

"Oh, Gods! Get out of here!" I cried, shooing them away— hopefully before they saw me blush.

"Look! She's turning red!" Ortheldo hollered. All of them went on laughing.

I turned toward them again with a smile. "Shut up and go get me some food!" I hollered playfully as they headed into the trees. "Stupid men," I muttered to Forfirith, who made another laughing noise. "All right, boy, how about you and the girls go for a frolic?"

I unhitched his saddle and took off his reins and tack, setting everything on the ground. I slapped his bottom and he headed straight for some ripe-looking grass a few feet from the creek. I unhitched all three ladies as well, and they joined him.

I sighed and put my hands on my hips. "Off we go then," I said and started for a jog along the water.

NINETEEN

…Two hundred forty-eight.

…Two hundred forty-nine.

…Two hundred fifty.

With a growl, I pushed myself back to my feet after the push-ups and slapped my hands together to knock off the dirt. Sweat dripped down every inch of my skin—my face, my back, my stomach, my legs, my arms, everywhere. I exhaled, wiped my brow with the back of my hand, and tried to catch my breath.

"Whoa!" Ortheldo suddenly said. I turned to see him and the other two coming out of the trees, all of them with kills slung over their backs. "Lords of Light, Azrel, you're showing an awful lot of tantalizing skin today."

"Are you complaining?" Norka asked. He and Rabryn started laughing.

Ortheldo's eyes locked on mine. "Not at all," he said as he passed me.

I rolled my eyes and shook my head while they all gathered around the "fire" I'd started for them when I'd taken a short break; it was barely a pile of embers now. I twisted my mouth to the side in annoyance.

"Great fire, Sis." Rabryn said flatly crouching near it.

I grinned. "Hey, I did all the hard stuff. You just have to fan it." He chuckled. I looked at the other two. "How was hunting?"

"Great!" Ortheldo replied. "Norka has something to tell you."

"Oh?" I looked at Norka. "He does?"

Norka smiled shyly. "I killed mine myssself."

I grinned. "I knew you could do it!"

He beamed a smile and looked me up and down with his brows drawn. "Have you been working out thisss whole time?"

"Are you kidding?" Ortheldo asked as he sat on the ground and started plucking feathers from his pheasant kill. "Just smell her, and you won't have to ask." The three of them burst into laughter again.

I bit my bottom lip, trying not to smile, but I did anyway. I playfully cuffed him upside the head as I passed behind him toward my pack. "Shut up!"

He grinned up at me and winked.

I gathered my bathing needs and a new set of clothes. "I'll be back," I said and headed around the creek bend to bathe.

The sky had already turned a dark grayish blue when I sunk under the water for my final rinse and headed for shore. I dried myself off completely and started pulling on my clothes: brown leggings and a deep red tunic with the three buttons undone at the top. I pulled out the necklace from the pocket of my discarded shorts and shoved it into my clean pocket. I strapped on my belt and sword, and tossed the remains of workout clothing into the river. There was no salvaging them.

Norka was already eating his kill while the other two cooked their prizes over the fire on a spit. The smell of the warm meat made my stomach growl embarrassingly loud. I went straight to my packs, put everything where it belonged and pulled out a comb, running it through my stringy wet hair. It was more tangled than I was used to; even the Salynn liquids couldn't defeat this nest. I brought a large piece over my shoulder and tried to work the comb through it as I made my way toward the fire. I deeply inhaled the aroma of the cooking meat as I sat on the ground beside Ortheldo.

"It's almost done," Rabryn said.

"You guys got this ready fast," I said, looking at the stubborn tangle.

"That battle burned off the next four meat meals I'll eat," Ortheldo said, making us all chuckle. "I wanted this one done as soon as possible."

I held up the piece of my hair I was working on and gritted my teeth, annoyed, as I frantically tried to comb through the mess. For the love of Heaven's Light, it wouldn't come out!

"Having difficulties?" Ortheldo asked.

"You think?" I replied, not taking my eyes from my work. He smiled and then got to his knees and moved behind me. I looked at him over my shoulder. "What are you doing?"

"Give me the comb," he said and reached for it.

I pulled it away from his outstretched hand. "No."

He froze and looked at me, confused. "I'll help you." He reached for it again.

"No," I said, pulling it farther away.

His brows dropped. "Azrel, let me see it," he said and reached for the comb again.

I dropped my elbow to the ground, keeping it out of his reach. "Why should I?"

"Because I said so."

He leaned over me to try and get it, but I squirmed away and got to my feet, clutching the comb.

"And what makes you think I'm just going to do what you tell me?"

He also rose to his feet. Both of us glared at each other while trying not to laugh. "Azrel," he said in a tone of warning.

"No."

Suddenly the comb was snatched out of my hand! I spun around in time to see Norka throw it over my head to Ortheldo. I turned back in time to see Ortheldo catch it with both hands.

"Ha, ha!" he taunted.

I laughed and ran after him. He didn't even try to run. I threw myself at him, reaching for the comb, but he held it above his head. As I fought to get it, we both ended up tumbling to the ground.

"Oh, no! No!" he cried as we hit the ground, both of us laughing.

Rabryn and Norka were in hysterics, too, as they watched us wrestle each other for the comb. I had the advantage because I was on top of him. I almost had it back when Ortheldo suddenly freed his powerful legs out from under me and wrapped them around my stomach, crossing his ankles behind my back. He pushed me over to the side until I was lying on the ground, and he rolled on top of me. I tried to continue to fight him for the comb, but I was laughing so hard that I couldn't keep a grip on it.

He finally pulled it out of my hands and wagged it arrogantly at me. "I win. You have to let me comb your hair now."

I chuckled. "Fine!"

He gave me a warm smile, got off me, and held out his hand to help me up. I let him pull me to my feet, and we made our way to the fire again. Now that Rabryn knew what I was and didn't hate me, I felt oddly free. I felt so much lighter and happier without this thing between us.

Ortheldo kneeled behind me and began the seemingly

impossible task of combing through my hair. It wasn't very painful. Or maybe it was but I just didn't notice. I may have been too busy shuddering every time Ortheldo's fingers grazed the back of my neck.

"Are you cold?" he asked me once.

"No, I'm fine," I replied, turning red.

Norka finished his meal, discarding the remains, and lay back on the ground with a sigh.

I smiled. "Feels good eating your own kill, doesn't it?"

"Indeed, it does," he replied, making us all laugh.

"Ours is done," Rabryn announced.

"Just let me finish Azrel's hair."

Rabryn nodded and reached for some plates and eat ware, and began serving up the food. Ortheldo finally managed to get the comb through the rat's nest. I thought he was finished, but then he placed his hand under my chin and lifted my face skyward.

My brows dropped. "What are you doing now?" I felt small tugs and pulls of separate pieces.

"I've never seen your hair in a braid before. I think you'd look gorgeous. Not that you aren't gorgeous all the time."

I laughed. "You're insane."

"Ah, that may be so, my dear, but I'm still lovable."

I giggled stupidly. "That you are, my friend. That you are."

He suddenly froze in his work, but after a moment he began braiding again. When he was done, his face appeared next to mine, and he was beaming a smile.

I ran my hands over it. "How do I look?" I said, striking various poses, which made them all laugh.

Ortheldo sat by my side and took the plate of food Rabryn offered him. "Gorgeous. Like I knew you would."

I smiled. "All right, gentlemen, let's eat and then make camp. I want to leave early tomorrow to make up for lost time. Beldorn will have a fit if we're late."

They all nodded their agreement. As we sat around the fire talking and laughing together, I felt better than I had since my dad had died.

———

We rode all day the next day and even for a couple of hours into the night to make up for lost time. After we'd ridden for a few hours with only moonlight to guide us, we stopped to rest at the foot of the Mongerst Mountains. I was glad we'd made it here tonight because the plant I needed thrived in shady areas under rocks. The flatlands behind us didn't yield much shade.

Everyone started making camp, and Rabryn and Norka were talking about magic—Rabryn's Salynn magic, to be exact—as they dug at the ground to make a ditch for the fire. Ortheldo was setting up sleeping mats as I made my way to a nice rocky area. I pawed around the ground near some boulders, feeling for the fuzzy texture of the Viiweth plant.

"Ah-ha," I said when I felt it. I plucked it from the ground and went back to the group.

I sat down next to the fire pit as Norka placed the last piece of wood on it to complete the teepee. "Try it," he said as Rabryn threw some dry leaves in the middle. My brother glanced nervously at Norka and back at the fire pit.

"Try what?" I asked.

"I'm going to try to light the fire with my magic," Rabryn said.

Sympathy washed over my face. "You don't know how to use your magic."

"Norka's been trying to teach me."

"I don't know how ssssuccessful I've been though. I think it takes a Sssalynn to teach another Ssalynn to use his magic."

I opened my mouth to speak, but Rabryn beat me to it. "There's no harm in trying."

I pressed my lips together and sighed. "Okay," I said with a shrug.

He smiled and held his palm up toward the fire pit. I saw his eyes glaze over and take on a deep look of concentration. I waited with my heart pounding. My brother, able to wield magic? *My* brother? The thought was as exciting as it was terrifying.

He stayed frozen that way for a long time before he finally let out a heavy sigh. "I can't do it."

"Magic comesss with time, my friend," Norka comforted. "You will find your niche, but I really think it takesss a member of your kin to teach you. I'm ssorry I can't do more to help."

Rabryn smiled and pat the snake's broad shoulder. "It's not your fault. You're trying. Thank you."

I bit my lip, not wanting to do what I was about to. I didn't want him feeling foolish, but I had to. I touched my fingertip to a dry leaf in the middle of the teepee and muttered Beldorn's spell. A yellow and orange flame ignited at my fingertip and caught the leaf on fire. Soon a full fire was ablaze.

I looked up at Rabryn who, surprisingly, smiled at me. "Don't show me up or anything, Azrel."

I gave him a small smile. "I'm sorry. It's just a simple spell Beldorn taught me. Anyone can use it. I'll teach it to you if you want."

His shook his head. "No, thanks. I'd rather learn to use my magic."

As Norka and Rabryn continued talking, I began pulling the leaves and purple flower petals off the Viiweth plant's stem. When only the stem was left, I put them into a bowl that I'd retrieved from Forfirith's pack and set the bowl on top of the teepee of logs to cook over the fire.

"Rabryn, lie back and lift up your tunic," I instructed, keeping my eyes on the bowl. He hesitated, and I could imagine the look he was giving me, but he did as I asked. "Ortheldo, could you hand me—" Before I finished my sentence, he held out the small cup of cold water I needed. I smiled and took it. "Thank you."

When the contents started smoking, I dipped my fingers into the cup of water and flicked the excess into the bowl. It steamed and sizzled, and I watched as the once-solid structure of the leaves and petals break apart and melt away into a fine powdery substance. Then I took the naked stem and began stirring the powder. After a moment, I split the pile in half. I pinched out one half, trying not to burn myself, and sprinkled it into the cup of water. I stirred that around with the stem as well and handed it to Rabryn.

"Drink this," I said, not taking my eyes from the bowl.

"What's this for?"

"It's to help your horrendous bruise."

He smelled the water and looked up at me skeptically. "How's it taste?"

"It doesn't matter. Just drink it."

I pinched out the rest of the powder from the bowl and sprinkled it into my opposite palm. Rabryn downed the water in a gulp. His face twisted in disgust at the bitter taste. "Yummy," he said and set the cup down.

I went over to him and studied the massive bruise that began at the lower left side of his stomach and wound around to his back. I rested my palm on his skin and began rubbing the powder slowly around in circular motions over the huge mark. Soon the bruise faded under my touch.

Rabryn gasped as it completely disappeared before his eyes. "What the…"

I smiled triumphantly and took my hand away. Nothing was left of the mark. "Better?"

He looked up at me with wide eyes. "That couldn't have been a simple plant!"

"You'd be surprised what simple plants can do," Ortheldo said as he crouched down next to me and handed me a cup of water.

Rabryn looked down at his stomach. "I already am."

We all started to laugh, but it was quickly cut short as that damned dark shadow grew in my mind again. My brother and I looked up at each other at the same time. Somehow he could feel it whenever I did, and this one was strong!

Deep cackles suddenly rose up all around us. We were surrounded! We all jumped to our feet, prepared to draw weapons, but we didn't have a breath of a chance. From every possible angle, bodies plowed into us. They were everywhere! Some stood back, not even bothering to attack us because there was so many of them!

A burly body slammed into me, knocking me to the ground. I heard my shoulder crack, and I screamed. Searing sharp pains, like knives raking my bones, shot down my arm and back up through my neck. I had barely caught my breath before a pair of huge hands rolled me onto my back. Another pair of hands held my shoulders down. I screamed again as fingers dug into my broken shoulder.

The world was racket of noise, and my shoulder throbbed with blinding pain. I barely even realized that a slimy, heavy body was on top of me, straddling my thighs.

"Ortheldo!" I screamed. I couldn't move! I couldn't fight! "Rabryn! Norka!" Where were they? Were they okay? Oh, Gods, they couldn't be hurt!

Ignoring the huge hand wriggling down my pants, I strained my ears through the noise and provocative cheers to listen for them. I only wanted to hear my boys. I wanted to make sure they were okay. I heard a struggle nearby. The unmistakable sound of a fist slamming into bone came from two directions. I hoped it was Rabryn and Ortheldo throwing the punches.

When a meaty finger was inches away from touching the virgin flesh between my thighs, a loud commanding voice rose over the commotion. "Break it up!"

The man immediately yanked his hand from my pants, and everything fell silent. A friend! Someone was here to help! Relief flooded through me but then just as quickly drained out of me. "Let them up," came the same voice, only more softly.

Sad moans broke out, and the world stirred a bit. The huge man straddling my hips got off me while the other holding my broken shoulder ruthlessly pulled me to my feet. I cried out in pain again. They spun me around, and the fat one grabbed my wrists, twisting them around my back and making me scream again in pain. He took a fist full of my now-messy braid, digging deep under my hair, and forced my head still. I could hardly breathe from the pain I was in. I'd never broken a bone before—I'd gotten cuts, pulled muscles, twisted wrists and ankles, yes—but this was way worse. I panted through clenched teeth, trying to focus.

My eyes darted around, surveying the crowd, and I realized there weren't as many men as I had first thought—maybe only a couple dozen. All of them looked dirty and oily and wore stained clothes and rotted smiles. Then I saw the source of the voice that had halted the commotion. He was looking at me with bright interest.

"Well, well, well," he said as he washed his eyes up and down my body. "What do we have here?"

His voice was cool and confident as he lazily strolled over to me. He had potential to be ruggedly handsome if he cleaned up. His dark brown hair was plastered firmly to his head, falling in little ringlets of greasy curls that just grazed his shoulders. He was tall and lanky, with no real air of power about him except for the multiple scars on his face, neck, and what I could see of his arms. But his filthy appearance, thick, unkempt mustache, and stubby facial hair made him ugly. To each side of him were two men who seemed to play the part of bodyguards. They were the only two who looked relatively clean. They had Ortheldo's thick, muscular build and sported a head of spiky blonde hair. They wore black, sleeveless leather tunics and pants. Weapons were strapped to every part of their bodies, including straps around their forearms and upper arms.

I weakly fought against the hand that held my wrists behind my back, but it was useless. I glanced around the clearing, hoping to get a glimpse of my friends and brother. Finally, to my left, I saw Rabryn. He was on his knees, his chin level with the ground, surrounded by three men and with his hands tied behind his back. My chin started to quiver when I saw the trickles of blood dripping from his nose and over his lips.

Ortheldo. Where was Ortheldo?

The sudden cold touch of fingertips on my cheek made me jump. I looked forward to see the scummy leader standing in front of me. His gray eyes were stone cold, yet they filled with a strange light as he stared at me. After he swept his gaze down my face, his eyes flicked over to the man standing behind me.

"Bumbli, you weren't thinking of claiming this luscious prize before me, now were you?" His voice was smooth and rather gentle, but now that the surprise and shock had worn off from the ambush, I was getting angry.

"N-no, Master Jaravel," Bumbli stuttered.

The man before me, Jaravel, gave him a meaningful look. "Don't lie to me, Bumbli," he said, sounding like a mother chastising a child.

I felt the man's big hands start to tremble. "I—I'm not, Master. I—I just wanted to scare her, that's all."

Jaravel peered at the man a moment before nodding. "That's a good boy, Bumbli." Then he addressed the crowd. "You all know that when we find a woman, she is mine! None of you may have her until I do!" He looked back at me with a cold smirk and grabbed my face with one hand. "I want to spoil you first," he whispered and then mercilessly crushed his hot, sticky mouth against mine.

I whined and tried to pull back, but Bumbli was behind me. I tried to turn my face away, but Jaravel held my face firmly in place. I couldn't breathe with his face pressed so hard against mine. I nearly vomited when I felt his tongue pry open my mouth, and I desperately tried to back away from it. The rancid smell of him filled my nostrils and made me feel faint as his tongue swirled around the inside of my mouth. I'd never expected my first kiss to be so unpleasant.

I heard Ortheldo scream in rage, and the sound of a renewed struggle came to my ears from behind me. Ortheldo was alive! He was okay! Or at least he had been a moment ago. The sounds of hard grunts came from him as punches were thrown at his body. I heard him cough up liquid. It had to have been blood! They were killing him!

Jaravel finally pulled away from me and ran his tongue elaborately over his mouth. "You taste delicious," he hissed. "I'm going to thoroughly enjoy you, my dear."

I glared hard at him. I gathered all the phlegm and goo into my throat that I could manage and hocked it into his face. He froze and then absently wiped it away before giving me a look to freeze boiling water. Suddenly, he belted me across the face. It was like getting a two-by-four whacked across my head. The shock of the pain prevented me from even crying out. I went completely deaf for a moment before the silence was filled with a ringing in my ear. My cheek pulsated with stinging heat, adding to the pain in my shoulder.

Before I could even recover from that blow, he grabbed the side of my hair, digging his fingers deep underneath the braid to get a good grip, and forced me to look at him. "You don't know who you're dealing with, dear. Don't do that again."

I was determined to stay defiant. "I'm not an object you can claim like a spoiled child."

He smiled evilly. "Oh, but you are," he said softly. "Now you are."

His wolfish expression melted into one of mock sympathy. "Oh, listen to me rambling on, and we haven't even introduced ourselves." He walked away and gestured widely with his arms to the surrounding men. "We"—he faced me again—"are the Dirty 30. Like the name? I thought of it myself." He hooked his thumb into his brown leather belt and took a few long, lazy strides toward me, grinning that slimy arrogant grin that made me want to break his jaw. "Perhaps you've heard of us. We are the most successful band of criminals ever known. We are a mix of murderers, kidnappers, robbers"—his greasy lips twisted up in an ugly smirk—"and rapists." He placed a hand on his chest and bowed slightly. "My personal specialty." I wanted to break his skinny neck. "We are the grandest blend ever constructed. I"—he bowed deeply, with a big sweeping motion of his arm—"am their leader, Master Jaravel." He straightened and pressed his lips together, clasping his hands and holding them to his chest. "With all that in mind, I think it's safe to say that you kids have landed yourself in a great deal of trouble."

He spoke like were children who had misbehaved. I wanted so badly to beat the confidence out of him. With my teeth clenched, I stretched out my neck toward him, straining against Bumbli's grip.

"Forgive me if I don't tremble in fear, but you are no threat to me." My voice was a mix of a hiss and a growl. I refused to be afraid of them. I refused!

His smile widened, and his brows went up. "Spirit. I like spirited women. They're much more interesting in bed."

I shot my foot out to kick him between the legs, but he thwarted my simple attack easily. I thrashed against the man holding me, desperately wanting to crack Jaravel in his mouth. The broken bone in my shoulder stabbed my skin and muscle from the inside repeatedly, but I didn't care. I wanted to hit him so badly!

Jaravel laughed at my feeble attempt to get free. I hated being laughed at.

"Master," a voice said behind me, "this one is more trouble than he's worth. Can we dispose of him?"

Jaravel waved his hand to the side and Bumbli immediately stepped out of his path, pulling me with him. I winced and let out a growl of pain through my clenched teeth as he moved me, turning me to the right to watch where Jaravel was headed.

Bile rose up into my throat. "Ortheldo!" I screamed and frantically tried to get out of Bumbli's hold. He pulled my arms tighter behind my back, and I screamed in pain. I had to hold still. I couldn't move to help him!

Ortheldo was on his knees, his hands tied behind his back and eight men surrounding him. All of them were glaring down at my friend and were sporting some bad wounds of their own. Ortheldo, my warrior. Blood gushed from his nose and mouth and dripped off his chin to the ground. One eye was swollen already. Sweat beaded on his forehead, and he was breathing heavily through his mouth, his nose clearly broken. One man gripped the top of Ortheldo's hair, forcing his head back at a nearly impossible angle, and pressed Ortheldo's own sword hard against his throat.

"Let him go!" I screamed without thinking.

Jaravel looked over his shoulder at me, studying me for a moment, and that loathsome smirk spread across his face. "Ah, she has a weakness for this man, does she?" He looked back at the creep holding Ortheldo. "We'd better keep him around to ensure she cooperates."

"Very well, Master." he replied, and then threw his knee into Ortheldo's chest once, twice, three times.

"Stop it! Stop! What do you want?" I screamed.

Jaravel turned toward me and started walking. "Well, my dear," he began, looking down at his fingers interlaced against his chest. "We were just planning on robbing and then killing you." He looked up at the sky a moment and shrugged. "Or vice versa." He grinned wolfishly. "Now, however, I'm considering another alternative." He stopped in front of me, traced my collarbone with his fingertip, and dragged it down in between my breasts. "You see, we're a group of thirty lonely men, who are always on the move, so we don't get many chances for...pleasantries." He rested his fingers on my lower lip. "Unless we stumble across a young woman who can indulge us." He leaned closer to me. "That's where you come in," he whispered.

"I will not be your whore."

He lightly dragged his knuckles down my throat. "You'll do exactly what you're told," he said softly, "or we'll kill your boyfriend."

He pulled away suddenly and held a finger up. "You're partly right, though. Not all of us want you." He held up his hands in mock innocence and backed away a few steps. "Oh, it's not that you aren't deliciously tempting, because you are. Some of us just have different tastes." He looked at one of the men holding my brother. "Isn't that correct, Relrand?"

The creature grinned broadly, revealing a mouth of mostly missing teeth. "That's correct, Master."

Jaravel faced me. "You see, we know that your Salynn friend over here, for some reason, can't use his magic." He gave me a sickening grin. They must have seen that Rabryn couldn't light the campfire. "And Relrand here has a weakness for Salynns, men and women alike. But because they are so powerful, poor Relrand doesn't get to enjoy Salynns very often. Sometimes we catch one wandering alone and mange to overwhelm him or her, but not often enough to slack Relrand's lust. So, this one will be the source of Relrand's pleasantries."

I felt the seams of my sanity stretching as I looked up at the beast behind my brother. "You touch my brother, and it will be the last mistake you ever make," I warned in a throaty voice that I hardly recognized as my own.

"Brother?" Relrand asked brightly, probably at the possibility that I might be a Salynn, too.

Suddenly Jaravel punched me across the face again. My head snapped to the side, and blood and broken teeth exploded in my mouth. There was no pain this time, though. No deafness. No ringing ear. I just felt the boiling heat of my rage spilling over. I balled up the blood and broken teeth in my mouth and spat the wad into Jaravel's face, sending him staggering backward.

"You bitch!" he wailed, frantically wiping it away. He grabbed my throat with one hand, the cool confidence in his composure gone, which gave me a little satisfaction. "For that, I'm going to let you *watch* how Relrand enjoys your brother." He nodded in their direction.

Relrand gripped Rabryn's hair and put one foot on each side of his body. He rocked his hips back and forth, rubbing his crotch over my brother's clenched fists, letting out a shaky sigh. Then he leaned down close to Rabryn's ear. "I like Salynns 'cause they're tighter than humans," he said in a breathy whisper. "Are you nice and tight?" His hand slid down the back of my brother's pants. My eyes and Rabryn's both went wide.

I started to shake. Rage pounded in my temples to the point of pain. All that I could see were my baby brother's big blue eyes begging me to help him.

"Oh, yeah," Relrand sighed, probing my brother. "I'm gonna use you in every creative way I know how."

Rabryn screamed in such sudden rage that even I jumped. He butted his head backward, nailing Relrand in the nose, which gave a resounding and satisfying pop. When Relrand dropped to his knees in agony, Rabryn dropped down to a shoulder and, with another animal scream, slammed his foot up into Relrand's nose again.

I stared, mouth gaping, and eyes wide. *How did you know how to do that?* I wondered. That move was part of the weaponless combat style with which only my father and I were familiar. Kicking or hitting someone in the nose from that angle sends the bone fragments shooting up into the brain, killing a person immediately. My brother, *my* brother, just *killed* someone!

The other men nearby quickly restrained him from doing any more damage, but Relrand was dead. Rabryn's expression was nothing I'd ever imagined on my brother's handsome, delicate face. His teeth were bared widely and his brows were drawn together so tightly that he resembled a vicious animal more than anything human or Salynn. I barely recognized him, but I felt oddly proud of him.

Jaravel released me and stormed toward my brother as the other men pulled him to his feet. He gripped a handful of Rabryn's hair behind his head. "For that, I'm going to handle you myself! Just so your sister can watch." He brought his face close to Rabryn's ear. "And I'm going to rip you in half."

Unfazed, Rabryn stared straight at Jaravel. "You should listen to my sister. If you touch me, it will be the last mistake you ever make."

A strange kind of calm came over me with the declaration of my brother's confidence in me. He trusted me to get us out of this mess. The calm didn't take away the rage pounding through me, but gave validation to it.

Jaravel punched my brother in the stomach. The seams of my sanity were snapping. Jaravel grabbed another fistful of Rabryn's hair and forced his head back so that Rabryn looked up into his face. "Bend over, Salynn."

Rabryn spat in his face.

Jaravel screamed and frantically wiped it away, then brought his fist back and sent it full force into Rabryn's face. I heard the sickening crack and crunch of my little brother's facial bones getting pulverized into dust.

And that was all I needed to hear.

The seams of my sanity burst. I opened my mouth wide, and I screamed long and loud into the sky. The very mountains seemed to shake with my voice as it ripped through the night. A bright white light surrounded me, and suddenly my hands and arms were free. I dropped to my knees while I screamed until my voice was raw.

When I had no air left, I clenched my teeth and looked at Jaravel. He was mine.

I stood and started over to him, barely noticing that I was in full White Warrior attire — white hair and clothes, glowing skin. My shoulder and broken teeth were healed, too.

Jaravel quickly got to his knees, putting his face to the ground and bowing to me with his arms stretched out in front of him. "Please, White Warrior! Have mercy! I am your servant!"

Cacophony spread through the area. Some of the Dirty 30 scattered, grabbing what they could from our packs before heading for the hills. I looked at my brother lying on the ground. His hands were still bound behind him, and his facial bones were so completely broken that his skin hung limp, swollen and deformed.

I looked back at Jaravel and pulled out my sword without moving to do so. I suddenly realized that I was in that weird detached state of mind I'd experienced when I'd cracked Ortheldo's skull open.

I didn't trust myself when I was this way. I had no control!

My arm placed the tip of my sword behind Jaravel's neck. "You are no servant of mine, you blackened wretch!" my voice said, though I hadn't thought to speak. "Evil consumes your heart. I can see it as clearly as I see the sun during the day."

Do it! Do it! I willed my arm to push. If I just added some pressure, it would be done!

Instead, my body spun around, and I saw a man running at me with a sword raised, ready to strike. Suddenly his head jerked back in a strange way, as if the wind had grabbed a fistful of his hair and then twisted his neck until it snapped. *Crack!* The man fell dead.

As I stood there confused, another man ran at me. He stopped suddenly, his body jerking in a way that looked like he'd run into an invisible wall. Then his head, as if on its own, twisted sharply and his neck was also broken.

Norka! It was Norka! He must have gone invisible before we were ambushed!

My body suddenly spun around, but Jaravel was gone. Damn.

When I turned around again, two more men were after me. I killed them with ease. My first human kills...sort of. *I* wasn't really killing them since I wasn't in control of my body.

Suddenly a high-pitched whistle caught my attention. It had come from a man still holding Ortheldo. He gave me an evil smirk while holding Ortheldo's own sword at his throat. "Didn't want you to miss this."

Then he dragged the sword across Ortheldo's skin!

Ortheldo's eyes went wide as fresh hot blood spilled out of the gash, looking like black ink in the moonlight. It soaked the front of his tunic and spilled onto the ground in a sight I wouldn't wish upon my worst enemy.

I screamed! But no sound came out of my mouth. My body started running. I eventually dropped to my knees at his side. Before I could do anything, bits of glittering brown magic formed around the wound in Ortheldo's throat, taking the shape of a hand. I watched in astonishment as the gash closed before my eyes.

Ortheldo fell forward, gasping and coughing for air, but the sounds of life coming back into him were drowned out by Norka's screams of agony. Before I could even get on my feet to help him, I saw it. As if in slow motion, the creature holding Ortheldo's sword slashed across the air where the screams were coming from, and a spray of blood and bone appeared out of thin air. Norka's hood fell back, and he became visible again as he fell to the ground.

My head throbbed with such wrath I nearly felt faint. Beyond any control of my own, my palm came up toward the man holding Ortheldo's sword. He had enough time to widen his eyes before a stream of white fire shot like lightning from my palm and buried itself deep into the man's chest. He arched outward, his jaw stretched wide open in a silent scream as the fire seeped into his skin. He looked at me in disbelief before his head jerked back and he screamed in agony. Long bumps formed under his skin and traveled like snakes throughout his entire body. As they spread into his face and head, his screams ceased, and all that was left of him was a reddish-pink spray of blood.

I thought I was too stunned to think or move, but my body stood and went to Rabryn. I kneeled at my brother's side, cut the ropes binding his wrists behind his back, and rested my hands on his shattered cheeks. White fire enveloped my hands, and I felt the bones in his face draw together and heal. They took the correct shape of his beautiful face and hardened into solid bone once again. He opened his eyes at last.

My White Warrior form faded, and I could feel myself about to snap back into control of myself, leaving me to tell my brother that his friend was dead.

Rabryn slowly sat up. "Azrel, what is it?" he asked, picking up on the tears that filled my eyes.

"Can you walk?" I asked as they streamed down my cheeks.

"I think so."

I put my arm around his back, draped one of his arms behind my neck, and pulled him to his feet. Where did I take him? To Norka's body?

"Azrel," Ortheldo called softly. "Bring Rabryn. Quick."

I saw Ortheldo kneeling next to Norka holding his hand. Norka was alive! I could heal him!

"Come on," I said, pulling Rabryn along.

Rabryn gasped when saw what had happened. "Norka!" He hurried to Norka's side and fell to his knees.

Norka was gasping for breaths to stay alive. I couldn't keep myself from glancing at Ortheldo. He was alive, and he was okay, but my heart sank at the price of that.

Rabryn looked up at me, hopeful. "Can you —"

I got on my knees beside my brother and placed my hand in the middle of the two-foot-long gash in Norka's torso that revealed bone and gore, only to have Norka place his hand over mine.

"Pleasse don't," he whispered.

"Let her try!" Rabryn cried.

Norka's eyes stared deeply into mine. "Your sssister knowss why I don't want her to."

I swallowed hard. I recalled the desperate sadness I'd seen in his eyes since the day we met. It was gone now, replaced with joy and hope. He wanted his painful life to come to an end.

"She can help! She fixed me!" Rabryn argued desperately.

Norka took his hand from mine and placed it on Rabryn's cheek. "Thank you, my dear friend, for making my lassst few days worth living." Rabryn's tears spilled over as Norka hooked a finger into the top of his black robes, taking out the beaded heart necklace his daughter had giving him. He sent a small stream of his brown magic into the leather thong, breaking it, and handed it to Rabryn. "Pleassse take care of this for me."

Rabryn gazed at it a moment before taking it and nodded. "I will."

His yellow eyes turned to me, and my chin started to quiver. "Sssee your sword for the true gift it was meant to be." He smiled. "The position of The White Warrior went to the right perssson."

I squeezed my eyes shut, letting my white tears stream freely down my face. *Please let me help you*, I wanted to say, but I didn't.

"Will you allow me to marvel at your magic onccce more before I go?" I opened my eyes. "Will you use it to heal my friend Ortheldo"—Norka placed a hand on Ortheldo's shoulder,—"sso I don't have to again?"

Though he smiled, and meant for Ortheldo to smile also, Ortheldo didn't. Instead, he closed his eyes to restrain his emotions and started trembling from the effort. "I'm sorry," Ortheldo said, opening his eyes. "And thank you for..." his voice cracked. I'd never seen him cry before, and he was trying really hard to keep it that way.

Norka smiled. "You can repay me by not letting me ssee your ugly face in the Sssky Sanctuary for at leasst another ssixty years." Both of them chuckled softly.

"Please, White Warrior?" Norka asked, looking back at me.

"Okay," I whispered. I was about to grant his last wish when suddenly that detached state of mind came to me unbidden, and my appearance gently faded into the White Warrior's.

"You have done what you were sent to do," my voice said. "Be proud as you enter the Sky Sanctuary, for you have aided me in my battle. Know that you will always be bonded to me through the power of Goodness, my dear Norka."

"Thank you, White Warrior."

I felt my face smile, and Ortheldo and I looked at each other. He swallowed hard and leaned over Norka, coming within my arms' reach. I placed my hands on his cheeks, and white fire appeared around them. I felt his wounds heal under my touch, even the blood disappeared, and he was restored to normal.

When I removed my hands from his face, he looked like his usual handsome self. I snapped back into my normal human form, and we both looked down at Norka. He had passed.

———

We buried Norka that night. Rabryn stayed at his grave to compose himself over the loss of his friend while I helped Ortheldo pack up our stuff, which the Dirty 30 had ransacked. We didn't have much of value to begin with, so they hadn't taken much. Neither of us said much to each other as we cleaned up, but I felt like I had a lot to say.

The image of that sword slicing across Ortheldo's throat tormented me. It played in my memory over and over again. The horror lingered. I'd almost lost him; I *should have* lost him.

I suddenly burst into tears and walked toward Ortheldo who was packing Urylia. He watched me approach, and when I threw myself into his arms, he quickly and eagerly gathered me into a tight embrace. I would have blushed if I hadn't been so emotional. Pressing my face into his shoulder, I sobbed like a newborn while he kissed my head, my cheek, and my hair several times.

"Why aren't you dead?" I cried. "Three times now you've been delivered to me from death! First the Legan`dirs, then myself, and now the Dirty 30. How can you still be with me? How?"

"Are you disappointed?" he asked softly.

What was he saying? I jerked away from him and looked up into his face. "Gods, no! Why would you say that? Of course I'm not!"

He smiled and gently wiped my tears away. "Then what does it matter why I'm still here?"

I squeezed my eyes shut again and rested my cheek against his chest, trying to compose myself while he held me tight. I finally managed to calm down enough to open my eyes. I looked at his neck where he'd been cut. I realized gratefully that there wasn't even a scar. There was no trace whatsoever of what had happened. I reached my hand up and gently ran my thumb over the base of his throat, reassuring myself that it was solid.

With a soft sigh, I stared up into his periwinkle eyes. Such a gorgeous, unique blend of purple, blue, and gray. He was really alive. He was here with me.

"Azrel, I have to… I want to tell you something," he said softly.

I just stared at his face, grateful that I could. "What?"

I realized that he had that intense look in his eyes, the look that warmed my heart to the point where my knees felt like liquid. I would normally look away, confused and maybe even a little frightened at what he was trying to tell me, but I didn't want to look away this time. I wanted to indulge in it tonight and be grateful that I could experience it, grateful that I could say I felt it, because he wasn't dead.

As my heart pounded from the excitement, I glanced at his lips and suddenly felt an overwhelming urge to kiss him. I wanted so desperately to pull his lips against mine, to rid me of the foul feeling left by Jaravel. I wanted to know what a pleasant kiss could feel like, a kiss given to me by someone I cared for and who cared for me.

But now wasn't the time. Too much had happened. Besides, I had no right asking for a kiss, never mind making an attempt for one.

His eyes suddenly faltered in sending his message and his confidence faded for some reason.

"What is it?" I asked gently.

"I just…well…I just wanted to tell you that maybe we should, um, go talk to Rabryn. Actually, I'd really like to talk to him alone, if you don't mind."

"Why alone?"

"I just feel that maybe…if I had a talk with him about losing a friend, hearing it from me, someone who's been through it before, he might…understand."

I'd never seen Ortheldo so unsure of himself. He was tall and muscular with a natural regal air about him that he had always pretended wasn't there—he was rightfully a King, after all. It seemed strange for him to be so insecure.

I placed my hands on his cheeks. "Go on then. I'll watch the fire."

TWENTY

I dipped my hands under the water again and splashed it all over my face, letting it land wherever it would. I was soaked through, but it still wasn't doing anything to cool me off. I splashed more water on my face, putting some behind my neck, and sighed heavily. So much had happened, but all I could think about was how she hadn't looked away from me this time.

I had to force my tender thoughts for her from my mind, though. There were too many other pressing things to think about. Norka was dead. He died saving my life. I'd had my throat slit tonight, too. I also desperately needed to talk to Rabryn, and it wasn't about losing his friend.

Since the night Azrel had attacked me, I'd known something about her magic had gone haywire, but I hadn't known to what extent until tonight. In the brief words we'd shared as we'd buried Norka and cleaned up camp, I'd gathered that she'd had almost zero control over herself from the minute she'd transformed until she'd transformed back.

For the first time, I saw a truly deadly side of Azrel. For the first time, I saw the White Warrior in her. Having no control over *that* was in no way a good thing.

How could she not have control over it? It was *her* magic!

More disturbing was the fact that the White Warrior in her, that part of her that came to life when she lost control, seemed to be progressing, strengthening.

It had begun with shocking displays of her temper. Then it had gone a step further when she'd attacked me, using a little bit of her magic to cut off my breathing. Tonight she'd screamed so insanely, so unnaturally, that I'd thought she had gone mad. Then her magic had ignited, and I'd watched the seven men closest to her *literally* turn to ash. Freed from their grip, she'd fallen to her knees, looking like she was kneeling in a white bonfire of her magic as she'd transformed into her White Warrior form.

I shook my head. Maybe Rabryn could make sense of what was happening to Azrel, but I sure couldn't.

I absently placed my hand on the hilt of my sword—the sword that had cut my neck, the sword that had killed Norka. I was tempted to throw it into the pond in front of me, but I felt a strange connection to Norka through it. Norka had given his life to save mine. The only comfort I found in that was that he was at peace now and would never have to return to Tribletwel. I wasn't much for religion, but Norka had been, so I said a soft prayer asking the Light Gods to care for him.

"That was a nice prayer," Rabryn said from behind me.

I spun around. He walked up to me and sat down at my side. "Are you okay?"

He nodded without lifting his eyes. "I need to talk to you."

"I need to talk to you, too."

The night breeze gently blew around us, making the tall reeds along the edge of the pond sway.

"I need you to tell me what happened after I was mercifully knocked out."

I blew out a breath and ran my fingers through my hair. "You missed all the fun."

"What happened?"

"I think your sister went temporarily insane," I replied. I told him what had happened with Azrel's unnatural scream, her transformation, and the details of the fight. Rabryn particularly liked hearing that Azrel had made Norka's killer explode, but his teeth clenched when I told him that Jaravel had escaped.

"How was Norka discovered? His hood was up, so no one could see him."

I rubbed my hand over my face and then gripped my throat as if my head still might fall off my shoulders. "One of the Dirty 30 gang slit my throat."

"What?" Rabryn cried.

I nodded and clutched my neck more firmly. I recalled how it felt, how it sounded—the light hiss of the blade slitting open my skin. I remembered the gush of my own blood running down my throat and the front of my shirt like I'd swallowed hot syrup. I swallowed heavily, trying to forget the taste of my own blood.

"Norka grabbed my throat and used his magic to heal me. While he was screaming in pain, the one who cut me slashed at the air where his screams were coming from and killed him."

"That's the one Azrel exploded into pink mist?"

I nodded.

"Good."

Aside from the breeze and the water gently lapping the bank, it was quiet for a long time. I looked up at the crescent moon shining brightly in the clear night sky and thought about Azrel. She loved the moon. It was her favorite heavenly body. She thought it was more beautiful than the shining sun. She also loved rainy days more than sunny ones. She was so different in such beautiful ways.

"Have you told her you love her yet?" Rabryn asked.

I sighed and looked down at my lap. "Not yet. I wish I..." I stopped and looked at him quickly, realizing what he'd just asked. He had a soft, knowing smirk on his face. "How do you..."

"Oh, please," he said with a gentle smile. "I see it every time you look at her."

I smiled and looked out over the water. "I didn't know it was that obvious. It's not obvious to Azrel."

Rabryn shrugged. "She'll understand someday. She just has too much happening right now."

I nodded. "What did you need to talk to me about?"

"Something that will make you think I'm insane," he said without emotion.

I grinned, thinking he was joking about something. "Why would I think that?"

He nodded without looking at me. "Because it might be true."

The seriousness of his tone concerned me. "What happened?"

He brought his interlaced hands up in front of his mouth and stared out over the water as he spoke. "Do you believe in ghosts or spirits?"

My mind immediately went to the glowing white mist I'd seen after Azrel attacked me, and I felt my expression harden. "Why?"

"Because I think I saw one." I stayed silent and he sighed heavily. "You're going to kill me for talking like this."

"Rabryn," I said firmly, maybe too firmly. "What happened?"

He looked at me quickly. After studying my face, his eyes went wide. "You've seen one, too, haven't you?"

I didn't answer him. "Just tell me what you saw."

He kept his eyes on me for a moment, gazed out over the water, and finally gazed down at his lap. "When Relrand was...touching me"—he winced, recalling the horrifying moment—"I was looking up at Azrel, begging her to help me, even though I knew she was just as helpless as I was, at least without her magic. And the ghost appeared."

"What did it look like?"

He looked at me and shook his head. "There wasn't really a shape to it. It just looked like a small patch of bright white fog."

I blew out a breath and rubbed my hand over my mouth as I gazed out over the water. So this fog phenomenon was a thing. Both Rabryn and I had seen it. What was the story of it? Talking fog. If it was some strange ghost or spirit, what was it doing here? And how could I sit down and have a talk with it?

"You've seen it, too, haven't you?" Rabryn asked.

I sighed again. "Keep talking. What did it say to you?"

"How did you know it could talk?"

I froze and looked over at him. He studied my face for a moment and let out a relieved breath. "Good. If you've seen it, then I'm not crazy."

I smiled slightly. "What did it say?"

He shrugged. "I guess it saw me begging Azrel for help because the first thing it said to me was, 'She cannot help you, but you can help her. By helping her, you can help yourself and the rest of the quest. Muster all the anger you can in your heart, and release it as I tell you to.'" Rabryn shook his head slowly. "Rage suddenly overcame me unlike anything I'd ever thought possible to feel. I don't know where it came from, but I doubt it came from me alone. Suddenly the voice cried out, 'Butt your head back with all your strength!' So I did. I hurt my neck a bit with how hard I hit him. Next it cried out, 'Drop to your shoulder!' So I did. 'Kick into his nose at an upward angle!' So I did. I knew right away I had killed him." Rabryn began wringing his hands together as he stared wide-eyed over the pond. "I've never killed anyone before."

I sighed softly and patted his shoulder. There was nothing I could really do to help him cope with taking a life. I wished there was. But it was a process he had to deal with inside his soul, and that was a place I couldn't go. I could only support him while he came to terms with it and hope he didn't fall apart.

"What happened after that?"

Rabryn shrugged. "Well, there wasn't much more I could do

because I was restrained pretty quickly. The voice went on, 'Stay angry. Keep feeding the rage. Don't let it waver yet.' So I didn't. What I said to Jaravel"—he looked at me and nodded—"the fog told me to say. It also told me to spit in his face. I saw what he did to Azrel when she'd spat at him, so I was a little hesitant, but something compelled me to do it anyway. I don't know if it was the ghost, but in my heart I felt I should do it, so I did." He sighed. "And just before Jaravel started pummeling my face, I saw that the mist was gone."

My head pounded with so many questions and the need for answers. I massaged my temples to ease the stress that was starting to give me a headache. Whatever this fog was, it had seemed to genuinely want to help, though. It had told me to remind Azrel who she was, which was why I'd started that battle with the Gibirs. After that, Azrel certainly had seemed lighter and happier, despite Rabryn's almost fatal wound. Now it had kept Rabryn from being molested.

I sighed. Perhaps when Rabryn heard about my encounter with the fog, he could make some sense of it.

I looked at him. "Yes, I've seen that glowing fog before—two nights ago."

"What happened?"

I sighed and told him about Azrel's attack on me, what the mist had said, and what Azrel had said about not being in control of attacking me. "It was the same thing tonight," I told him. "In the few words we shared, I got the impression that she yet again had no control over her actions." I swallowed nervously. "Maybe that fog-mist-thing knows what's going on with this weird disconnect Azrel is experiencing when she uses her magic and thinks that the issue somehow puts Azrel in danger. I don't know. I was hoping you might think of something."

Rabryn turned his thoughtful gaze across the water. He seemed to be searching the swaying reeds for an answer. A frog croaked in the distance, followed by a soft plunk as it leapt into the water.

Finally, Rabryn shook his head. "I don't see a connection yet, but we need to keep an eye on her, note everything she does, and bring this up to Beldorn when we get to Rocksheloc."

"Yeah. If we make it there alive," I said flatly.

"Yeah." He gazed across the water again. "If."

TWENTY-ONE

AZREL

I stroked Forfirith's nose and looked up at the mountains, almost wishing that the mouth of Crox Path wasn't in front of us. I wouldn't have minded taking a rougher route up into the mountains, but the cost of time wasn't something we could afford.

I looked at Ortheldo as he finished packing Urylia. "How long until we reach Hellsville?" I asked, meaning Narcatertus.

He threw his head back and laughed, and I couldn't help but smile at the sound of it. Even Rabryn, who was already mounted on Eleclya, smiled broadly.

"It's ten days," Ortheldo replied. "Rocksheloc is an additional three."

I nodded and mounted my horse. "Stay north of Crox and we can avoid it, right?"

"Yes."

"All right," I said as Ortheldo mounted his horse. "Let's go, boys."

Crox Path was a well-traveled pass through the Mongerst Mountains, constantly used by merchants and hawkers and travelers of all kinds. Villages were spread throughout the mountains and valleys that made traveling businessmen wealthy. Some villages were rather elegant, and others weren't very different from The Pitt. Some had a significant history; others were so small that they were barely known to exist.

We traveled the entire day and had yet to come across another person. "Ortheldo, shouldn't we have seen someone by now?" I asked.

He shook his head. "The nearest town is still a few hours away."

I nodded, surprised at how much I'd forgotten.

Once night fell, we finally came across a few people in a small village. Seeing different faces was a breath of fresh air. For eight years, I'd seen the same ugly, hateful faces day in and day out. Even Rabryn gazed about in wonder at the different faces. He'd seen the same faces for seventeen years.

We passed though that village. An hour later, another village opened up to us, but we passed right through that one as well. I began to wonder what Ortheldo was waiting for.

"Are we going to stop for the night or what?" I asked.

"Soon. The Oaksher Inn in Oaksher village is just ahead."

"Is the Oaksher Inn some place special to you?"

"Yeah, right," he said flatly. "Hoibur, the inn keeper, owes me a favor. Considering we have no money thanks to the Dirty 30"— he gave me a wide toothy grin—"I'd say now would be a good time to cash in that favor."

"Why does he owe you a favor?"

He shrugged and looked away. "I saved his daughter from being raped and probably beaten to a pulp."

I stared at him in wonder.

"How did you do that?" Rabryn asked before I could.

Ortheldo shrugged again, not taking his eyes off the wide dirt road ahead. "Some drunken passerby came into the inn while I was there and started a ruckus. He grabbed Hoibur's thirteen-year-old daughter, threatening her life and innocence, so I broke his jaw and threw him out."

"How long ago was this?" I asked, suddenly wondering what else he'd been up to since we'd been separated.

His eyes turned up to the sky as he thought about it for a moment. "Three years maybe."

"Will Hoibur remember you?" Rabryn asked.

"I think so. If he doesn't, Ibalissa will."

I tightened my jaw. She'd be sixteen now, and probably a prostitute. "Well, you've certainly been busy without me, haven't you?" I didn't mean for my tone to come out like it did, but he didn't seem to notice.

"Yeah, you could say that."

I bit the inside of my cheek to keep myself silent. The Gods only knew what that man had been up to over the past nine years. My insides twisted with a suddenly thought. He could have a woman somewhere out there, a wife even. He couldn't have been alone all that time. I suddenly felt ill.

Snap out of it! I scolded myself. *What did I care if he did or not?*

I was jealous—that's how much I cared.

I wasn't jealous!

My mind was in turmoil until we finally arrived at Oaksher village and saw the weather worn wooden sign with faded black paint indicating the Oaksher inn.

We dismounted and walked our horses to the rear, where two stable boys were tending other horses. As soon as one boy spotted us, he ran up and took the reins from each of us. "Hello, my lords and lady."

"Hello," I said and handed him the reins. "Now listen, son, I want you to take extra good care of these beasts." Forfirith snorted, stomped his front hoof, and nudged me with his nose, clearly not happy with my choice of words. I smiled and petted his cheek. "They have a long way to go on a very important journey." I reached into my pocket and pulled out two coppers the Dirty 30 had dropped in their hasty escape and placed them in the boy's hand. His eyes lit up. "One for you and one for your friend. You have to take good care of our horses, though."

"Oh, I will! I promise!" he cried and closed his fingers over the coins before taking the horses to the stables.

"Where did you find money?" Rabryn asked softly.

"They were lying in the clearing. The Dirty 30 must have dropped them in their hurried escape." I actually had two more, but I wanted to save those for the stable boys when we left.

We rounded the building heading for the front door. The inn was small but didn't look rundown. It actually looked pretty homey, with rugged brown wooden shutters and a whitewashed exterior. We pushed open the front door and were immediately greeted by a cloud of smoke. I coughed and waved it away. Wooden tables were scattered about a small, plain common area. The thirty or so people there didn't bother concealing their curiosity as they gazed at my brother, wondering what a Gold Flowered Salynn was doing in a place like this. The bar sat on the far wall to the right. Smoke stained the once-white walls, but nevertheless, it was a well-lit friendly looking place.

A heavyset man with a thick black mustache, black stubble darkening his round cheeks, and short black hair with a receding hairline stood behind the counter, drying out a mug with a rag. When he spotted us, his eyes brightened. Before he could offer us a greeting, though, a feminine voice squealed Ortheldo's name.

From the right corner at the back of the inn, a young girl ran up to greet us.

I wanted to slap her for being so beautiful.

Her fine red hair came pin straight down past her shoulders. A small patch of brown freckles on each cheek stood out against pale, light skin. Her brown eyes were huge, reminding me of a young doe's.

"Ortheldo, how wonderful to see you again. It's been so long, but you're still just as dashingly sexy as I remember."

I think I actually flinched. How dare she be so bold? I wanted to slap her for that, too.

"Hello, Ibalissa. You look lovely."

I wanted to slap him for acknowledging her beauty.

She licked her full, pink lips, gave him a seductive look from under her brows, and rested a hand on his chest. "You know"— she batted her thick eyelashes—"I was only a young girl when you saved me from that icky man." She wrinkled her nose. "And, well"—she licked her lips again, letting her tongue rest in the corner of her mouth as her hands roamed his chest and one shoulder—"I never got to thank you properly for that. I'm hoping you'll give me a chance tonight."

He just stood there letting the little whore press against him and offer herself! I didn't know whose neck I wanted to wring more, his or hers. I felt myself turn red and deliberately pushed myself between them. She stumbled away and then looked at me as if just realizing I'd been standing there the whole time. She gave me a flat look of boredom and crossed her arms under her full bosom.

I gave her a tight, fake smile. "You can 'thank him' later. Right now, I'm tired, and Ortheldo needs to get us a room so I can sleep. So, if you'll excuse us." I grabbed Ortheldo's collar in a tight fist and dragged him over to the bar.

The man behind it beamed a smile as we approached, and the two of them clasped hands over the counter. "Ortheldo, my friend. Nice to see you, nice to see you. What can I do for you?"

"Well, Hoibur, I need that favor you owe me." The man nodded. "We were robbed by the Dirty 30 and —" The entire room gasped. Ortheldo, Rabryn and I looked around as astonished whispers broke out. "And uh"—Ortheldo looked back at the man behind the bar—"we need a room for the night."

Hoibur gave a thin laugh. "One room for one night? That's not the favor I owe you. My debt goes deeper than that." He pulled out a key from behind the counter and handed it to Ortheldo. "You can have a room free of charge and still call upon me when you have more dire need." His smile melted, and he shook his head. "Especially after an encounter with the Dirty 30. Ortheldo, it seems you haven't changed a bit."

Ortheldo smiled. "Thank you, Hoibur, very much."

Hoibur nodded. "Third door on the right." We headed toward the stairs when Hoibur called Ortheldo's name. "Did you ever find that girl you were looking for?"

I felt my face flush.

Ortheldo smiled. "Yes, I did," he said and glanced at me with that special look in his eyes. He placed a hand on my lower back and looked again at Hoibur. "This is Azrel."

Hoibur nodded. "Pleasure, ma'am."

"Pleasure's all mine," I said and thanked him again for his kindness in letting us stay the night. As we headed up the stairs, I barely felt the wood under my boots. I felt like I was walking on a cloud—even with Ibalissa in tow.

The room wasn't bad. Simple, but not bad. There was a bed in the middle large enough for two people. A small round table was to the left with two chairs and a lit lantern. A large couch was on the far right wall that would serve as a nice bed.

I sighed, eyeballing the couch. "Rabryn, you and Ortheldo take the bed."

Rabryn looked at me strangely. "I'll take the couch, Azrel."

Ortheldo stepped through the door with Ibalissa attached to his hip. She was washing her eyes up and down the side of his body and licking her lips.

"Well, from the look of it, Ortheldo is going to be preoccupied with this little girl tonight," I said. "And after he's done thinking he has enjoyed himself, he won't want to share a bed with a woman."

Rabryn turned away quickly to hide the smile that spread across his face from Ortheldo. Ibalissa's face turned red and she glared at me, but I hardly noticed because I was too busy fuming at Ortheldo, who only stuck his tongue inside his cheek and tried not to laugh. He didn't deny that he was going to take this little girl up on her offer to "thank him."

I tightened my jaw and looked at my brother. "Rabryn, I'm so tired the floor looks comfortable to me. The couch will be fine."

I sat myself down, and only in that instant of complete comfort did I realize my feet were killing me. I was hesitant to take off my boots for fear that Ortheldo would see my feet, but he was too busy with Ibalissa to notice. With an effort and grunt of pain, I removed each of my boots with a jerk and dropped them onto the floor. I tried to massage the ache from my mangled toes as I watched Ortheldo from the corner of my eye to make sure he wasn't looking. No problem there. He was looking at Ibalissa, who was pressing herself against him again.

"So, darling, are you going to let me thank you properly?" I watched her trace his jaw lightly with her fingertips. When Ortheldo glanced at me, I focused my sight on my throbbing feet, pretending I hadn't noticed.

"Ibalissa, I'm really tired."

"Oh, I don't doubt it, love. Well, after coming across that band of icky criminals." Her constant use of the word "icky" was getting on my nerves. "But I promise you'll forget about all your *problems* while you're with me."

She hardened her voice at the word "problems," which told me she was probably looking at me as she said it, or at the very least indicating me.

"Ibalissa, I…"

She gently shushed him. "Just come for a walk with me in the gardens and think about it," she whispered.

I clenched my teeth and looked up. He was pressed against the door frame with his hands resting on her hips. Her full chest was pressed against his, and her knee was between his legs. After a moment of gazing into her face, he nodded his agreement to go for a walk.

I wanted to scream. Throw up. Cry. Do something! Anything not to feel this aggravation that I didn't understand.

I watched them head out the door. A scream that I couldn't release burned my throat. I wanted to be going for a walk with him. I wanted to feel the comfort of his strong arms around me, to feel safe in his embrace. I should have run up and pulled him to me and then beaten the stuffing out of her. Pulled her pretty red hair out of her head. She was a pipsqueak. I could take her.

"Ortheldo," I said instead. He paused and looked at me. I caught sight of Ibalissa's glare and flaring nostrils behind him. I swallowed hard. "Try not to stay up all night. We have a long way to go tomorrow."

He responded only by drawing his brows together and pressing his lips together, looking annoyed, before shutting the door. I jumped at the sound of the click when it closed. Though it shut softly, he might as well have slammed it.

———

He came back in the early hours of morning. I couldn't see anything behind my closed lids, but I felt him, and was immediately comforted. The constant uneasy feeling that had plagued me the entire time he was gone quickly subsided with his return.

No matter what he did with that girl, he was my friend. We'd grown up together. Ibalissa was a passing thrill. She could never appreciate him for the truly amazing person he was. I could, and I did. He and I were friends and would always be friends, which meant I had more with him than she'd ever have. He and I had spent years of blood, sweat, and tears training together with my father. What was Ibalissa compared to that?

Thank the stars for Rabryn. He had pointed all of that out to me while Ortheldo had been gone. He'd done it in an offhand manner, too, so I wouldn't feel embarrassed about how much pain I was really in with Ibalissa around. It had made me feel a lot better, but the constant uneasy feeling without Ortheldo's presence had kept me from falling solidly asleep, though I'd been dead tired.

He was back now, though, and I should be able to sleep. I was about to do just that when I heard his soft boot falls coming in my direction.

I felt him standing right over me, watching me. What was he doing? I waited and found myself wishing it weren't such a warm night so I might have kept some of my clothes on. Though I was covered with a sheet, I still felt like he was looking at me naked.

He drew closer, and I had to remind myself to breathe when he rested his hand on my cheek. His face was directly in front of mine, the heat of his breath warming my lips. I thought my heart might explode from how close his face was to mine. He couldn't have been more than an inch away. I wanted to hold my breath but didn't dare because then he'd know I was awake. He then pressed his soft lips to the corner of my mouth, which sent fires licking up and down my spine. His lips lingered for a long moment before he pulled away, let out a soft sigh, and pressed his forehead to mine.

"Goodnight, Azrel," he whispered.

When he walked away, all the heat seeped away with him. The air around me suddenly felt cold, and I began to shiver. I lay still and listened to him undress. He pulled his boots off, followed by his tunic. I heard the clicking of metal and rubbing of leather as he removed his belt. I listened to him sink into the mattress and ruffle the sheets as he pulled them over himself.

My teeth were chattering by the time his breathing became steady and I threw the sheet off of me. Sitting up, I stuffed my legs into my pants and threw on my tunic before lying back down. With a frustrated sigh, I curled up, clutching the sheet tightly around myself. The night eventually warmed up again, but the loneliness I felt was bitter cold, so I drew the sheet around myself more tightly.

TWENTY-TWO

"Tell me what happened," Rabryn whispered.

Ortheldo sighed. "I swear, nothing. I went for a walk with her. Then we ate dinner, and that was that. She was hardly around while I mingled with Hoibur and some old friends."

"She just left?"

"Yes, well…"

I held my breath as the two went on talking.

"Well what?"

"When I came back upstairs she was outside the door in a very, very sheer nightgown and made the offer again, just a little more boldly."

How in the world that girl could have been any bolder than she already was I didn't even want to know.

"You turned her down, though, right?" my brother asked in a tone of soft warning.

Ortheldo sighed again. "Of course I did."

"Good." Rabryn clapped him on the back. "I'm glad."

My brother came toward me and gently laid a hand on my shoulder. "Azrel, wake up. It's time to go."

I breathed in deeply through my nose and stretched as I opened my eyes with fake effort, making it look like I was just waking up. I sighed and placed a hand over my eyes as if trying to block the brightness of the sun. "What time is it?" I asked in a groggy voice.

"It's a little past seven."

I sat up and looked around the room with squinted eyes. When they rested on Ortheldo, sitting on the bed putting his boots on, I forced myself to stay calm and put myself in the same sarcastic, flippant mood I'd been in when he'd first left with Ibalissa, so he wouldn't know I'd been awake when he returned.

I smirked. "And how did *your* night go?"

"Fine," he said plainly without looking up at me.

My brows dropped. "Fine? That's it? You're not going to relish in every sexual detail?" I looked at him smugly. "Or will

Rabryn hear all about that later when I'm out of earshot?"

He sighed heavily in irritation. "He's not going to hear anything, and neither are you, because there's nothing to tell. Nothing happened."

I grunted and looked away. "Whatever you say, pal." I kept the sheet over my lap as I put my boots on underneath it so Ortheldo wouldn't see my feet.

"Azrel?" he asked.

"What?" I responded without looking up.

He didn't answer. I laced up my boots before I looked up at him. Surprisingly, he had a sly grin on his face and a picnic basket dangling from the tips of his fingers. "Care for a picnic?"

———

The stable boys did as they'd promised and had taken very good care of the horses. Forfirith's coat had never before gleamed so brightly. I gave each boy one of my last two coppers, and we were off. Ortheldo had already said goodbye to his old friends and had even managed to get some charitable donations so that we were no longer penniless. As we rode away from the inn, I realized I hadn't seen Ibalissa since last night. I couldn't say that I was disappointed.

The sun was shining bright, but out in the east a dark gloom foretold a nasty storm coming. I actually cringed.

After about an hour on the road, Ortheldo turned right off Crox Path into a thicket of trees. After maybe five minutes more, a beautiful round clearing opened to us with bright well-tended green grass rather than the usual brown dead leaf debris of a forest floor. Across the top was a small creek so flooded with plant life that you could hardly see the water beneath the tall blossoms and ferns. To the right, through the trees, I could see a large lake. The water was calm, and the sunlight twinkled off the surface in a yellow dance. I felt serene pleasure from the sight of the mountains rising high beyond the water.

We stopped at the edge of the creek, and Ortheldo dismounted first. Before I could dismount, he was at my side, holding out his hand to me. I looked at him skeptically for a moment and reluctantly placed my hand in his.

"What's this all about?" I asked when I was on my feet.

"Nothing," he said with a shrug and started walking toward

the creek, holding the basket. "I just thought you might enjoy a nice, peaceful picnic for a change."

"I'd much rather prefer a nice, peaceful bath." I gave him a sidelong glance, seeing if I struck a nerve. The hurt in his eyes made my heart sink, and I sighed. "I'm sorry. I just think I would enjoy it more if I was clean."

He brightened. "The lake is just beyond those trees."

I nodded and gathered up my bathing needs, including the robe Norka had given me upon our first meeting. "I'll be quick." Ortheldo nodded as he and Rabryn sat on the ground and started digging through the basket.

I walked a short distance through the trees until I was on the shore of the lake. I stood there gaping at the scenery for a moment before I smiled and shed my clothes. I wrapped the necklace chain around my wrist a couple times, checking to make sure the orange soul of the gem hadn't died yet, and submerged myself in the water. It was surprisingly warm. I washed my hair quickly and felt the same exhilarating feeling I got every time I used the strong floral-scented liquids.

I was enjoying this bath immensely when that damned dark shadow came into my mind again.

I froze, and my eyes went wide. With no sudden moves, I slowly turned to look over my shoulder. Nothing was behind me. I slowly turned fully around, putting one foot in front of the other, wading to shore without splashing.

I stooped down and picked up my robe, put it on, then grabbed my sword. I slowly made my way through the trees back toward the clearing. Each step sounded like thunder in my ears, though I knew it wasn't. I wished I could walk like a Salynn, silent and light.

When I reached the edge of the trees, I crouched just inside of them and peered out into the grassy area. Ibalissa was there! She kneeled in front of the boys, seeming engaged in conversation. Ortheldo lay casually on his side, propped up on one elbow. Rabryn sat with his arms wrapped around his knees.

As I lifted my foot to run and beat the life out of her, I was suddenly thrown into that awkward detached state of mind.

No, no, no! I screamed in my mind, though my mouth didn't make a sound.

Rather than take a step like I had intended, my foot silently lowered back to the ground, and I continued to look out into the clearing.

What am I looking for? I screamed in my head, extremely frustrated that this happened again and that I didn't even know exactly *what* was happening.

Suddenly figures in the trees around the clearing began to glow black. I felt my eyes widen, but I doubted my face reflected my surprise at seeing them. The darkness of the figures seemed to suck the very light and warmth of the sun. I studied them, trying to make out what they were. Finally, an elbow moved. They were humans—humans holding loaded bows at the clearing.

I wondered if the others had noticed. I considered what I could see of their eyes. Rabryn's were filled with terror, but not for himself—for someone else. He was…worried for someone else's safety. I looked in Ortheldo's eyes and realized he was saying something with them. He kept glancing away, so the words came broken and mixed up, but I finally got the message.

Don't come out, Azrel! They'll kill you, they said repeatedly.

I looked at Ibalissa and saw only one side of her face. Then I felt myself willing her neck muscles to turn so she could face me, though I didn't understand why. I couldn't believe it when Ibalissa indeed began to turn her head. Her eyes were now full of fear for the force that was making her move against her will. When the other side of her face came into view, I saw blood dripping down the side of her head.

I looked again at the scattered black lights in the trees. *Do something!* I screamed at myself.

I took the necklace off my wrist and wrapped it around the hilt of my sword and then placed my sword on the ground and hid it under some dead leaves. I stood to my full height and walked out into the clearing, the flowing satin of my white robe gently caressing my ankles.

I screamed at myself to stop, but of course my body wouldn't obey. This was it. I was how I was going to die. How stupid!

As soon as I stepped out onto the field, all three heads spun in my direction, "Run, Azrel!" my two companions screamed.

"Fire!" a familiar voice commanded.

Fifteen arrows came at me from the woods across the

clearing...or fifteen arrows were *supposed* to be shooting at me.

Suddenly the air in front of me became very thick. Pressure formed around me like I was trying to make my way through a block of clay. Everything slowed to a near stop, including the arrows flying at me. I casually looked at each one in turn as they hovered in mid-air a few feet from where I stood. Then I raised my palms and pushed them forward as if I were shoving a person rather than air. Amazingly, the arrow tips went straight up and then turned backward, pointing in the direction from which they had come. In that instant, there was a soft snap as everything returned to normal and the arrows flew back into the trees.

Most hit a mark, but three men managed to duck in time. I placed my hands on my hips and waited for them to charge. Two men rushed forward with clubs raised—the two blonde guards from the Dirty 30.

The one out front swung his club at my head, and my arm shot up to block the blow. My other fist went into his gut with three quick jabs, breaking a couple of ribs. Then I grabbed his huge wrist and twisted his arm behind his back, breaking the bone in the process as I bent him forward.

I couldn't help being surprised at my own strength and speed. It was ridiculous! This man was huge, and here I was handling him like a rag doll.

The second blonde guy's club came at me from the side. While still holding the first one's wrist behind his back, my leg shot up, blocking it. He immediately brought the club back to swing again, but I had enough time to do a backward summersault over his companion's back, so the swing missed me. Before he could even straighten, and before the second guy could get another swing off, my fist went straight down into the back of the first guy's neck, breaking the bone. He fell dead, face down in the grass.

The surviving blonde guy brought the club back again, and I punched him in the nose, breaking it on contact. Blood exploded from his face, and he staggered back. Before he could regain his senses, I spun my body around with my leg out, and my heel caught him square in the jaw. He stumbled to the side but didn't fall. I spun again and wrapped my leg around his neck and then changed the direction of my momentum, slamming my knee forward into the ground, taking him down with me.

Suddenly a blade sliced at me from behind. I ducked in time, but I could hear the soft whistle of the metal slicing through the air as it missed me by centimeters. Apparently this third adversary had a death wish. He knew who I was, yet he still challenged me in open battle. I looked up as Jaravel changed his sword's direction with incredible swiftness, but when it came within arm's reach, my hand shot up and I grabbed the blade before it got near me.

I wanted to scream from the pain of getting my hand chopped off—but my hand was still there! My bare flesh had stopped the blade mid-swing! I felt a stream of blood running down my arm, but there was no pain and I was still in one piece.

Jaravel's eyes got so wide that they looked ready to roll out of his head. My arm holding the blade trembled, but whether it was from rage or the effort of holding it, I couldn't say.

I looked down at the man wrapped up in my leg as if I had all the time in the world and gave a powerful twist, snapping his neck in two.

I looked up at Jaravel again and slowly rose to my feet. He stared at me in horror. Then, with a twist and a yank downward, I snapped the blade I was holding in half. The steel blade just broke at my will as if it were made of bread! Jaravel could only look at his broken sword and tremble.

"You know I'm going to kill you, don't you?" my voice asked.

He gave a small nod, still looking at his broken blade. In the time it would take someone to blink, my fist flew up under his nose. The powerful hit knocked him clear off his feet, and he landed dead fifteen feet away.

I casually looked at my bleeding palm with a smirk of satisfaction. "That was invigorating," I said and started wiggling my fingers. A white flame appeared from inside my sleeve and traveled up over my palm to my fingertips, and I watched as the gash in my hand seemed to knit together and heal in seconds. I sighed and placed my hands on my hips, evaluating the damage I'd just done.

"Um, excuse me," Rabryn said beside me.

My head turned from the dead bodies to him. He held Ibalissa by her wrist and around her waist as he pulled her toward me. As soon as my eyes fell on her, she shrieked and cowered away as if I were about to kill her with my gaze, but Rabryn had a firm hold on her. Her heels dug into the grass as she tried to break his hold and get away.

"This is my friend, Ibalissa. I was wondering if you would mind healing her? She's got a few nasty injuries on her head."

He was speaking to me as if he didn't know me! Why?

"Of course, I will," my voice said. I arched my brow. "If you stop talking to me as if you didn't know me, little brother. It doesn't help my purpose."

Rabryn's eyes flooded with as much confusion as my mind did. What in the name of the Sky Sanctuary was I saying? Help what purpose?

Rabryn looked back at Ortheldo, who was on one knee with an arm resting across his raised thigh. At my words, he closed his eyes and shook his head before giving Rabryn a helpless shrug.

What was *that* about?

Rabryn looked back at me. "Uh, sorry about that, Sis. Would you just heal Ibalissa please?"

I felt myself smile, and then I looked at Ibalissa. She screamed and stubbornly sat on the ground so that Rabryn couldn't pull her toward me. Screaming and flailing frantically, she tried to get out of my brother's grip. Rabryn soon lost his hold, and she scrambled to her feet and ran toward Ortheldo...*toward Ortheldo!*

"Stop!" my voice boomed.

The sound of my voice more than my words stopped her, no doubt. She slowly looked back at me over her shoulder with wide eyes. I strode toward her, and she sat again and began screaming. She began to crawl backward, but a wall of white fire suddenly sprang up behind her. She bumped into it as if it were a solid surface and stopped her retreat. She began screaming in short repetitive bursts, which was incredibly annoying.

I closed the distance between us and squatted down in front of her. Still screaming, she covered her face with her hands as if I might strike her, and a little sympathy washed through me as I looked at the ugly wound on her head. I sighed through my nose, and brushed my fingertips down the back of her hands. Her screams stopped immediately, and she slowly brought her hands down and looked at me, stunned by the fact that she had calmed down against her will.

"I'm not going to hurt you, child."

I slowly raised my hand, making her flinch and cower, and rested it over her wound. She squeezed her eyes shut and made frightened squeaking noises as white fire enveloped my hand. She sucked in a gasp and then sighed heavily as her whole body relaxed, as if a great calm had come over her. When I lifted my hand, she opened her eyes and looked a bit dazed—peacefully dazed.

"That was wonderful," she whispered. She started to come to her senses and focused on me. "Who are you?"

My face smiled at her. "If you have Goodness in your heart, I'm your best friend." I turned to look at the three dead bodies on the grass before I returned my gaze to Ibalissa. "If you have Evil in your heart, I'm your worst nightmare."

Rabryn kneeled at my side, placing a hand on my shoulder. "Are you okay?"

I looked at him with a smile and then stood. "I'm fine." My eyes fell on Ortheldo. "Thank you for your warning."

He flinched a little. "Warning?"

"I read the warning of the ambush in your eyes before I stepped out into the clearing."

"Oh. You're welcome," he said a bit awkwardly.

As he came toward me, I wondered what I was still doing in this horrible detached state of mind. Why hadn't I snapped out of it by now? The battle was over, so why was I still…like this?

"I didn't want anything to happen to you," Ortheldo said. I could tell he wanted to say something else. He was looking at me so strangely, like he didn't know me.

My face smiled, and my hands went on my hips. "What is it you wish to ask, my friend?"

He smiled, still looking a little awkward. "Curse you and your ability to read eyes so well." My smile widened. "I actually have a lot of questions."

"I can only hear one at a time."

His smile widened, but he quickly grew serious. "Rabryn and I think that Az…uh, your magic…um, well, we think something is wrong with it. Is there something wrong with it?"

All right! This had gone on long enough! I wanted control back! Ortheldo and Rabryn were scaring me. It was still me, despite the awkward detached situation I was in. I needed control of myself! I wanted it! I demanded it!

Unexpectedly, I found myself coming back into control, back into myself.

"Yes," my voice managed to say before I snapped back into myself.

I collapsed to the ground, suddenly having no strength to hold myself up. Then the pain came! I gasped, clutched my head with both hands, and screamed. My head felt like it was on the verge of exploding! I could almost feel cracks running across the surface of my skull, breaking the bone. I was in agony.

Ortheldo and Rabryn were quickly at my side. Both of them were talking a mile a minute, asking me what was wrong, and trading questions between each other about what it could be. I could barely make anything out.

Another blast of pain ripped through my skull, and another scream of agony tore from my throat! I had never wanted to die more in my life! As if some merciful being decided to grant the request, darkness overwhelmed me, and I was certain I was dead.

TWENTY-THREE

AZREL

When the world came back to me sometime later, I was very surprised to be still alive. The pain was gone, but I felt incredibly tired. I slowly opened my eyes to see the graying sky above me. Gray? How long had I been out?

A hand was suddenly under my head, lifting it, and a cup was placed against my lips. I shifted my eyes to see who it was—Ibalissa.

"Go on. Take a drink," she said softly and gave me a barely-there smile. "I promise it's not poisoned."

I would have laughed had I the strength or voice. I think I managed a small smile before I took a few small sips. "Thank you," I said in a raspy voice, and she rested my head back on the ground. I looked around. We were still in the grassy clearing, but Ortheldo and Rabryn were gone. "Where are the boys?"

"They're tending the fire."

"Fire?"

She nodded. "They burned the bodies of those men that, well, that...that you killed." Her uneasy expression softened into a forced smile. "They've been gone since"—her smile faded—"since you've been out, so...um...they should be back soon."

"How's your head?"

Ibalissa was quiet a moment. "It feels better, thanks to you."

"Good."

I studied the sky. It looked to be about afternoon. Crap. I'd been passed out all day. The storm I had seen earlier was closer. This was going to be a nasty one. I was not looking forward to traveling in this, but it looked like we had hours of wet riding ahead of us. We'd lost so much time in getting to Rocksheloc. We had to make it up. Beldorn was going to be upset if we were late.

Suddenly, I heard soft sobs. I looked at Ibalissa again. Her chin rested on her chest, and her eyes were closed. Tears spilled down her face and dripped off her chin.

"What's the matter?" I asked.

She sniffed and tilted her eyes to the sky before looking back down at me and speaking. "Here you are, lying in enough pain to make you pass out, and you're asking how I am."

"You're okay, aren't you?" I asked with sincere concern.

She looked down and shook her head. "I was terrible to you, though, and you…and you were so kind to me. You saved me from those…men. And healed my wounds." She broke down into heavy sobs, covering her face with her trembling hands. "Can you ever forgive me?"

I slowly got to my knees in front of her and pulled her into an embrace. "Of course I can. I understand you acted the only way you knew how."

"Not only for my actions at the inn"—she paused and swallowed heavily—"but for this."

Suddenly pain exploded in my back!

My jaw snapped open.

I couldn't breathe.

I couldn't even scream.

It took a moment for me to realize she'd driven a knife into my back. I was frozen, stunned, feeling the metal buried into my tissue and muscles.

Ibalissa's tear streaked face came into my line of sight. "I'm sorry!" she wailed. "He said he'd do terrible things to my father if I didn't do this! He said he'd torment me even as I slept! Please don't hate me! I'm sorry!"

I couldn't respond. All I could feel, all I knew, was that a knife was in my back. I felt a river of blood soaking though my beautiful robe. Norka's gift. My face trembled with the silent scream I wanted to let out, but I couldn't muster a sound.

Suddenly the most amazing, frightening pair of eyes imaginable filled my vision. They were an incredible, intense, green color that was so bright they appeared to glow! There was an unspeakable challenge in those eyes that dared me to die right now, a challenge that also said if I *did* die, this person would bring me back to life just to kill me again.

I was about to take the dare and die when the green eyes shifted to Ibalissa and seemed to grow deadlier. I forced the blackness of death away so I could look at those eyes a little longer, curious as to what they were going to do.

The face they belonged to, I realized, was covered from the

nose down with a tan cloth. The head was also covered by a snug matching tan hood. Not a single strand of hair peeked out from that hood. When I focused more, I saw that this green-eyed person was consumed by bulky tan garments. In the tan gloved hands was a wooden paddle with the edges sanded to a deadly thin edge.

With a mighty swing, the stranger brought the paddle across Ibalissa's head. I flinched as it exploded in a cloud of bone, brain, and other gore. Unable to hold myself up, I fell face forward over Ibalissa's remains.

Ortheldo and Rabryn burst through the trees with their weapons drawn. "No!" Rabryn screamed and ran toward me.

He was quickly behind me, pulling my limp body up by my shoulders. Ortheldo grabbed two fistfuls of Ibalissa's dress and heaved her remains aside like a bag of garbage. He was soon on his knees in front of me, and that green-eyed stranger was gone.

Rabryn's hands gingerly touched the part of my back where the knife was embedded. "Gods of Light, don't you dare take my sister away from me," he whispered with tears choking him up.

"I'll...I'm...I'm okay...Rabryn," I said between labored breaths.

Ortheldo lifted my hanging head so my eyes met his. He was crying! Seeing his tears for the first time gave me the strength to keep my head up. He cupped my face in his hands, his fingertips in my hair.

"You...you're," I whispered, and with an effort, brought my hand up and touched the tears on his cheek. "You don't...you don't cry."

His eyes took on a pleading look. "Azrel, I—"

Before he could finish, I screamed long and loud as the knife was suddenly yanked from my back. I fell forward against Ortheldo as I began to bleed out. Quickly my vision faded to black, and sound faded from my ears.

"Rabryn! What did you do?" I faintly heard Ortheldo scream.

Suddenly healing magic started dancing in and around my skin where the knife had been. I felt my wound pinch together, and the bleeding stopped. Stunned, I slowly looked over my shoulder at my brother, who was still kneeling behind me. He was staring wide-eyed at the spot on my back where I'd been stabbed.

"Rabryn," I whispered, astonished. He looked up at me, and

we stared at each other in silent shock. "Did you just…?" I couldn't even finish my sentence, but with my brother I didn't have to. He nodded slowly, looking terrified of the fact.

"What's wrong? What just happened?" Ortheldo asked.

I looked at him. "He just used his Salynn magic to heal me."

Ortheldo's wide eyes went to my brother. "I thought you didn't know how to use your magic."

"I don't," Rabryn said, shaking his head. "It just…worked."

I turned around and embraced my terrified little brother. "I'm so proud of you," I whispered. I pulled away and kissed his forehead. "Thanks for saving my life."

He smiled a little awkwardly, still stunned by what he'd done. "Well, you've saved mine more than your share of times. I'll save yours when I can. Maybe we'll make it through this in one piece."

I smiled and rested my hand on the back of his head. "Thank you."

"Azrel," Ortheldo said behind me, "we really need to talk about whatever is happening here."

I nodded and placed my hand on my brother's shoulder and pushed myself to my feet as Rabryn guided me by one of my forearms. "I'll get dressed."

"I'll clean up this mess," Ortheldo said, indicating Ibalissa's body.

I nodded and went to where I'd left my sword and the necklace and put my clothes on, trying to fight the strange exhaustion that still had a hold of me. When I went back to the clearing, the boys and Ibalissa's body was gone. Good. I needed to check something.

I went over to the two puddles of blood in the grass—mine and Ibalissa's—and crouched low to the ground. I looked at the grass a moment and lightly ran my hand over the top. Indeed, the grass was bent and broken with fresh boot prints, smaller than Ortheldo's, and heavier than Rabryn's.

The unearthly green eyes hadn't been a dream.

I scanned the trees surrounding the clearing but saw nothing.

What distracted me now was why I hadn't seen Ibalissa's attack coming. Usually when danger was near, that familiar shadow in my mind would tell me about it.

Perhaps it didn't work because Ibalissa wasn't the danger.

Her final words echoed in my memory. "He said he'd do

terrible things to my father if I didn't do this! He said he'd torment me even as I slept! Please don't hate me! I'm sorry!"

I blew out a breath and ran my fingers through my hair. I hated to think of who "he" could be, but I feared I might already know. One question remained though: If it *was* him, why send a silly innocent peasant girl to assassinate me?

Why not come after me himself?

TWENTY-FOUR

"A woman?" I asked skeptically. That was all he had for me? After a month on the hunt for the White Warrior all he had was her gender. "Are you sure it's her?"

"Yes, my Lord. She uses the same fighting style."

"Have you *seen* her use that fighting style?"

The big man began to sweat and tremble. "Well, my Lord…that is, well…no. I…"

I slammed my fist straight down into the marble table, putting a crack down the length of it. "How *dare* you come to me with this and have no evidence!"

He was shaking like a leaf. "My Lord…I…I…"

Gritting my teeth, I held out a fist and released a cord of black fire. It coiled around his thick neck, lifted him off the floor, and brought him closer to me. "Have you seen her *at all?*"

Choking and sweating, he managed to shake his head no.

I squeezed his throat harder, feeling the blood vessels break under his skin. I put myself into his mind in order to continue this conversation.

How, then, can you tell me she uses the same fighting style?

M-my Lord, Glessar recently showed me the results of a battle that some Gibirs got into. One creature managed to escape and described the woman's fighting style to Glessar, and he described it to me.

But neither you, nor Glessar saw it for yourself?

N-no, my Lord.

You're getting my hopes up by telling me what an ignoramus like a Gibir thinks it saw?

I really wanted to squeeze until his neck was as thin as my little finger. Unfortunately, this one had proven the most gifted of my minions in the art of mind magic.

I'm sorry, my Lord! he cried, finally realizing his mistake. *I just wanted to keep your hopes alive. Please say they still are! I didn't mean to upset you! I just wanted to give you hope! Forgive me, I beg you!*

I dropped him to the floor, leaving him gasping and coughing. "No hope is better than false hope. No one can steal from you what you don't have." I put my back to him and went to one of the tall arched windows. "Don't disappoint me again, Jonoic. I don't want to look at you until the White Warrior is found. I want either you or Glessar to personally see the fighting style, the white magic, or the white tears. Do you understand?"

"Yes, my Lord. Thank you, my Lord," he said and quickly retreated out of my throne room.

I sighed. Something was wrong. I had felt an odd disconnect with the White Warrior for a long time. It was as if he'd completely fallen off the face of the world 3,000 years ago. This...new creature wasn't like the other.

My lip twitched in disgust, and I turned my gaze up to the overcast sky. The Light Gods had to be getting involved again.

I shook my head and gazed back over the landscape of my kingdom. It didn't matter. A Second Shadow was coming, and what I had in store was something the White Warrior was wholly unprepared for. Hell, the Lights Gods weren't even prepared for it.

I still wasn't sure what had brought my Shadow creatures out of hiding prematurely, but if nothing else, the game was on, though a bit sooner than I would have liked. For now, I would just watch them and see if they led me anywhere interesting.

TWENTY-FIVE

Rabryn gave a low whistle. "Guys, we seriously need to work on our communication skills."

I still felt drained, so Rabryn had me lying down again on the grass with my head on his lap. I stared up at the graying sky as I digested what they had just told me—the talking white mist, what had been said, what had happened.

"Have we decided that this theory is definite?" Ortheldo asked.

"Nothing is definite," I replied halfheartedly. The madness of what they were suggesting was not something I could deal with right now, and I didn't have the energy to argue.

"How else can you explain it?" Rabryn asked.

I shook my head lightly. "I don't know."

"I still don't understand why she said 'That doesn't help my purpose' when Rabryn was talking to her as a separate person."

"Because maybe she's not a separate person like you're suggesting!" I cried, which made my head throb from overexerting myself. I squeezed my eyes shut and rested my hand over my eyes. Why was I so tired?

Apparently they had been mulling this theory over for days about my magic and why I felt so detached in my own body whenever I used it.

"Ortheldo," I said, lowering my hand, "we don't know anything for sure. Right now, my least concern is what's wrong with my magic. I want to know what terrified Ibalissa so much that she was motivated to kill me. I also want to know who those strange green eyes belonged to."

"Well, that tan stranger scared the wits out of us when she told us you were about to be murdered," Rabryn said.

"I was rather concerned myself when I felt that knife go into my back," I said, making them chuckle gently.

I sighed and took my brother's hand, pressing it to my cheek. Then I took Ortheldo's hand and pressed it to my other cheek. My boys. I relished in the comfort of having them both with me. I was seriously getting concerned that this search for the necklace's owner would take them away from me, and the thought of losing them made me tremble. I pressed Rabryn's palm to my lips and kissed it, then Ortheldo's.

"Azrel, are you okay?" Ortheldo asked gently.

I nodded and fought the tears that threatened to burst forth.

I couldn't lose them. I wouldn't!

I made a vow to myself, then and there, that my mission now consisted of only keeping my boys alive. I would give my life before harm came to them. The necklace was no longer my primary concern.

I kissed their hands again and gave them a squeeze before slowly sitting up. "We should get going. We are running so late, and we need to make up some time."

They both helped me to my feet, and my eyes went to the dark sky. That mean storm was nearly on top of us.

"Hey, boy," I said when I reached my horse and petted his nose, "a really nasty storm is coming, and we've got some time to make up. You feeling up for a long, cold, wet night?"

He blew out a breath and held his head high, seeming to peer down at me and scold me for questioning his bravery.

I chuckled and rested my forehead on his nose. "Forgive me, my friend. I spoke without thinking."

He made a throaty noise, which I took for a laugh, and I mounted with a little bit of help from my brother.

"Are *you* up for this?" Rabryn asked.

I shrugged helplessly. "No choice. Let's go."

TWENTY-SIX

The rain came down in sheets. It had already soaked through my cloak and my clothes, and it seemed to seep down into my very bones. My hands, one clutching my cloak at my throat, the other leading Eleclya, had lost feeling hours ago. This storm had even defeated my Salynn shoes, which always had kept my feet warm and dry. Mud oozed between my toes, which I wiggled so they wouldn't go numb. If I kept them moving, maybe I could warm them up. I was regretting very much that we'd lost a day of travel and had to endure this.

People in their homes who happened to be looking out as we passed must have thought we were mad. Some of them even came outside and asked if we needed a place to stay for the night. Thinking about their warm fires and hot food, I sighed. Azrel or Ortheldo kindly turned them all down, using the excuse that we had a sick relative to visit. That sick relative would be me before long. The longing was almost unbearable as I watched those people head back inside. I wished they would take someone up on his or her offer. Anyone!

The night was pitch black, save for the jagged bolts of lightning that raked across the sky every few seconds. The wind constantly blew my hood off my head. Since I was already soaked down to my entrails, after the eightieth time I just let it be. The lightning served as our only light for the path we trod. In a way, it was good that it was pretty constant, or all our horses would have broken legs by now.

I turned my thoughts to other matters. Maybe, just maybe, I could take my mind off my misery. I turned them to what had happened in Oaksher with Ibalissa.

I could not escape the memory of seeing my sister with a knife buried in her back. I couldn't escape the terror I'd felt in that moment, the terror that I might actually lose her. Azrel didn't know it, but she was my whole world. She was all I had left of anything that mattered in my life. She had looked out for me in The Pitt. She had protected me from the abuse she'd endured. She'd taught me everything about weaponry and adventure and travel. Everything I knew, I owed to her. Everything I was, I owed to her.

I hoped the messenger that Ortheldo snagged had gotten his letter to Hoibur about his daughter. When he and Azrel were writing it, Azrel had insisted that Hoibur not know that Ibalissa tried to kill her. When I'd asked her why, she'd said, "When a person's strings are pulled by another, only the puppeteer can be blamed." Whatever that meant.

My feet suddenly slid on a patch of mud. I landed hard on my butt with a thick splash. I groaned from the rude awakening back into reality. I stood up slowly, shook the mud off my hands, and blew out an annoyed breath as my body adjusted to the new cold feeling on my butt and back of my legs. Finally, I trudged on. So much for getting lost in my thoughts. I couldn't walk correctly unless I paid attention. The icy hot feeling in my feet, the freezing cold rain, and my stomach growling, all brought me back to our miserable path.

I resorted to beating myself up again for not having stayed with Azrel and Ibalissa. I should have been there. I should have protected her. I'd had a bad feeling about Ibalissa right off. Every instinct I had told me not to leave them alone. Why hadn't I listened?

That dark feeling I couldn't explain had presented itself as soon as Ortheldo had asked me to go with him to burn the bodies of the men Azrel had killed. I'd wanted to scream at him, "Are you crazy? Don't you feel that something is wrong here?" But I'd gone with him. I had ignored that bad feeling, dismissing it as brotherly love, perhaps even paranoia at being out here in the world for the first time in my life. But it hadn't been simple brotherly love! Something had been very wrong, and it had nearly cost me my sister!

I certainly had someone to thank, though. That tan stranger, whoever that was, had saved Azrel's life. The words she'd said when she'd come into sight against the distant trees had sounded so indifferent, so casual. "Your friend is about to be murdered by the red head." Then she'd just disappeared. Ortheldo and I had bolted just in time to be too late.

I smiled, though, at recalling how I had saved Azrel with my magic. My magic! I'd used it! Effectively! I still wasn't sure how

I'd done it. I clutched the beaded heart necklace I was wearing and wondered if Norka was somehow still protecting us from beyond the grave.

The storm hadn't ceased by morning. I painfully watched the sky grow lighter and lighter as the hours dragged on for eternity. Finally, when I was about to pass out from exhaustion, Azrel and Ortheldo decided we'd made up a good amount of time, so we stopped in a village called Blesska.

We put the horses up at the first inn we came across and then staggered into the common area, all of us barely able to stand. While Azrel and Ortheldo went to inquire about a room, I actually did lose my legs for a moment. By reflex, I grabbed the first thing my hands touched, which turned out to be a tabletop.

After the dizziness faded, I got a very evil feeling in my soul. I turned my eyes up slowly and found myself looking into the coldest pair of dark blue eyes I'd ever seen. I flinched as those eyes seemed to rip through my very soul. I knew I would never forget the horrible feeling I got from those eyes. It felt like a thousand tiny ice snakes with spikes along their entire bodies were swimming though my veins. The face was no softer. The man sitting at that table had sharp, strong, defined features that a fleet of men would cower before. His thin, hard white lips were almost completely covered by a thick blonde mustache, and he had short blonde hair that was plastered down with the rain. His clothes were soaked through, showing hard, defined muscles under a medium build.

I straightened quickly and dropped my hands from the top of the table where he sat. We stared at each other. His eyes seemed to freeze me in place. The tension grew, and neither the clattering noise of the inn nor the storm outside could ease the silence between us.

The tension broke briefly when he glanced away from me toward Ortheldo and Azrel. I didn't like the way he was looking at my sister. His cold eyes seemed to brighten with some dark delight at the sight of her.

He shifted his eyes back to me. "Are you okay, son?" he asked. His voice was deep and kind, but I saw right through the false concern.

"Yes," I replied, trying to keep my voice from shaking and

betraying my fear. "I'm sorry for disturbing you. We've traveled for a long time, and I'm weary."

He gave a slow, careful nod, his eyes fixed on me intently as if absorbing my face. Then he looked back at Azrel. "I have no doubt."

I took a careful step back, dreading those horrible eyes falling on me again. He didn't even notice. His gaze was fixed on Azrel even as he lifted a mug of hot ale to his lips and took a sip. I moved to stand beside my sister, not daring to turn my back to that man.

I finally turned toward her and protectively placed my hand on her lower back. "Let's go somewhere else."

Her tired, ashen face looked at me as if I were daft. "What?"

I glanced back at the man. He was still staring at her. I looked back at my sister. "I have a bad feeling about this place. Can't we go up the road a little more?"

I had Ortheldo's attention now. He and Azrel exchanged glances and looked back at me. "Rabryn, you're just tired," Azrel said. "All of our nerves are on end. We just need to sleep. Everything is fine."

I exchanged glances with Ortheldo while she went back to talking about getting a room. Ortheldo didn't look so certain that it was just my nerves. I mouthed "look" to him and turned my gaze to the man. He hadn't even moved, and his eyes were still on Azrel. He wasn't even trying to be inconspicuous about staring at her.

Ortheldo and I looked at each other again. He placed his hand on Azrel's back. "I have a bad feeling, too," he said. "Let's go up the road a little bit."

Azrel gave an exasperated sigh. "You're both just tired." She looked to each of us. "We'll get some sleep and everything will be fine. We're not staying that long anyway. Nothing is going to happen."

I gazed around the inn. It looked friendly enough. It was wide open and clean. Not too many goons were hanging around here, just the one behind us. Maybe he was just deeply attracted to her. A few other men around the common room were shooting glances her way, particularly eyeing her figure, which was very apparent under the soaking wet clothes that clung to her body.

I sighed and nodded. "Maybe you're right." I turned to look at the man again, but he was gone. Feeling instantly relieved, I nodded. "Okay, we'll stay here." I didn't care much to take another step anyway, never mind walk the Light Gods knew how far down the road to another inn.

Once we had a room, we all trudged heavily up the stairs, each of us barely able to lift our feet onto the next step. We opened the door and went in. It looked a lot like the Oaksher Inn, only a bit brighter and homier. It had a fireplace on the back wall to the right of the bed, too. Ortheldo got busy right away starting a fire as Azrel went out in the hall for something. I plopped heavily onto the wood floor, leaning up against the bed, and weakly started to pull off my wet clothes.

"Should we set up watches?" Ortheldo asked quietly.

I considered it while I pulled my shirt over my head. I let it drop to the floor in a sopping heap, along with my cloak, and then started to pull off my mud caked Salynn shoes.

"No," I said at last. "I think it'll be okay. He left."

He started poking at the fire. "I didn't like the way he was looking at her."

"Neither did I." I reached over my shoulder and pulled one of the thick blankets off the bed and wrapped it around my shoulders. "His eyes were terrifying." I threw Ortheldo one of the other blankets to wrap up in.

He caught it and set it aside and looked at me seriously. "Rabryn," he said, "you told me you had a bad feeling when we left Azrel alone with Ibalissa, and look what happened. Neither of us took your bad feeling seriously." He shook his head. "I don't intend to make that mistake again. Now tell me, is this another one of your bad feelings?"

I studied him a moment and thought about it. His usually bright and charming eyes were drooping with the dull, lifeless look of utter exhaustion. I knew he'd walk off a cliff for Azrel if she needed him to. He'd deprive himself of much-needed sleep and stay awake all night if I told him it *was* another bad feeling.

Since I wasn't really sure if it was, I shook my head and finished taking off my pants under the warm blanket. "No, it's not another bad feeling. Like Azrel said, I'm just tired."

He studied me a moment to be sure I was telling the truth. Though he clearly wasn't fully convinced we were safe, he stood and began peeling his clothes off anyway. As he did, Azrel returned carrying a wide rack with long pegs. She placed it in front of the fire with the pegs facing the warm heat.

"Put your clothes on this so they can dry," she said as she scooped up my pile of wet garments.

"I'll do it, Azrel."

"I've got it," she replied without looking at me.

Too tired to argue, I just clutched the blanket around me and stared into the fire. I found myself thinking about those incredibly bright green eyes I'd seen in Oaksher Village. I'd only seen them from a distance, but even then, they were striking. I wished I'd seen them up close to see if they really were as unearthly as Azrel had said.

"I'm taking the couch this time," Ortheldo declared as he sat wrapped up in a blanket. He stared intensely into the fire.

I looked up at Azrel to ask if it was his turn or mine for the couch and my words were frozen in my throat. She'd peeled off her shirt and stood there naked. I couldn't help looking. I'd never seen the soft curves of a woman's bare flesh before. Despite the fact she was my sister, Light Gods, a woman's body was such an incredibly beautiful thing. When her eyes met mine, I felt myself turn bright red and moved my eyes to the floor immediately.

"It's all right, Rabryn. You would have seen a naked woman eventually," she said.

I cleared my throat and desperately changed the subject. "No arguments about Ortheldo taking the couch?"

I saw the blanket swish around her feet as she wrapped herself up in it, and I figured it was safe to look at her again. She sat on the floor and gazed into the fire. "Do you think I'm in any condition to think of a witty argument?" She glanced at me and we smiled.

We all sat in silence for a long time, letting our bones unfreeze. As I stared into the flames, I soon found it was taking a lot of effort to hold my head up. Without a word, I forced myself to my feet, using the bed for aid. I dropped my shoulder onto the mattress and was asleep before I even remembered getting comfortable.

———

Rabryn! Help! Raaaaabryyyn!

I awoke with a start, sitting straight up in bed, gasping for air and dripping with sweat. I quickly looked down at the bed beside me and found Azrel sound asleep. I sighed, and my shoulders sagged in relief.

Her screams had seemed so real. *She* had seemed so real.

I lay back down, rubbing my eyes and trying to catch my breath. I looked across the room at Ortheldo, who was asleep on the couch, glad to see he hadn't stayed awake to keep watch. I curled up onto my side with my back to Azrel and tried to go back to sleep.

The storm was still raging. Thunder shook the building, but that's not why I was uneasy. That dream had been terrifying. I hadn't seen anything very frightful, but the feeling of terror just seemed to consume the entire world of the dream.

Azrel was standing alone in an eerie green light. Her hand was reaching out to me, and she was screaming my name. As I ran to her, not making any ground, her image started to pulsate from her normal form into that of the White Warrior. The terror in her face, as both herself and the White Warrior, was like nothing I had ever seen, and my not being able to even get near her was the most wretched feeling I'd ever felt in my life.

Suddenly, I heard floorboards creak. My eyes snapped open and shifted to the door of our room. A shadow was cast underneath it from someone standing in the hall. I held my breath, knowing exactly who it was without setting my sight on him. I could feel the cold, dark blue eyes coming through the door as if it were wide open.

I slowly sat up and silently got to my feet. I went over to the rack in front of the fireplace, took my pants from one of the pegs, and pulled them on. They were still damp. I returned to the bed, guided only by pale daylight filtering through dark gray storm clouds. I reached underneath it and grabbed my hunting knife, holding it in my grasp tightly, trying not to tremble as I slowly approached the door.

I was halfway there when Azrel suddenly awoke in a screaming fit that nearly turned my insides out. I snapped my head around to look at her as she writhed around on the bed as if she were being murdered by the air!

I ran back toward her as Ortheldo closed the distance from the couch. Each of us was on one side of her, and I looked back toward the door again. The shadow was gone, so I turned my attention to Azrel. Ortheldo was standing over her, shaking her, and I realized she was still asleep! She was having a nightmare?

"Azrel! Wake up!" Ortheldo screamed.

I joined in trying to wake her, my heart beating faster every moment she was in this horrible state.

The thundering of feet running up the wooden stairs of the inn was louder than the thunder outside as Azrel finally opened her eyes. She was gasping and panting, sweat dripping off her face like she was coming in from the rain again. She looked around the room as if she'd forgotten where she was.

The door was suddenly kicked in, and six heavyset men filled the hallway. I could only imagine what they thought was happening. Azrel was lying naked and exposed since she'd kicked off her blanket. Ortheldo was completely naked as he stood over her, holding her shoulders firmly from trying to shake her awake, and I was standing half-naked on the other side of the bed with a knife in my hand. The big men charged forward, immediately making Ortheldo and me cower against the back wall.

"No! No!" Azrel cried, her voice high pitched, a sound I'd never heard in her voice before. She sat up and held a hand out to them, desperately clutching the blanket to herself with the other. "It's okay. They're fine. They're not hurting me. We…"—she glanced from me to Ortheldo—"um…we just got carried away with our, uh…game," she said. She looked at Ortheldo. "Right?" He hesitated and then gave a nod. She turned to me and nodded her head. I looked back at the six men and nodded my agreement.

The men fumed. "You sounded like you were being murdered!"

"Well," she began awkwardly and looked at them with false bashfulness. "That was the scene. I was a damsel in distress about to be…"

"All right!" the man cried, not wanting to hear the details. "Keep it down! No one wants to hear what you do up here!" We all nodded as the men shook their heads in disgust and left, slamming the door behind them.

Azrel dropped back down onto the bed, still trying to catch her breath, and placed her hand on her forehead. She stared up at the ceiling as her eyes began to fill with white tears.

"Azrel," Ortheldo said softly, kneeling beside the bed. "What happened?"

Azrel looked at the ceiling again. "I—I don't know." She closed her eyes again, and two large white tears fell from the corners of her eyes. "It was so real."

What in the world had my sister seen that had terrified her so badly?

She opened her eyes again and looked at me. Her brows dropped when she saw my knife in my hand. "What happened?"

Before I could answer her, or even comfort her, her eyes suddenly went wide and she threw the blanket up over her head. I was about to ask her what she was doing, when I realized that someone was standing in the doorway, though I hadn't even heard the door open.

It was him.

"Is everything all right?" he asked, coming forward.

I quickly moved to stand at the foot of the bed. "We're fine. Leave."

He blanched. "No need to be rude. I just want to check on the lady."

He tried to step past me, but I quickly put myself in his way. "She doesn't want to be checked."

"Please. I'm an Herbest. I can help her."

He tried to get past me again, and again I stepped in front of him again. He was my height, so it was easy to get in his face. "She doesn't need help."

He had something to do with her nightmare. I knew he did.

"I'd like to hear that from her, if you don't mind."

Again, he tried to go around me, adamant about seeing her for some reason. Just by being in the room he was too close to my sister.

I took up the front of his shirt with my free fist and held my knife to his throat with the other. "I'm not going to tell you again," I warned venomously. "She's fine. Now get out."

I forced him backward, away from the bed, away from Azrel, and toward the door. I shoved him into the hall and slammed the door in his face.

I turned and saw Ortheldo in front of the fireplace pulling his pants on. "Couch," he said as he buckled them.

We each ran and took an end of the couch, lifted it, and set it down in front of the door, blocking any entry. Then we went to Azrel. She was sobbing. In all the years that Azrel had lived with Mother and me in The Pitt, she'd never cried. Not once. I'd never seen one single white tear of hers, though the monsters there often did things to her that would make a grown man bawl like an infant. She had cried more times since this journey had begun than I'd ever seen in my life, and I hated it.

Ortheldo rubbed her back. "Azrel, he's gone."

Azrel slowly lowered the blanket from her eyes and looked at the doorway to be sure, then removed it from her face and rolled onto her back.

"Why did you cover your face when he came in?" I asked, picking some strings of her damp hair off her cheeks.

She glanced at me before looking back up at the ceiling. "Beldorn told me a long time ago, before I even met you, that if I ever found myself in a position where I had to cry, I should hide my tears." Her eyes narrowed thoughtfully. "His words came so clearly to me all the sudden, as if he was standing right in the doorway, screaming them at me."

"Azrel," Ortheldo said, taking her hand. "Why did you wake up screaming and struggling?"

Azrel shook her head. "It was just a nightmare," she replied dismissively.

"Just a nightmare?" Ortheldo pressed. "Tell me what happened."

Her brows dropped as she looked at him. "What does it matter? It's over. I'm awake."

"Azrel," Ortheldo said with obviously strained patience. "Tell me what happened in your nightmare. I want every detail."

"Don't worry about it! It's over!" she cried, throwing the blankets off of her and storming over to the clothes rack.

"Azrel, please," Ortheldo begged, standing. "At least tell me if your dream involved a strange green light."

I felt my skin crawl and quickly looked at Ortheldo in disbelief. Why was he mentioning something that had appeared in my own terrifying dream?

Azrel sighed and rubbed a hand over her face. "No," she replied shortly and began to get dressed. "We might as well get going. I won't be able to go back to sleep." She dropped a tunic over her head and looked at both of us. "Did you both sleep enough?"

Though we had only slept a couple of hours, Ortheldo and I nodded. Ortheldo looked troubled as he got dressed. Something was obviously on his mind. When he caught me looking at him, he just shook his head to dismiss the matter for now. He'd likely tell me later.

We moved the couch, but before opening the door to leave, I pulled out my knife again, lest that stranger be waiting around to torment my sister further. I opened the door, poked my head out, and looked up and down the narrow hallway. No one was in sight, but that didn't mean he wasn't nearby.

As we made our way down the stairs, my stomach suddenly growled so loudly that Azrel and Ortheldo laughed. I smiled self-consciously. "I don't suppose we could get something to eat before we leave?"

Chuckling, Azrel put an arm around my waist. "Of course. We can't have you starving to death, now can we? Besides"—she looked over her shoulder toward the window at the end of the hallway—"I'm in absolutely no hurry to go back out in *that*."

Ortheldo and I chuckled our agreement, and all of us walked down the stairs to the common. It was after lunchtime, so the common was nearly empty. The three of us sat ourselves in the far back corner, Ortheldo up against the wall between Azrel and me.

The server girl must have sensed our starvation because she quickly came over to us. "What can I get you gentle folks?"

There wasn't much of a choice, roast beast or deer, but the thought of getting food in my stomach made me not care. I was ravenous. After we put our requests in and she walked away, I suddenly wished I'd ordered some onion soup to go with my meal.

"I'll go tell her for you," Azrel said suddenly.

I looked at her smirking face and chuckled. "Thank you."

She got up and went after the server girl. I shook my head, amazed that she could read eyes so well.

Suddenly Ortheldo gripped my arm so hard and so fast that I jumped. I looked at him, and his expression was so full of alarm that my heart started to beat faster. "Rabryn, we have to find out what Azrel's nightmare was about," he said in a low tone. "Please, somehow, get it out of her."

"What's wrong?" I asked, trying to keep my voice steady.

He released my arm and looked down. "Just do as I say," he whispered.

I was about to ask why again when I saw Azrel coming back. Brilliant! Scaring me to death just before the best eye reader in the world sits down at the table. I forced a smile on my face, which she would see through like glass in a window.

Her smile faded. "What's wrong?"

"Nothing," Ortheldo lied in a cheerful tone.

My mind raced. She wasn't going to buy that. How could I get the details of her nightmare while burying this bone of worry she now had in her teeth?

"Guys," she said in a warning tone.

I knew Azrel. She wasn't going to let this go.

Finally, an idea came, and I let out an exasperated sigh. "Ortheldo, just tell her."

He looked at me sincerely confused, wondering what I was doing.

"Tell me what?" she asked suspiciously.

I looked at Azrel. "He had a nightmare last night, too, but he's afraid to tell you about it because he doesn't want you to think he's weak. But I think he needs your comfort more than he needs mine."

I looked at Ortheldo. As he caught on, the corners of his mouth were turned up, rather impressed with me. Before Azrel noticed, he changed his expression to look ashamed, quickly frowning and getting into character.

"Rabryn, I confided that in you as a friend." His hands fidgeted in an act of nervousness, picking at his nails and such. I had to hold back a smile.

"Since when can you confide in my brother and not me?" Azrel asked, clearly offended. "You've known me for more than half your life, and you've known Rabryn for barely over a week!"

"Azrel, it's not that I didn't want to confide in you. It's just…I thought you'd see me as weak, like Rabryn said." He paused and acted like he was debating whether to say the next thing on his mind or not. "I…it's just," he sighed and his shoulders sagged. "I woke up crying."

I pressed my tongue tightly inside my cheek and kept my eyes on the tabletop to keep from laughing. I thought for a minute that Azrel wouldn't buy that, but his performance had worked.

"Ortheldo"—Azrel rested her hand on top of his and stopped his finicky picking—"I have seen the mighty side of you far more often than the sorrowful side. I would never consider you weak. Please tell me."

He and I glanced at each other. My idea wasn't working. My mind raced, wondering how to get her talking first. "Azrel, you never show weakness," I said at last.

Her face went solemn. "I did upstairs, didn't I?" Bingo! That's what I wanted. She looked back at Ortheldo. "Would you feel better if I told you what made me cry?"

Both our eyes lit up, but Ortheldo kept his gaze on the tabletop so he wouldn't seem too eager. "Maybe, but I doubt your weakness compares remotely to mine."

Nice touch, I mentally congratulated him.

Azrel sighed. "It just might come close." Her face scrunched in thought. "It was so real." After a moment, she put her elbow on the tabletop and rested her head in one hand. She drew on the table with the other, seeming a little absentminded. "I've forgotten most of it already." Ortheldo's shoulders sagged with disappointment. "But what I do remember is that I was standing in a building of some sort. The details of the building are gone, but a man was standing across from me, clad entirely in black and wearing a black mask. He was watching me with this strange, alien, evil intensity. His eyes burned into me. We watched each other for a long time. Then he raised his hand, and snakes shot out from his palm." She winced. "They were huge snakes with dripping fangs, and they came right at my face. They bit me and burrowed their way into my skin. One of them even went up my nose and another into my mouth."

The table shook a little bit with all three of our horrified shudders. I found myself rubbing my arms to warm the chill that had crept over me from imagining what she was describing.

Her eyes narrowed. "I could feel them. I could *see* them just under the surface of my skin. The long bumps of their bodies were swimming up my legs and arms until they got to my head." Azrel held her head in both hands as if she were feeling the snakes right now. "Then they started breaking my skull bones to get into my brain. I could—" her face scrunched in horror and she pointed to her head—"I could *feel* them in there." She paused and swallowed heavily before gently shaking her head. "The next thing I knew, I was on my back and the man in black was on top of me. He was"—she squeezed her eyes shut—"inside of me, having his way with me." Just as I was about to console her, she blinked rapidly, looked at us, shook her head, and stared down at the table. "Then I woke up." She composed herself quietly for a moment and looked back up at us with a forced a smile. "It's stupid to get upset about this, I know. It was only a dream."

Ortheldo gently cleared his throat. "While he was…doing that to you, was he angry? Or was he laughing and…or something of the sort?"

"Oh, he was angry," she replied with a firm nod. "No doubt about that."

Ortheldo visibly relaxed at her response. He must have concluded something, but I was lost.

"Okay, your turn," Azrel suddenly said.

"My turn?" Ortheldo asked.

"Tell me about your nightmare."

"Oh," Ortheldo shrugged. "It wasn't as bad as yours, and I don't remember much of it. All I remember is that my brother somehow came back to life and butchered all my friends and my parents right before my eyes."

Before I could take that to heart, Ortheldo winked at me so Azrel couldn't see, and I had to hold back another smile.

"Oh, Gods," Azrel said, taking his hands into hers. "Are you okay?"

"I'm fine." he replied and adopted a sad, innocent expression. "I just wish Rabryn hadn't forced me to tell you. Do you think less of me now?"

"Of course not," she said gently. "I count on you for comfort when I need it. I'll never hesitate to comfort you if you need me."

That look came into Ortheldo's eyes again—that look where a total stranger could tell from ten thousand miles away that he was hopelessly and deeply in love with my sister. To be looked at like that would have burned a hole into the soul of any other woman in the world, but not Azrel. She was blind to it. What baffled me more was how Ortheldo could keep such strong feelings inside. It seemed to me he should be on every mountain peak, screaming at the very top of his lungs about how much he loved her so the entire world could hear him.

Our meal was set before us. "Ohhh," we all crooned in pleasure at the sight of it. We each voiced our sincere thanks to the server girl and dug in heartily.

Halfway through, I went rigid. I felt those cold, dark blue eyes on me again. I subtly shifted my eyes around the common, looking for him. I didn't see him. But I felt those eyes on us as we finished our meal. I felt them as we gathered our horses. And I still felt them after we'd been on the road for more than two hours.

TWENTY-SEVEN

"What do you think?"

He shook his head and then bowed it until his chin was resting on his chest. "I don't know, and I dare not guess for fear of Lord Hathum's wrath. He nearly choked the life out of me the last time I gave him false hope."

"Jonoic, please trust me. It's her."

He looked up at me like a scared child. "You said yourself that you searched her mind and found nothing."

I tried to keep my composure. If I lost control, he surely wouldn't take my information to Lord Hathum. "You know how conniving and powerful the White Warrior is. She may have somehow hidden her magic if…"

"Not possible," he interrupted with the most confidence he'd displayed since I'd called him to this mental meeting.

I bit back an urge to scream at him. "Jonoic, I know you fear Lord Hathum. Who wouldn't? But you must trust me. Take my information to him. Tell him that he was right about the White Warriors companions and that only he can find her magic in…"

"I can't," he sobbed.

My thread of patience finally snapped. I punched him in the mouth, knocking him down. "Stop blubbering, you damn fool! You sound like a little girl who just wet herself on stage!"

He looked up at me with big, frightened eyes, and I realized just how afraid of Lord Hathum he was. No matter what I said right now, he wasn't going to tell the Lord my information.

"Fine!" I shouted. "Take me to Lord Hathum then! I'll tell him myself, and I'll take the heat if I'm wrong, which I'm not!"

Jonoic shook his head. "You can't get to Lord Hathum's mind without my leave, and if you're wrong, he'll kill me for delivering you to him."

I clenched my fists at my sides and absently started cracking my knuckles, desperately trying not to lose my temper on him.

"Please, Glessar," he said pathetically and finally stood up. "I just need proof. Then I will be more than happy to take you to his

Lordship."

I relaxed a bit. I couldn't blame him for fearing Lord Hathum so much. I didn't deal with him on a daily basis, so I wasn't fully aware of what he was like. Jonoic was.

"And seeing the white tears would be enough?"

Jonoic's mood brightened. "Have you seen them?"

"No, but I almost did. I made her cry once. I can do it again. It should be easy enough, if that blasted Salynn stays out of my way."

"What about the Dwellingpath heir that Lord Hathum foresaw?"

I smiled smugly. "That whelp may have royal blood, but he's no King. He's little threat." I considered Jonoic again. "Will you not reconsider telling the Lord that his visions proved true? He may accept that and try to find the magic in her that I couldn't."

The big man shook his head. "Lord Hathum isn't too keen on his visions right now. He recently checked on two people that he foresaw crossing the White Warrior's path, and both have vanished. He's now developing a way to look at all his servants' last few minutes before they vanish so that he might know what happened to them. He was hoping to also see what happen to the two already missing."

"Which two are lost?"

"Jaravel, a known criminal, and Ibalissa, a peasant girl he mentally tortured to ensure her cooperation."

"He doesn't know what happened to them?"

His brows drew together almost defensively. "They'd have to be dead to prevent Lord Hathum from entering their minds."

It made sense, but my patience was running thin dealing with him. "Very well, I'll get the proof Lord Hathum wants. You just be ready to take me to him when I call you back to a mental meeting."

I was about to pull back from my subconscious to end the conversation when Jonoic called my name. I looked back to see a sly grin on his face. "Is she attractive?"

I kept my face neutral. "Why?"

He shrugged. "I know Lord Hathum, and if this woman is indeed the White Warrior, I'm sure it would please him if she's attractive."

I smiled. That was certainly the truth. "She is beyond a sight his eyes have ever seen," I stated honestly. "And I know how long he's lived."

Jonoic's grin widened excitedly. "Can you show her to me?"

I smiled and then concentrated, bringing forth the image of the woman I was right now watching. Jonoic's jaw fell open. She had hypnotizing bright blue eyes, long brown hair down to the middle of her back, and peach porcelain skin that shone with rainwater. The shape of her body was exposed through the wet clothes that clung to her sinful curves. She smiled right then, and Jonoic dropped to his knees. She ran her fingers through her soaking wet hair and laughed as she pulled it to the side. Even I felt my knees tremble. If Lord Hathum wanted the White Warrior to be attractive, he was going to be the furthest from disappointed he could possibly get.

"That's the White Warrior?" Jonoic said in a breath.

I could only nod, not wanting to look away. My eyes went to her shapely hips and then settled on the sword at her left side. That was the sword my Lord Hathum was after, the sword that held the element of the Light Gods, the power of Goodness. My jaw tightened. It was so near, yet so far away.

"Can I hear her? Please let me hear her," Jonoic begged pathetically.

I curled my lip in disgust and pulled the image back out of view, leaving us surrounded by blackness again. The man looked distressed beyond reason as the image disappeared.

"I can't hear her now. I'm too far away. If I open this mental meeting to sound, all you'll hear is thunder and the rain pouring down. Speaking of which, I'm getting soaked. I'll call you back here when I have Lord Hathum's proof."

Jonoic barely nodded a response as he stared at the spot where the image had been. I found myself also wishing it was still there, but I had the real thing waiting for me on the outside.

I focused my eyes and slowly came back into myself, keeping watch on the three travelers as they led their horses over the flat clearing. That rotten Salynn immediately turned to look over his shoulder again in search of me. Too bad he was looking in the wrong direction.

I twisted my mouth to the side in annoyance. Somehow he

could sense me nearby. The other two were oblivious, and the Salynn didn't have the guts to tell them about it. I'd have to wait until the Salynn was away from her before initiating another night terror. Just one of her white tears was all I needed to see, and he couldn't be with her every second of every day.

I turned my horse around and continued on the path ahead of them.

TWENTY-EIGHT

RABRYN

"What is the matter with you?" Azrel cried out.

The storm hadn't ended by a long shot, but the wind had slowed. Now the rain just fell in straight heavy sheets instead of whipping at us from all sides.

"We couldn't stay north of Crox Path because of the landslides! What would you suggest we do?" Ortheldo cried in response, holding his arms out to his sides.

"A baboon wouldn't have come up with this harebrained solution!"

Ortheldo rolled his eyes and rested an elbow on top of his horse's saddle. "Well, aren't we *quite* the drama queen today?"

I chuckled at their little lovers' spat. They really were cute together. I let them have it out as I looked through the rain at Narcatertus. It was set widely at the bottom of the hill where we stood now. It was big—huge, in fact! I never knew one place could be so big. It spanned from the bottom of the hill out about ten square miles before the mountains rose up behind it.

Even more impressive, visible behind the Mongerst Mountains, was the top half of the most monstrous mountain I'd ever seen: Rocksheloc. A few days ago, we could see Rocksheloc's peak just over the Mongerst mountain range. Now, being only a few days away, I could see just how enormous that mountain was.

I turned my eyes onto Narcatertus again. It didn't look so bad, though a little overwhelming in size, but I saw no harm in staying one night. Then again, Azrel hadn't seen the harm in staying a few hours at Blesska, and I still felt the lingering harm from that encounter.

I looked over my shoulder again, though I knew I wouldn't be able to see more than I had when I'd looked the first thousand times. Thankfully, we hadn't had any more adventures at any inns since leaving Blesska more than a week ago.

"You know what they do to Salynns who pass through here!" Azrel hollered.

"Whoa, whoa!" I interrupted before Ortheldo could reply. "Is that what you've been worried about?"

"What?"

"You wanted to avoid Narcatertus because I'm a Salynn?"

She looked at me as if I were hopelessly thick. "Well, yeah!"

I sighed and gave her a pitying look. Then I closed my eyes and reached into the soft core within myself, the soft center of my soul where the life force of my magic lay. I caressed the outside of it, which was all I'd learned to do, then opened my eyes to see their astonished faces.

I grinned gleefully as I stood in my human form. "You both have a really poor memory."

Ortheldo's astonishment turned into a triumphant grin as he looked again at Azrel, who glared hard at me and then at him. I had to bite my tongue to keep from laughing out loud at her expression.

"Shut up and walk!" Azrel hollered, thrusting her arm out toward Narcatertus.

They both passed me, and I took up the rear. It felt really strange to be in my human form, even after the short amount of time I'd spent as a Salynn. The ends of my hair that had before fallen to between my shoulder blades now made the back of my neck itch. The shorter pieces of my hair in front scratched my cheeks. The boots I wore felt heavy and clumsy compared to the light Salynn shoes I was now used to, and I wore a simple maroon tunic, gray pants, and cloak.

Oh, well. We'd only be here one night. I could survive that long.

————

Noise exploded in my sensitive ears as we crossed the town borders. Though it was near evening, and rain still poured down, it was impossibly busy! The main dirt road was wide enough to allow two wagons to pass each other with a wide gap between them, but the hordes of people congested it so much that barely one wagon could get by.

Wooden buildings lined each side of the main road. Some buildings were tall, some were short, some were square, some were triangular. They were all so close together that there was barely any room for alleyways and other roads between them. Between the buildings were heaps and heaps of garbage and waste and some shady and unsavory activity it was probably best I didn't understand.

People went about their business, to and fro, in every direction, stepping in mud puddles and cracks in the wooden sidewalks as if they weren't even there.

It was utter chaos, everywhere.

As we led our horses along the road, I almost felt suffocated by the body heat emitted from this place. We couldn't take three steps without rubbing shoulders with someone. Wagons squeaked by, horses clopped past, people stood and talked and walked, never apologizing for bumping into us or even acknowledging our presence.

Some women were standing at the corners, seeming to approach any man that happened by them. One approached me and another Ortheldo, without even a glance at Azrel. The two of them looked younger than me!

"Well, hello, dahlin'," the girl in front of me said, and pressed her thick bosom to my chest. "You gonna be lonely tonight, honey?"

Before I could say no, Azrel gripped both girls' hair in her fists, and with a powerful yank, laid them flat on their backs on the muddy ground. I looked up and around immediately, expecting someone to come running to their rescue, but no one so much as glanced our way.

Azrel gave the girls a tight, mirthless grin. "We're all set, ladies," she said and then stepped between them, leading Forfirith around.

"Why did they do that?" I asked.

"They're called prostitutes," Azrel replied. "Men pay the women to sleep with them."

"What?" I cried. "That's absurd!"

She shrugged. "It's a living, for them anyway."

I wrinkled my nose. I'd never heard of such a thing.

A fight suddenly broke out between two big men on the other side of the road. My eyes desperately searched the area again for anyone who might help, but no one made a move to intervene. Instead, some people formed a circle around the fight and began to cheer it on. Others looked away and went about their business. Farther down on our side of the road, an elderly man was thrown out of a window, landing at Ortheldo's feet, battered and bloody. I nearly jumped out of my skin, but he and Azrel went on as if this was normal behavior.

"He's dead," Ortheldo said as he stepped around the body. Azrel gave a jerky nod.

I swallowed hard. "We're not staying here, are we?" I asked, though it was a ridiculous question. I now realized why Azrel deliberately wanted to avoid Narcatertus.

"Yup!" Azrel said without sincere excitement. "You can thank Ortheldo for this."

"What? Me?" he countered. "This isn't my fault! Blame the rain!"

"Uh-huh," Azrel said with her tongue in her cheek. "Whatever you say, pal." Ortheldo sighed heavily and looked away with a roll of his eyes, not bothering to argue.

Suddenly, two men came directly at us. They looked at us in front of them, stared at us really, but made no attempt to move around us even though we had three horses. I sighed and was about to lead Eleclya around them when Azrel placed her hand on my forearm to stop me. She fixed a determined glare on the two men. When they were a few feet in front of us, Azrel picked up her pace and plowed between them, separating them aggressively as they stumbled around her, then around Forfirith, and then around Ortheldo, me, and our horses.

"Bitch!" one yelled from behind.

Azrel's response was an obscene hand gesture over her head without a glance back at them.

"Being courteous and polite here won't earn you respect, Rabryn. It might even cause you more trouble than it's worth. People here, first of all, aren't used to it. Second, city folk view it as a weakness."

I nodded, though I didn't completely understand that concept.

We soon stopped in front of a ratty-looking inn. After tying our horses to the hitching posts out front, we headed up the short set of stairs to the wooden sidewalk. Azrel and Ortheldo both groaned their displeasure before they pushed open the thin wooden door.

We didn't take more than two steps into the rancid smelling common before the crowd fell silent. Everyone stared at us, particularly Azrel. I could kind of understand why. The women I'd seen here so far had thick, round figures, and filthy, tired appearances. Azrel, however, was very lean, with a soft, angular face.

With her jaw set, Azrel started for the bar on the left side of the room. The men broke out into whistles and cheers and shouted provocative comments at her. A few made kissing faces at her as she passed. Some tried to make a grab for her but were stopped by my or Ortheldo's icy glares.

The smoky pit of the inn was full of barrel tables with round, crudely cut tabletops. The chairs looked frail enough to splinter under the men's bulky weight. Not a full foot could have stood between each table, and it was so packed that some people stood with their mugs of ale or beer.

Azrel shouldered her way between two men sitting at the bar. "We need a room," she said plainly to the huge innkeeper.

Beside him stood a lanky young man with a mat of curly red hair. He looked at Azrel with wide eyes, as if he'd never seen a woman before in his life. Both wore aprons that looked like they hadn't been washed in months.

The innkeeper stared at Azrel's chest shamelessly. "We're full."

The young man on Azrel's left was staring at her. He looked about my age, maybe a little older, with pin straight black hair that was cut one length at his jaw. He was very clean, unlike most of the people in this place, with a pale, sort of beautiful face, and he wore red velvet robes that were decent looking. He had a thin build, too, unlike the burly, barrel-chested men that appeared to populate this town. He had large, fiery brown eyes that seemed to have more depth than he wanted anyone to know about.

He stood from his barstool and ran his hand up the back of Azrel's thigh, over her bottom, and up under her shirt to caress the small of her back. "You can stay in my room," he whispered seductively in her ear.

The common room broke out into laughs and cheers for the young man, which encouraged him on. He licked my sister's earlobe and pulled it gently between his teeth.

Ortheldo looked ready to explode. I just stuck my tongue in my cheek and smiled. I knew how my sister would handle this.

Azrel turned to him with a sweet smile, which made

Ortheldo's eyes go wide with disbelief. She ran her hand lightly up the boy's chest. "Think you can handle a woman in your bed, young one?"

The room exploded again in laughter and hollers.

The boy cupped Azrel's bottom with both hands, and with a small jerk he pulled her against him. "You'd better believe it, sweetheart."

"Good. There's just one tiny problem, though," she said seductively, bringing her hand up over his shoulder, and behind his head.

"What's that?"

She grabbed a fistful of his hair, and in one fluid motion, dropped down to one knee, with the boy bent backward over her raised thigh. His head was tilted so far back he could barely breathe. The entire room watched with wide eyes.

Azrel brought her glowering face down to his. "The problem is that the only part of my body I'd let near your twig dick is the heel of my boot." She bent his head farther back. "Do I make myself clear?" Choking, the young man managed to nod. Azrel's brow twitched up. "Good."

She then pushed him up, and as she stood, she drove his forehead into the edge of the bar counter. Blood exploded from his face, and Azrel let him crumble to the floor, unconscious. The entire common let out a startled shout. She crouched next to the boy and rummaged through his pockets.

She stood with a key in her hand and gave a tight, mirthless grin to the innkeeper. "He needs to see an Herbest all of the sudden, so we'll take his room if you don't mind." The innkeeper shook his head vigorously. "Good. Wouldn't want the poor boy to have paid for nothing."

With a fake smile lingering on her face, Azrel stuffed the key into her pocket, and we headed for the narrow stairway in the back right corner of the room with every pair of eyes watching us. We were halfway up the stairs when the soft noise of conversation finally resumed.

"My lady! My lady!" we heard above the noise.

We all stopped and turned. The redheaded young man from behind the counter bolted up the stairs after us. He stopped in his tracks halfway between us and the bottom, his gray eyes filled with what looked like admiration.

As soon as he realized he was staring hard at my sister, he flushed bright red and looked down shyly. "That was incredible, what you did."

Azrel and I glanced at each other, silently acknowledging the strangeness of this boy. "Thank you."

"He had no right to touch you like he did. No right! Why, if I'd had the gall, I would have given him a lesson in respecting a beautiful lady myself."

Azrel forced a smile on her face. "Is that why you called after me, or was there a reason?"

"Oh, of course," he said, turning even more red. "I thought you should know, well, the boy you just injured—that's Addredoc, the son of Thrawyn."

"So?"

"Um, well, Thrawyn is the best known and most highly skilled sword master in these parts. He may come after you, my lady, to even the score."

Azrel walked down a few steps and rested her hand gently on his cheek. He froze for a moment and looked like a lovesick puppy as he stared up at her. "What is your name?"

"L-Loir, my fair lady."

"Loir, thank you very much for your warning." She bent down and kissed his forehead.

He let out a long breath and smiled. "You're—you're welcome."

Suddenly, someone downstairs shouted Loir's name. The boy jumped and then quickly turned and booked it back into the kitchen, looking up at Azrel one last time before he disappeared from view.

"Well, that was interesting," I said as we continued up the stairs.

"I thoroughly enjoyed that myself. Though I expected Ortheldo to jump in any second."

Both of us smiled at him, and he slightly blushed. "I was going to, but Rabryn didn't seem too upset, so I figured you'd handle it." We all chuckled.

When we reached the top of the stairs, Azrel looked at the tag attached to the key. "Room four."

We unlocked the door to find that that room had been used but wasn't a mess. The bed was next to the door on the right, the couch against the left wall. A closet was in the back left corner and a chair was on the back wall facing the foot of the bed. The windows were on the right wall. Some of Addredoc's clothes were draped neatly over the arm of the chair, and the wire bed was made. It would do for a night.

Azrel stripped down to her underclothes, and Ortheldo and I stripped out of everything but our pants. "I get the couch this time," I said.

Azrel nodded without complaint, but Ortheldo shot a nervous glance at my sister, like he did every time it was their turn to share the bed. The sun was still a couple hours from setting, but she and Ortheldo wanted to get a very early start, as in a pre-dawn early start, before the streets became too crowded.

"Goodnight, boys," she said in a sigh as she lay down on one side of the bed.

"Night."

"Goodnight," Ortheldo said. He looked at me intently as he as he closed the distance between us. "I'm kind of hungry. Do you want to get something to eat?"

By the look he was giving me, I knew he really meant, "I need to talk to you alone, now!"

"Sure." I glanced at Azrel, who was already asleep, before stepping into the hall with him and pulling the door closed. "What's wrong?" I asked.

"I've needed to talk to you for days." He looked up and down the hallway. "I know you can sense that man nearby, the one from Blesska. Is he here?"

I shook my head. "I haven't felt him since we entered this town, but that doesn't mean he's not close by."

Ortheldo nodded. "Why do you think he wanted to see her so badly that night?"

I blew out a breath and shrugged. "All I can think of is that he wanted to see her tears."

"Why do you think so?" His tone told me he had his own ideas about the answers to these questions and he wanted to confirm them with me.

I shrugged and started down the long hallway toward some

chairs at the far end. "I don't know," I said, sitting down. "My only guess is that someone is on the hunt for her—not the necklace, but her, the White Warrior." Ortheldo nodded and sat in the chair beside me. His expression was intense, and I couldn't help asking, "You know something, don't you?"

"I only have guesses."

"Well, tell me. I've been wondering why you wanted to know about Azrel's nightmare so badly."

He straightened and faced me. "All right, you know the bulk of Hathum's magic is the power of mind corruption, right?"

I flinched and stared at him, stunned. "Um, no. I don't really spend my leisure time studying up on the entity of all Evil."

"Well, it is. It's what he does best. He gets into people's minds in different ways and can do different things with them."

My heart jumped up between my ears. "Okay, wait. Before you get to your point, tell me how in the Shadow Gods' Lair do we protect ourselves from magic like that?"

He shook his head. "Details on that later. Just know we're safe right now."

"Right now?"

"Mind corruption magic has its limitations. You have to be corruptible, and we're not right now."

"How do you know?"

"Just trust me. We're safe. But I think Hathum might have taught his minions some mind magic. Not full corruption, but the ability to enter minds for lower-level purposes, like seeing things about the person whose mind they've entered."

I narrowed my eyes, still worrying about how someone could remain unsusceptible to a magic that took over the mind. I'd never heard of such magic!

"Bear with me," Ortheldo said. "I think you're right. I think Hathum is on the hunt for the White Warrior. He wants her sword badly because it's the only thing standing between him and complete victory. Whether he knows about the necklace, I can't say, but the sword is far more important to him than the necklace. I think the man from Blesska is one of Hathum's hunters."

"But why would Hathum have to be hunting for her? Isn't he all-powerful? Can't he just conjure up a spell to point her out?"

"The White Warrior's magic has been inactive for 3,000

years. Probably during the majority of that time, Hathum was healing from his creation of The Nameless One, which sapped him of almost his complete life force. My theory is that he lost track of the first White Warrior, Azrel's father, while he took time to heal, and now he can't find Azrel, the new White Warrior. I don't know if he's aware that Azrel's father is dead or not. He might not even know who he's looking for, Azrel's father, or Azrel."

"Well, if this guy is one of Hathum's hunters, he's sniffing a little too close. Do you think Hathum knows who she is now?"

He gave me a wary look. "I think if Hathum knew who Azrel was, she would already be dead."

My brows dropped. "So this hunter in Blesska found her and Hathum doesn't know? Why would the hunter keep it from him?"

"I don't know. But—"

"How did the hunter even know where to look for the White Warrior in the first place?" I asked urgently.

I was becoming more and more concerned for my sister. I really didn't like how close Hathum might be getting to her. This hunter, whoever he was, was directly responsible for putting her in danger, and that enraged and terrified me at the same time.

"Remember what Beldorn said back in the woods of The Pitt? Any pure enough power of Shadow can feel the presence of an equality pure power of Light and vice versa. The two extremes are constantly at odds. Both are like a force of invisible pressure on the other. They pull and rub at each other naturally, creating supernatural friction just by existing. Hathum and Azrel are each other's natural opposite. Hathum, however, has much more experience as a Shadow Wizard, while Azrel is still very new to being the White Warrior. I don't know if she can feel him when he use his Shadow magic, but I'd bet our last coin that he can feel her when she uses her Light magic."

I rubbed my forehead firmly with the heel of my hand as the dire situation started to sink in. This hunter was an immediate threat to her.

"If Hathum and this hunter can feel Azrel's Light, how come they haven't attacked us yet? What are they waiting for? And what does this have to do with Azrel's nightmare?"

"I think the hunter you feel following us used his power to search for any evidence of the White Warrior in Azrel's mind."

"What? Why would he have to do that?"

Ortheldo shrugged. "Maybe Hathum wants proof of who she is. Azrel rarely uses her magic. She's been told to hide it since the day she received it. Because she so rarely uses it, she doesn't give Hathum a lot of her Light to pick up on."

I nodded as understanding dawned on me. "That's why he's searching for her." Ortheldo nodded. "That's the reason for the hunter." Then panic set in, and my eyes went wide. "But that nightmare! If the hunter got into her mind like that, he must have proof of who she is now!"

Ortheldo held up his hands as a gesture for me to stay calm. "That's why I had to know the details of Azrel's nightmare."

"And?" I pressed. It felt like a dam had broken in my chest, and a flood of worry and panic for my sister filled me up to my eyeballs.

"I don't think any of them know exactly who Azrel is yet."

"Why not?"

He shrugged. "I have no doubt that the hunter got into Azrel's mind. I think the snakes represent his power as it swarmed around her mind, looking for evidence of the White Warrior. Afterwards when…when he was…having his way with her"—he cleared his throat—"she said he was angry. I think he was angry because he couldn't find anything. Also, consider the fact that he came into the room afterward. You and I agree it was probably so he could see her white tears. It was a desperate attempt to get physical proof because the mind search failed."

My face scrunched in confusion. "But how could he not see proof of the White Warrior in her mind? It's who she is."

"Is it?"

I pondered that for the longest time. Then cold realization washed over me. As I thought about it longer, my face went slack when a single memory came to my mind.

"Beldorn…" I managed, and Ortheldo nodded.

I was about to open this for further discussion when I felt that shadow of dread fill my mind. My keen hearing allowed me to detect Azrel's small whimper from our room.

"Something's wrong!" I cried and bolted to the door with Ortheldo on my heels. I tried to turn the knob. "It's locked!"

Panic gripped me. I desperately yanked on that knob while

Ortheldo pounded on the door.

"Azrel! Open the door!" I screamed.

"Azrel! Azrel!" Ortheldo hollered, pounding his fists into the door.

We frantically kicked and pushed and pulled. We drove our shoulders into it numerous times, making as much noise as we could so she'd wake up before she could cry.

"Azrel!" I hollered.

No. Not my sister. I had to protect my sister!

"What's wrong?" a frightened voice asked from behind us.

We both spun around to see Loir.

"Do you have keys?"

"Do you have spare keys?"

Our shouts made him jump. "Y-yes, of course. What's…?"

"Give us the key!" we both yelled.

Loir jumped again and shakily pulled a ring of keys from his belt. Ortheldo snatched them away and frantically searched for the one labeled "4."

Azrel began to cry.

I sucked in a breath and held it. *Get in! Get in! Get in!* kept screaming in my ears. If the hunter saw her tears, Hathum, a powerful, ancient, ruthless entity of Shadow, would come crashing down on my sister's head!

Finally, Ortheldo found the key and stuck it into the lock. When it clicked, I nearly knocked him over as I ran into the room. Azrel wasn't my first thought, though. I pulled out my knife from under the bed and looked around the room while Ortheldo kneeled at Azrel side.

Where was he? I knew he was here somewhere. My jaw hurt from how hard my teeth were clenched. My muscles were taut and I was ready to kill anything that came near me. I pulled open the closet—nothing. Then, suddenly, I felt the wind on my back and spun around. The window was wide open with the rain still pouring down. I ran to it and looked out.

I instantly felt those cold eyes on me. I searched the crowded street, using my keen Salynn eyesight to my advantage.

There he was—standing stone still in the middle of the busy main road, looking up at the window where I stood. He gave me an arrogant, toothy grin and raised his hand, wiggling his fingers in a knowing wave.

My breath caught, and I spun around. Azrel was curled up in Ortheldo's arms with her face pressed against his chest. Ortheldo looked up at me somberly and pulled away from Azrel enough to show me the white tears dripping down her face.

TWENTY-NINE

"NO!" I screamed. Fear for my sister devoured me so quickly that I couldn't even think. I saw red—his blood. His blood would save her life.

I spun toward the window again. I leapt onto the sill and out onto the overhanging roof and then went quickly to the edge and jumped down to the muddy ground.

"Rabryn!" Ortheldo called after me, but I wasn't listening.

He couldn't live!

Ignoring the freezing rain on my bare upper body and the cold mud under my bare feet, I searched the crowd. I finally spotted him walking down an alleyway across the street. My teeth clenched, and my fist tightened around my knife. It was either his death or my sister's, and it would be his *long* before Azrel's if I had anything to say about it!

Two wagons crossed in opposite directions in front of me, and then I ran. Shouldering through the crowd, I made my way toward him. My soundless Salynn steps didn't alert him that I was coming, and I tackled him hard to the ground. I lost my knife, but I didn't care. I didn't really want to use it anyway. I wanted to beat him to death. As we got to our feet, my fist flew out and broke open his mouth in an explosion of blood. He stumbled back into some garbage cans, and I was quickly on top of him. I slammed my fist into his jaw, one, two, three, four times before he managed to gather his senses enough to throw me off him. I hit the wall of a building behind me, smacking the back of my head, but I felt no pain. With my teeth bared, I waited for him to come at me.

He only made it about halfway when the narrow edge of a wooden paddle came flying into view. A sickening thunk filled my ears, followed by the sound of splattering gore. I cringed a little when I saw the hunter fall to the ground with barely a head left.

Shifting my gaze to the source holding the paddle, my face went slack at the sight of two intense green eyes. Big, beautiful eyes, yet terrifying at the same time. They were as unearthly and overwhelming as Azrel had said, seeming to radiate with an unseen light.

I tried to swallow past the lump in my throat and gave a goofy smirk. "I'm glad you're on our side."

The corners of the stranger's eyes went up as if there was a smile hidden behind that thick, tan cloth around her face. She carelessly tossed the bloody lumber to the ground and then placed her hands on her hips. One eyebrow went up inquisitively as her eyes rested on my naked upper body and bare feet. I blushed. She probably thought I was mad, being half naked and barefoot in the rain like this.

I indicated the hunter's dead body with my chin. "I was in a hurry."

She laughed. Though it was muffled, it sounded light and gentle. Suddenly I found myself mentally begging her to take off her tan hood and mask so I could see her.

"Who are you?" I asked.

She indicated to my body with her chin. "You'd better head indoors, handsome. We don't want you to catch cold."

I felt my knees start to tremble at the graceful, fluid sound of her voice. When she had come to warn us about Ibalissa, her yells had come across a distance. Choked by some emotion I couldn't understand, I managed to nod, but before I'd even finished the gesture, she disappeared.

I was stunned at first, looking up and down the alley, seeing no sign if her, or any sign that she'd even *been* there, save for the dead body. I realized my heart was racing and my lungs hurt because I'd forgotten to breathe. I smiled, thinking about how I'd made her laugh, and that she'd called me handsome. When some strength had returned to my legs, I made my way back to the inn.

Before I'd even crossed the street, Azrel, Ortheldo and Loir came running out to meet me. They were fussing and asking a thousand questions, but I didn't hear a word they were saying. I was lost in thought of those green eyes and that lovely laugh.

"Rabryn!" Azrel shouted, cupping my face in her hands.

"Huh?" I finally focused on her concerned blue eyes. "Oh, hi, Sis."

Her brows dropped and she smacked my bare, wet shoulder.

"Ow!" I said and rubbed it. Cold water made skin extremely sensitive!

"'Hi, Sis?' That's all you have to say?"

Ortheldo stepped up beside her. "Are you okay?"

Before I could answer, Azrel gasped. "You're bleeding!"

I looked down at my hand. My knuckles were bleeding. "Oh," I said, not really caring about what was happening outside of my mind, where the tan stranger wasn't with me.

"'Oh?!' What's the matter with you? What happened?"

Loir came running out of the inn with a blanket and threw it around my shoulders. I shuddered at the sudden warmth and pulled it tightly around me, only now realizing how cold it was out here.

"Is that better, Master Rabryn?"

"Yes, thank you."

Azrel gave me a shove toward the inn. "Get inside before you freeze to death. Then you can tell me what happened."

I found myself smiling about those green eyes and her laugh, despite the fact that Azrel was yelling at me like this. Where had she come from? What was her name? I made a mental note to ask her the next time I saw her.

A sudden commotion in the street made us all stop before entering the inn. We looked down the main road to see a heavily armed group of men coming toward us. They were the least filthy bunch I'd seen so far in this scummy town. They looked like a group I would take for soldiers, but brutal. They deliberately shoved people out of their way who weren't quick enough to move out of their path.

The man leading the cavalry was an imposing figure. He was a little taller than Ortheldo and had broader shoulders, but Ortheldo was far more muscular. This man was a little on the slight side. He wore five swords on his body. One large sword was at his left hip, two more slightly smaller ones were on his back, and he had two daggers strapped to the outside of each thigh. Over his black leggings, shiny black boots came up to under his kneecaps. He wore a dark blue coat that came down to the middle of his thighs. It had two rows of gold buttons running all the way down the front, and he wore a red sash around his waist.

He seemed heedless of the rain, and he was angry. Oh, he was angry. His face was set in a grim, unmoving expression, but his widened gray eyes betrayed his rage, and his face was so red that I half expected his pencil-thin mustache and his short black hair to catch fire.

As the crowd wisely parted, a familiar figure walked with hunched shoulders and bowed head next to the proud man in the lead. It was Addredoc with what had to be his sword master father. Great.

"It's Thrawyn," Loir whispered, confirming my thoughts.

All of us faced the approaching party. Azrel looked bored, crossing her arms and heaving a sigh. Ortheldo's muscles were tense, and his jaw clenched in preparation for a fight. I just waited to see what was about to happen.

Addredoc bore the expression of an abused puppy and had a bandage wrapped around his head. I couldn't help but to notice that walking seemed to take effort for him.

The big man in the lead, Thrawyn, grabbed his son's red robes in two fists. "Where is he?"

Addredoc looked terrified and pointed in our direction. Thrawyn looked at us and stormed in our direction, nearly dropping his son flat in the mud.

Thrawyn stopped in front of Ortheldo. "You did this to my boy?"

Ortheldo was going to say yes. I knew he was. He was going to say yes to protect Azrel. I glanced at Addredoc, and from the pleading look in his brown eyes, I could practically *hear* him begging Ortheldo to take the blame. But, unfortunately for him, I knew my sister better than that.

Azrel pushed herself between the two men, facing Thrawyn. "I did."

Thrawyn regarded her with disgust. "Step aside, princess. I have to kill your boyfriend." He raised a hand to shove her aside.

"Touch me, and I'll do to you what I did to your disrespectful son."

Thrawyn narrowed his eyes, studying her hard expression, considering what she was saying. He glanced at Ortheldo behind her and then back at Azrel. His eyes bulged and he drew back a fist, but instead of striking Azrel as I'd expected, he spun around with a scream and slammed his huge fist into Addredoc's mouth. Addredoc went down like a sack of bricks. Everyone cringed or gawked at the sound of his jaw splitting in half.

Thrawyn reached down and picked up his barely conscious,

heavily bleeding son off the ground by the front of his robes. "You let *a woman* beat you up?"

He brought his fist back and sent it crashing full force into the young man's face again. I blanched at the sound of his facial bones getting pulverized. Then Thrawyn hit him again.

"Hey!" Azrel screamed as he brought his fist back a fourth time. Azrel grabbed his forearm in mid-swing and, unbelievably, stopped him from busting Addredoc's face again.

I couldn't keep my jaw from hitting the ground—everyone's did.

Thrawyn's sharp glare at her could have cut stone. But it was no match for the dangerous look in Azrel's eyes.

"Hit him again, and I'll break your arm."

The rage and hate in his expression vanished into a loud belly laugh. Oh, it was not a smart idea to laugh at Azrel, especially when she made a threat. Azrel hated being laughed at, no matter what the circumstances, and she wasn't forgiving of anyone who did so.

Thrawyn let go of Addredoc, who crumpled lifelessly to the mud, and lifted an open palm to slap Azrel. I clenched my teeth and nearly grinned, knowing what this hateful man was in for. As his hand came down, Azrel's arm went up, blocking the blow, and her other fist shot forward and slammed him hard in the mouth. The crowd gasped and jumped back with a start as Thrawyn stumbled backward with blood dribbling from his lip. He touched his fingertips to the blood and examined it, rubbing it in his fingers as if to make sure it was really there.

"Now that you know what I can do with my bare hands, care to take it a step further?"

She pulled out her Salynn blade from the holder attached to her thigh and dragged her tongue along the broad side of it! Even I blanched at the gesture!

Thrawyn's eyes went wide for a moment, but he quickly composed himself and scowled. "I don't have time for this. My son needs to see an Herbest."

Azrel crossed one arm over her chest, rested her other elbow on top of it, and lightly touched the tip of her Salynn blade to her temple. "Gee, I wonder why that is."

Thrawyn only deepened his scowl, his pride apparently

bruised enough for one day. He picked up Addredoc, who was just coming to, and threw him back in the direction they'd come. Addredoc stumbled and fell to his knees in the mud. His father roughly pulled him up again by the back of his robes and shoved him on forward. Addredoc nearly fell again but forced himself to stay on his feet.

I felt horrible for Addredoc about having a father like that. How had the boy survived this many years? He looked about nineteen.

I was suddenly aware that Azrel was looking at me, and not in a soft manner. "Move!" she barked, thrusting her arm out toward the inn.

I scowled at her back as she headed for the building. I hated it when she spoke to me like I was four years old.

"You should talk to her about that."

I realized Ortheldo had stepped up beside me. I sneered at Azrel as she disappeared in the door. "Talk to her about what?"

I didn't mean to take my aggravation out on him. I was just tired of Azrel's nonsense.

"Treating you like a simpleton, incapable of thinking without her aid."

I pressed my lips together and sighed, only a little surprised that he already knew what was bothering me. "What good would it do? She won't listen to me for the mere fact that she *doesn't* believe I can think for myself."

"She's a stubborn one," he said, nodding. "I've tried to talk to her about not babysitting you."

I looked at him. "You have?"

He nodded. "But she won't listen to me."

Big surprise, I wanted to say, but didn't.

If she wouldn't listen to Ortheldo, she certainly wasn't going to listen to me. I wouldn't bother challenging my sister. We'd never gotten into a serious argument before, and I doubted it was even worth the effort, considering her quick tongue, her merciless temper, and her overprotectiveness of me.

"I see it, Rabryn," Ortheldo suddenly said. I looked over at him. "I've seen it since the night you encountered those Feariters."

My brows dropped in confusion. "You've seen what?"

"You." I flinched slightly at the unexpected response. "The

real you. The Salynn you. It's been buried deep inside of you your entire life. Even as I look at you, now, your eyes are a little sharper, your instincts are surfacing, and your back is even a little straighter, stronger, with beginnings of the infamous Salynn pride."

He smiled, and I just stared at him. I couldn't believe he was saying this to me.

"You can't stay sheltered under her wing forever. It's impossible to keep someone safe inevitably out here anyway, even for Azrel."

I shrugged. "What do I do?"

He shrugged. "Tell her, first of all. She won't expect you to challenge her. Perhaps that will be a first step. But if you let her go on protecting you, she'll always think you need protection, and you'll get nowhere."

I was proud that the man I looked up to was treating me like a man. It replaced the childlike scolding I'd just gotten from my sister. Ortheldo clapped me on the shoulder, and we headed into the inn. I decided I'd tell Azrel the first chance I got. But after one look at her face as we entered the common area, my courage and conviction withered.

"Sit!" she barked, pointing her Salynn blade at a corner table. I grudgingly obeyed. "Loir, would you please bring my brother some hot soup?" She sat down and glanced at my bleeding hand. "And a bandage."

"Absolutely," Loir replied, then headed into the kitchen.

"Well?" Azrel asked eyeing me mercilessly.

"Well what?" I asked annoyed.

"Well, explain to me why you jumped out of a window, half naked, in a rainstorm."

Here was my opening! I couldn't believe it! She was actually *asking* for an explanation. "Because I—"

My hopes deflated when she closed her eyes and held her hand up. "If you tell me you did it for me, I'll rip your spine out."

I snapped my mouth shut. It was quiet for a long time.

"Well?" she barked impatiently.

"You said you would rip my spine out!"

Azrel let out an exasperated sigh and lowered her forehead to the table, putting her interlaced hands behind her head. "Why would you do such a stupid thing?"

I didn't bother answering. She was going to jump down my throat regardless of what I had to say.

She removed her hands and sat up suddenly looking tired. "Rabryn, I don't want you to risk yourself for me under *any* circumstances."

"Why?"

"Why?" she repeated looking perplexed. "Rabryn, I can't lose you on such a foolish errand. I can take care of myself. I'd rather die anyway then try to live without the one person left in the world who loves me."

I glanced at Ortheldo as pain shot through his eyes. He loved her, too. She just didn't let herself know it.

I looked back at Azrel. "Well then, we have a problem, Sis. Because I'd rather give my life to save yours." Her eyes narrowed, and I shook my head. "I don't know where you got this ridiculous notion that I should just stand by when your life is at stake. As if I could. If I have a chance to keep you from harm, I will."

"Don't!"

We stared at each other for a long, silent moment. I wouldn't cave on this issue. I couldn't. I did love my sister, and I would save her life if it came down to it. She needed to understand that.

Loir set a bowl of steaming hot soup in front of each of us and placed a long bandage next to Azrel. "I thought you might all need a little something to warm you up."

"Thank you, Loir," Azrel said without giving him a glance.

Loir remained a moment, looking like he wanted to be offered a seat. When no one did, he strode away.

Azrel picked up the bandage and starting dressing my bleeding knuckles. It was awkwardly silent.

When she finished, I picked up my spoon and took a bite of my soup. "Azrel," I began, feeling slightly braver than I had upon entering the inn. "You couldn't stop me from jumping out that window. If you're in danger, I will do everything in my power to prevent it from reaching you."

"I wasn't in danger!"

"You were!" I fired.

"I don't care!" she fired back, and it fell silent again. She eventually looked at Ortheldo. "Will you help me out here, please?"

He looked at her a second before leaning over his soup and picking up his spoon. "You're on your own, Azrel," he said with a shrug. "But just for the record, he's right."

"Right about what?" Azrel cried.

Ortheldo pointed his spoon at me after taking a bite. "He knows about the danger you were in as you slept. But you would already know that if you had any listening skills at all."

I was shocked by his vague insult but not angry. I felt proud that he had the guts to stand up to my sister.

"He was right to go out that window and kill that man."

Azrel, her face red hot, stood from her chair so quickly that it fell over. "You *killed* a man?"

My eyes went to my bowl, and I nodded. I wasn't going to bother explaining the tan stranger's involvement. She wouldn't have listened anyway.

"Why?" she barked, making me jump and making me wish I'd kept my mouth shut.

Ortheldo made the oddest sound then. He laughed. "Oh, *now* you want to listen? Well, wonders never cease."

He was looking directly into Azrel's eyes, which gave me strength—and blinded me to reason.

I scoffed a laugh, too. "Really. I wonder if I should bother wasting my breath, though. I'm sure she'll just scream at me anyway."

"She definitely doesn't care about the fact that you were saving her life."

My breath caught in my throat immediately when I realized what I'd just done. I looked up at Azrel quickly as memories of her abuse in The Pitt flashed across my mind, as the pain of betrayal filled her face.

We shouldn't have ganged up on her! We shouldn't have laughed at her! I knew better! I wanted to take my words back and hug my sister. I wanted to apologize. But I knew that wasn't going to happen.

Rage flooded her face. She screamed and picked up the edge of the table, throwing it onto its side with strength I didn't even know she possessed. Ortheldo and I jumped up to avoid the hot soup that went flying to the floor. She kicked another table over behind me, sending it through the air before it crashed onto its side five feet away. My insides twisted with wretchedness when she dropped to her knees and started pounded her fist into the wood. With only two bone-breaking punches, she put a gaping hole the size of her head into the barrel and then, with another scream, picked the entire thing up and heaved it against the wall. The wood splintered on contact. She was out the door before we could stop her.

Ortheldo and I exchanged glances before running toward the doorway. We got there just in time to see Forfirith's rear end as he galloped at full speed down the main street with Azrel hunched low over his back.

"What did you do?" a voice shouted from behind.

We turned around to see Loir scowling at us. Without waiting for a reply, he shouldered his way between us, mounted his own horse and galloped after Azrel.

"What *did* we do?" Ortheldo asked as we watched Loir disappear down the main road.

"We humiliated her," I choked out. "We ganged up on her. We made fun of her."

I couldn't believe I'd done that to Azrel. I knew better!

"Well, she does have a listening issue," Ortheldo stated as he headed back inside to clean up the mess Azrel left.

He said it so coldly, so heartlessly. I couldn't be angry with him, though. He didn't know what it was like for Azrel in The Pitt. I did. This was my fault. I knew what she'd been through. I shouldn't have let him talk to her like that. *I* shouldn't have talked to her like that.

I shook my head, nearly choking on the lump in my throat. "You don't understand," I said and went to help him.

I desperately tried not to think about what I might have just lost with my sister: closeness, love, an unconditional trust. Everything we had.

"Understand what?" Ortheldo asked bitterly.

I shook my head. "If you had lived with her in The Pitt, if you had seen what they put her through, you would understand what we've just done."

"What we've just done?" he asked spinning on me. "You make it sound like she's going to kill herself or something." All I did was look at him, and he saw it in my eyes and expression, and his eyes went wide. "You've got to be kidding me!"

I shook my head slowly, keeping my eyes firmly locked on his, as if I could push the images and memories of her torture there into his mind so he could see, so he could understand! "You can't begin to understand how she was treated, what I watched them do to her. Then you and I, the two people she trusts most in the world, the two people she was sure would never do things like that to her, make a laughing stock out of her. We find a reason for more ridicule and *make* her endure it." I felt myself getting angry—angry at myself, angry at the people of The Pitt, and then angry at myself again. "Can you imagine what that feels like? We've betrayed her, and now she feels like she has nothing."

He stared at me in confusion and horror, unable to grasp the entirety of what I was saying. No one really could. I decided to put it into terms he would understand. "Ortheldo, you may have just lost her forever." His eyes went wide. I sighed and bowed my head as a tear rolled down my cheek. "*I* may have just lost her forever."

THIRTY

AZREL

The dark was nothing. The rain pelting my body and soaking me was nothing. The cold mud I was lying in was nothing. The putrid smell of the alley was nothing. I didn't care. I just stared up at the night sky, not moving, not wanting to. I was utterly and completely alone. There was nothing left for me here. I was done. I couldn't do this. I refused to do this. The only two men I loved and trusted in the world had turned on me.

Yes, I loved Ortheldo. I knew it the second I woke up in tears and saw him cradling me in his arms and singing to me. I loved him, deeply. I always had. Love was the warm, exciting feeling I got whenever I looked into his eyes. Love was why I couldn't catch my breath when he smiled. Love was why I felt out of sorts when he looked at me in that special way. Love was why the sight of him made me—

No! I pushed thoughts of him away. I was empty. Hollow. That was all I felt right now. Nothing. They had made fun of me. They had laughed at me. My brother.

I closed my eyes and let my tears slide down my temples and into my hairline. The one person who had seen what the people of his hateful land had done to me had betrayed me. I thought Rabryn understood. I thought Rabryn knew!

No. This was my fault. I was stupid to get so close to either of them, stupid to let them in! I knew what I was. How dare I think anything good could come my way?

Someone suddenly took hold of my upper arm.

I opened my eyes and saw the black outline of a person above me, and recognized the mat of curly hair. "Loir?"

"I couldn't have planned this better myself," he said with surprising surety. He didn't sound like the bumbling boy I'd seen at the inn.

My brows dropped. "What?" He pinned my shoulders down roughly and straddled my thighs. "What are—"

He silenced me by crushing his mouth to mine. He groaned in pleasure, then pulled away and sucked in a deep breath between his teeth, which made a wet hissing sound. "I have been dying to be inside of you since I saw you walk in the door."

I sighed in numb defeat and went completely limp. He was going to rape me. I closed my eyes again. Whatever. My brother had betrayed me. What effect could this stranger possibly have on me?

Loir lifted my tunic, exposing my entire upper body to the cold rain, and I waited for him to begin. "You won't fight me?" he asked.

I halfheartedly shook my head. "Get on with it."

Loir chuckled. "I was hoping for a little more sport. You seemed like a fighter. But, okay." He leaned down and took the flesh of my breasts into his mouth, suckling my skin like an infant. He moaned, and I felt his body tremble. "Oh, I'm going to enjoy you," he said around my skin.

I wondered if I could die. If Ortheldo's father could will it to happen, maybe I could, too. There had to be a way. I didn't want to open my eyes again until I found it. I had no real good reason to open my eyes.

Suddenly Loir gasped. Then, "N—!"

He didn't even get the rest of the word out before I heard the unmistakable metallic ring of a sword coming unsheathed and the sound of a sword slicing through flesh and bone. A warm splatter of blood and gore showered down onto my face and naked upper body, which made me shiver.

A pair of fingers grasped the bottom of my tunic and gently pulled it back down, covering me again. A hand slipped under my thighs and another under my shoulders, and I was lifted out of the mud. Filth and water dripped off my clothes and the ends of my hair, but I refused to open my eyes, still trying to figure out how to will death.

The person carrying me ascended a short flight of stairs and carried me through a doorway. Warm light fell on my face and slightly lit the blackness behind my eyelids.

"Oh, dear me!" a woman's voice said. Heavy footfalls quickly came toward me, and I felt hands on my face. "Dear Gods!" The hands left my cheeks. "Bring the poor thing in here." The footsteps walked away, and the person holding me followed.

I heard a fire going, and then the sound of someone pumping

water, no doubt under a tub. Oh, a hot bath! I hadn't had a hot bath since I'd left The Pitt. My arms broke out in goose pimples at the thought.

A woman chuckled. "I think she likes the idea of a hot bath. I'm going to hurry supper along so the poor dear can eat. Start undressing her and put her in." There was a silent pause, and then the woman said, "Darling, don't worry. We're taking care of her." Footsteps left the room.

I was gently set down on a floor. I was tempted to open my eyes, but I really didn't want to be fooled by these people's kindness. I didn't want to burden them either. I wanted this emptiness, this loneness, to just go away for good.

I was quickly yet gently undressed, and then I was picked up again. The steam from the warm water hit my cold, dirty, clammy skin, and I shuddered violently. The person slowly lowered me into the bathtub, and I curled up into a ball with my knees in my chest and my arms tightly wrapped around them. Sitting there, I felt the dirt and mud and Loir's blood start to melt away.

Unintentionally, I let a soft moan escape as the person started gently rubbing my back with a small cloth, working their way up my shoulder blades and neck, adding some pressure like they were giving me a massage, and it felt good. I sighed softly. I guess I wasn't going anywhere tonight.

I cupped my hands under the water and splashed it on my face, washing away the blood and mud, then slowly opened my eyes. The large bathing room was lit with warm yellow light. It had a wooden plank floor and light-colored walls. In front of me was a tall shelf filled with numerous folded cloths stacked high. A wooden chair sat beside it. To my immediate left was the pump that had filled the tub, over which was a large window. On the right wall, in the far corner, was the door to the hall.

I sighed and looked down into the gruesome water. Dirt had settled on the bottom of the white tub, and the water was tinted pink. The person behind me continued to gently massage my back while I tried to think of something to say.

"Not much of a talker, huh?" I asked.

The massaging stopped for a moment. Then a small piece of parchment with writing on it appeared in front of me. *I could say the same for you.*

I smiled and turned to face the stranger. When I saw him, my jaw hit the floor. "Addredoc?"

I couldn't believe the degree of his father's beating. I actually covered my mouth with both hands. The skin on one side of his face was almost entirely black and swollen beyond any forgivable standards. When I saw his jaw, I pressed my hands tighter to my mouth to keep from screaming, or throwing up. He couldn't speak because his jaw was wired shut. The thick, black wire weaved in and out of his skin in hideous crisscross designs with a small pool of clotted blood surrounding each entry and exit wound of the wire.

"Gods," I whispered, unable to imagine the pain he was in. For his sake, I hoped he was on at least fifty different painkilling herbs. With that thought my mind quickly went to the necklace. It was in my pants pocket. I wondered if I should grab it now and risk —.

"Oh, the lovely dear decided to join us in this world," a gentle voice said.

In the doorway stood the woman. She was a little taller than the average woman and wore a blue, simple, knee-length wool dress and yellow shoes. Her thick, shoulder-length blonde hair was wavy and disheveled. She was rather beautiful, though she looked overworked.

She came to the tub, pulled a bucket out from behind it, and dipped it into the water. "Close your eyes, dear, and we'll get you all cleaned up."

I closed my eyes, and she emptied the bucket over my head. I felt the last of the blood and mud wash away from me.

"There, there." She kneeled beside the tub and began washing my hair with a handful of gel. It was weird not using my Salynn liquids. "Addredoc, honey, why don't you go watch over the supper? We'll be out in a minute." Addredoc nodded and left, closing the door behind him.

The woman looked after him sorrowfully. "Oh, my poor boy." She faced me with a soft smile and started scrubbing my hair again. "Thank you for stopping my ex-husband from killing my son." She swallowed uncomfortably. "Though I know what Addredoc said and did to you upon your first meeting." She smiled privately for a moment and chuckled. "Thank you most of all for publicly bruising Thrawyn's pride."

"You know about all that?"

"Oh," she cooed, looking at me tenderly, "your voice is even sweeter than I thought." She resumed with scrubbing my hair. "Yes, I know. Addredoc was sent to an Herbest after your first encounter. I met him there, and he told me what he'd said to you. He said, 'Mama, that girl had every right to crack me like she did. A brave lady like that deserves respect.'"

"Then why did he talk to me like that?"

She sighed and dipped her hands under the water, rinsing off the suds. The bucket followed, and she poured three full ones over my head before the suds were washed out of my hair. She put some cream in my hair next.

"As you saw for yourself, my ex-husband is a jerk." I smiled. She paused and looked at my face again. "Oh, you have a pretty smile, too." I blushed a little as she continued with my hair. "Well, Thrawyn wants to 'make a man' out of Addredoc. In order to do that, my son needs to be a jerk like him. Addredoc only treated you that way to please his father and avoid a beating. Addredoc gets beatings anyway, which is why I keep him safe at home as often as I can." She tucked a strand of her short blonde hair behind her ear. "I wish I could let him out to experience the world, but I'm so afraid for him. Thrawyn only lives across town." She sighed and rinsed her hands off under the water again. "I think if he lived across *the world* it wouldn't be far enough away." She filled the bucket again and dumped it over my head a few more times.

Now I understood why Addredoc had blamed Ortheldo for his knock on the head, and why Thrawyn had been so upset that it hadn't been Ortheldo. I scrunched my face in pain at the thought of Ortheldo and quickly abandoned it.

"Darling, are you all right?"

She didn't need to know about my problems, and I wasn't about to tell her. "Yes, I'm fine. Thank you."

She stared at me for a moment longer and her eyes softened. "Oh, listen to me rambling on, and we haven't even exchanged names. How thoughtless. My name is Meddyn. You can call me Meddy."

"I'm Azrel."

"Azrel. What a beautiful name. What does it mean? Mine means 'melody' or 'music.' I've always liked my name because of that."

I smiled. "I was once told my name means 'victory.'"

Her mouth dropped, and she gasped softly. "That is *so* beautiful." I smiled.

The door suddenly squeaked open, and Meddy and I looked to see Addredoc poking his head in. He gave a little nod.

"Supper's ready," Meddy said to me as Addredoc closed the door. She walked to the shelf that was full of cloths and came back to me, clearly holding back tears. "Damn you, Thrawyn."

"What's wrong?" I asked as I stood from the filthy water.

She wrapped a large white cloth around me and wiped some tears from her cheeks. "I've been preparing dinner since this morning. Its Addredoc's favorite. Now because of his injury he can't eat it. I made it especially for him."

I gently placed my hand on her shoulder and smiled a little. "Maybe I can help."

I went to the door, pulled it open, and followed the hall to the left until it opened up into an empty front room. A dining room was deep to my left, up two stairs and against some windows at the back of the house. The front door was to my right.

Addredoc was setting two plates down on the table. In a third spot was a single cup with a straw. My heart sank. When he spotted me, he started, then bowed his head shamefully.

I walked up the two short stairs, hoping I'd be able to use my magic, even if it meant going into that awkward, detached state of mind. "Your mother told me why you acted the way you did. You have no reason to be ashamed. I forgive you."

His eyes brightened, and he tried to smile, but his forehead wrinkled in pain.

"Besides," I said and shrugged, "you stopped Loir from taking something from me that didn't belong to him. For that, I thank you."

I reached out with both hands and, not wanting to hurt him, held them just over the surface of his face. I didn't care anymore who saw my magic. If Hathum wanted to kill me, I was willing to make it as easy as possible.

That awkward state of separation came to me, and white fire surrounded my hands. Addredoc's big, brown eyes went wide, and his injuries vanished.

When I was done, I snapped back into control, and lowered my hands, smiling at his newly healed face. I realized for the first time how truly striking Addredoc was. He was younger than me, maybe twenty years old or so, but he was beautiful to a degree I found stunning for a human.

He placed his hand on his newly restored jaw and opened his mouth a few times, testing it out. Satisfied, he smiled at me. "Thank you, White Warrior."

I nodded, feeling a little uneasy about revealing myself, when a door to my left was suddenly thrown open and a monstrous form came out. It took me a second to realize it was Thrawyn, and panic set in. I stumbled backward, horrified, until I hit a wall, my mind racing with questions.

He thrust a finger toward Meddyn. "We *told* you it was her!" he shouted.

"Oh all right, Thrawyn, calm down. You're scaring her," Meddyn replied.

Addredoc gently took hold of my upper arms. "Please don't be afraid. We mean you no harm."

The tenderness of his voice seemed sincere, but I couldn't help thinking otherwise. I looked past Addredoc to see Meddyn and Thrawyn down on a knee. Addredoc, seeing what they were doing, quickly did the same and kneeled.

"What—what's this?" I asked in a breath.

All three rose to their feet and smiled. "It's an honor to have you in our home, White Warrior," Meddyn said. "We're glad you have returned to us."

I closed my eyes against the pain of being addressed so formally. I wasn't worth any special attention, least of all anyone kneeling. "Please. My name is Azrel," I said, opening my eyes.

They glanced at each other nervously, as if they weren't sure they should be calling me by my first name. "Very well, Azrel," Meddyn said awkwardly.

Thrawyn came forward and gently cupped Addredoc's face in his hands. A soft smile came to his face. "He's perfect," he said in an emotional whisper, and the two embraced. "Can you ever forgive me, my son?"

Addredoc clapped him on the back. "There's nothing to forgive. We did what we had to do to."

My confusion exploded into anger. "What is going on?"

All of them jumped and faced me, then bowed at the waist. "Forgive us for angering you, White Warrior," Thrawyn said.

I closed my eyes and rested a hand on my forehead. "Please stop bowing and kneeling and treating me with this ridiculous air of respect. Just"—I dropped my arm and opened my eyes, seeing them staring at me like I was speaking another language—"treat me like you would a normal person."

Meddyn swallowed heavily as if she wasn't very fond of that idea. "Very well. Let's get you some clothes. Do you prefer dresses or pants, dear?"

I was glad to hear her call me *dear*. "I never wear dresses."

She smiled, though it seemed slightly forced. "All right. Addredoc, go get your best outfit. She'll have it, if it's okay with you."

"It will be an honor." He disappeared down the hallway that I'd come from.

"Won't you sit and eat with us?" Thrawyn offered, pulling out a chair.

I gazed at him suspiciously. "I'd rather you tell me why you broke your son's face today. And what was that mess with hiding in the closet?" I looked at Meddyn. "Why is he hugging the son he just beat within an inch of his life?"

It was quiet a moment. "That was the most difficult thing I've ever had to do," Thrawyn said, bowing his head in shame. Meddyn quickly went to comfort him.

I was barely hanging on to my sanity. "Then why did you?" I cried, throwing my arms out to my sides.

Addredoc came out of the hall with a set of clothes draped over one arm. "You can dress in the bathing room if you'd like."

I shook my head in confusion and frustration and then followed Addredoc back into the bathing room. He placed the clothes on the wooden chair and headed for the door again.

Just get dressed and get out of here, I told myself. *Get to Rocksheloc. Give Beldorn the necklace and go home.*

What home? I also wondered.

I heard the bathroom door shut, but saw Addredoc still in the room. He faced the door with his arms clasped behind his back like he was guarding me. I narrowed my eyes at him.

He must have felt the heat of my glare because he glanced at me over his shoulder. "I'll explain everything over dinner." Then he smiled affectionately. "I've waited a long time to serve you, White Warrior." He faced the door again.

I shook my head, trying to rid myself of this madness, and then glanced around the room. My clothes were still in a filthy wet heap next to the tub. Picking each smelly item up with only two fingers, I finally got to my pants and shoved my hand into the right pocket. I sighed in relief when I felt the cold, hard, metal chain of the necklace. Pulling it out, I was disturbed to see that the orange glow had slightly dimmed. Crap. I had to get out of here.

Glancing to my left, I froze when I saw my weapons laid out in the corner of the room. My sword was on top of a beautiful purple velvet cloth with gold trim, and it had a sheer white mesh cloth wrapped around the hilt. I remembered seeing the same kind of white mesh cloth around the hilt of it when I woke up in Galad Kas for the first time. My Salynn blade was laid out next to it on a smaller velvet dark red cloth with gold trim.

It suddenly dawned on me that I had left my sword unattended for the first time ever. My heart sunk low into a pit of shame in my stomach. How did I do that? How *could* I do that? Had these people been Shadow beings...I blinked, unable to comprehend the damage that might have occurred. How could I have *done that?*

"Addredoc?" He looked over his shoulder again. "What's with the white cloth around the hilt of my sword?"

"It's ancient by-spelled cloth."

I flinched. "Ancient magic?"

Addredoc nodded. "A few strips of it remain from your father's time." My eyes went wide. "It protects the sword in case the White Warrior gets injured, faints, or accidentally drops it. If any hand except the White Warrior's tries to grab it, the magic throws the person fifty feet."

"Why do you have these?"

"I'll explain everything to you," he said again and faced the door.

I hurried to my weapons, tore off the cloth from the hilt, and watched it float to the floor. A piece of something from my father's time. Okay. I could buy that. But how had he gotten his hands on such an item? I glanced suspiciously at Addredoc again and began putting the clothes on. The outfit consisted of fine satin silver leggings and a silk white tunic. I tied the sliver sash around my waist and put on the shiny black boots with some discomfort. These were clothes for a ball, not for traveling in the rain and mud.

"Addredoc," I said, making him turn as I strapped on my own belt. "I'm leaving tonight, and these are very fine clothes. Do you want to get me some others?"

"Not at all. The White Warrior deserves the best, and I'm honored you're wearing mine."

Suddenly my entire being exploded with madness. I had no idea where such insanity came from. I dropped to my knees, grabbed two fistfuls of my hair, and screamed at the top of my lungs.

What is he talking about? I left my sword completely vulnerable! My father never *would have done that!* He *was the White Warrior!* He *should be doing this! I wasn't right! I wasn't worthy! I was a mistake!* My mind screamed at me like some feral beast.

"Stop telling what you think I deserve!" I screamed. "I don't deserve anything! My magic destroyed my life! I hate what I am! I hate it!"

Addredoc was on his knees in front of me, trying to release the grip I had on my hair. The door burst open a moment later, and two people came running in. All of them started talking at once. At first it didn't make sense, gibberish, until I realized they were speaking in Ancient Salynnian!

"Has she been harmed?"

"What happened?"

"I don't know. She just started screaming!"

When the three of them realized I was looking at them in astonishment, they drew nearer and started speaking in the common tongue.

"Are you all right?" Meddyn asked.

"You…you were speaking Ancient Salynnian." They all glanced at each other. "Not even the oldest generation of Salynns today knows that language. It died over 3,000 years ago."

Thrawyn gently took hold of my shoulders. "Please come into the dining room. We will explain everything."

I picked up my sword and Salynn blade and shakily got to my

feet as the other three started out of the bathing room. I felt riddled with shame and embarrassment. Today had not been a good day. I glared at my sword and all its hateful beauty, roughly thrust it into my white scabbard, and attached that to my belt. I quickly attached my Salynn blade hilt to my thigh and dropped the blade in before following them into the dining room.

"May I serve supper, or do you wish to talk first?" Meddyn asked, holding out a chair for me on the left side of the table closest to the windows.

"I don't care," I said, shaking my head and plopping down into it. "It's your house. Do whatever you want."

She stared at me for a moment and then glanced up at the other two. "Sit down," she said in Ancient Salynnian.

They all looked rather nervous now. They probably weren't expecting to deal with this—a White Warrior who hated her magic with every fiber of her being.

Addredoc sat next to me, while Thrawyn sat across from me. Meddy hurried to and from the kitchen, bringing numerous items of food to the table. When all the food was on the table, she sat herself next to Thrawyn and began serving each of us.

"Okay, explain. And please be quick about it. I need to go." I didn't even glance at the plate of food Meddyn placed in front of me.

"As you wish," Thrawyn said.

He looked at his wife, who nodded. Then he looked at Addredoc, who also nodded. They closed their eyes, and a magical red light began to shimmer around each of them. I watched in astonishment as they changed from their overworked, tired human forms into the graceful beauty of Salynns.

Thrawyn's black hair now fell perfectly straight to rest between his shoulder blades, the top part held at the back of his head by a thin gold barrette. His thin mustache was gone, and his face was far more clear and youthful. His build became more slender and his gray eyes brighter. Meddyn's ash blonde hair fell smooth and straight all the way down her back to her bottom. The top of it was also pulled back behind her head by a far more elaborate gold barrette. She now wore a light blue, floor-length gown made of silk, with sheer white sleeves that belled out to fall nearly to her knees. Addredoc didn't change at all. He was still beautiful with short, straight black hair, only now it was dotted with small bursts of Red Sallybreath flowers; all their hair was.

I didn't have to think very hard about where Red Flowered Salynns lived. It was a Humount realm called Godel, the largest mountain cluster in Casdanarus, way down south.

Humounts were a mix of Salynns and humans. In ancient times, even before my father existed, the two races had left their segregated homelands to mine mountains, building grand and beautiful cities within them.

When a Salynn decided that he or she wanted to become a Humount, a magic user was summoned, usually a Wizard, and the user was paid a handsome fortune to change the color of Sallybreath Flowers, to the color of the being's new Humount home. It cost mounds of gold because the Wizard would lose some amount of their power for such a service. The power lost was gone for good. Lost power meant a permanent weakness, since a magic user's existence, his or her very life, was based solely on his or her magical energy.

However, Wizards in ancient times were far, far more powerful than today's Wizards, whose power was diluted. As weakened Wizards passed their weakened gifts on to their offspring, and their offspring also lost power to change the color of Sallybreath Flowers, the whole force of magic in the world diluted. What would cause an Ancient Wizard a barely noticeable drain of power before would probably take away more than half the life force of a Wizard today.

Ancient magic was something of legend. Hardly fathomable. That was why the ancient magic in those white strips of cloth around the hilt of my sword was so suspicious to me. That kind of magic didn't exist anymore.

"Well." I looked at each of them in turn and cleared my throat uncomfortably. "Okay. So, what does being very, *very* far from your homeland have to do with you beating up your son?"

"I knew your father, Azrel," Thrawyn said.

My blood ran cold. I tried to take a breath, but an invisible fist cut off my air.

"We fought together in the Nameless War."

The invisible fist closed tighter around my throat. Had he been there the day my father fled? If so, why was he talking to me? Why was he bathing me and feeding me?

"Do you…did you…how…how do you…" I bumbled.

Thrawyn reached across the table and rested his hand over mine. "I believe he was the bravest man on that battlefield."

My eyes went wide. Was he serious? After all the hateful things written about my father, the White Warrior, someone was actually speaking fondly of him? Someone who saw him leave the battlefield? Someone who'd been there? And this person was reaching across a table and holding my hand and smiling at me? He didn't hate my father? I thought *everyone* hated my father!

I could hardly breathe as I stared at him. I wondered what my father would do if he knew these three Salynns still thought highly of him. Maybe he wouldn't have hated himself so much. Maybe he wouldn't have felt so alone.

"You…you don't believe my father was a coward?"

The three Salynns grimaced slightly at the ugly word. "No," Thrawyn answered. "Meddy and I have ever since been loyal to the White Warrior, and we will carry that loyalty to our graves, even if it should send us there."

"We were banished from Godel because of that loyalty," Meddy added. An unbelievable determination hardened her eyes. "They cut off our hair for it."

My hand came up to my mouth as I stared at her. I couldn't believe she was saying this to me. Salynns who lost their Sallybreath Flowers lost their magic. Since a magical being cannot live without the energy of his or her magic, having that hair cut off amounted to a slow and painful death sentence. It was the most profound gesture of loyalty for a Salynn, and I could hardly believe they'd done that for my father!

"How did you get your Flowers and your magic back, though?"

"After the war," Thrawyn said, "I'm sure you're aware of what most people thought of your father." I nodded. "Well, Meddy and I defended him from all the hatred we could for more than 200 years. Thus, we got ourselves banished." He smiled ruefully. "Meddy and I often wondered if we were the very reason the laws were passed against speaking highly of the White Warrior." I grinned at that. "Anyway, we weren't sure how long we were going to live after our hair was cut off and decided to travel with whatever time we had left. It was during these travels that Meddyn became pregnant with Addredoc."

I glanced at Addredoc and back at Thrawyn.

"Meddy and I were just beginning to feel sick from our magic loss when we came across two young Wizards. They were on the riverbank, recently tortured, half drowned, and barely alive. Despite our own wilting strength, we nursed them back to some state of health. When they could talk, they told us how they, too, along with many others in many other lands, had been banished from their homeland for their loyalty to the White Warrior."

I started shaking in the chair. Again, I found myself wondering what my father would have done had he known about these people—people so loyal to him that they would allow themselves to be tortured and banished and killed!

"The two Wizards—"

"What were their names?" I asked in a breath, feeling the need to be familiar with these two unconditionally loyal Wizards.

"Isal and Fyril. Though they looked youthful, about twenty human years, they were wise, powerful and very clever. They told us that other Wizards of their homeland had tortured them and cast a spell on them so that their magic would slowly deteriorate until they died from its loss."

"The spell on them had sort of the same effect of our hair being cut off," Meddyn added. "Except the Wizards kept their magical abilities, which would slowly dwindle over time, killing them in the same span. But Salynns lose their magic immediately and slowly die without it."

I nodded my understanding, still fascinated by the fact that my father had people who were this loyal to him, loyal enough to *die* for him!

"They told us," Thrawyn continued, "that since they could no longer be of service to the White Warrior, we had to be." Meddyn's eyes filled with tears. "So, they took all of their magic and allowed our Sallybreath Flowers to grow in our hair again, restoring our magic and our life force and passing away from the sacrifice."

I was confused. Restoring Sallybreath Flowers to a Salynn's hair would not have killed an Ancient Wizard. It could kill a Wizard today, for sure, but not an Ancient Wizard.

Thrawyn nodded, reading my face. "We didn't understand

why they died either until Addredoc was born."

I nodded. "Go on."

"Well, before they died, they said we would get instructions from them on what to do after our child arrived. We didn't know what they meant. After that, we spent some time on the road to allow our hair to grow back and used our magic to hide our race."

My heart twisted sharply as I thought about my brother and how he'd done the same—hidden his race.

Suddenly the pain of why I was there, in that house, became very raw. To take my mind off Rabryn, I tried to picture again how different things would have been if my father had known about these people who were so loyal to him. Would I have even been born? Would he have destroyed Hathum? My father was probably turning in his grave right now.

"Eventually we settled here, believing it was the last place in Casdanarus we might run into our own kin. We enlisted the help of a few Wizards over the past 3,000 years to tamper with memories of the people here to keep them from questioning why we never aged or died."

Meddyn picked up the story. "After Addredoc was born, and as he started to mature, we noticed something"—she searched for a word— "*peculiar* about him. We couldn't exactly say what it was we were sensing, but there was something different about him.

"When he was about 600 years old, we finally came to realize why Isal and Fyril had died while restoring our Flowers and magic." She gave a mischievous grin, which looked odd on a Salynn face. "It was because they had passed their magic on to Addredoc."

My eyes went wide, and I slowly turned to stare at Addredoc. He smiled almost smugly and then turned up his palm and ignited a ball of liquid red Wizard fire. I couldn't help staring in awe and horror. Addredoc had the gift of two Ancient Wizards! Plus his own Salynn magic on top of that! He had to be the most powerful being in Casdanarus! If not the most powerful being in the world!

"You see," Thrawyn continued, "Isal and Fyril could only pass their gifts onto Addredoc because he hadn't been born yet. In doing so, they outsmarted the Wizards of their homeland by allowing their magic to survive through our son."

I'd stopped listening to him as I stared at Addredoc, unable to look away. How could one fathom such power? Did he even realize how powerful he was?

"You have the gift of two"—I held two fingers up at him, as if he didn't know how many two was—"*two* Ancient Wizards?"

"Two Ancient Wizards," he replied.

"Two Ancient Wizards?" I asked again. Maybe if I asked enough times his answer would change.

"That's right."

I looked at Thrawyn and Meddyn, astonished. "You have *got* to be kidding me."

Addredoc's Salynn magic was completely irrelevant. He didn't even need it. No Salynn was a match for a modern-day Wizard, never mind an Ancient one. Never mind *two* Ancient Wizards!

Salynn magic was basically concentrated energy that Salynns could use for different things to suit their purposes. A Wizard's magic, however, went far beyond just energy. Wizards could control the elements and weather. They could even control time to an extent, among other things. I'd never seen an Ancient Wizard in action, but if a modern-day Wizard could do all that, Ancient Wizardry was something I couldn't even fathom.

Now, this Red Flowered Salynn sitting beside me was telling me he had two gifts of Ancient Wizard magic.

I rubbed my forehead vigorously with the heels of my hand. This was too much to wrap my head around right now, so a change of subject was in order.

"Okay, so what does any of this have to do with me and what you did to your son today?"

"Isal and Fyril's instructions guided our actions today," Addredoc said.

I flinched. "Isal and Fyril were dead before you were born, weren't they?"

"They were."

I blinked hard and shook my head, feeling completely out of my depth. Then again, I was dealing with Ancient Wizard magic, so the hope of anything making sense really went out the window from this point on. "All right, what did their 'instructions' say?"

Addredoc looked at me with a soft smile. "See for yourself, White Warrior."

He held his fingers up toward the wall behind his parents. Tiny red currents of energy formed around them and then, like lightning, shot out from his hands, making them jerk. The small red lightning currents squirmed and wiggled and started spelling out words in Ancient Salynnian.

I read them once and then read them again. "Okay. What does all that mean?"

Thrawyn's brows dropped in confusion. "You can understand Ancient Salynnian but you can't read it?"

I narrowed my eyes at him. "I can read it just fine. I just don't understand what it's saying."

"It's speaking to the recent events that have brought you to us," Meddyn answered.

The words were definitely scripted by two Ancient Wizards. They seemed like a meaningless riddle, which was the staple of even modern-day Wizards. Untangling this verbiage would be interesting.

VICTORY WILL STAND OUT IN A STORM WHEN BLOOD IS SHED BY HIDDEN WHITE HANDS.

THE HONEST AND THRICE BETRAYED WILL STOP BLOOD IN THE FACE OF THE DISHONORABLE.

THROUGH THE BEAST, SEEK THE WINDOW HELD SAFE BY A BLADE. VICTORY WILL LIE WITH DEFEAT NEAR AT HAND.

A KIND LIGHT WILL ILLUMINATE THE SHADOW, AND THE WHITE HANDS WILL BE REVEALED.

THEN SHADOW SHALL BE THE BETRAYED, THOUGH ITS POWER GROWS.

I eventually shook my head. "I don't understand this."

Addredoc sighed, appearing irritated with me, which made me glare at him. "I got these instructions over 1,300 years ago. I was fooling around with my magic, trying to develop it more, when these suddenly shot out of my fingers and into view. I pondered over them for more than a hundred years and came to realize that these were instructions to help us locate and save the life of the new White Warrior."

"Okay, I don't get that. Explain."

Addredoc sighed again and pinched the bridge of his nose, seeming on the verge of losing his patience. He sighed heavily and looked up at the glowing words on the wall.

"'*Victory will stand out in a storm,*'" he began. "We still weren't exactly sure what 'victory' meant until you told my mother what your name meant."

How interesting, and terrifying. These two Ancient Wizards had known what my name was going to be 3,000 years before my parents had even met.

"'...*will stand out in a storm,*'" Addredoc went on. "Meaning that you would make yourself obvious in a rainstorm. You did a nice job of that, laying out those prostitutes, bullying your way through the streets, approaching an innkeeper before the men you were with. Women here are not so bold. All of that made you stand out."

I nodded again, feeling a creepy, crawling feeling that these Ancient Wizards had known these things about me in such detail.

"I had been waiting for you at the inn as soon as this storm began. It was an unusual storm, as you know. Never has it rained so hard for so long. I knew this was the storm that would bring you to us. So I guided you on your travels a bit to make sure you passed through Narcatertus."

It took me a moment to catch his meaning. When I did, my jaw dropped. "*You* caused the landslides to the north, didn't you?"

Addredoc nodded. "'*When blood is shed by hidden white hands,*'" he said, reciting the next line of the prophecy.

He looked at me and waited to see if I would make sense of it. When I stayed silent, he shook his head and looked back at the wall.

"'*Hidden white hands*' means the hidden White Warrior. Your '*hidden white hands*' slammed my face into a counter which '*shed my blood.*'"

I looked at him, stunned.

He shrugged. "It had to happen. It was the proof I needed that you were the White Warrior. I was purposely as crude as I could be, knowing that the White Warrior, and a woman as bold as you, wouldn't put up with it." He looked back at the wall. "'*The honest and thrice betrayed.*'" He looked back at me. "I know you've been betrayed three times. You don't have to tell me anything, but it's in the instructions, so I know."

He was right. Ibalissa, Rabryn and Ortheldo. I wanted to

scream as the sting of those betrayals came back to me. What made these people so bloody special that I had to suffer such betrayal to be brought here?

"'*Honest*' refers to how I accused Ortheldo of my knock on the head but you took reasonability for it, even in front of my father, who was counseled to look as dangerous and as intimidating as possible."

I shook my head and glanced at Thrawyn. "I wasn't afraid of him."

"It doesn't matter. You were honest. Which brings us to '*will stop blood in the face of the dishonorable.*' You stopped my father from shedding the blood of my face, even though I treated you '*dishonorably*'— badly."

Addredoc sighed heavily. "'*Through the beast seek the window.*' A horse came to my front door, stamping his hooves and snorting frantically, and I realized you had arrived. So, I went searching for you at every 'window' of the house until I found you lying under that one." He nodded toward the window beside me. "'*Held safe by a blade,*'" he continued. "So I brought my sword, '*saving*' you from Loir. '*Victory*'—again, referring to your name—'*will lie with defeat near at hand*' is talking about the defeat of yourself. You were giving up. You came pretty close, too. But if you had, that would have meant the defeat of everything of Light."

He looked away, and I narrowed my eyes at him when a thought passed through his eyes. *Your father would never have selfishly put such pettiness before the survival of Light.*

That was it. I didn't need to hear anymore. I could understand the last part of the prophecy well enough. '*Then Shadow shall be the betrayed, though its power grows.*' I stood quickly from my chair and headed for the front door.

"Wait!"

"Where are you going?"

"Azrel?"

I pulled it open and glared back at them, particularly at Addredoc. "I'd hate to *selfishly* bother you in your home any longer." They all blanched, and I walked out into the rain, slamming their door shut.

I was so enraged that I was surprised the rain didn't sizzle when it touched me. Heading for the road, I silently dared anyone to cross me. Just one more little push was all I needed to unleash my hazardous temper on some poor soul; too bad it had to be Addredoc.

I heard the door behind me open and close. "Azrel, wait!" Addredoc cried. I heard the splashing of his footsteps as he ran to catch up to me.

I was ready to whirl and break his jaw again when I spotted Forfirith beside the road, looking expectant but patient. Pelts of rainwater splashed off his body and reflected in the soft glowing lamps around the town, which created a halo of water and light around him. Just looking at him calmed me immensely.

Addredoc finally appeared in front of me. He was back in human form, soaking wet already, with small locks of his black hair sticking to his face in heartstopping beauty. "Azrel, please forgive me. I didn't mean—"

"Get out of my way, Addredoc."

"Azrel, please! Come inside and we will—"

"Move!"

He swallowed hard, then bowed slightly and stepped aside.

I continued without a glance at him and approached my horse, petting his wet face. "I'm sorry I sent you away. Can you forgive me?" He responded by butting his nose gently against my cheek, which made me smile. "Thank you."

He turned his head toward the saddle and my packs and took up something in his teeth. He yanked on it a few times until it came free and he was holding my spare cloak out to me. Such a human gesture.

I smiled and took it from him. "Thank you." I threw it over my shoulders and continued petting his face. "Think you can travel for a bit? I want to get as far away as we can as soon as possible. I promise we'll stop before dawn so I can feed you and give you a rest from those heavy packs." He nudged me firmly with his nose, which I took to mean, "Let's go then."

I mounted my horse and checked him around, putting myself back in the direction of the inn. It was the only way through Narcatertus without going all the way around. Hopefully Rabryn and Ortheldo would be asleep. I didn't want to see them again.

THIRTY-ONE

---◦◦◦---

HATHUM

Jonoic was on both knees before me and my two comrades, shaking and sweating. I could see, playing in his mind, the horrifying thoughts of what I might do to him. Some of them were rather creative, which I'd have to remember for future consideration.

"Report, Jonoic," I commanded.

"M...my Lord," he began, periodically taking in quick jerky gasps of air. "I h...I have failed you. I haven't the...right to ask...ask your forgiveness. The man I had on the hunt... Glessar...he's dead."

I knew this already. I had been angry at first, but since having recently conjured a way to see the last few living moments of beings under my command, I was in better humor.

The redhead was dead. Jaravel was dead. Now the hunter, Glessar, was dead.

It was the method of death I'd seen for the redhead, and the hunter, that had put me in a better mood. They had been killed with wooden planks and boards. I smirked internally because that could only mean one thing: the White Warrior's Deralilya was now unleashed. Another piece of my scheme that had fallen into place. It was happening much more quickly than I'd anticipated, but it wasn't yet time for the main event. We were at the point in the game where my patience was going to be deeply tested.

"When did you last hear from him?" I asked.

"A week and five days ago."

"What did he tell you in his last report? I want every detail."

Jonoic hurried into the tale of Glessar's last report. He said Glessar believed he had found her. He also said that my vision about the White Warrior's travel companions had proven true—a Gold Flower and the heir to Dwellingpath's throne. Jonoic also stated that Glessar had said he would need my aid in finding the woman's magic in her mind.

"He couldn't find a memory of her using it?"

"No, my Lord. He managed to get into the woman's mind but

found no evidence of her magic. He would have searched deeper, but he's not so skilled."

"What else?"

"Well—" Jonoic's eyes went slightly unfocused, and his voice became wistful. His attention was so focused inward that I felt myself leaning forward, drawn by the intensity of what he was seeing in his mind.

"Well, what?" I screamed.

He snapped back from whatever dream he was having and looked at me with a queer smile on his lips. "Well, my Lord, Glessar showed her to me."

"You've seen her?"

"Yes, my Lord."

I had tried to see the White Warrior through the redhead's eyes before she was killed, but her tears had blurred everything. Jaravel's last moments were of him soaring through the air before falling dead. The only face before Glessar's eyes was that of the Gold Flower in human form. That foul Salynn made me cringe slightly. I wasn't sure yet if I needed to worry about him too much. In all three visions, though, I had missed seeing the White Warrior's face.

"Show me," I commanded Jonoic sharply.

He jumped. "I can only show you the image Glessar gave me, which is nearly two weeks old. I'm afraid it might be a bit faded, my Lord."

I smirked. "Oh, I doubt that. You've probably been using it to self-indulge, hmm? Late at night when you're all alone?" Jonoic flushed red. "I doubt it's even *close* to fading from your mind." My eyes went wide with an overt threat for him not waste my time. "Now show me."

Jonoic looked deep into my eyes, a terrifying feat for anyone under my command, and I pushed my magic through his eyes. I wrapped it around the image he was concentrating on and drew it forward. Slowly it developed between us. It was hazy at first, but soon it became as clear as if she were walking right in front of me.

My face relaxed in awe at seeing such a beauty, and my body responded in such a fierce way that I could hardly think straight enough to remind myself not to react. There was not a flaw to be seen on her face or in her curvaceous figure. No woman, not even the alluring female by my side, Glondra, could compare to the impossible perfection of the woman I saw before me.

"Jonoic," I said roughly, meeting his eyes as the image slowly disappeared between us. "Find her. I don't care how. Just find her, and get her here anyway you can. Break her legs if you have to! Just bring her to me."

"Yes, my Lord," Jonoic said, rising to his feet and bowing, excited for another chance to prove he was worth more to me alive than dead.

He started out of the palace until I called his name, stopping him. "Be wary and quiet about your business with the White Warrior," I smiled devilishly. "The Deralilya is about."

Jonoic went instantly pale. "My Lord?" he squeaked.

"That's what killed Ibalissa and Glessar." He sucked in a breath through his teeth, and I waved him off dismissively. "Leave." Biting his bottom lip, Jonoic reluctantly walked out the door.

Thaybo, my male companion, looked at me. "You've got to hand it to the Light Gods. They certainly know how to create beautiful things." I nodded in full and utter agreement.

With the White Warrior this stunning, my patience was really going to be tested. I wanted her, and I wanted her now. But now was a really bad time.

Not yet, I had to remind myself silently. *Not yet.*

THIRTY-TWO

So much for my hope of leaving during the night. Dawn had risen, ugly and gray, and for some reason a huge crowd had gathered around the inn where Rabryn, Ortheldo and I had been staying. The one place I wanted to avoid.

I sighed heavily while at a full standstill among the heavy crowd. "Doesn't this figure."

I had my dark gray hood up, looking for any small opening to take advantage of in my attempt to get to the other side of the town. I kept my eyes on the path in front of me and away from the inn, in case one of the boys happened to be looking out the window while I sat here.

Forfirith suddenly went into a soft state of panic, snorting, neighing, and stomping his hooves eagerly.

"What? What is it?"

He jerked his mouth in the direction of the inn.

"I don't want to be seen, Forfirith."

He threw himself into a more violent fit, nearly throwing me from the saddle, and jerked his head more feverishly toward the inn.

"Okay, okay! Sheesh."

I drew my cloak up higher onto my shoulders, gathered it tightly under my chin, and turned my head to look. My eyes went wide, and my heart sank down into my stomach and through my toes, plopping down onto the wet dirt road. Two ropes were strung up in the rafters of the inn. One was securely fastened around Ortheldo's neck. He stood on a short stool with blood dripping from his forehead and nose. My brother was being forced up onto the second stool with his hands tied behind his back.

Was this a joke? They weren't really about to…they weren't really about to be *hanged,* were they? I squeezed my eyes shut for a moment and then opened them again to see that the scene hadn't changed.

"Hey," I called down to a small group of gossiping women. "What's going on?"

A younger lady, who would have been beautiful if not for her missing and rotted teeth, looked up at me. "The boy is being hung for murder. The other is being hung for attacking the sheriff when he tried to take the boy." She looked at the other women with her, who seemed to find this hilarious. "What a shame, too. Two good looking men at once? I pity their women having to suffer such a dashing loss." They all giggled absurdly. "I'd be in tears for months to come!"

Without thinking, I hopped off my horse, grabbed the front of her dress, and yanked her toward me. "*I'm* their woman," I growled and began to shoulder my way violently through the crowd.

This was my fault. Rabryn had killed that man to save me. I wouldn't let them die over this. I wouldn't let them die, period! Especially not on my account.

I aggressively threw back my hood as I emerged from the front of the crowd just as the stools were about to be kicked out from under them. "STOP!" I commanded in a voice I barely recognized.

Thankfully, the men about to hang Ortheldo and Rabryn heeded my word and froze. Whether from shock or curiosity I didn't care.

One man standing off to the side, apparently presiding over this event, looked at me curiously. He had thick white hair and a neat white beard. His eyes were a hard, icy blue, and his build would have been intimidating if not for the similarity to that of Thrawyn, whose lip I had split just yesterday. He was dressed in all black with a thick black wool cloak over his shoulders. I assumed this was the sheriff from the way he scowled at the other men, who had hesitated at my command.

"What are you waiting for?" he yelled. "Get on with it!"

"You would do well to heed my word," I said menacingly, narrowing my eyes at the men, whose feet came up again to kick the stools out from under my boys. Unbelievably, they stopped again, and glanced from me to the sheriff nervously.

The sheriff looked at them, stunned. "You fools! Why are you listening to a worthless woman? Kick those stools and let's get this done!"

"What is your name?" I asked the sheriff, halting the other two men once again.

His eyes narrowed on me. "Sheriff Kodeyer."

"Kodeyer, your men are smarter than you give them credit for." My glare deepened. "Because they listen to me." The Sheriff looked both angry and astonished. "Now, I'm telling you, let these men go."

"These men are murderers! They must be punished by law as such." He gave me a steady gaze. "Unless you think you are above the law—above the Sheriff of Narcatertus." A few people in the crowd laughed.

"I acknowledge no law outside of my own, and I have no respect for authority until they earn it." My voice dropped into a low tone of warning. "I will gut you, Sheriff, with no more thought than I would give to cutting off a chicken's head."

The crowd gasped as the sheriff and I stared at each other. He was measuring me up, wondering if I was telling the truth. I could see him debating with himself whether he should do as I said or rope me up beside the boys.

"I wouldn't take her threats lightly, Sheriff," a familiar voice said from the crowd.

Everyone turned to see who was speaking. Thrawyn, in his human form, emerged at the front of the crowd a few feet away from me. Addredoc was by his side, looking broken and swollen, with his jaw wired shut again, which I knew was only an illusion.

"What are you talking about, Thrawyn?" Kodeyer growled.

"She is without a doubt a danger to you, sir." He tapped his busted lower lip, another illusion. "This was because I threatened her yesterday." Astonished whispers broke through the crowd that a sword master like Thrawyn had gotten a busted lip from someone like me. "I'd release these men if I were you, sir, for your own safety. The sooner she and her companions can move on, the better."

Kodeyer's face was red. "They're murderers!"

"Only one of them is!" I hollered, desperately trying not to unleash the rage I felt pounding in my temples. "And he only did it to protect me. It was a defensive kill."

Surprisingly, Kodeyer smirked. "You expect me to believe that? You hit a sword master in the face, and suddenly you need protection from danger?"

I looked up at Ortheldo and Rabryn for the first time. Both of them were looking at me apologetically, and Ortheldo's eyes had that intense, special look in them. For the first time, though, I felt nothing in response. I felt empty. I looked at Rabryn again and saw him mouth, "I'm sorry," and the corners of my mouth went up in a small smile. I knew he was, too.

I looked back at Kodeyer. "I was unaware that the man was a threat to me. Otherwise I would have taken care of it myself. He was plotting a later kill. My brother knew about it and killed him to prevent future harm from coming to me."

"The law doesn't recognize intent. It recognizes deed, and your brother did the deed."

"And I already told you that I acknowledge no law outside of my own. Now release them."

"I will not follow the orders of a woman!" he screamed.

My eyebrows jumped up. "You'd better, or you'll be very sorry."

Kodeyer started heaving breaths through clenched teeth. With a yell, he kicked the stools out from under my boys' feet.

As if time had slowed, I saw them drop. I watched the rope tighten around their throats. I saw them dangle by the nooses.

My mind exploded! I would not lose them!

I was thrown into that detached state of mind so quickly that I didn't even know what happened. All I knew was that I was on my knees, screaming, and white fire had erupted all around me as I changed into my White Warrior form.

I glanced at the ropes suspending Ortheldo and Rabryn, and they snapped. My hand shot out, sending a bolt of white light that caught them before they hit the ground. I slowly and safely lowered them down. Only then did I become aware that the crowd behind me was screaming and running in every direction. I kept my eyes on Kodeyer.

He cowered against the wall of the inn as I got to my feet. "It's my job to enforce the law, White Warrior! I'm not evil for doing my job!"

I slowly approached him. "I know that," my voice said, "but you did defy a direct order from me, didn't you?"

"How could I know it was you? I only recognize you now from ancient stories, legends! I would never defy you!"

I really wanted to get out of there, and I started to prepare myself to demand control back of my body. The pain of the headache be damned if I tried to hurt this man.

"You may repent your mistake," my voice said. "I want this town cleaned up before I return."

"But…when will you return?"

"I don't know."

"Then how can I fix it in time?"

"I guess you'd better get started now." His face shadowed with doubt and fear. "This had better be a nice place for me to visit when I come back."

He nodded. "As you wish, White Warrior."

He hurried away, eager to get out of my sight I'm sure, and I turned around to a gruesome scene. All around the place where I had dropped to my knees were dead bodies. Some were sliced up savagely, some were halfway melted into a gory puddle, some had heads smashed in, but all of them had some sort of weapon in their hands.

Now in their Salynn form, Addredoc, Meddyn and Thrawyn stood in the misty rain with the Tan Stranger. All of them had blood dripping off their weapons. What was going on? Why were the four of them surrounded by dead bodies for which they were apparently responsible? Of course in this awkward state I couldn't ask them.

My head gave a little nod of approval to them and I headed over to Ortheldo and Rabryn, who sat upon the ground against the building. I noticed they were completely healed. The blood was even gone from their faces. Both of them looked at me with wide eyes as I smiled and crouched down in front of them.

Rabryn quickly gathered me in his arms. "I'm so sorry! I wasn't thinking, I swear! I didn't mean to hurt you! I'm so sorry! Please forgive me!"

"Of course I forgive you," my voice said.

I pulled away and touched his shoulders. My white fire magic dripped down his wet, half-naked body and grew into a warm wool white blanket for him. He quickly clutched it around himself, his teeth chattering from the cold.

"Thank you."

I looked at Ortheldo. He was so wounded. I could tell he had no idea what to say to me. Finally he said, "I didn't know…" *I would hurt you,* were his unspoken words.

I smiled and then leaned forward and kissed him!

I couldn't breathe! I couldn't think! What was I doing? I didn't want to kiss him! Well, not *now*, anyway.

It was quick and soft, and when I pulled away, Ortheldo looked at me with huge eyes, probably feeling as stunned as I was. Suddenly, I leaned forward again with my face turned toward his neck. I almost panicked, thinking I was about to start kissing him there, but instead, I started to whisper.

My eyes narrowed suspiciously, though I doubt my face did, because I couldn't even hear what *my own* voice was saying! Now I was *really* tempted to risk the blackout headache and demand control back!

Before I could, though, I pulled away. He and I stared at each other a moment before he nodded in what appeared to be some sort of understanding. I straightened, pulling Ortheldo to his feet with me. Rabryn was already standing, clutching the blanket around himself and staring at the Salynns in the street. The Tan Stranger was gone.

"Azrel, are those Salynns?" he asked.

"They are."

His eyes got wider. "Is that Addredoc and Thrawyn?"

I nodded.

Ortheldo stepped up to my side and crossed his arms. "*Red* Sallybreath Flowers?" he asked softly.

I looked at him and nodded. "Oh, you haven't even heard the best part yet."

His brow cocked up. "Looking forward to it."

All three of the Salynns came up to me and dropped to one knee. "On your feet, my loyal followers," my voice said. They all stood. "Well, it's nice to see you all in this world at last."

In this world? What did that mean?

"You, as well, White Warrior," Addredoc responded.

"Where did the Deralilya go?" I asked.

Deralilya? What in the Shadow Gods' Lair was that?

Ortheldo suddenly snatched my arm. "The Deralilya is out?"

I felt like the whole world was spinning out of control and I could hardly catch my breath. What was happening? Damn to the depths all the forces, including Addredoc's, which brought me here! I hadn't wanted to come to Narcatertus! And since arriving, my world has completely fallen apart.

"Yes, but she isn't officially named yet. I haven't given her a weapon, which is why I was asking where she was."

I was going mad. That's all there was to it. I had to get out of here. I had to get *out* of here!

Meddyn gave a small curtsy. "Acalith wanted me to relate to you her apology. She had to leave right away, lest she be caught and discovered by her people."

"Acalith? Deralilya? Who? What?" Rabryn asked, looking from me to the Salynns, and back.

My face smiled at him and then I looked at Ortheldo. "Would you mind getting some clothes on him and explaining what you've learned? When you return, just remember what I told you, and savor that kiss."

Sadness flashed in his eyes and he nodded before he and my brother headed for the inn. I faced the Salynns and gazed at the scattered bodies in the street.

My lips pursed and I nodded approvingly. "I see your talents precede you, Thrawyn and Meddyn. Very nicely done. Addredoc, you will serve me well, I have no doubt."

"Thank you, White Warrior." His forehead wrinkled with concern. "What do we do now?"

Once again, my body leaned forward, and I began whispering to Addredoc words I couldn't hear. Addredoc occasionally nodded or shook his head, and at last I pulled away.

"Of course, my Lady," he said. He looked back at his parents. "Did you hear?" They both nodded and mounted their horses and rode away.

This was beyond maddening! Something was very wrong! Why could they hear from a distance, but I couldn't hear my own voice speaking? Was my magic blocking my hearing? The thought made my stomach turn. What if it was? Was my magic plotting something evil? No, that was absurd. Rabryn and Ortheldo would stop me if I were. But then what was the big secret?

"I'll wait out here," my voice said to Addredoc. "I won't give up control until I see you."

"Yes, my Lady," he said and headed toward the inn.

I sat on the wooden sidewalk in front of the inn and gazed out toward the street. I suddenly realized the main road was completely empty. Everyone appeared to have barricaded themselves in some building. I'd never thought I'd see a day when Narcatertus was even remotely calm, but the street was completely deserted now and disturbingly silent. I felt thousands of eyes on me, though, peering from windows or doors.

I sighed heavily. "Well, Azrel," my voice said, stunning me, "the secret is out. It only has to reach Hathum, and you're done for."

Well, I thought to myself bitterly. *This is what the Light Gods get for not looking out for me—a nice, big, fat defeat! Serves Them right if you ask me.*

Forfirith approached me slowly and laid himself down on the dirt road next to my feet, with his chin resting on my lap like a puppy.

"Hey," I said and stroked his head. "How about taking a breather from those packs?"

"I wouldn't mind one bit."

I blinked. Did…did my horse just talk? I really was losing my mind!

I held my hand over him as it began to glow with white fire. I heard belts unbuckle and leather pull across leather as everything came undone. The entire bundle floated in the air a few feet away, and with a heavy thud, everything dropped onto the wooden deck. I removed his harness and reins with my own hands and tossed them aside with the rest of the heap.

Forfirith rested his head on my lap again. "That's much better. Thank you."

"You're welcome. I bet you're hungry, too."

"Famished."

My face smiled, and I held my palm up. A small flash of white fire erupted from my hand, and in its wake appeared a small white cake. "For some strength replenishment."

"Ooo, thank you. I'll be needing that."

I placed the cake under his mouth and he swallowed it in one gulp. He rested his head on my lap again as I stroked him between his ears.

"We're in big trouble, aren't we?" he asked suddenly.

I sighed heavily. "That we are, my faithful friend. That we are indeed."

THIRTY-THREE

I stood at the window with my arms crossed, gazing down at the empty street and the alleyway where the tan stranger had killed that hunter. Ortheldo was sitting on the bed with his back against the headboard and Addredoc sat on the couch against the wall on the other side of the room behind me. He had just finished explaining who he was and the instructions he had to follow to find Azrel.

"Why was it so imperative that Azrel be brought to you? And what, or who, is Deralilya, or Acalith, or whatever?"

"Acalith is her name. The Deralilya is the name of the position she holds. She's the White Warrior's Deralilya. The hunter she killed was named Glessar," Addredoc explained.

Acalith. What a pretty name.

"What position does she hold?" I asked, looking at him over my shoulder.

"She's the leader of the team that protects the White Warrior. Bodyguards, if you will, very unique bodyguards. My parents and I are a part of this team, which is why it was necessary that Azrel be brought to us. The people that protected the first White Warrior 3,000 years ago bound following generations to protect Azrel, the new White Warrior."

I faced him, my brows drawn in confusion. "But Acalith found her over a week ago, in Oaksher Village. She saved Azrel's life. Why did we still have to fulfill your prophecy to prove who she was?"

"The Deralilya is not officially named yet. Azrel will do that when she's ready. Acalith's capabilities are limited until then. She can sense evil disturbances and can teleport herself to them quickly. The White Warrior being murdered certainly qualifies, which is why she was there when Azrel was stabbed. Acalith had an idea who Azrel was then, but the proof came when Azrel fulfilled the prophecy."

I looked out the window again. "Tell me more about the Deralilya," I said, not sure if I wanted to know for Azrel's sake or my own.

"Well, she's only outranked by the White Warrior herself in the Light Gods' chain of command. They are the most dangerous and ruthless beings in existence when it comes to protecting the White Warrior. They must be ready to sacrifice anything, and everything, even their lives, in order to protect the White Warrior. Aside from the White Warrior herself, the Deralilya is the most feared being in the Lights Gods' ranks."

I shook my head. What a mindful I was getting. "What's with the bulky tan clothes and wooden weapons?"

"Acalith isn't officially named yet. Once she is, the White Warrior will provide special clothing and a weapon of distinction, marking her as the official Deralilya. Acalith is only lacking these things now because of Azrel's...unique situation. Azrel chose Acalith but didn't name her officially."

"Whoa, hold on," I faced him with a hand up. "Azrel *chose* this Deralilya? When did she do that? And why didn't she tell us?"

Ortheldo cleared his throat. "I don't think Azrel knows she chose her Deralilya." I looked at him. "Our theory that Azrel and the White Warrior are two separate people is true. The White Warrior just told me outside."

My eyes went wide. I slowly went to the foot of the bed and sat down with my back to both of them. Stunned, I ran my fingers through my hair. We were right. I couldn't believe we were right. Azrel's magic had developed its own personality in her mind, the White Warrior. We'd had our suspicions for days, but to actually have the notion confirmed that my sister's mind was truly broken, it was heartbreaking.

I looked over my shoulder at Ortheldo. "Beldorn," I said, finishing our thought from yesterday before that hunter had attacked. "Beldorn said your subconscious can abandon you while you sleep."

"That's how the White Warrior communicates with us," Addredoc said suddenly, making Ortheldo and me look at him quickly. "She calls us, her team of protectors, to another world almost. It's a safe meeting place where we can't be overheard by Shadow beings. We can only go there when we are asleep."

Ortheldo looked at me again. "That's why Azrel—or the White Warrior—said, 'How nice to see you in this world at last' to the Redians."

I looked back at Addredoc as I came to an unreal conclusion. "Does this meeting place look anything like an endless void of green light?"

Addredoc flinched, and Ortheldo's eyes went wide. "Yes. As a matter of fact, that's exactly what it is."

I looked at Ortheldo again. "In Blesska, when Azrel had that night terror, you had a dream of green light too, didn't you?" He nodded slowly. "So did I."

"But why?" he asked.

"Think about it," I said, standing from the bed and facing him, as things started clicking into place. "Hathum, a master of mind magic, has a hunter on the loose to find the White Warrior. But this hunter can't get anything out of Azrel's mind. So, what does he do? He turns to her companions and searches their minds for memories relating to Azrel being the White Warrior. To protect herself, the White Warrior pulls us both into that safe place, that green light world, so Glessar can't find anything."

"That…actually makes an odd kind of sense," Addredoc said.

I found myself thinking about the Deralilya again. "Is Acalith a Salynn or a Wizard? And why doesn't she just stay with the White Warrior?"

That question, I had to admit, was more for my sake than Azrel's.

Addredoc shrugged. "She could be either. I've never seen her use Wizard magic, and I've never seen her hair since it's always covered by that hood. She could very well be a human, too."

My brows dropped. "But her teleporting ability—that's magic, isn't it? Humans can't use magic."

"Every Deralilya has that traveling ability, magic user or not. That way if they are sent on a mission, and then sense trouble, they can instantly return to the White Warrior's side. As for why she doesn't stay with Azrel, Acalith is probably just not ready yet."

"Not ready?" Ortheldo and I both asked.

"Well, in almost every country in Casdanarus, it's a crime punishable by death to even *think* highly of the White Warrior due to, well, his history. I reckon Acalith lives in one of those countries. If she was discovered to be serving the White Warrior, the Light Gods only know what they'd do to her."

"Why doesn't she just run away?" I asked rather foolishly.

Addredoc shrugged. "She's probably someone of high rank or position and would be missed."

How interesting. More mysteries surrounded those green eyes. Who and what was she, and where was she from?

"All right, there's another issue I need clarified," I said, looking at Ortheldo and then Addredoc. "What did the White Warrior whisper to you both? I heard her say, 'Remember what I told you and savor that kiss.' What did she mean? And why did she whisper it?"

Ortheldo sighed. "She wanted me to savor that kiss because Azrel hasn't forgiven me yet for betraying her. The White Warrior knows our betrayal was necessary to bring her to her protectors, but Azrel's still hurt." His brows dropped in confusion. "I'm not sure why she whispered it, though."

"Is that all she said?"

"That, and she told me that she and Azrel were indeed two separate people."

"She whispered that to me as well," Addredoc piped in.

"What else did she say to you?"

"She just told me to follow you in here and explain things and answer any questions you have. She also gave me instructions to pass to my parents, but they heard anyway. They were to get on their horses and ride back toward our house, making it seem to Azrel that we were leaving her alone. But when you leave, we are to follow at a distance. The White Warrior whispered it so Azrel wouldn't know we'd be following. She's a little anxious to be rid of us."

"Okay," I said and ran my hand over my mouth thoughtfully. "So then Azrel can see and hear everything the White Warrior does."

Addredoc nodded. "Yes. Just as the White Warrior can see and hear everything Azrel does."

I looked at Ortheldo. "And she hasn't rationalized that the reason for this 'detached state of mind' is because her magic has taken over her body as another person?"

Ortheldo rolled his eyes. "Is there anything really 'rational' about what you just said?"

I had to smile at that.

"She probably doesn't *want* to know what's wrong with her,"

Addredoc said. Both Ortheldo and I looked at him. "She hates her magic so much that she just doesn't want to think about it, never mind think about the possibility that the thing she hates most in the world is another person inside her mind. If she were to believe that, she'd only hate herself more, and she's already on the brink of self-destruction. She only deals with her magic, the White Warrior, when she must. Then she tries to forget anything even happened so she can pretend her magic isn't there."

Unfortunately, that made perfect sense. I knew Azrel well enough to know how much she hated herself and her magic. "How did you know she hates her magic so much?"

Addredoc gave a small humph. "Considering she was on her knees in my bathing room screaming about how much she hated it, I kind of guessed."

I turned to look out the window again with my hands on my hips. "Well, since Azrel can see and hear everything the White Warrior does, we've got some explaining to do about what happened on the street."

"She can't be told the truth," Addredoc said, making me turn around.

"What?"

He shook his head. "She can't be told that she and the White Warrior are two separate people. She needs to learn it for herself. That will make it easier for her to accept."

Ortheldo and I kept to ourselves that we'd already brought the possibility to her attention. Knowing her, and how dismissive she was regarding issues of her magic, she'd ignored it.

I studied the powerful Wizard–Salynn before me. Two gifts of Ancient Wizards was staggering. Ortheldo told me that made Addredoc was probably the most powerful being alive! I wish I had *half* of his knowledge, and I was grateful for the loyalty and protection he gave my sister.

I considered the Red Sallybreath Flowers in his hair. "What realm are you from again?"

"Godel," he said, as if that was the last question he expected me to ask.

"And you were banished for being loyal to the White Warrior?"

"My parents were, yes."

I pressed my lips together and touched the surface of my magic. A cocoon of heat formed around me as I started to glow gold. The cotton and wool clothing against my skin gave way to the soft, slippery satin of typical Salynnian fashion. My hair lengthened and was restyled, and my clumsy, heavy boots faded into light Salynn shoes.

Back in my Salynn form, I looked at an astonished Addredoc. "I thank you for that."

He suddenly stood from the couch, touched his fingertips to the middle of his forehead, and bowed at the waist.

I flinched at the unexpected gesture. "There's no need for that." I knew my kin of White Veilvin were the most powerful Salynns in Casdanarus, but I didn't know that other Salynns *bowed* to them.

"This was unexpected!" Addredoc said as he straightened with a smile. "Your magic will come in handy."

I scoffed. "Sure, if I knew how to use it."

Addredoc's brows dropped. "You just did."

"Transforming my appearance is all I can do. I'm half human, and I was born and raised among humans. My father was a Salynn, but due to the prejudice of the people where I was raised, he never let anyone know what he, or I, truly was, and he was never able to teach me how to use my magic."

Addredoc's eyes brightened. "I could teach you! If you'd like, of course."

I grinned. "Would you?"

"It would be an honor." His grin quickly faded though. "Oh, but my parents and I were ordered to stay out of Azrel's sight. I can't teach you from a distance."

"Don't worry about my sister. I'll just tell her that you're going to help me, and she'll be fine."

"But it wasn't your sister who gave me the order."

"In a way it was. If the White Warrior has anything to say about it, then she can deal with me." I turned back to the window and pressed my palms against the cold glass. "Ortheldo, you said you were in a green light when you received that necklace, right?"

"Yes."

The White Warrior must have given it to him. But how did she get it in the first place? I bet the White Warrior knew who the necklace belonged to. Why give it to Ortheldo, send him to Azrel, and tell us to return it, but not say who to return it to?

"I'm sorry, what's this about a necklace?" Addredoc asked.

Ortheldo and I looked at each other, confused, and then back at Addredoc. "You don't know about it?" Ortheldo asked.

"Depends on what you're talking about."

I felt waves of anticipation ignite in my toes and travel up to heat my face. Maybe Addredoc knew something about it!

I pushed away from the window and walked toward him. "It looks a lot like a diamond, but it's perfectly round. It's warm to the touch and has an odd orange glow inside of it."

Addredoc's eyes went wide. "How—how did you say you got it?"

Ortheldo and I glanced at each other again. "The White Warrior gave it to me in that green 'other world.'"

"Gave it to you? That doesn't make sense. Why would..."

Suddenly a deathly blank look came over his face, and he passed out instantly. Ortheldo just barely caught him before he hit the floor too hard. He and I exchanged concerned glances before Ortheldo picked him up and laid him on the bed.

"What was that about?"

"I don't know. But we're going to have to find out," I replied.

We stayed quiet a moment, pondering all we had learned.

"So, what do you think about this whole business?" he said.

I went to the window again. "I'm not sure yet."

"Well, you've been on a roll since we came upstairs. Don't stop now."

I sighed and ran the facts through my head again. The White Warrior was a separate person in my sister's mind. She could go to a protected "other world" of green light that kept her hidden and safe from the master of mind magic, Hathum. She surfaced after nine years and gave Ortheldo a priceless healing gem, and then she sent us on a quest to find the owner, though I was fairly certain she already knew who the owner was. And yet...

My eyes went wide!

...and yet the White Warrior had steadily been growing stronger since we'd left The Pitt.

I recalled the White Warrior's words in Blesska: "Don't talk to me as a stranger. It doesn't help my purpose."

What purpose?

Then it dawned on me. "The White Warrior needs to be one with Azrel," I whispered.

"What?" Ortheldo asked.

I spun to face him. "The White Warrior needs to be one with Azrel."

"Why?"

"Because that 'other world' in Azrel's subconscious is a huge weakness."

He looked at me, confused, and shook his head. "How so? That hunter couldn't get the proof he needed of who Azrel was because we were all hidden there."

"He was just a lowly hunter, but Hathum could get in if he knew who Azrel was!" Ortheldo's eyes went wide. "Hathum could annihilate the White Warrior if he got in there!" Ortheldo put his hands on his hips and licked his lips anxiously. "The White Warrior sent us on this journey to strengthen herself, and Azrel, in hopes of fusing them together again. They *cannot* be separated when she faces Hathum!"

It was quiet a moment as we absorbed this.

"You're right,' Addredoc said suddenly. We both looked and saw him sitting up on the bed with his knees raised and his arms wrapped around them, as if he'd been listening a while. "Hathum's specialty is mind magic, and that 'other world' is deep in Azrel mind. He could completely destroy the White Warrior in there, and she would be defenseless to stop him. All of us would be defenseless to stop him since she is, in a way, trapped there until Azrel lets her out. The only way that will happen is if she accepts her magic as a part of her and allows herself to use it freely—magic that she hates with every fiber of her being."

"Are you okay?" Ortheldo asked, sitting on the bed.

"The White Warrior needed to speak with me urgently, so she forcibly pulled me into our meeting place, even though I wasn't asleep." He smiled. "Thanks for keeping me from falling on my face."

"Why did she need to speak with you so urgently?" I asked.

"I can't tell you."

My jaw went tight. "It has to do with the necklace, doesn't it?" Addredoc just looked away. "She knows who the owner is, doesn't she? And she doesn't want you telling us."

Addredoc didn't answer, but he didn't have to. "Azrel must finish this journey with no knowledge of the necklace's owner or what is wrong with her magic," he said. "She needs to find all this out on her own. That's all the White Warrior wanted me to tell you."

Ortheldo looked up at me. "Probably to strengthen her."

I nodded. "Probably."

"I don't understand, though," Ortheldo said. "Why doesn't the White Warrior just take permanent control of Azrel, putting *Azrel* in that other world of green light so that if, the Light Gods forbid, Hathum *does* find his way in there only Azrel will be, well, destroyed? Hathum may even see her as no threat and spare her."

"The White Warrior isn't cruel," Addredoc said with distaste. "She would never subject Azrel to that, knowing Azrel would be defenseless against Hathum."

"Okay," I said with a heavy sigh. "We need to get out of here. We need to get to Rocksheloc and talk to Beldorn about all of this."

We made our way down the stairs to the common area, which was completely overcrowded with cowering people who didn't dare chance the streets after today's events. All eyes fell on us, and everyone gasped and murmured at seeing Addredoc and me in our Salynn forms.

"Salynns? Here?" one man whispered.

"Quiet! Don't you know they can hear you?" another scolded softly.

Most just stared in horror and disbelief, pressing themselves as close to the walls or as close to the person behind them as they could in order to clear a path for us to the door like we had some contagious disease.

Addredoc was handling this well. He'd lived here for the however many hundreds or thousands of years he'd been alive. Narcatertus had been his only home. Now the faces and families he knew so well were looking at him with hatred—a feeling I was familiar with. Addredoc had spent much more time here than I had in The Pitt. He'd seen grandparents of grandparents die and knew their grandkids and so on. Yet he held himself with confidence and dignity.

We stepped out into the gray, drizzly day but stopped in our tracks when we saw that Azrel and Forfirith were gone. Our eyes darted around feverishly, wondering where she could have gone.

"Addredoc! Addredoc!" a female voice called.

We all looked to see Addredoc's beautiful mother galloping toward us from down the street.

"Mother, where is Azrel?" Addredoc asked, but her wide eyes were fixed on me. She dismounted quickly and bowed in the same fashion Addredoc had upstairs.

I gently took her arm. "There's no need for that. Tell me where my sister went."

"Thrawyn and I were watching from a distance, as we were instructed, and she seemed content for a while, feeding and talking with Lightning, when—"

"Lightning?" Ortheldo and I asked—me with confusion, Ortheldo with excitement.

"Yes. When suddenly she collapsed over his neck and her White Warrior form faded into her human form. She sat up again and began packing him quickly, mounted, and then rode off."

"Where did she go?" Ortheldo cried.

Meddyn shook her head. "I don't know. Thrawyn is following her. I stayed behind to let you know."

"How long ago did she ride off?" I asked.

"Not long. Please hurry. We can catch Thrawyn."

Ortheldo and I ran as fast as we could to our horses while Meddyn and Addredoc mounted theirs. We mounted and quickly started following the Salynns. Side by side, we dashed down the center of town.

"The White Warrior must have lost control of Azrel when she pulled me in for that urgent meeting," Addredoc called over the thunder of hooves.

I didn't care. I just had to find my sister.

"Meddyn, when we catch up with Thrawyn," I said, "you stay behind with him. Ortheldo and Addredoc will come with me."

"May I ask why?" Meddyn said.

"Because your son is going to teach me how to use my magic." I narrowed my eyes on the road ahead. "I'm going to need it."

Continue Reading for a Preview of Book II....

THE BLAZE
IGNITES
the white warrior series: book two

Nichelle Rae

Available now on Amazon Kindle, Barnes & Noble Nook,
and iTunes

ONE

They would need to rest for the night. Not me. I wasn't stopping until I reached Rocksheloc Mountain. Forfirith was doing very well under my abusive driving. Though we'd rarely stopped over the past two days, and then only for water, he was still in a good mood. Still, it didn't make me any less angry at him.

I glared down at his head, staring between his pointed ears. "I know you spoke, you overgrown ass! I may be a little thick sometimes, but I'm not mad! You spoke!" He snorted and shook his mane. "Yeah, if you say so. I know what I heard."

After nearly two weeks straight, the heavy rains finally seemed to be over. Though I was glad for it, the storms had left behind a ghostly mist that hovered just above the ground of the already ominous forest we rode though.

"This place gives me the creeps," I said to myself. I looked down at Forfirith. "Feel up for a run, buddy?" He neighed and stomped his front hooves. "Alright then," I said, gripping the reins tighter. "Let's get out of here."

He immediately bolted forward, despite the rough woodland terrain and the thick mist hiding the forest floor from view. With the ground not visible and no path laid out, I feared he might trip on something and break a leg. He maneuvered the woods though, as if it were a grassy plain.

I was really impressed by the way he was flying at a remarkable speed without missing a stride. Suddenly, I sensed it. I hadn't felt that dark shadow deep in my soul for nearly two weeks, but now it grew inside me quickly. Something was wrong.

I panned my eyes over to the right, but I saw nothing but a blur of trees as we sped by. I looked to my left where a single shadow caught my attention. I narrowed my eyes. It looked like the shadow of a person, a person running. But it was keeping pace with Forfirith's speed. No human could do that!

My face burned with apprehension and my mouth went completely dry. The shadow in my soul deepened. I tried to lick my lips, but my tongue felt thick and heavy. On my right, just inside the thick of trees, another shadow was running. Its arms were pumping and its head kept turning and looking in my direction. I held back a cry, unable to admit to myself what they were. It couldn't be! It just couldn't be!

In a flash, the shadow on the left jumped out from a thicket of bushes and thrust its arm upward in an arc. I screamed as the knife ripped through my left side. I lurched back and nearly fell off Forfirith, blinded by the sizzling pain. I scrambled for the reins and pulled myself upright again. I couldn't think or breathe. This wasn't happening! I covered the gash with my hand, biting back a scream. Thick, warm blood gushed out between through my fingers and onto my pants.

I looked over my shoulder. Four shadows now ran behind me! As I watched in horror, lumps of shadow material developed between their legs. The lumps grew and grew and soon took the form of shadow horses.

Legan'dirs!

Legan'dirs were after me! No one ever had survived an attack from one of these things, let alone four!

"Run, Forfirith! Get us out of here!" I cried, clutching my wound. Somehow, he went even faster. I glanced back at the Legan'dirs. They were catching up!

I faced forward and was suddenly hit by a wave of nausea. I'd lost a lot of blood already, and I was losing more. But I would not allow myself to throw up. I looked back at them again. One was riding on the far right, heading straight for a tree. It looked solid enough to make an untrained eye think it was about to crash, but I knew better. It passed through the tree as if it wasn't there at all. It watched me as it drew out its weapon, the only solid part of a Legan'dir.

I held the reins with my free hand, my other clutching painfully at my wound. The creature rode up to my right side, its arm raised ready for a strike. I screamed and yanked Forfirith's reins to the left as its arm came down. The blade missed me but cut a shallow gash in Forfirith's side. He cried in pain and stumbled, but he quickly regained his footing and galloped even faster. I couldn't believe this was normal speed for a normal horse. No way.

"Are you okay?" I called to him over the howling wind. He

merely gave me a grunt and continued on. He was a lot braver than I. I found myself struggling to keep from passing out. My entire left thigh was covered in my blood. Every foot of terrain we covered seemed to rip my gash open another quarter of an inch, and soon my eyes were going to start rolling back. I managed to get a foggy glimpse to my left and saw another Legan'dir next to me with its arm raised high. I couldn't even attempt to move.

Helplessly, I watched its arm come down. Suddenly, I was blinded by a red explosion of light and nearly deafened by a BOOM. I recoiled, closing my eyes in horror and shock. When I opened them again, the Legan'dir was gone. I was still alive!

I looked behind me and couldn't believe what I saw in the distance. Addredoc, remnants of red light on his palm, was riding behind me. So were Meddyn, Thrawyn, the Tan Stranger, Ortheldo and my brother, Rabryn. They'd come after me. They'd caught up with me? Their horses looked to be on their last legs, foaming, panting and sweating profusely. I was surprised they were on their hooves at all.

Addredoc moved his hand to the side, and a current of liquid red fire shot like an arrow from his palm. The flash nearly blinded me again as another Legan'dir that had gotten too close to me was hit by his magic.

When I opened my eyes again, I saw the misty woods ahead of me were about to open up into a narrow clearing. Two more Legan'dirs were waiting on each side of the opening. With no strength left to scream, I ducked my head until my forehead was touching Forfirith's back and covered my head with my arms. My heart pounded. I waited for the pain of sharp metal to rip through my back.

The grey light of day fell on me and I knew we were out of the trees, yet there was no stabbing pain. All I heard were the battle growls from two men, then the clang of metal on metal. Shocked, I sat up. Ortheldo and Rabryn were riding beside me now, blocking the Legan'dirs' knives with their swords and allowing me to ride through unharmed. Ortheldo's eyes met mine for a moment, they were soft but determined.

Unable to hold his gaze, I quickly looked behind me at the other four, who were riding hard as the Legan'dirs surrounded them on all sides. They tried to fight, but the creatures were nearly invincible. One of the shadows broke free from the throng and sped after me. The Tan Stranger was quickly in pursuit. But why?

The Tan Stranger's warhorse was large, powerful and extremely muscular, allowing it to easily catch up with the shadow. As the creature raised its weapon above its head, a tan gloved hand reached out. With a high-pitched cry of effort, the Tan Stranger took hold of the very blade of the weapon and yanked it backwards, flipping the Legan'dir off the rear end of its shadow horse.

That cry—it had been a feminine sound. I couldn't believe it, t it was a woman under those bulky tan garments.

All of them injured, the three Salynns abandoned the vain battle, but the Legan'dirs followed.

Even Addredoc, as powerful as he was, couldn't completely destroy Legan'dirs. He could just temporarily dismember them, forcing them to reform. Only one thing could kill them. My magic.

Rabryn and Ortheldo had gashes in their shoulders and upper arms. The Tan Stranger held her arm against herself, not daring to touch the leather reins with her sliced-open palm. Her blood-soaked the front of her tan tunic, a garment so thick that there was no evidence she had breasts at all.

I fought another wave of nausea, this one stronger than the first, and the edges of my vision began to darken. I squeezed my legs against Forfirith to stay on. Much as I hated the idea, I knew what had to be done.

Still holding my wound with my left hand, I released the reins in my right and reached across my body to my left side for my sword hilt. I braced myself, squeezing my eyes shut and anticipating the pain, then yanked out my sword. The gash opened further. I screamed and clutched my blood soaked left hand tighter to it.

Rabryn was suddenly at my side. His eyes went wide. "Azrel is bleeding badly!" All heads turned to me. I held back another scream of anguish as I pressed my hand tighter to the wound. Ortheldo pulled his horse, Urylia, back, then moved behind Forfirith to ride up to Rabryn's far side. His eyes went wide at the amount of blood I'd lost. It was now dripping off Forfirith's side to the ground.

"I'm fine! Just ride!" I cried. I didn't want to, but I had to do it. I released my wound and took up Forfirith's reins with my blood-soaked hand. I slowed Forfirith down so the others would go ahead of me. All of them pulled on their reins, too, slowing their horses down. "No! Just go!" I cried. They hesitated, stared back at me, but continued on.

I glanced behind me. Four of the shadows were gone, but I knew they weren't far off. I scanned the patches of woods that ran along the sides of the narrow clearing. When I saw one of the creatures in the trees to my left, I looked away, pretending I hadn't seen it at all. As subtly as I could, I switched sword and rein hands, putting my sword in my left hand and held the reins with my right.

It was getting closer. Closer. Almost.

It burst out of the trees. In an instant, my sword was ablaze with white fire. With an agonizing slash backwards, my flaming sword cut right across the shadow's throat. The shadow exploded in a white burst of light and an eerie scream of agony. I screamed in pain, more blood spilling from my wound. I didn't have time to think about it. Clenching my teeth, I quickly switched hands again as another Legan'dir approached my right. I swung my sword up. When it ducked like I knew it would, I switched the direction of my swing and sliced forward, cutting through its back and out its chest. It exploded like the first.

I screamed again in pain and had to hold my wound. I'd lost too much blood. I was dizzy and my sword felt heavy. The arm holding my sword dropped to my side and my entire upper body slumped forward over Forfirith's back. How I hadn't fallen off yet I couldn't imagine.

Death. Finally death was coming. The thought made me happy. Peace was waiting for me now. But the Legan'dirs were still out there, going after them. I couldn't die now! Not until I killed all the creatures and my brother and the others were safe.

I tried hard to sit up, but my weakness was like an anvil on my back. I could barely even breathe. I was going to die now, when I didn't want to? I couldn't yet. I had to save them! But slowly the edges on my vision darkened. I felt myself relaxing, seeping into silence.

"Help! Someone help her! She's dying! Fix her!" a vaguely familiar voice screamed. I fought off my impending death just slightly to try and see who it was. "Help her!"

It was Forfirith. I knew he had spoken in Narcatertus. But still I couldn't help wondering if being so near death was making me hear things.

Fight! I screamed at myself. Fight it, Azrel! Get up and kill the Legan'dirs. Then you may have your peace! But I just couldn't do it. My sword slipped from my grip. I didn't even hear it clatter to the ground.

I felt a small warm tingle in my palm and shifted my eyes down to look. A thread of white magic was suspended from my hand to my sword, keeping it from falling. Though I supposed that was good, what help was it when I couldn't move?

A set of running hooves suddenly filled my clouded vision. I forced my eyes upward to see the rider. It was my brother, wearing the fiercest look of determination I could ever imagine. He rode so close to me that it was a marvel the two horses didn't trip over each other. He kicked my foot out of Forfirith's stirrup so my leg hung limp in the wind. He swung both legs over Eleclya's back so he was riding sidesaddle, and then put his own foot in Forfirith's stirrup. He took the reins from my limp, blood-soaked hand and heaved himself into my saddle behind me.

"What . . . do you think . . . you're doing?" I managed in a few small breaths.

He gripped my shoulders and yanked my body up, putting my back against him, and resting my head against his shoulder. "Shut up, Azrel. For once in your life, just shut up!"

If I'd had the energy or strength, I would have screamed at him for talking to me like that. Suddenly, a Legan'dir appeared next to Forfirith. I gasped, but before I could scream it exploded in a flash of blinding red light. Addredoc came back into view and gathered up Eleclya's reins to lead her on.

"Lie back! I can't reach the wound!" Rabryn cried over the pounding hooves.

I arched my back and pushed my torso out as best I could. I felt him peel up my torn and blood-soaked shirt and rest his hand on my wound. I gasped from the hot sting of his touch, but then sighed as a gentle tingling sensation crawled over my skin. I felt my gash pinch together. Strength came back into my body. I sat up in my saddle, feeling fully alert. There was still a pool of blood on my shirt, leg, saddle that dripped down Forfirith's coat, but when I lifted my shirt I found not even a bruise left where I'd been savagely cut open. I spun my head around and looked over my shoulder at my brother, who smiled sheepishly. He looked so innocent yet so devious to me at that moment.

"Did you . . .?" I didn't get to finish my question because I realized that two of the six Legan'dirs were no longer behind us. I faced forward, searching for them.

Suddenly, I felt them. They were hiding in the patch of trees just ahead, where the clearing through which we rode now bent to the left. They were going to attack us from the side when we made that turn . . .

But we weren't going to make that turn.

I clenched my teeth and yanked up my right arm, making my dangling sword jump. I snatched the hilt out of the air. I took the reins from my brother and bent over Forfirith's neck. "Ya!" I said and sped him up. I fixed my gaze straight ahead. "All of you fall back! Stay behind me!" I called to the others as we passed them. They obeyed without question. An odd feeling came over me for a moment, but I hardly had time to ponder what it might be. I began to pull my legs up. I grabbed Rabryn's shoulder as I got to my knees in the saddle.

"What are you doing?" he cried.

"Listen to me," I said, as I looked down at him and handed him back the reins. "When I jump, I want you to pull Forfirith's reins hard to the left. He can turn on a coin, so pull as hard as you can. He won't lose his balance."

"Why?"

"Just do it!" I yelled. I looked down at Forfirith. "You hear that, boy? Help him out with the turn. Use whatever hidden capabilities you might have to make that maneuver." He grunted in understanding.

I pushed myself up so I was standing in a low crouch in the saddle. I kept one hand on Rabryn's shoulder with my sword out behind him and reached with my other into the sheath on my thigh, pulling my Salynn blade free. I concentrated on feeling for the evil these things radiated. I watched for them as we approached the trees.

As I'd predicted, the two Legan'dirs rushed from the shadows, knives raised in their fists. I set both of my blades aflame with white fire and leapt off my horse's back, while Rabryn pulled hard on the reins to get Forfirith out from underneath me and away from the creatures' falling blades. I twisted my body to avoid their weapons, flipping my legs over my head in an airborne backwards summersault. In midair, I back slashed both of my weapons across the throats of the shadows.

I tucked myself again before I hit the ground and did another backwards summersault snapping myself up on one knee, ready to leap up if I was suddenly attacked. My sword and Salynn blade were up, ready for anything, but nothing came. The echoes of the Legan'dirs' death screams faded away.

Rabryn finished the tight circle he'd put Forfirith in and came back towards me at full speed. My eyes widened. What was he doing? I had to get back on! As Rabryn flew past me, he bent to the side, reached down, and pulled me up by the arm, throwing me behind him in the saddle.

I stared at him. "How did you do that?"

"No time to explain. In case you forgot, we're still riding for our lives." I looked behind. Ortheldo and the Tan Stranger were riding together in front, then Addredoc and Meddyn, and then Thrawyn in the rear. "I don't know about Forfirith," Rabryn said, "but the other horses are on their last leg." Indeed everyone, especially the horses, looked to be in bad shape. The remaining Legan'dirs were still in pursuit and gaining fast.

"I've had enough of this," I said, and turned to face backwards in the saddle. I held my palms out. My comrades glanced at each other, seeing my eyes turn white from my magic in use and the white flames suddenly surround my hands, then pulled their horses to opposite sides making a clear path down the middle. I released my magic, the blasts of fire hitting the Legan'dirs square in the chest. They exploded in a white flash and a collective scream.

Everyone slowed down their horses to a brisk trot. Rabryn looked over his shoulder. "Ortheldo, where is the nearest water source? These horses need to rest."

Ortheldo nodded his chin outward. "About two miles ahead."

I sat forward in the saddle and my arms slipped under Rabryn's. He gently patted my hands, and I rested my cheek against his back. I suddenly felt very tired, which was odd because thanks to Rabryn's healing I'd felt perfectly fine a moment ago.

I closed my eyes, deciding to catch a wink of rest until we reached the water source. I suppose it had been a long enough day, or two days rather, since leaving Narcatertus. I hadn't slept or rested. Apparently these six hadn't either, if they'd managed to keep up with me as well as they had.

Why were the Salynns here? The question echoed in my mind as I drifted off into sleep.

Find Me On-Line!
Facebook: www.facebook.com.NichelleRaeAuthor
Twitter: www.twitter.com/Nichelle_Writes
Web: www.nichellewrites.com
Email: Nichelle_Rae@yahoo.com

www.ingramcontent.com/pod-product-compliance
Lightning Source LLC
Chambersburg PA
CBHW020904200626
46814CB00001BA/167